9/16

Anna Smith has been a journalist for over twenty years and is a former chief reporter for the *Daily Record* in Glasgow. She has covered wars across the world as well as major investigations and news stories from Dunblane to Kosovo to 9/11.

Also by Anna Smith

The Dead Won't Sleep
Screams in the Dark
To Tell the Truth
Betrayed
A Cold Killing
Rough Cut

Anna Smith

Kill Me Twice

Quercus

First published in Great Britain in 2016 by

Quercus Editions Ltd
Carmelite House
50 Victoria Embankment
London EC4Y 0DZ

An Hachette UK company

A CIP catalogue record for this book is available
from the British Library

PB ISBN 978 1 78429 479 3
EBOOK ISBN 978 1 78429 480 9

10 9 8 7 6 5 4 3 2 1

Typeset by Jouve (UK), Milton Keynes

Printed and bound in Great Britain by Clays Ltd, St Ives plc

For the Smiths, who helped shape my life through education and example: Uncle Pat, Uncle John, Aunt Jeannie, Aunt Ellen and Aunt Anna.

'Ethics is knowing what you have a right to do, and what is right to do'

Potter Stewart

Madrid, March 2000

Millie raised her glass in the direction of the barman, signalling for the same again. As she knocked back the dregs
of her gin and tonic, she caught a whiff of her breath, a
little stale still from last night's booze as well as having
nothing to eat. She'd forced down half a croissant at breakfast in the hotel dining room, conscious of guests eyeing
her with a cross between mild disgust and pity as her
hands trembled when she lifted her coffee cup to her lips.
She'd encountered those furtive glances before when she'd
travelled alone. People would view the middle-aged woman
she had become and think she must have been a striking
beauty in her day, but was now ravaged by time and, probably, drink.

To hell with them, she thought. Who were they to judge?
What did they know of her life? The barman put her glass

on the solid mahogany bar and slid a dish of mixed nuts across, making eye contact as though he were trying to tell her to eat something, that it was only four in the afternoon and she was on her third gin. She looked away from him, picking up her packet of Marlboro Lights and flipping it open. Three left. That should be enough.

She pushed away the nuts without looking at him, and put a cigarette between her pale pink lips. She flicked the lighter and inhaled deeply, stifling the urge to cough when the smoke hit the back of her throat and burned all the way to her lungs. She cursed the racking cough she'd woken up with for the last four days. Too much smoking and drinking, combined with walking around late at night in the chill of a Madrid evening. She'd stumbled from bar to bar, lost and hopelessly adrift. She'd always felt dwarfed by the magnificence of the buildings and architecture of the city, which held so many special memories for her, but now they seemed to underline the sheer emptiness of her life. Not for long, though. Not long now.

In the heavy silence of the gloomily lit hotel cocktail bar, she hadn't noticed that anyone else was there. It was only when she heard the sniffing that she looked across the room and saw a blonde girl, sitting in an alcove. She was crying into a tissue, dabbing her eyes. The barman shot Millie a glance and disappeared into the back room, leaving them alone among the plush burgundy-velvet easy chairs and shiny mahogany tables. She peered across at the blonde girl as she pushed back her hair a little, and the striking high cheekbones caught her eye. She watched as the girl seemed to compose herself and light up a cigarette. Millie took a long look at this beautiful waif-like figure, her blonde hair cascading onto her shoulders, the sharp features and hollow cheeks. There was something familiar about her, but she couldn't work out why.

The girl glanced up at her, then away, picking up her drink and downing it in one. She was crying again, sobbing now. Millie shifted on the bar stool, resisting the urge to go over and comfort her – a mother's instinct. It had always been there, but the child part was too painful. Don't go there, Millie told herself. There was no point now and, really, she should be past caring. But as she watched the girl sob uncontrollably, Millie got off the stool and stood, unsteadily, at the bar. She was about to move towards her when the doors opened and a horde of people bustled in.

'Bella! *There* you are, my darling!' The man leading the charge – he had dyed black hair – breezed through the bar as though he were on castors. 'We've been calling your mobile, sweetie.'

The girl looked up with a start, and swiftly composed herself, blinking nervously as she eyed the approaching throng.

'Oh, lovey. What's the matter?' He put up a hand to halt the army at his back, then turned to them. 'Give us a couple of minutes, peeps.'

The gang of what looked like media and camera crews stopped in its tracks and turned to each other, lowering their voices. The man glided across to where the girl was sitting and slid into the alcove beside her. His back was to the crowd, his body shielding her. 'Come on, sweetheart. Oh, Bella! Come on, love,' he whispered. 'You need to get your act together. There are dozens of press out there waiting for the fashion shoot. You should have been up at Plaza Mayor ten minutes ago. Come on! Pull yourself together, darling.'

Millie saw her nod, sniffing, and it dawned on her who she was. Bella! She was Bella Mason, the supermodel, the face that had launched a thousand products, from perfume to airlines. Her piercing green eyes gazed bewitchingly from billboards across the country. Those famous razor-sharp cheekbones and the lush blonde hair could turn any mediocre product into a bestseller. Any magazine with Bella Mason on the front cover leaped off the shelves. Yet here she was, looking like a broken, vulnerable kid, weeping in a hotel bar far from home. Millie climbed back onto her stool and watched as Bella took a deep breath and got to her feet. She painted on a dazzling smile, took the man's arm and they strode off towards the waiting crowd.

Millie finished her drink and walked out after them. She followed, curious, as the media people walked briskly ahead of Bella, who hung back, still linking the man's arm, until they reached Plaza Mayor, the late-afternoon sunshine throwing shadows on the buildings and cobblestones. Millie went to a cafe to watch as the media crowd set up pictures and three make-up artists fussed around Bella.

A few minutes later, as Millie sipped her coffee, Bella posed and swaggered confidently under the flashing lights and whirring cameras, as though the girl she'd been half an hour ago didn't exist.

It was nearly eleven when Millie walked slowly back to the hotel. She had almost drunk herself sober, going from cafe to bar around the Latin Quarter, along streets where she and Colin had strolled a lifetime ago, so much in love, untouchable, utterly possessed by each other. She'd wanted to capture the atmosphere one last time, then wander back through the front door of the hotel that held so many cherished memories of precious weekends together. But now she was ready. She wasn't drunk, but she wasn't sober. She just wanted all the hurt to stop.

She walked past the doorman into the massive foyer. She'd left everything in her hotel room, her small leather overnight case and passport. Her clothes hung in the wardrobe. They would find them later. She got into the lift with three tipsy men, who hit the button for the roof, not asking her which floor she wanted. She didn't care. She was going to the roof anyway.

When the doors opened the men got out and walked along the corridor to the rooftop restaurant, where there seemed to be a party going on. Out of curiosity, Millie followed them, but stood outside the door where a flunkey was ticking off names on a guest list. Through the small window she could see white-coated waiters gliding among the revellers with trays of champagne and canapés. Flushed with drink and self-importance, the guests stood chatting and laughing. There were beautiful girls and handsome, androgynous young men, who looked as if they were straight from the pages of *Vogue*.

Then she saw Bella. She was exquisite in a petrol-blue gown that glittered beneath the lights. She was smiling and laughing as people approached her and air-kissed both cheeks. Millie stood for a moment, entranced by the scene, but whenever someone moved away for a fleeting moment and Bella was on her own, the frozen smile would vanish and the green eyes seemed full of hurt. For a fleeting second, Bella looked beyond the crowd towards the door, and her eyes locked with Millie's. They held each other's gaze for a long moment. Then two people came up behind Millie and opened the door, holding it for her. She backed away, then went down the corridor towards the fire-exit door she had seen when she was up there yesterday, planning.

Now she opened the door and stepped onto the roof, the din of the traffic muffled, six storeys below. A chill ran through her, and she pulled her coat around herself. What difference did it make now, being cold? She opened her packet of Marlboro and lit up one last time.

Millie stood leaning against a pillar, gazing out across the city, a million lights twinkling and stretching for miles. She thought of Colin and what he would do when he heard the news. His first reaction would be how to manage it – it always was. How things looked was important to him. He would have to explain that his wife had been missing now for over five days, and he hadn't reported it. Get out of that one, Millie mused, glad of her parting shot.

She wished she didn't hate him so much. All of the love, the trust, had been chipped away by his countless affairs, and now she could take no more humiliation. The rejection tore at her heart. The secrets of his life as a politician and Tory cabinet minister, how things were hidden, brushed away, made her ashamed that she had been a part of it, because she was his wife. Image was everything. Nothing was sacred to him. Even if it was innocent children who suffered.

Millie flicked her cigarette away. It was over now. She just wanted peace. She took a step towards the edge of the roof and felt the cool breeze in her hair. Her story ended here. Tears began to flow down her cheeks and they felt warm against the chill. She swallowed, weeping now as she took another step towards the edge.

Suddenly, on the other side of the roof, a door burst open. She whirled round. It wasn't the fire exit she had come through so it must lead into the function room. She could hear arguing and loud, angry voices.

'No! You fucking listen to me, Bella.'

Millie's ears pricked up and she stepped back behind the pillar. She could see two burly men and an older man, silver-haired, wearing glasses. He was stabbing a finger towards where Bella must be standing.

'I can fucking ruin you, bitch. You were nothing until I found you. I own you! Don't you forget that. You're nobody without me!'

'I . . . I can't go on like this.' She was weeping.

Millie moved forward until she could see Bella in her blue gown, wiping her eyes with her hand.

'I need some help,' she pleaded. 'I can't cope. I'm going to the police. I want to tell them everything. I've had enough of this shit.'

Millie noticed her Scottish accent, and vaguely recalled some rags-to-riches story about the girl, who had come from nowhere to conquer the modelling world.

'You're fucking going nowhere. Nowhere!' the silver-haired man barked, then turned on his heels and walked away.

Millie watched as the two burly men grabbed Bella's arms. Startled, she struggled, but she was no match for them.

'Leave me alone! Get your fucking hands off!' she protested.

They said nothing, dragging her to the edge of the roof. 'Jesus Christ,' Millie whispered. They picked her up, and she watched in disbelief as they threw her off. Millie felt her legs buckle and she stood, barely breathing, her back to the pillar, terrified to move in case they spotted her. She stayed that way for a few seconds, listening to their footsteps fading. When she could see that the roof was deserted, she took a couple of steps towards the other edge. Even from up there, she could hear the screams of people below, and imagined Bella spreadeagled on the ground. Millie's blood ran cold. Everything stopped, and she was suddenly completely sober.

She ran back to the fire exit, down the deserted corridor and into the lift, bashing the button for the second floor. She opened her bedroom door and slammed it behind her, locking it twice. She could hear the plaintive wail of sirens as she closed her eyes to shut out the image of Bella's blonde hair billowing in the breeze in the second before she disappeared.

CHAPTER ONE

It was going to be a long day. The last time Rosie Gilmour had been up so early for a flight during the night was when Princess Diana had died, and she was on her way to Paris before the princess was even cold. Bella Mason wasn't royalty, but in the shallow world of celebrity that engulfed the media these days, she was near as damn it. The last place you would find Rosie was anywhere near the trough of frippery that surrounded that tacky world, so when the call from the night news editor had woken her at three that morning, she'd had to think for a moment before she remembered who Bella Mason was. 'She's taken a swan dive off the roof of a Madrid hotel,' he had declared, as she answered her mobile, her mind foggy from last night's red wine. 'Looks like suicide,' he'd added. The taxi would pick her up in twenty minutes for the five o'clock flight to Madrid.

Matt had been next, shouting, '*Hola*,' down the phone, as she was pulling on jeans and a sweater.

In fifteen minutes she was ready to roll, having flicked on Sky News to see the commotion outside the Hotel Senator in the centre of Madrid. Poor Bella. She'll know all the answers now, Rosie thought, as whatever was left of her was stretchered into a blacked-out ambulance.

Rosie stepped out of the taxi and paid the driver as Matt hauled their bags out of the boot. She gazed up at the Hotel Senator, its sculpted white façade magnificent against the bright blue sky, and counted six storeys to the rooftop. For a second she pictured Bella tumbling through the air, and wondered what would drive a beautiful kid like that, with the world in the palm of her hand, to take her own life. If she had. Suicide seemed to stalk stars and celebrities like the Grim Reaper, and barely a year went past without some actor or rock star found hanged, or dead from a lethal combination of drink and drugs. It seemed to go with the territory.

Her mobile rang as she walked through the revolving doors into the hotel foyer. 'Gilmour, howsit going there? Have you got the lowdown on Bella's story yet?'

'Yeah, right, Mick! I just got here. Give me a break. I've hardly woken up yet.'

Rosie knew McGuire was only winding her up, but the fact that he was on the phone so early in morning, before he was even in the office, meant Bella Mason's death was the only show in town. She had been a massive figure alive, and the newspapers had devoured her every move. Dead, she was even bigger news.

'Well, get some breakfast into you and let me know what the sketch is. It's number one on every news bulletin. Bella was one of our own, Rosie. A Glasgow girl. What the fuck happened to the kid?'

'That's what I'd love to find out, Mick. But bear in mind that the Spanish cops will tell us bugger all as usual. The real story here is, did she fall or was she pushed? Unless there were injuries on her other than the ones she got when she hit the ground, they'll not be able to find out if there was foul play. Are you hearing anything from the showbiz people on the features desk? What about London? Her life's been down there for years. That might be where the real story is.'

'I know. I'm not going to keep you in Madrid long, but we need to have a presence there for a day or so. Just dig around a bit. See if you can get a one-on-one with any of her people – though I doubt you will. But at least if we're there we can run a big colour piece, so get to work on the writing as soon as you can. A lot of newsy stuff will come in on the wires, so I'll have that dealt with here. See if you can get something nobody else has a sniff of.'

'Sure. No pressure there, then! I'm on it. But we need a better picture of who she was back in Glasgow before she hit the big-time. It's always been a bit vague. Maybe ask someone like Declan to look into it.'

'Thanks for the advice, Gilmour. I hadn't thought of that.'

Rosie smiled at his sarcasm. 'No problem. I'll call you later.'

She hung up. Typical McGuire. It wasn't enough that the first four pages of his and every other paper would be chock-full of Bella Mason tomorrow. He wanted something different, an exclusive. Didn't they all? she thought, as she and Matt went towards Reception, stepping over cameras and luggage from the various media crews arriving, all of them after the same exclusive.

The press conference had been two shades of shag-all, and a complete waste of time, Rosie told Matt, as she met up with him in the hotel bar that afternoon. The Spanish police had read a brief statement and taken a couple of questions – a pointless exercise as the stock answer to each was: 'It is under investigation.'

'We're not really any further forward,' Rosie said, as Matt studied the menu. 'They're having a post-mortem to determine the cause of death, but I'll be surprised if it says anything other than "striking the ground from a great height", or words to that effect.' She paused and flicked at the menu in Matt's hands. 'Are you listening to me?'

'Of course, boss,' he joked. 'But I'm starving.'

Rosie waved the waiter across, and Matt ordered a burger and chips.

'When in Spain . . .' Rosie said, rolling her eyes. She ordered some kind of stew that sounded Spanish enough to be home-cooked.

The bar was quiet, despite the posse of press around for the Bella Mason story. Most of them would be out taking pictures or trying to chase up Bella's publicity people, who'd been doing their best to avoid everyone. All the information seemed to be carefully orchestrated by her PR team in London. They'd put up some bloke with ridiculous dyed black hair – apparently her publicity agent – to read a brief statement, and he'd taken no questions. Rosie sipped her mineral water and tried to think outside the box. She had managed to get a guest list for the rooftop party on the night of Bella's death from the friendly concierge, whom she'd tipped heavily when he'd brought her bag up to her room. He'd confided that he'd been on duty that night, and said he'd heard Bella had been crying in the cocktail bar earlier in the afternoon. She asked him to try to remember everything he'd seen that night, and if he'd meet her later for a drink.

Rosie heard an angry voice trying and failing to keep the volume down on whatever he was bitching about. It was the publicity manager from the press conference, and he was berating some young female who was clearly close to tears.

'I don't give two fucks who wants a sit-down interview, or who claims to have the inside story. It's all crap! That's what these parasite journalists do, for Christ's sake. What planet are you living on, Sarah?'

'He looks like a pantomime dame,' Matt said. 'Is he wearing make-up? And is that a wig he's got on? Surely there must be better ones than that!'

Rosie watched as the pair of them went to sit in the far corner of the room. 'I think it's all his own creation, tons of backcombing and hairspray. He's a weird-looking bastard,' she said. 'I don't think there's much point in approaching him for an interview. He'll probably be hysterical.'

Rumours of cocaine and depression had been whispered about Bella Mason for the past three years, but no newspaper ever had anything concrete to publish. Whoever was supplying her must be getting well paid off by her handlers because nine times out of ten a dealer, or someone further down the food chain, approached the newspapers to make a few quid by selling a celebrity down the river. Cocaine and celebrities went together like bacon and eggs. It was more or less compulsory. Rosie had never been to a showbiz party, but her colleagues on Features said the toilets were like a blizzard every time you went in.

Rosie waited in the cafe off the Calle Preciados pedestrian precinct, hoping the concierge would show up. He'd no doubt expect some extra cash. There was always the possibility he was a chancer, and that she wasn't the only reporter he was passing information to, but that was the risk you took. She watched the tourists enjoying being outside in late-afternoon sunshine as she tried to get her head round what had happened. Her gut instinct told her that Madrid wasn't where Bella's story had its roots. It had only ended here, tragically.

The concierge was coming through the door. He raised his chin in acknowledgement when he saw her, then pointed to an empty table in the far corner. He went across and sat down. Rosie followed, taking her coffee with her.

'Thanks for coming. I'm sorry my Spanish isn't good enough to have a real conversation. Do you mind speaking in English? Yours is better than my Spanish . . . Er, I didn't get your name?' Rosie stretched her hand across the table. 'I'm Rosie Gilmour. I work for the *Post* newspaper in Scotland.'

'José.' He shook her hand and smiled. 'Thanks. I learn my English from talking to all the tourists.' He frowned. 'But please, first, Rosie, you must promise me that nobody will know I talk with you. I would lose my job, and I have a family.'

'Don't worry, José. That won't happen. I promise.'

The waiter came and José ordered a black coffee and a brandy. 'I'm finished for the evening now. I'm meeting my wife for dinner.' He scanned the room. 'Okay. I can tell you some things that maybe you are interested in.' He leaned closer. 'I told you the dead girl, Bella, was crying earlier in the afternoon, in the cocktail bar?'

'Yes. You did. Who told you that? The barman?'

'*Sí*. Yes. Pablo. He's my friend. But he told me something else.'

Rosie raised her eyebrows in anticipation. 'What?'

'In the bar that time, there was another woman. Older. British woman. I see her too. She was staying in the hotel for three nights, before Bella is dead.'

Rosie's radar pricked with all sorts of possibilities. 'Do you know who she is? Her name? Is she still there?'

'No. She checked out the next morning. Very early. I know her name was Chambers. But I don't know the first name. I can get it for you. But it will be difficult.'

He looked Rosie in the eye, and she knew where he was coming from.

'I'll make it worth your while, José. Just a name would be fantastic. Her address, too, if you can get it.'

He nodded. 'I will get it by the morning.'

'Terrific. What else can you tell me about the bar that afternoon and the woman? Was she there when Bella was crying?'

'Yes. Pablo says the British woman is, well, I don't want to be unkind . . . but maybe a bit of an alcoholic. She had three gin and tonics in the afternoon and was a bit drunk. She was in the bar by herself, drinking. She was in there every afternoon when it was quiet, drinking alone. She looked sad, Pablo said. I sometimes see her go out in the middle of the morning, and if I was working at night, I saw her come in. She was all the time quite drunk.'

'Okay. If you can get me some details on her I'd be grateful.' Rosie paused, lowering her voice. 'Now, the night it happened. You said you were on duty. Did you see anything that you think would interest me? Anything unusual?'

He shrugged. 'Lots of cocaine, of course. In the bathrooms, in the corridors. Many people snorting it like crazy. Is normal at these things.'

'What about Bella? Did you see her?'

He nodded. 'I see only one thing. Some guy passing her a packet. Like the kind of packet I see people with cocaine. I see it a lot. People get a small packet from the dealer, then they go to the toilet for snorting.'

Rosie watched his face for any signs that he was making this up. He looked genuine. 'You saw this?'

'Yes, I tell you. But I cannot say for sure if it is a drug. It could be anything. But it was the same guy I saw earlier giving a couple of packets to someone else.'

'Do you remember anything about him?'

'Yes. He was big. Like a bouncer or doorman. Very strong. Like maybe he takes the steroids. You know what I mean?'

'Yes,' Rosie said. 'Was he Spanish?'

'No, no. He is British. English. I'm not sure. But not Spanish. I heard him talking. The problem is he and the other friend with him – same with the big muscles – they are not on the guest list of Señor Mervyn Bates, who was organizing the party. So when they came to the door of the rooftop restaurant, I had to tell someone to go and get him. He told me not to worry, that it had been a mistake, and that these men were with him.'

Rosie was hooked. Something was taking shape here. Whether any of it was provable, or relevant, was another story. 'So it was one of those guys you saw giving Bella the packet?'

'Yes.' He looked surprised. 'But not just Bella. I saw him giving two other men and one of the model girls a packet also. But, to be honest, that is the kind of thing I see here all the time at parties. Always the drug dealers.'

'I don't suppose they gave their names when they were allowed in.'

'No. Señor Bates said they didn't have to, that they were with him.'

'Have you seen them around the hotel since?'

'No. They went away later. After Bella fall from the roof it was all panic. Everyone shocked. People left the party and began to go from the hotel. Many police were arriving.'

'And you didn't see the two guys at all?'

'Yes. I saw them go down the fire escape.' He paused. 'But other people did that too. I think maybe people who had been taking cocaine wanted to get out because police would be asking all the guests some questions. That's just my opinion.'

'Can you remember anything about these men that would stand out?'

José nodded. 'The one who gave the packets. He had

very blond hair. Like the bleached hair. Very short hair, and a small beard.' He drew a goatee on his face with his hands.

'Great. What about the other guy?'

'He has a small scar under his eye. Like here. Almost like a small hole.' He pointed to his cheek.

'Listen, José. Is there any CCTV of the hotel that I could maybe get access to?'

He puffed a sigh. 'That is too difficult. I think. So much CCTV, the whole day and night every day. Would take a long time to go through it. But I think anyway the police have come and taken everything.'

Rosie nodded. 'Okay. It was a long shot.'

José knocked back his brandy and finished his coffee. He looked at his watch. 'Rosie, I have to go. I am meeting my wife close to here. Do you mind?'

Rosie went into her bag and brought out two fifty-euro notes. She slipped them across the table to him and he took them, sliding them under his hand. 'Not at all. Thanks for your help. Tomorrow when you get the name of the lady, we'll sort things out. You understand?' She looked him in the eye. 'But it's really important to me that you only talk to me.'

'Of course.' He looked a little wounded. 'I am not a false person. I will see you in the foyer tomorrow. I start at eight.' He stood up. 'I am very pleased to meet you Rosie. And to help. I think, I hope, from your eyes that I can trust you.'

He shook his head. 'I am very sorry for that young girl. I have a daughter only maybe a few years younger. To die like that. Kill yourself.'

'Perhaps she didn't kill herself, José.'

He stared at her for a long moment and nodded slowly. 'Maybe not.' He turned and left.

CHAPTER TWO

Millie stirred as the pilot announced they were about to land at Gatwick. For a frantic moment, she couldn't work out where she was, or if she was dreaming. She was afraid to open her eyes, the images unfolding as though she were watching someone else's nightmare. She'd lain on the bed in the hotel, terrified to move, wide awake and waiting for the darkness to lift so that she could get out of Madrid and as far away as possible. As soon as it was light, she slipped downstairs with her case and checked out. She'd had no idea where she was going when she got into the taxi. She was wrecked from shock and lack of sleep, her body trembling because she hadn't had a drink in several hours.

She told the driver to take her to the main Madrid Puerta de Atocha railway station, where she went to the bar, ordered a gin and tonic, and looked up at the departures board, wondering where to go. She wanted to get out of Madrid quickly but didn't want to go to the airport. There was bound to be press passing through, and she didn't want the tabloids getting any inkling she'd been there. Barcelona seemed the easiest choice, and once the gin had steadied her nerves, she purchased a ticket and got onto the train for the long journey. When she got there, she took a taxi to the airport and bought a flight to Gatwick. She had a vague plan that she would go to Eastbourne and book into a small hotel out of the way until she could get her head around what she had witnessed.

She'd been a fugitive from the moment she'd walked out of her home in London while Colin was away on business. But she'd known then exactly what she was doing, that her trip to Madrid would be one way. But now she was still a fugitive, still running with nowhere to go, and with no desire to go back and face Colin. His people would have been discreetly looking for her for days now. Once the Spanish police began trying to trace all the guests at the Hotel Senator as part of their inquiries, she would be absent. If they contacted her home to track her down, Colin's first priority would be to work out how he could keep this under wraps in case the press got hold of it. He'd have to find her, though. That much she knew. He couldn't have his flaky lush of a wife being linked in any way to the death of Bella Mason, without having his story ready in case he was approached by the media.

She blinked back tears of frustration, anger and disgust as she pictured her husband. If only the media knew the kind of bastard Colin Chambers really was. The former Tory golden boy who could outperform any opposition, whether on his feet in the House of Commons or in front of a TV camera, with his wit and acerbic put-downs, had lost his seat when Labour had swept to power three years ago. It had been nothing but a minor irritation for him, because he was now a sought-after consultant and speaker everywhere, from London to the United States, and was probably richer now than he had ever been. If only those people who hung on his every word knew that he was a wife-beater, a ruthless adulterer, who had bedded at least two of the wives of the ministers he'd sat with at the cabinet table in Number 10. Millie had concealed bruises and scars for the past twelve years that would prove what he really was. But she had more than that.

Millie sat on a seafront bench in Eastbourne, hypnotized by the gentle roar of the sea washing over the pebbles, recalling long, sultry summer holidays there as a child with her parents. She'd booked into a small hotel close to the pier, knowing it would be the last place Colin would look for her. She picked up a discarded copy of the *Mirror* from which a picture of Bella Mason stared out at her, the jewel-green eyes transporting her back to the hotel roof. She shuddered, recalling Bella's face as she'd met her gaze across the crowded room. Had this girl seen something in Millie's eyes that made her recognize the sadness? The vulnerability of her own self? A pang of remorse niggled. Millie had turned her back on Bella; she'd been so self-centred, only concerned only with going out on the roof to take her own life. If she'd stopped, perhaps she could have in some way befriended the girl . . .

It was a ridiculous notion, given that Bella had been surrounded by an entourage whose job was to keep her under wraps until the next prearranged photo shoot. But guilt had been part of Millie's psyche for most of her life. Guilt and lack of self-belief. Now, the newspaper headlines screamed that Bella Mason was a tragic beauty, hinting that she had killed herself and supplying tales – digging up stories of drugs and depression that the poor girl wasn't there to deny. But the real truth, if only they knew it, was that Bella hadn't wanted to die. Millie was the only person who could tell the world the truth, the only witness to Bella's desperate struggle with her killers on the roof. Yet she had scurried off to save herself.

Shame engulfed her. Even though she'd been about to take her own life when it had happened, Millie's basic instinct, when the chips were down, had been to save herself. How fucked-up was that? If Colin found out what had happened, he'd berate her that she was even a failure at suicide, a coward who had run off to protect herself. Something had been very wrong with Bella Mason: she'd clearly wanted to go to the police and report whatever was going on. Now nobody would ever know what it was. Bella's frantic struggle for life in her final moments made Millie see how trite and shallow her own suicide plan had been. She needed a drink.

Colin Chambers could hear the telephone ringing in the hallway, but he let it ring. Conchita, his Mexican housekeeper, would get it. He knew somehow it wouldn't be Millie. Wherever the Christ she was, she'd be either too pissed or too strung out to call at this time of the morning. And even if she did, she would ring his mobile. The phone rang and rang.

'Conchita! Telephone!' he barked, from behind his *Daily Telegraph*. Where the hell was the bloody woman? He knew she wasn't far away. She'd only put his breakfast in front of him twenty minutes ago, and she wouldn't have gone out without telling him.

The phone stopped ringing as Conchita burst into the dining room, flushed and out of breath. 'Sorry, Mr Chambers. I was downstairs in the basement putting some washing in. I didn't hear the phone.'

Chambers looked over his reading glasses and shrugged. 'Well, whoever it was, they've gone now. Can't have been that important.' As soon as he'd said it, the phone was ringing again. 'Bloody hell! It's all go this morning. Can you get that, please, Conchi?' He watched as she went out of the door, her tight jeans hugging her pert little bottom. He sipped his coffee. He reckoned he could get into those jeans, with a bit of charm.

She came back in, holding the cordless handset. 'Is for you, Mr Chambers.'

'Who is it?' He sighed. He really didn't like to have conversations until he was properly fed and had eased into his day.

Conchita spoke into the handset: 'Who is calling, please?' She frowned, confused. 'Is a foreign accent, sir. Like maybe Spanish or Italian.'

Chambers beckoned for the phone and she handed it to him, then left the room. 'Hello? This is Colin Chambers. Who is this, please?' He could hear crackling on the line and some activity in the background. 'Hello?' he said again.

'Oh. Hello. Am I speaking with Señor Chambers?'

'Yes, you are. Who is this?'

'Are you the husband of Señora Millie Chambers?'

Chambers felt his stomach twist. Millie. Something had happened to her. His mind went into overdrive. What the hell had she done? Was she in jail? He knew she wouldn't be dead, because protocol stated that the foreign police force would contact their UK counterpart, who would come round in person and knock on the door. So she was alive. Stupid bitch had obviously fucked something up royally if the Spanish police were calling him.

'Yes, I am.' His voice was sharp, businesslike. He was in charge.

'Hello, Señor. I am sorry to trouble you. My name is Juan Alonso. I am the official interpreter for the Policia Nacional in Madrid.'

'Yes. What's going on?' Chambers pictured his wife in some police station confused and pissed out of her head. It wouldn't be the first time he'd had to have someone pick her up and make sure it stayed under wraps.

'The police are investigating the death of Bella Mason, a young lady, a British model. She fell to her death from the roof of the Hotel Senator on the Gran Vía in Madrid.'

Chambers knitted his eyebrows in confusion. He vaguely remembered something on the news last night about the girl falling from a roof in Madrid. It didn't interest him. Just another coked-out celebrity who couldn't hack fame and fortune, he'd thought.

'What has that to do with my wife?' he asked, looking at his watch. He was due in the city for a meeting in the next hour. 'Just get to the point,' he said, under his breath. 'Where is my wife?'

'We are trying to contact her at this address. That is why we are phoning, Señor. She was a guest at the Hotel Senator on the night of the girl's death. The police are trying to trace all the guests of the hotel so they can interview them as part of the investigation. Is it possible to speak with Señora Chambers to arrange an interview?'

Chambers felt a flush rise in his neck. This was all he fucking needed at a time like this. Fucking Millie, out of her head somewhere in Madrid, manages to be in the same hotel where some silly tart tripped off the roof. The press would be all over the story of the model, because that was what sold newspapers. But the fact that a fucking Tory ex-cabinet minister's wife was staying there at the same time took the front page to a whole new level. What a stupid cunt that woman was. If he could get his hands on her right now he'd wring her bloody neck. He was in the middle of negotiating a six-week speaking tour of America, and being in the papers for having a nutcase wife would not help seal the deal. He tried to compose himself. Thinking on his feet was, after all, his speciality.

'I see. Well, I'm afraid my wife is not here at the moment. Didn't anyone speak to her before she left the hotel? I mean, in the immediate aftermath of the tragedy?'

'No. She left very early in the morning so she was already gone by the time the police were looking for her. There were more than two hundred guests in the hotel, so the police are going through them. Most of them were interviewed the same night or the next day, but now they are trying to speak to the others.'

Chambers allowed the pause while he worked out what to say.

'Can you tell me when she will be available?'

'Well, the problem is, my wife is travelling at the moment in Europe. She was only in Madrid briefly.'

'Yes, Señor. For three nights at the Hotel Senator.'

'Yes.' Chambers pictured Millie staggering from bar to bar in a stupor. Then, for a second, there was an image of the two of them, carefree and in love, in Madrid many years ago, before it had all gone tits-up. 'Er . . . Yes. But I know she's on the move now and, to be honest, she doesn't check in with me every day.'

'Does she have a mobile telephone?'

'No. She didn't take it with her. She would normally phone me every few days to keep me abreast of her travels,' Chambers lied. He had been ringing her mobile for days and it was switched off. Millie had either lost or thrown it away.

'Oh. I see. Well. If it is possible, the next time she gets in touch, could you please ask her to call this number?' He reeled it off.

Chambers wrote it down, anxious to get off the phone. He walked out to the hallway. 'I'm sure she'll have nothing to tell you, other than the fact that she stayed at the hotel. She probably isn't even aware of the incident.'

'I understand, Señor. But we would like to speak to her, as we are speaking to everyone.'

'I'll let her know.'

'*Gracias.*'

'I have another call coming in. Thanks for getting in touch.' Chambers hung up and leaned his back against the staircase. 'Holy fucking shit!' he said aloud.

CHAPTER THREE

Rosie's mobile rang as she and Matt stepped through the doors at Heathrow Airport. It was Mickey Kavanagh. She'd given her private-eye contact Millie Chambers' name and address before she'd left on the early flight from Madrid.

'Are you sitting down, Rosie?'

'Hi, Mickey. I'm just off the flight. I was going to phone you as soon as I got moving. Have you got something exciting to tell me already?'

'Oh, yes, you bet I have.'

'Well, go on, then. Spill.' Rosie stopped in her tracks and signalled to Matt not to hail a taxi yet.

'Millie Chambers,' Mickey said. 'Did the name not ring any bells, Rosie?'

Rosie thought for a moment. She could tell from his triumphant tone that it should have. But when José the concierge had slipped her the piece of paper with the name and a London address scrawled on it, plus a photocopy of the credit card, she had squirrelled it away in her pocket in case anyone spotted it.

'Nope. Not at all, Mickey. Can't say it did.'

'Well. You'll have heard of Colin Chambers, won't you?'

Rosie's jaw dropped. 'Colin Chambers the ex-Tory cabinet minister? The pretentious git with the face you'd never get tired of slapping?'

'The very one.'

'Are you having a laugh, Mickey?'

'Nope. Millie Chambers is his wife.'

'Fuck me!'

'All in good time, sweetheart.'

'Are you telling me Colin Chambers' wife has been floating around Madrid for days on her own, three sheets to the wind?'

'Without seeing a picture of her in the hotel, I can't be a hundred per cent certain that it was her, but the credit-card details check out to Colin Chambers' address in Notting Hill. So unless someone has stolen his wife's card and fucked off to Madrid, we can be sure as shit that it's her.'

'Holy Christ, Mickey! This is a whole new ball game.' Rosie knew McGuire would be doing cartwheels when she told him. She felt like doing one herself.

'Do you think you've got this to yourself, Rosie? If you have, then it's some fucking result.'

Rosie pictured José's smile as he helped her to the taxi with her bag. She'd slipped two more fifty-euro notes into his coat pocket. 'I hope so. My source seems like a good guy.'

'Okay. Here's what I'm going to do. I'm going to fax you a picture of Millie Chambers, a recent one, and if you can get your man in Madrid to ID her, you're laughing.'

'Brilliant. I'll be at my hotel in about twenty minutes, and will call you with the number.' She paused. 'Mickey, I'm very grateful for this, but is there any chance a man of your means could get the lowdown on Chambers' marriage? And anything else on the wife?'

Rosie knew that ex-cop Kavanagh had contacts from the streets to the secret service. She'd never asked him how he dug anything out, but he always managed to surprise her.

'Already doing it, pet. I have to go. Phone me with that hotel number.' He hung up.

Rosie turned to Matt. 'The Bella Mason story just got a whole lot better. Millie Chambers, the woman in the bar I told you about? She's Colin Chambers' wife – the Tory former cabinet minister.'

'Is he the prick with slicked-back hair who looks like a Wall Street broker?'

'Yep.'

'Oh, Christ!'

In the hotel bedroom, Rosie kicked off her shoes and opened the curtains to gaze down at the bustle around the

Embankment and the pleasure boats gliding up the River Thames, the sun bursting through the clouds. She took her mobile out of her bag and lay back on the bed, punching in McGuire's phone number.

'Gilmour. You've arrived!'

'I have, Mick.'

'Listen. I don't propose to keep you in London forever on this, but this morning's news said that a statement is coming from Bella Mason's PR people.'

'I wouldn't worry about that too much. I've got some great news for you.'

'Well, let's hear it, because all the papers, including ours, have the same old shite this morning. More pics of Bella in all sorts of sultry poses. A few weeping celebs claiming she was their best friend. All crap. If they were so close to her, how come she ended up so miserable she took a dive off the fucking roof of a hotel?'

Rosie could tell he was on a rant, and she was bursting to give him her line. 'Mick. Listen. I got a break with a friendly concierge at the hotel this morning. I'd already given him a few quid last night when he told me there was some Brit woman in the hotel bar hours before Bella died. Apparently she saw Bella alone and crying.'

'I like the sound of that. Have you found her?'

'I only found out last night! But it gets better. Guess who she is!'

'Come on, Gilmour. Don't keep me hanging around.'

'She's Millie Chambers – the wife of Colin Chambers.'

'You're kidding me!'

'That's right.'

'Fuck me!'

'That's what I said.'

'Who told us this?'

'I got the name from the concierge. Then I gave it to my private detective contact in London. Her name didn't register with me. She was never really in the spotlight.'

'Are you seriously telling me Colin Chambers' wife was in the same hotel as Bella Mason?'

'Yes. I am. And she was pished. Drunk for three nights running, according to my source.'

'For fuck's sake, Gilmour! I can't believe this! Have we got it to ourselves?'

'I think so. Hope so. I paid the concierge.'

'Well, get back onto him and tell him to keep his trap shut, and there'll be a lot more where that came from.'

'I will. I have to get him to ID a picture of Millie Chambers, just to make sure, though. But it was her name on the credit card, and the address is Colin Chambers' place in Notting Hill.'

'Fucking belter!'

'What do you think, Mick? This is so hot, I'm not sure we should break it just yet. Maybe see if we can track the wife down.'

'She's not still in Madrid, I presume?'

'Not at the hotel anyway. She checked out at six in the morning after the tragedy. She could be back home by now.'

'I don't want to hit Chambers' door just yet, though I'm tempted to tell him that his wife might have been one of the last people to see Bella Mason alive, just to fuck up his day.'

'Me too. But my pal down here is trying to find out a bit about the Chambers marriage. He'll dig up something.'

'Great. And give our esteemed political editor Pettigrew a ring at Westminster. He'll know a bit of background about the Chamberses – how they lived and stuff. Privileged fucker, silver spoon and all that. I wonder what his wife was doing staggering around Madrid on her own.'

'Maybe she has a secret lover. Or they might have had a row . . . I could get dizzy with all the possibilities.'

'Yep. But let's play it close to our chests for the next twenty-four hours and see if we get away with it. I'll shoot myself if this appears anywhere else tomorrow.'

'I'm not even going there, Mick. I'm sure it won't.'

'Okay. Get back to your concierge and tell him he'll get a few hundred quid pronto. Make an arrangement. Just keep him quiet.'

'Sure.'

'Call me in the afternoon.' He hung up.

Rosie sent the faxed picture of Millie Chambers to José, and told him more money was coming his way. He seemed to be enjoying the intrigue and excitement, and promised he wouldn't speak to another reporter. In truth, she'd have felt better if she'd had her old Spanish ex-cop, private eye contact and *amigo* Javier to hoof it up from the Costa del Sol to keep José sweet. They worked together a lot in Spain and he'd have been ideal on a job like this, but when she'd phoned him, he was on a lucrative spying mission in Havana for a rich Spanish industrialist. His wife had told him she had gone to Cuba for a four-day cleansing session at a spa, when she was actually there with a twenty-five-year-old stud, who was taking better care of her between the sheets than her husband did. So she had to keep José on-side herself. It was working so far. He told her the police were still in the hotel interviewing people for their investigation and asked Rosie to send the photograph to a friend's office near the hotel.

Half an hour later, when she called him back, she heard the delight in his voice as he announced, 'It is the same woman I saw in the hotel. No mistake. I am certain.'

Rosie wasn't the only one whose day was made.

She decided to relax for a while before she called McGuire with the good news, and lay on the bed, scrolling through a list of missed calls. Her gut did a familiar flip when she saw one was from TJ. She smiled, leaning back on the pillows and closing her eyes, as she recalled the heart-stopping moment when he'd turned up out of the blue.

It had been two months since she'd walked into the cafe in Glasgow and there he was, sitting sipping coffee as if the last year and a half had never happened. The sight of him had nearly knocked her off her feet, and for a long moment the two of them had just stood there, staring at each other, their eyes fixed as though if they blinked for a second they would both disappear. Even after everything they'd been through together, they seemed afraid to take a step towards each other. Rosie had hung back, fighting off the urge to throw her arms around him, afraid he would reject her, telling her they could only be friends. Eventually he'd stepped forward. 'Come here to me, Gilmour. Let me hug the bones of you.'

She'd fallen into his embrace, the familiar arms around her, pulling her close to him and holding her tight. Then he'd kissed her softly on the lips. It was warm and tender, not the confident kiss of old, but slightly hesitant. She looked into his grey eyes as he pulled back, and before she could stop herself, she reached up and brushed her fingers against his cheek. 'I can't believe you're here, TJ. Jesus! I nearly passed out when I saw you.' She paused. 'When did you get back?' She was gripped with dread that he'd returned with a wife or lover. If he'd been intent on coming back for her, surely he would have got in touch, instead of this chance meeting in a cafe. She quickly regained her composure and chastised herself. She was doing this crap again, falling to pieces like a lovestruck teenager, and they hadn't even talked yet.

'I got back two weeks ago.' TJ motioned her to sit at his table.

'Oh.' Rosie barely heard herself say it.

TJ gazed at her without speaking, and she was conscious of him scanning her face. She wished he wouldn't look at her like that.

'I missed you, Rosie,' he finally said.

Rosie tried to swallow, but her mouth was dry. She hadn't expected to feel like this.

'Me too,' she managed. 'I missed you . . . too much, TJ.' She bit her lip. 'But . . . but why didn't you tell me you were coming? What's that all about?' She was trying to keep her emotions in check.

TJ waved to the waiter and Rosie ordered a coffee. What she really needed was a stiff drink.

He leaned forward, his hands stretching across the table, their fingers almost touching, but not quite. 'I just wanted to slip back into Glasgow and have some time out to think. Do you understand what I mean?'

'Not really, if I'm honest.' She looked away from him briefly, then straight into his eyes. 'When were you going to let me know you were here? Were you ever going to tell me? Or just wait until we bumped into each other . . . like we're acquaintances?'

Rosie felt her voice trail off and she had to bite back tears. Christ! This was the last thing she ever thought she'd do in all the times she'd dreamed of this moment. She swallowed as the waiter put down her coffee. Then she felt TJ's hand on hers.

'I'm sorry, Rosie. Really. I should have contacted you.' He took a breath. 'I . . . I just . . . For the past few months, I've been trying to go over in my head what happened to us. How can two people with so much . . . so much stuff going on inside for each other just let things slip through their fingers?'

'You're the one who went away, TJ. And stayed away.' Rosie put up her hand. 'Sorry. That's not fair. Look I don't want to fight with you. I . . . I just . . . Jesus, TJ! I'm so glad to see you.' Rosie felt tears in her eyes and brushed them away. 'Sorry. I've had a long week, and now this.' She smiled. 'It's all too much.'

TJ ruffled her hair and gave her a mischievous smile – the old TJ, digging her, goading her. 'Don't start weeping all over me, Gilmour. We haven't even had a drink yet. Listen, let's not pick everything apart or analyse the shit out of things. Finish that coffee and we'll go for a decent drink. I want to hear your patter.'

He brushed a tear from her cheek with the palm of his hand. Rosie drank some coffee and put the cup down. She saw the grey flecks in his hair, a little more than she remembered from a year ago. He was back. She stood up.

'Come on. Let's go.'

That was how it had happened. Rosie was back in, hook, line and sinker. TJ was back in her heart, and she was back in his bed, or him in hers, depending on how their evenings panned out. They hadn't put their relationship on any firm footing, but it never had been. He was just there physically, rather than the ache she'd had inside, wondering if he'd ever come back. They hadn't discussed how they'd lived their lives in the past eighteen months, and Rosie was glad he hadn't questioned her. They had made no plans, and while that suited Rosie, paranoia niggled: maybe he didn't want commitment. She knew she was being ridiculous because she was the one who had always stepped back from throwing her lot in with his. And even now she wasn't sure. What they had was here and now, but his return confirmed what she knew in her heart: that she had never really let him go.

She was about to call TJ when her mobile rang, and Declan's name came up on her screen. He was the rising star at the *Post*, keen as mustard and smart, too. He sat opposite her in the office and had become her sidekick as she watched him grow in stature. 'Declan. Howsit going?'

'Good, Rosie. Paper's full of Bella Mason, so I've been pitching in on that, pulling out birth certificates and any school records. It's hard, though. Doesn't seem to be a lot of history on her here . . . But I've just had a call from some guy. He's a junkie – that much I'm sure of. I could hardly make out a word of it, but he said something about Bella having a brother.'

'I don't remember seeing anything about a brother in cuttings, do you?'

'No. But this guy is saying he knows him and can find him.'

'Is he asking for money?'

'Yeah.'

'Did he give you a phone number?'

'Yeah. His mobile. Says he lives in a hostel some nights.'

'Christ! Sounds like a real operator!' Rosie sighed. 'Well. We can't just patch him. You never know, maybe Bella did have a brother. Did he give you a name?'

'No. He said he would when we met.'

Rosie was silent while she processed this. Her gut had told her that Bella's early background might throw something up. A long-lost brother would be sensational. She was going to get nothing in London, and once she'd established that the wife of Colin Chambers wasn't there, she didn't see much point in hanging around.

She looked at her watch. 'Okay, Declan. Thanks. I'll speak to McGuire when he comes out of conference. I'll be heading up to Glasgow tonight, so if you give me this dopehead's mobile, I'll call him and keep him sweet. What's his name?'

'Only gave a first name. Mitch.' Declan told her the number and Rosie wrote it down.

CHAPTER FOUR

Millie felt sleepy, sitting next to the fire in the pub off the seafront in Eastbourne. She'd surprised herself by how quickly she'd polished off the steak pie, as she rarely finished a meal, these days, and was conscious that she'd lost weight. Every time she sat down to eat, she felt nauseous after a few bites. The depression that had stalked her for the past fifteen years was creeping back, challenging her, as every morning she woke up unable to lift the blackness. She'd toyed with the idea of talking to Colin about it, but whenever they'd sat in the stony silence of their dining room, the atmosphere had been so thick with tension and resentment that she couldn't even begin. She would push the food around her plate, then make an excuse to have an early night. Colin had snidely remarked that she managed to finish her wine, but never her food.

He'd grown to despise her, even before this latest episode. He'd told her he was tired of her mood swings, that she was old and dragging him down. He was living a different life now without her, rejuvenated, travelling on lecture tours and acting as a consultant on the board of at least two companies. He probably had a young mistress tucked away somewhere. But she knew he would never divorce her. Image was everything. He'd lost his seat at the last election but he liked to be seen as a devoted husband. It kept everything neat and scandal-free – especially for the more conservative Americans on some of the squeaky-clean Bible-belt tours he'd done. Millie had accompanied him on a couple of them, smiling at all the right moments, but she'd hated it and later blamed it for making her drinking worse, and one night she'd told him so. She'd received a hard slap for those kinds of protests. But the next day he had been all smiles. If only they knew what he was. But they never would.

The bar was quiet, except for one couple and an older, distinguished-looking man sitting at the bar just a few feet away, reading the *Telegraph*. The barman had a copy of the *Sun* and was chatting to the couple about Bella Mason. Millie listened to their theories and kept her eyes on the magazine she was pretending to read so that she wouldn't look as lonely as she felt. She was conscious of the older man stealing little glances at her. He was silver-haired and well dressed, his camel coat folded over the stool next to him. He sipped a whisky and smiled when Millie looked up. She finished her drink and signalled for the bill. The last thing she needed was to be drawn into conversation.

The barman came across to her and handed her a slip of paper, then went into the office to answer the phone.

'Can I buy you a drink? For the road?' the older man asked.

'No, thanks,' Millie said. 'That's kind of you, but I must be off.'

'Not from around here, are you?'

'No.' Millie shook her head.

He looked beyond her and scratched his chin. 'I feel I know your face from somewhere. Do you come here on holiday?'

Millie half smiled. 'Not for a very long time.'

'That's a Scottish accent, isn't it?'

Christ, Millie thought. What a nosy bastard. 'Yes. But I left Scotland a very long time ago.'

'You live in London, then? Brighton?'

Millie felt the colour rising in her neck. 'You do ask a lot of questions, don't you?' She gave him a look that was a clear putdown. But it seemed to bounce off him.

'Just curious. A beautiful woman all alone in a place like Eastbourne. I just wondered, that's all.' He began to get off the stool. 'Would you like some company?'

Jesus wept! What do I have to do here? Millie thought. Tell him to take a flying fuck? In her day, she would have been capable of that and more, but these days she felt vulnerable, weak, so lacking in self-confidence. Colin had knocked it out of her years ago. She was relieved to see the barman coming out of the office so that she could pay him.

She handed him the cash and his eyes lit up when she told him to keep the change. She just wanted to get out of there, fast. She stood up and pulled on her coat, conscious that the man was watching her. She had to walk past him on the way to the door, so she put on her best frosty smile.

'I'm Michael, by the way.' He stretched out a hand, almost blocking her way. 'Born and bred here, but spent a lot of time in London working. I'm retired now. Not much to do, these days. Sorry if I was asking too many questions.'

'Not at all. I have to go now. Have a lovely evening. Good-night.'

Millie woke up in a pool of sweat, and could feel her whole body trembling. She'd ended up in another pub last night and downed three large gin and tonics before staggering back to her hotel, where she had sat up in the bar drinking until the barman yawned and told her he was calling it a night. At least he hadn't asked any questions, and had just kept pouring her drinks. In his job, he'd probably seen it all before. He didn't seem remotely interested in her, unlike that nutter in the other bar with his twenty questions. Even the thought of him made her nervous, the way he was probing, trying to find out more about her. She'd always been uncomfortable with over-familiarity, but these days she was much worse.

She sat on the side of the bed, trying to work out where she could go from here. Anxiety gnawed at her. She was running out of options. It was only a matter of time before Colin put a stop on her credit card. He wouldn't let this go on indefinitely because, sooner or later, people would start asking where she was. He'd allowed her to go off on another of what he called her 'depressive episodes' to let off steam before, but always made sure she'd have no financial means to keep it up. He knew she would come back when she ran out of money. That was why he had kept her monthly allowance at a frugal minimum. He'd told her she couldn't be trusted.

She looked at her watch on the bedside table. It was nearly eleven. She stood up, head pounding, and opened the bedroom curtains. The sun streamed in, almost blinding her. She took a deep breath. She'd go out for a long walk to clear her head. She couldn't stop thinking about Bella Mason and her struggle with the brutes who had murdered her. She could still see them in her mind, the bleached blond and the shorter, squat dark-haired man. When she'd been bladdered last night it had all seemed so straightforward. She would go to the police and tell them what she had seen. But now the very idea terrified her. She knew that as soon she told them who she was they would contact Colin. She went into the bathroom and drank a glass of cold water, holding the tumbler with both of her trembling hands. Then she turned on the shower and stepped in. She had to be strong.

*

Millie had walked for nearly an hour, stopping briefly to buy a bacon roll and a cup of tea in a cafe, eating the roll quickly in case anyone spoke to her. She was fine when she was on the move, the sea breeze in her face and the sun warming the day. But she was still jittery inside. She walked the length of the promenade, then back into the town, now busy with lunchtime business and cars. She stopped at a news vendor and saw the front page of several newspapers declaring that Bella Mason had been a drug addict. 'Coke Binge Led to Bella's Suicide', said one headline.

'It wasn't suicide,' she nearly said aloud. How could they just make that up? She felt a little light-headed.

'Hello there! We meet again!'

Millie jumped when he touched her arm and for a second she had no idea who he was. Then the penny dropped. She felt nauseous. She glared at him.

'You don't remember? In the pub last night? Michael?' He smiled. 'I'm sure I know you from somewhere. I've been racking my brains all morning. I'm glad I bumped into you . . . I know who you—'

Millie heard distantly what he was saying. She felt unsteady on her feet and took a step away from him. Fear and panic swept over her and she could feel a full-blown anxiety attack coming on.

'Are you all right, love?'

'Go away! Leave me alone!' She heard herself whimper.

'Are you all right? You don't look at all well.'

He came towards her and she backed away, then turned, panicking, and stepped into the road. She heard him shout, 'Wait!' But it was too late. She felt the thud of the car on her hip and suddenly she was flying through the air. For a second she thought she was dreaming. Then she hit the ground. Something cracked, and everything went black.

Colin Chambers came out of the meeting at the Connaught Hotel and into the afternoon sunshine with a spring in his step. It couldn't have gone better. The Yanks were a push-over for a bit of clipped English class, and he had given it all the gravitas he could muster. The six-week tour was more or less agreed. His fee was five grand a day plus expenses – he knew they would put him up in the most lavish hotels, where he could avail himself of high-class hookers as well as fine cuisine. His mobile rang in his pocket: Pete, his assistant, who managed all his mail and calls and put newspapers in touch for quotes.

'Morning, Pete. I've a missed call from you.'

'I was trying to get hold of you. Are you out of your meeting?'

'Yes I am. And very well it went, too.'

'Good. Er . . . I'm afraid I've got some rather bad news, sir. It's Millie.'

Something reached inside his gut and twisted it. But it was more fear of a scandal than concern for his wife. 'Oh, Christ! What has she done now?'

'She's in hospital.'

'What? Is she all right? What's happened?' He felt a sting of sweat under his arms.

'She was hit by a car, sir. Crossing the road.'

'Where?' He pictured her in Madrid, drunk in the afternoon.

'In Eastbourne.'

'Eastbourne? What the fuck is she doing in Eastbourne? When . . . Where is she?' He had to get on top of this immediately and smother it. 'Is she all right?'

'A head injury, cuts and bruises, a damaged hip, but she's not in any danger.'

'Thank God for that. Which hospital?'

'Eastbourne District General.'

'Okay, leave it with me. I'll be back in the office in twenty minutes. We'll have to work something out. Any idea what happened?'

'Not really, sir. Best if we speak when you come in.'

'What do you mean?'

'Well. They've had to sedate her. She's been a bit hysterical.'

'Fuck me! Bloody woman's been hysterical for years. I've had fucking enough of this, Pete. Enough! I'm on my way. Don't answer any media calls. You know the drill.'

CHAPTER FIVE

Rosie was on her second mug of tea in the greasy spoon off Glasgow Green, her heart sinking further by the minute. It was eleven in the morning, and she had to admit it was the wrong time of day to have arranged a meet with a junkie. At this hour, most heroin addicts would be wrecked, barely able to stumble to the city centre for a spot of shoplifting to pay for their next fix. Junkies didn't have the luxury of a surplus of heroin to inject or smoke when they woke up. They went from fix to fix, their entire day spent trying to get their next hit sorted. So she'd been surprised when Mitch, the guy claiming to know Bella Mason's brother, had asked her to meet him at this time.

Rosie watched the door. The old Italian guy, who was slapping fish into a bucket of white batter and firing up the fryer, watched her. So did the waitress. She hated this side of the city: its grim shop fronts and bars were the kind of places you didn't wander into in the dark. Through the grimy windows she could see an emaciated half-naked girl on a street corner, leaning against a wall, eyeing up the passing cars hopefully for business. Down here where cars cruised, looking for the cheapest of thrills, a couple of hand-jobs would be enough for her next tenner bag.

Rosie let out a long sigh. The sight of these kids depressed the hell out of her. No hopes or dreams, just the cold light of day to face every morning, when they woke up in whatever stinking junkie den they'd passed out in. They must know that one day they wouldn't wake up. Mitch had told her he was staying in the hostel around the corner, and that they turfed them out at half ten. So, unless he'd been thrown out last night, he should have got here by now.

She was about to call the waitress for the bill when the door opened. A tall figure came in, his hollow cheeks and sunken eyes making him look like a ghost. He looked haunted, desperate. This had to be him. Rosie coughed and made eye contact as he scanned the room. He bounced across to her on rubbery junkie legs.

'Mitch?'

'Aye. Rosie?' He glanced over his shoulder.

She motioned him to sit down.

'Awright, man? Sorry I'm late.' He sniffed. 'I was rattlin' when I woke up, had to get a wee toot. Sorry.'

'No problem, Mitch. I was just enjoying my tea.'

Rosie smiled, studying his face to get a handle on his age. It was always hard to tell with junkies, ravaged from years of living the way they did. He looked about thirty-five, but he was probably ten years younger. His eyelids were heavy and his pupils like two pinheads. He'd had a recent hit. Christ, Rosie thought. He looks like he could fall asleep on me.

'So,' she began. 'You want something to eat? How about a bacon roll.'

'Nah!' He puffed. 'No lumpy stuff. Can I get a Coca-Cola iced drink? They do good ones in here. Big dollop of ice cream, man. Just what I need.'

She knew all about a junkie's craving for sweet things. She beckoned the waitress and ordered.

'Oh, and a chocolate biscuit too. One of them Orange Clubs,' Mitch ventured. 'Is that all right?'

'Sure, Mitch. Let's push the boat right out.'

Rosie hoped he had something interesting to say – and soon, because he smelt like he hadn't had a bath in a month. He wiped his nose with the back of his shiny jacket cuff. 'You staying in the hostel, then?' she asked, thinking she might as well start somewhere.

'Aye. So far anyway, till they kick me out.' He sniffed. 'That's where I saw Dan.' He looked into Rosie's eyes. 'That's his name. The boy I told you about. He's Bella Mason's brother.' He shrugged. 'Or so he says. Could be fuckin' lying, but I don't think so.'

Rosie's stomach tightened.

'Did you get a second name?'

'Eh?' He seemed surprised. 'Mason. Same as hers.' His drink arrived and he took a long suck from a straw, then started spooning the ice cream into his mouth. 'Fuckin' magic this!'

'Have you met him a few times or just once? What I mean, Mitch, is that I want you to tell me when you met. Everything you know.'

'Am I getting paid, by the way?' He wiped his mouth.

Rosie locked eyes with him and said nothing for a long moment. 'You'll get paid. Sure. But only if you can take me to him. I want to meet him.' She hated telling a junkie they'd get weighed in with cash, because it could mean there was no end to how they'd embellish a story to up the ante.

He looked a little crestfallen. 'But I'm here now. I mean, I've got work to do, man. I could be out earning instead of sitting here.'

Rosie leaned forward and stretched her hand over the table, so that she touched his wrist. He looked down as she held it. 'Listen, Mitch. I want you to know something so we're absolutely clear. I didn't come up the Clyde on a banana skin. I'm no soft touch. I know plenty of junkies who would tell me the sky was falling in, like Chicken Licken, just to get a few quid for a fix. Now, so you know, I'm not that kind of reporter. So if you're making any of this up in the hope of upfront cash, then forget it. But if you're telling me the truth, I'll look after you. Don't worry about that.' She paused for effect. 'And the deal is, you don't talk to a single soul about this or you get nothing.' She'd find a way to tell McGuire about the cash.

'Aye, right. I get your drift, man.' He scooped out more ice cream. 'But I had a wee toot about an hour ago, so it's beginning to wear off. I need something to sort me out in the next wee while or I'll be fucking useless. Can you not give me something now?'

Rosie ignored the request, sipping her tea. 'Tell me the last time you saw this guy Dan. Tell me everything you know.'

He stared at the table for a few beats, as though he were trying to piece it together in his head. 'Right. Okay, then. Here's the sketch.' He took a long breath and let it out slowly. 'It was about two months ago, maybe three. I don't know, really, because I lose track of time. The weeks and months all roll into one. Sometimes you only know what season it is if you're sleeping outside and freezing your balls off.'

Rosie waited patiently. She didn't need to hear tales of a junkie's lifestyle. She'd seen and heard it all before.

'So,' he continued, 'I was in the hostel the first time I saw him. He's just a wee guy, a bit younger than me. Twenty-one, I think. Blond hair. Nice-looking wee guy. He got a bit of a doing from some cunt that was just out of jail, and his face was all bruised. I jumped in to help him and broke a chair over the cunt's head. We all got thrown out, so me and Dan slept under the bridge that night. Fucking freezing. Then in the middle of the night I heard him greetin'. Sobbing, so he was. After that we used to cut about together. He used to sleep next to me in the hostel and that's how I got to know him. He woke up one night sobbing again, and I had to try and calm him down. He's a bit fucked-up. He does a bit of rent-boy stuff, he told me, and he gets picked up a lot because he looks young.'

Rosie nodded, afraid to say anything now that Mitch was in full recollection mode. She stuck the tape on, and Mitch looked at it and shrugged as he continued.

'So I got up and we went into the wee corridor for a fag. Because if you make a lot of noise they just turf you out. I mean you do hear the odd guy greetin' or something at night, but mostly it's just farting.'

He sniggered and Rosie saw a dimple in one cheek. His face might have been beautiful once, a grin in a school photograph, sweet and innocent. She felt a wave of sympathy for the boy he had been. 'Go on.'

'We were talking outside and he said he was greetin' because he had all these nightmares about when he was a wee kid. Said he got abused by loads of people. He was in a children's home in Glasgow. Said he was with his sister for a while in the same home, but they got split up. They took her away . . . Then he started sobbing again. I mean, he's well fucked-up this boy. Been smoking heroin for a few years now.'

'Jesus,' Rosie said. 'Did he say which home?'

'Eastwood Park Children's Home. It's down in the East End. Or it was. It's not there any more. I know a few boys who were there. I see them in here or in the houses where I get my kit.'

'You mean a few of them are heroin addicts?'

'Well, put it this way, Rosie. Everybody I know is a heroin addict. I don't know normal people any more. I haven't seen my family in eight years. My da's dead and my maw's not well. My sister died from heroin two years ago and my maw's never been the same since.'

Christ! Rosie thought. The city's schemes were littered with stories like this, so many victims, no matter what hard line the government peddled to deal with the aftermath of the nineties heroin explosion that had swept the country.

'I'm sorry to hear that, Mitch. Must be tough for you. But you need to start looking at a programme to get off this shit.'

He nodded wanly. 'Aye. I'm going to get on methadone. At least it makes it easier – you've always got something to get you started in the morning if you've got a meth script.'

Rosie knew that was part of the problem. Half the junkies were hooked on heroin, stealing to get it, and the other half were hooked even deeper on methadone, using it as a crutch till they got their next fix. It was costing millions, and nobody was getting any better. It was just a more organized way to get spaced out, and it made social services feel they were tackling the problem, which they weren't.

'So where is he now? When did you last see him?' Rosie was as convinced as she could be that Mitch was genuine, however desperate he was for money. She'd been here before and she could usually detect a bullshitter, even a good one.

'A couple of nights ago. We ended up in a house down the Barrowfield. He was smoking heroin and was in a bit of a mess. Place is stinking, but at least it was a roof over our heads. We slept on the floor.'

'Did you see him in the morning?'

'Aye. About eleven or twelve or something we woke up and had another wee toot. Then we went out to go up the shops and see what we could blag. That was when he saw the paper.'

'The newspaper?'

'Aye. All the papers had the front page about this Bella Mason killing herself. Wee Dan just fucking went to bits. He collapsed and everything. I had to pick him up and drag him to a side street. That's when he started going on about stuff happening to the two of them. He said he should tell the cops again. Apparently he did when he was younger, but nothing happened. And now . . . I mean, who's going to believe a fucking wee junkie claiming he's the brother of a famous model? It's just not going to happen, is it?'

'It's difficult, I'll say that.'

'Aye. More like impossible.'

'Did he say when he'd last seen her?'

'Aye. He said they'd lost touch years ago. They took her away when she was thirteen, but she came back to Glasgow one time and found him. She was trying to help him with the drugs and stuff, but he was a junkie big-time by then. I don't know what happened after that. But he'd seen her a few weeks ago, he said, and they'd been talking about the stuff that happened years ago. The abuse.'

Rosie had to find Dan. Of course he might be a fantasist, making up stories about a sister, but her instincts told her different. 'So, Mitch, how are we going to find Dan now? I really want to talk to him.'

'I was looking for him the past couple of days, but to be honest, I got caught up in a few things. I was arrested for shoplifting and spent a night in the cells, so I haven't had a real chance.'

'Have you any way of getting in touch or digging him up through friends?'

'Nobody knows who he is or what his story is. We don't really have a lot of friends in this fucking set-up. We only have people who'll give you the time of day if you share your stash with them, then rob you once you fall asleep.'

'Can you start looking for him now? Take me to some places? Or at least have a serious look for him, and as soon as you see him, call me?'

'Aye. I can do that. But I don't think you should be walking into some of the shitholes we hang around in.'

'I've been in them before, Mitch. As I said, I've been doing this a long time.'

'You don't look it. You look quite young.'

'I'm flattered.' Rosie smiled. Even a down-on-his-luck junkie had the guile to try a bit of charm. Top marks for effort.

She noticed that he had started to look even more pasty-faced, and sweat was appearing on his top lip and hairline. He needed more heroin.

'Listen, Rosie. I have to go. I've got to get myself sorted, know what I mean?'

Rosie knew exactly what he meant. She went into her bag and took out twenty quid. It was more than enough to see him through the day. Half of her believed she might as well set fire to it for all the good it would do her. But something inside told her that she could put a glimmer of trust into the pathetic shambles in front of her. Right now, she didn't have a lot of options.

'Here's the deal, Mitch, and listen good. I'm going to be looking for you later this afternoon and tonight. I want to talk to you and you'll need to tell me where you've been and what you've seen. I need you to do that. Just text me on your mobile.' She asked him to let her see it, then keyed in her number and stored it. 'Are you understanding me?'

'Aye. Of course I am. I'm going to find wee Dan for you

and I'm going to bring him and get him to talk. I want paid, mind you, but I don't want him fucked about because he'll need paid too.'

'Don't worry about that. Just find him for me, and we'll take it from there.'

They stood up and Rosie paid at the counter. Then they left, and Rosie found herself giving his bony shoulder a friendly squeeze as he half smiled.

'Thanks for the iced drink. I'll text you.'

Rosie watched him bounce down the road towards the Barrowfield, hoping her twenty quid wouldn't be smoking out of his brains in the next two hours.

CHAPTER SIX

Millie opened her eyes but could see nothing. It was pitch black. Her eyelids felt like they were weighed down. Fear lashed through her. Where the hell was she? She shifted in the bed and a searing pain shot through her hip and back. Then she remembered. Eastbourne. The car had hit her and flipped her into the air. The squeal of seagulls before she hit the ground, before everything turned black. She brought a hand up to touch her face. Nothing hurt there, and she traced her fingers across her lips and cheekbones, then her eyebrows. There was a bandage on her forehead. She followed the path of it, wrapped around her head, and pressed lightly, wincing at the sharp pain. She began to move her feet and arms slowly, to make sure she could, then turned her head a little to the side.

Her body was clammy, trembling every time she moved. But that was normal for Millie: every morning she woke up with the tremors. But now she could barely lift her head off the pillow. She must be in a hospital. But how long had she been out? And why was it so dark? She could hear movement in the corridor and turned her head carefully towards the chink of light under the door. Her eyes were beginning to focus and she could see that the blinds on the window were pulled down tight. She wanted to get up, but pain burned through her when she moved. She thought she wasn't badly injured, perhaps just stiff from the accident.

All of a sudden, the room lit up, the ceiling lights dazzling her. Slowly the window blind rose and stopped halfway, sending in streams of daylight. The handle of the door turned and was pushed open. She closed her eyes, barely breathing. She could hear someone approaching her bed. She half opened her eyes.

'Good morning, Millie.'

A broad Irish accent. Millie opened her eyes to see the bright smile of a nurse, middle-aged with a round, friendly face.

Millie didn't return her smile. 'Where am I?'

The nurse was adjusting a drip at the side of her bed, and looked down at her, again with the smile. 'You're going to be fine, Millie. How are you feeling?'

'Where am I?'

'You're in hospital, pet. I'm Staff Nurse Bridget Casey. You're being looked after well here, so don't you worry about a thing. The doctor will be in to see you shortly.'

Millie swallowed and licked her dry lips. Her tongue felt like paper. 'I got hit by a car.'

'Yes. You did. You were very lucky.'

Lucky, Millie thought. Sure, I've always been lucky. 'I hurt my head,' she said. 'And my hip. My back is very painful.'

'It's no wonder you're sore, Millie. Your hip is very badly bruised, but nothing is broken, thank God. And you've a few stitches in your head. You're on some very strong painkillers. But I'd say you'll live.' She grinned, blue eyes twinkling.

The words stung Millie. Suddenly she was back on the hotel roof. All she'd wanted was to jump, to end it all, until she'd seen Bella being dragged by those brutes. Suddenly her chest felt heavy and tears spilled out of her eyes and rolled down her cheeks.

The nurse reached down and took her hand, squeezing it gently. 'There there now, pet. Just let it all out. It's the shock. Delayed shock. It happens a lot after a trauma. You'll be fine.'

'I'm so sad.' Millie was still weeping, and the nurse took a tissue from a box on her bedside cabinet and wiped her eyes and nose.

'Don't be sad. Everything will be all right, in time. You've just had a bad shock and your body is traumatized. Your husband will be in shortly.'

Panic rose in Millie's chest. Colin would come breezing in here with his caring face on, but he'd be raging that she'd upset his busy routine. Suddenly it occurred to her that it might have got into the news that the ex-cabinet minister's wife had been knocked down by a car. She didn't want to see him. She just wanted to go back to Madrid, or any place she could be by herself. She wanted to find the strength she felt when she was full of alcohol, so that she could go to a police station and tell them what she had seen in Madrid: that Bella Mason had been thrown off the roof. She turned her head to the side and tears trickled into her ears as the nurse left.

Half an hour later the nurse came in again and gave her a drink, fussing around her bed and plumping up her pillows. Millie sipped it. Being attended to like this, the simple acts of kindness, somehow made her aware of how lonely she was inside. Her eyes welled again and she had to swallow the lump in her throat.

The nurse left and Millie lay back on the pillows, anxiously watching the door. She was tense, but the painkillers must have taken the edge off it. She recalled last night, being held down, hysterical, while someone injected her. That was the last thing she remembered. She'd been fighting and demanding to get out. The medication made her feel sad, but that was manageable. It had happened before. She watched the door, waiting.

Eventually it opened and the nurse came in again. 'You've got visitors, Millie.' She beamed.

Millie saw Colin behind her, his face changing from flint to a caring smile. A doctor in a white coat and thick black glasses stood behind him.

'Millie, darling!'

Colin's voice was shrill, fake and cut right through her. She didn't smile, but caught the nurse, concerned, glancing from one to the other.

'My God, darling! Look at the state of you! Are you all right?' Colin rushed to her bedside and leaned in, kissing her cheek. He held her hand.

Millie swallowed hard and nodded. 'I think so. I . . . I was hit by a car.'

'I know! Goodness! What a thing to happen! Well, don't worry, Millie. You're in safe hands now.' He looked into her eyes and she could see the smiling assassin that he was. He lowered his voice, lip curling. 'I'm going to make sure you're looked after this time.'

If Millie hadn't been mildly sedated she'd have screamed, but she just felt a dull recognition that she was imprisoned.

The doctor gave her a sympathetic smile. 'My name is Dr Andrew Black. How are you today, Mrs Chambers?'

'I'm okay,' Millie said. 'Pain in my hip and back when I move. My head hurts a bit. And my neck.'

'Yes. The neck is the whiplash. That'll take a few weeks. You just have to rest. I've had a look at your X-rays on the hip and back and it's just deep bruising, nothing broken. The X-ray of your skull is the same. You gave that car a run for its money, I'd say.'

Millie tried to smile, but her stomach was churning.

The doctor moved closer to her. 'Mrs Chambers, I've had a long talk with your husband. We've discussed your situation and had a look at your medical history.' He was staring straight at her, and she felt as if she was being accused, judged. 'You've had some mental-health issues in the past. I don't want you to worry about anything, because you will get better. You'll be able to cope. But you need complete rest, and some therapy. In time you'll get through this and then you'll be able to go home.'

Colin nodded at his side, but his expression was cold.

'Where am I?'

'You're in the Eastbourne General District Hospital, darling,' Colin said. 'But we're going to get you moved so that you can have a long rest and recuperate. Where people can take care of you and get you back to your old self.'

My old self, Millie thought, as she looked straight at him. You ruined my old self with your putdowns and your philandering, your beatings and your lies. I can never be my old self again. She felt herself shaking, but she had to stay calm. The medicine was steadying her a little. She said nothing.

'Okay. I'll look in on you a bit later, Mrs Chambers, once I've finished my rounds. Meanwhile, we'll leave you with your husband.'

He turned and nodded at the nurse, who caught Millie's eye as she backed away.

When the door closed, Colin waited, and for a long moment Millie thought he was building up to the red rage she'd seen so many times before, which ended with a slap. But he was managing to contain it somehow – probably because he knew he couldn't get away with it here.

'Okay, Millie. The fucking game is up,' he snarled.

She said nothing, waited for the deluge.

'I've had it with this charade. This . . . I've had it with your drunken antics, disappearing at every turn. Taking off to bloody Madrid! Fucking Madrid? What the fuck, Millie?'

Millie didn't reply, swallowed the ball of dryness. She wanted to say, 'Please listen to me. I'm so unhappy. I just couldn't go on any more with the rejection and the lies, and I went to Madrid to go back to the places where it all seemed so possible years ago, when you were the man I couldn't wait to see day and night. But you are gone now, gone for ever, and I hate who you are. I went to Madrid to end it all.' But, of course, she couldn't say it, and her chest felt tight trying to hold it in.

'I like Madrid,' she managed. 'You used to love it too, Colin. In the old days, when you were a good man. When you loved me.' She felt the tears come as her voice trailed off.

'Oh, spare me the bloody waterworks! Listen to me! You're unstable, Millie! Have been for years! When we were young and carefree, I put your exuberance and mood swings down to your artistic nature and all that crap. But you're mentally ill, Millie. You know that. You'll never be the woman I loved and married, and you've made it much worse by turning into a bloody lush. I can't take you anywhere these days unless I bloody monitor you at every turn. You're the biggest disappointment in my life, and I want more than anything to be bloody rid of you. But you know what? I have to be the husband who gets you picked up from hotels and cafes blind drunk. I have to swallow all that. I've had it now, Millie. No more! You're going into therapy and you're getting some treatment, whether you like it or not.'

His rant was like blows raining down on her and she lay there, defeated. Any faint hope that Colin would come in and be the man she had once loved was gone. This was who he was. He didn't want her. He didn't care about her or where she'd been or what she'd seen in Madrid. If she told him right now that she'd gone to Madrid to commit suicide, he'd say she couldn't even get that right, smirking as he spoke.

'What do you mean? I'm not going anywhere except home,' Millie protested, her voice weak.

'No, you're bloody not. I've wanted to have you sectioned for years, and your latest antics have given me all the evidence I need. I should have done it that time you fell asleep, drunk, while you were cooking, and set fire to the kitchen. If Conchita hadn't come in we could all have burned to death. Or the time you drove bladdered drunk and hit the bus stop. If it had been in the middle of the day, you could have killed somebody. But I let it go, thinking you'd get some sense into that nutcase head of yours. Every time you did your disappearing act of late, I told the doctor you were a danger to yourself, but he was giving you time. He'll back me up all the way now, though. Especially with your meltdown last night, screaming like a fucking lunatic. You're going in and that's final.' He shook his head. 'I mean, this whole debacle could end up in a bloody tabloid newspaper. You inconsiderate idiot!'

'You can't do that!' Millie said, her voice hurting her throat. But she knew he could. There was enough medical evidence over the years of depression and alcoholism, as well as her erratic behaviour. No doubt he'd been storing it all up for a day like this.

'Yes, I can. Your history, and your latest escapades have confirmed it. I've already got my own man in Harley Street to sign the documents. So shut up and take what's good for you. We'll see what you're like after a few months of therapy.'

Millie burst into tears, her head throbbing with the pressure. 'Leave me alone! Get out! Oh, God, help me! I just want to die! Please, somebody help me.'

The door opened and Nurse Bridget came in. She glanced at Millie, then glared at Colin, her eyes telling Millie that she was on her side. She was the first person she'd had on her side for so long. Millie looked at her pleadingly.

'Whatever is the matter, pet?', she asked. The nurse looked at Colin.

'Christ knows,' Colin said, irritated. 'She gets like this a lot.'

'Well, she's had a real trauma, with some delayed shock. I think it's best if she has a little more rest now, Mr Chambers, if you don't mind.' Her tone was dismissive.

Colin looked at her and then at Millie. He went across and took her hand but she pulled it back, and twisted her head away when he bent to kiss her. He turned and left. The nurse closed the door behind him.

'It's all right, pet,' she said. You'll be okay. You're a good person and a fine-looking woman too. Don't worry.'

CHAPTER SEVEN

Dan Mason shivered as he stood in the doorway, sheltering from the biting wind. The long sleeved t-shirt clung to his skinny body, and he stood with his hands dug deep into the pockets of his jeans, watching every car that passed, hoping it would be his punter. When the text had appeared on his mobile asking him to meet, he would have patched it rather than hang around outside on a shitty night like this. But he was desperate, and his drug debts were mounting. He hadn't made any money for the last four days, not since Bella . . .

Even now, despite the newspapers running the story on their front pages, and the TV news with endless updates, Dan still couldn't take it in. He'd never see his sister again. Ever. The thought brought tears to his eyes and he blinked and swallowed hard. Bella was all he'd had. All they'd ever had was each other, and for nearly twelve years, while Bella was fostered and he was left in the children's home, they didn't even have that. He'd cried every day for six months when they'd taken her away. He hadn't even known where she was, and at one point had been told that she'd been taken to America and had been adopted by a couple there. Why couldn't they have taken him too? he'd pleaded to the social worker. They only wanted a girl. He was told to toughen up, that Bella was gone. He had to be a strong boy now, like all the others in the children's home. But despite not seeing her, year in, year out, Dan had never felt totally alone because he knew she was out there, somewhere. Now he had nobody. He wiped his nose with the back of his hand as the tears came.

Dan lit a cigarette and shook himself out of the gloom. Where the fuck was this punter? He peered out at the line of cars, I'm freezing to death. He took a long draw on his cigarette and coughed till he lost his breath, doubling over. The racking cough was like a knife in his chest. It had been that the way for more than a week now, and it was getting worse. Standing here without a jacket didn't help, and he cursed the robbing bastard who had stolen it from the hostel. It was Bella who'd given it to him as a present the last time they'd met, and he'd treasured it. He'd even slept in it most nights, wherever he could get his head down, which was often under the Jamaica Bridge along with the other junkies and down-and-outs. He'd only taken it off in the hostel because he'd woken up in a pool of sweat with a raging temperature. He'd folded it carefully and put it under his head, but when he woke up in the morning it was gone.

Dan was about to give up on the punter when he spotted a car flashing its headlights. He stepped out of the doorway and glanced up and down Waterloo Street as the blue Ford Mondeo pulled in to the kerb. He opened the door and got in.

'Awright, son?'

'Fucking freezing, man! Some bastard stole my jacket. The only one I had.'

The punter half smiled as he shot him a sideways glance, then pulled out into the traffic. Dan stared out of the window as the car went through Anderston bus station and along Argyle Street. He knew where they were headed. It was always a deserted car park in one of the side streets at the end of Broomielaw. Nearly every week, the same routine. The car pulled into the side street and up to the top of the road, then into the car park. Dan felt his body tense. This shit never got any easier. Not just with this guy, but with any of the punters. He hated putting himself through it, but it was all about survival. It always had been. Even the first time, when he was only eight, instinct had told him it was safer to say nothing.

The punter switched off the engine, and as they sat in the darkness, he could hear his breath quicken. Dan shifted his body so he was facing him, his knees apart. He knew the drill. The punter reached across and fondled his penis through his jeans. He didn't seem to mind that there was no response, and ran his hand down Dan's skinny thighs, caressing him. There was something almost tender about it. Then he unzipped his trousers and pulled Dan's hand across, pushing it inside. He was already hard. Dan began to move his hand up and down as the punter leaned back making little moaning sounds. He placed his hand on Dan's head, running his fingers through the blond hair and gripping it tight. He looked Dan in the eye. 'Come on, son. Get on with it. I'm dying here.'

He pushed Dan's head down. Dan took him in his mouth, closing his eyes tight as he worked. At least it wouldn't take long. He could hear the punter's breath come in short gasps as he muttered and cursed, then shouted, 'Fuck!' as Dan brought him to a shuddering climax. Dan opened the passenger door, spat on the ground, then wiped his mouth with a tissue from a box on the dashboard.

They sat in silence while the punter sorted himself and Dan stared out of the windscreen at the garbage swirling in the wind. He could hear the rustle of notes as the punter switched on the engine. Dan's eyes lit up when he handed him three tenners. 'Get yourself a jumper or something, son. You'll freeze to death.'

Dan had to bite his lip to stop himself crying at this simple act of kindness. In spite of all the shit, there was time for kindness. Then suspicion flooded him. 'I don't do anything else. Just the blow-job. Okay?'

The punter nodded. 'Fine by me. You want to be dropped where I picked you up?'

'Yeah. Thanks.'

They drove back to the city centre in silence. Dan got out of the car and looked back in at the punter.

'See you later, son. Take care of yourself.'

Dan closed the door and walked quickly towards the cafe where he knew he could get a burger and a tenner bag of heroin from the guy on the till.

Dan was woken by someone shaking him. He opened one eye. 'Fuck me, Mitch! I was asleep!'

'I know, man. Sorry. But I've been looking for you for four fucking days. I thought you'd topped yourself.'

Dan sniffed, his eyes focusing in the dark. He took a breath, but it hurt his chest and he started to cough.

'Fuck's sake, man. You got some kind of lurgy? You sound like my da before he died of fucking emphysema.'

Dan stopped coughing and took a short breath. 'Don't know. Think I've got some kind of infection.'

'You need to go to a doctor.'

Dan sat up. 'Aye, fine. Can you just phone my doctor and ask him to do a house call?' He shook his head, sweating but freezing. 'I don't have a doctor. I don't even have a fucking address, man.'

Mitch lay down close to him, pulling his own blanket over him. 'Well, we need to see the doctor tomorrow. We'll go up to the hospital.'

'I was coughing blood this morning,' Dan said matter-of-factly.

'Fuck me, man! I hope I don't catch anything from you.' Mitch sniggered and snuggled in. 'Come on. Back to sleep.'

From the park bench in Glasgow Green, Dan and Mitch watched the customers come and go into the People's Palace, an elegant city landmark straddling the line between the prosperous city centre and the run-down East End. They'd attempted to go into the cafe in the Palace's Victorian glasshouse for breakfast an hour ago, but were turned away at the door by a receptionist who could tell a mile off they were a couple of junkies. They'd bounced away with a one- finger salute, and headed for the cafe off London Road that served the best Coca-Cola iced drinks. They'd smoked some heroin in one of the boarded-up squats in the Calton, after Mitch had returned triumphant from Argyle Street with a padded jacket he'd shoplifted for Dan.

'It's nice this,' Dan said, admiringly running his hand down the sleeve. He zipped it up to the neck and sat back, his face upturned to the sun. 'Feels really warm.'

'No worries, Dan. I don't want you peggin' out on me.' He drew on his cigarette. 'Listen, mate. I've got something I want to talk about.'

Dan turned to him, blinking one eye against the glare of the sun. 'Aye? What?'

'It's about your sister. Bella.'

Dan said nothing for a while and they sat in silence. Then he looked at Mitch. 'What do you mean?'

'Do you really think somebody might have shoved her off that roof in Madrid? Like, murdered her?'

Dan sighed. He put a hand into his jacket pocket, took out a cigarette, lit it, and coughed as he inhaled. He spat on the ground.

Mitch leaned forward. 'There's fucking blood in that, man!'

Dan sniffed and composed himself, taking another draw. 'I know. Fucking hurts too.' He took a few shallow breaths, then turned to Mitch. 'Aye. I do think somebody killed Bella.' He leaned forward, his elbows resting on his knees. 'But listen, Mitch. Nobody knows she was my sister. That's how it was, how it had to be between us.'

'How come?'

'It just did, right? Bella . . . I didn't see her for twelve years. She was already famous when she found me. I was a fucked-up wreck, a junkie. That's why.'

Dan could still picture the moment he'd seen Bella after they'd been apart since he was nine years old. The image gave him a physical pain in his heart. He stared straight ahead.

'Listen, mate. I want to tell you something. Er . . . I don't want you to get mad at me. It was after that day when you saw the paper and collapsed and stuff. I was really shocked. And, well, I talked to somebody.'

Dan shifted his body to face him. 'What? You fucking told somebody? Fuck me! Who?'

After a few beats, Mitch answered: 'A reporter. From the *Post*.'

It took a few seconds to sink in. Then he leaned back, looking up at the sky.

'Aw, for fuck's sake, man! You spoke to a reporter? Are you fucking kidding me? What if the papers find me? That can't happen. It's too dangerous.'

Mitch was confused. 'What do you mean, too dangerous?'

'Just is.' He shook his head. 'Listen, Mitch. There's a lot more to this. It's . . . It's just . . . Aw, man, I don't know what to say now in case you go running to the fucking papers.'

'Maybe it's you who should go to the papers, Dan. Go to the cops, if you're scared. Tell them why.' He paused. 'Why are you scared, anyway?'

Dan shook his head and flicked his cigarette away. The last time he and Bella had met, she'd picked him up in a taxi and taken him to the hotel she was staying at, made him have a shower and given him a new set of clothes, including the new jacket that some other homeless fucker was now wearing. Then she'd made him eat some soup. He remembered her crying as he was leaving, hugging him close. He could still smell her perfume, feel the softness of her hair on his cheek. They'd talked for hours and she'd told him everything. It was the first time they had ever spoken about the abuse that had happened when they were children, the nights when they were taken away, the strangers who came in and took them from their beds. Not just them, but others too. Bella had said she couldn't cope with it any more, that she had been taking cocaine to get through her demanding work schedule, but also, because she was crying for days on end. They'd talked about going to the police then. And look what had happened.

'I can't tell you. I can't talk about it. Just leave it.'

'Why don't you at least meet the reporter? She's quite a nice bird.'

'You've fucking met her?'

'Aye. I'm sorry. I was trying to help.'

'Yeah, Mitch. Trying to get some fucking money out of her. Don't try to hump me, man. You're supposed to be my mate. I thought you were my friend. You . . . You're all I've got.'

Dan put his head into his hands. He jerked away when Mitch's arm went round his shoulders, but Mitch persisted. Eventually he turned and sobbed into his chest.

'Come on, man. I'm sorry. I *am* your friend. But listen, something's wrong. I can feel it. Something's wrong inside your head.'

'I'm scared, Mitch. I just want to die so I can be with Bella.'

'No, you don't, mate. I won't let you die. I'll look after you. I promise.'

They sat hugging each other, and Mitch gently stroked the back of Dan's head, as the midday sun warmed the chilly Glasgow morning, filling it with promise.

CHAPTER EIGHT

Rosie stood by McGuire's desk along with Bob, the picture editor, all three of them watching his screen, eagerly waiting for the pictures to drop. José, the concierge in Madrid, had proved to be a belter of a contact, going about his task like a detective, picking up any information at the Hotel Senator that he thought would be useful to her. The four hundred euro the editor's office had arranged to wire him was no doubt the driving force, but Rosie was more than impressed by his enthusiasm. He'd called her this morning to say his friend on the night shift had gone through the spare copy of the CCTV and found pictures of the two men he'd described to her, who had arrived at the party that night. One had given Bella a wrap of what he believed to be cocaine.

The pictures dropped onto the screen one by one. First, the muscled guy with the bleached-blond hair, then his squat mate with the brick-shithouse frame. A third opened, and Rosie's eyes popped. It wasn't the greatest shot in terms of clarity, but Bella Mason, in her blue gown, was clearly identifiable, and it looked as though she was being handed something.

'Can you pull that up, Bob?' Mick said. 'Make it less grainy?'

'I should be able to enhance it a bit. The more we home in on it, the less clear it is, but the geeks downstairs understand these things. I'll see what we can do.'

'Are these two gorillas the blokes he was talking about, who turned up and weren't on the guest list?'

The editor was addressing Rosie, but didn't take his eyes off the screen as Bob zoomed in on the faces.

'Yep. That's how he described them. In fact the pictures so far show exactly what José described when I talked to him that day, before he'd even seen the CCTV. So he's spot on with his information.'

'I might have to give the guy a job,' McGuire quipped. 'He's shit hot.' He sat back in his chair, hands behind his head. 'Of course, using these at this time will be a problem because the cops have taken the CCTV as part of their investigation, so it's evidence.'

'Yeah,' Rosie said. 'Evidence in a *Spanish* investigation. We need to speak to the lawyers and get the lowdown on how much we can use in this country. But even if we don't use the pictures, we can still tell the story, say it was from insiders who cannot be named but who witnessed everything. From what I see here, I can get a colour piece out of Bella's final moments. Not suggesting anything untoward, just that these are the last pictures of her alive.'

'Great! I fucking love it when this happens, Gilmour. Tell your man I'm very pleased with him. And get Tom Hanlon on the phone.'

Tom was the *Post*'s hotshot lawyer, whom Rosie regularly wrestled to the floor when she was fighting to get her more explosive stories into the paper.

'But, Mick,' Rosie said, 'We have to work out the impact of using this story at this point. It's a fantastic line and leaves the rest of the media in our wake, but I don't want to blow it too early. There might be even better ones to come, maybe even more pictures. I have to talk to José later. He's keeping his ear to the ground on the police investigation. If anyone can pick up a line, it's him.'

McGuire nodded at the picture editor, signalling that he wanted to talk to Rosie alone. Bob left the room, saying he'd have a look at what he could do with the images.

Rosie's mobile rang on McGuire's desk and she picked it up. It was Mitch.

'I have to take this, Mick.' She walked away from McGuire's desk towards the window and put the phone to her ear. 'Mitch? You there? It's Rosie.'

Silence.

Christ! Rosie thought. He'll be spaced out somewhere. 'Mitch. Are you there? Talk to me.'

'Rosie. Aye. It's me, Mitch.'

She was relieved to hear his voice, even if it was thick and slurring. 'Are you all right?'

'Aye, man. No' bad. Listen, Rosie. Can you come and meet us?'

A little punch of excitement in her gut. He had said 'us'. 'You found Dan?'

'Aye. I got him. He's not very well and stuff. But he's all right. I told him about you.'

'Sure. Just tell me where and I'll come right now. Do you want me to pick you up?'

Rosie didn't want to hear the details of what Mitch had told Dan and how he'd managed to get him to agree to see her. She wanted to be off the phone and out to meet them.

'Aye, well, maybe you could come and get us. It's pishing rain and we'd need to walk to the town.'

'Where are you?'

'Down in the Barrowfield.'

Rosie grimaced. Barrowfield, a run-down clutch of council houses, was deepest heroin territory. It wasn't the kind of place you just wandered into. Delivery men had stopped going there months ago, and GPs refused to do house calls, fearing for their safety. Rosie pushed away the memory of her last visit: she'd had to climb out of a bedroom window and make a run for it through the back gardens after some nutcase had held her prisoner, with a slavering Rottweiler watching her every move.

'Fine,' she said. 'What's the address?'

She could hear mumbling in the background. Mitch probably didn't even know what bloody house he was in.

'Number thirty-six. Text me when you're nearly here.'

'Okay. I'll be there shortly. Is Dan with you?'

'Aye. He's standing right here. By the way, if anybody asks, you're my cousin, right?'

'Fine. See you in fifteen minutes. Wait for me.'

'Aye, right. We're waiting.'

The line went dead.

Rosie took a long breath and let it out slowly, then turned to McGuire, who was staring at her, intrigued. 'Mick,' she said. 'I've got something to tell you.'

'Aw, fuck! I hate it when you say that, Gilmour. What's happened?'

'Probably the biggest story we've seen in a very long time – if it turns out to be true.'

'Tell me.'

'I went to see this guy the other day. He'd phoned in. A junkie. He said he had information about Bella, and wanted to meet.'

'How much dosh did you have to part with?'

'Nothing,' Rosie lied. 'Just listen. It gets better. I met this guy – his name's Mitch – in a cafe off London Road. The usual suspect, junked-up, skinny as a rat, but he only goes and tells me that Bella Mason has a brother.'

McGuire leaped to his feet as though he'd been stung. 'Yeah, right! A brother?'

'So this guy says. The brother's a junkie too. Homeless and living rough here. His name is Dan Mason.'

'Christ almighty, Rosie! Who was that on the phone?'

'That was Mitch. He hadn't seen Dan for a few days, but I told him to go looking for him, and he has.' Rosie headed for the door. 'He's with him now, so I'm going to pick them up.'

'Pick them up? Where are they?'

'Barrowfield.'

'Fuck's sake. You need someone with you.'

'I'll take Matt. We can't go in mob-handed and frighten them off. I have to go, Mick.' Rosie was almost out of the door.

'Phone me as soon as you're out of there. Do you hear me?'

'Yeah, I hear you.'

By the time she answered she was well out of McGuire's earshot and heading for the stairs.

Rosie gazed out of the window as Matt pulled off London Road and into the shambles that was Barrowfield housing scheme. In the shadow of the Celtic football stadium, it stood out like a rotting tooth. The streets were deserted, and in every one of the grim grey buildings, at least three of the flats were boarded up with steel. A couple of abandoned cars were propped up on bricks, the wheels having vanished long ago. As they drove into the street, Rosie sent a text to Mitch. He didn't answer, so Matt pulled up at the next block from number thirty-six and waited.

Rosie spotted Mitch standing outside the house, with a smaller skinny figure. 'That's my man there.'

'He certainly looks the part.'

Matt drove towards him and Mitch peered into the car. 'Who's this?' he said, suspicious. The guy with him was shivering.

'It's okay, Mitch. He works with me. Don't worry. Just get in and we'll go for breakfast.'

They got into the car. Matt glanced at Rosie and pinched his nose. The lads smelt like they hadn't changed their clothes in a week. Rosie turned to them as Matt reversed and headed out of the scheme.

'This is Dan,' Mitch said.

'Dan.' She stretched across to the back seat and held his cold clammy hand a second longer than she needed to. 'I'm Rosie Gilmour. You all right?'

He looked no more than sixteen or seventeen, but there was nothing of carefree youth in his haunted expression. He nodded, his eyes downcast, and said nothing.

'He's a bit worried,' Mitch said. He turned to Dan. 'It's all right, pal. You'll be fine.'

'Don't worry, Dan.' Rosie spoke softly. He looked up and she caught the striking green eyes, fringed with long lashes. Then she said brightly, 'You guys look like you need a good breakfast.'

'We had a wee joint.' Mitch also seemed to want to lighten things.

'I mean a real breakfast.' Rosie smiled at Dan, hoping for a response. His eyes softened and his lips twitched a little. It was as good as it was going to get for now. Rosie directed Matt to the cafe. 'They do the best Coca-Cola iced drinks in Glasgow.' she flipped down the sun visor and looked at Mitch.

When they pulled up outside, Rosie told Matt it was best if she went in alone with the two lads. If there was a chance that Dan was going to talk, he might respond better if it was just her. Matt was happy to give the greasy spoon a miss, and said he'd hang handy in the hope of a picture.

'He looks a bit like her,' he whispered to Rosie, as the boys got out of the car. 'Like Bella, but a half-starved version. I can definitely see a resemblance – the eyes.'

Rosie couldn't help but agree, though she didn't want to think that far ahead. Find the truth, an old news editor once told her, not what you want the story to be. She'd never forgotten it as she'd chased down stories as a young reporter.

Inside the cafe, Rosie walked to the furthest booth, tucked into the corner, and slid in. Mitch and Dan sat opposite. It was mid-morning and the place was empty, apart from an old man: he looked as though he'd been turfed out of the hostel round the corner. Two men in working boots and jeans were at the counter. Dan shivered as he loosened his padded jacket and took a packet of cigarettes out of his pocket. He handed one to Mitch, and Rosie waited while they lit up.

She was about to speak when suddenly Dan started to cough. She frowned and glanced at Mitch as Dan's face went crimson, coughing so deep in his chest he was on the verge of passing out. 'Christ! What's wrong? Are you sick, Dan?'

He managed to get his breath back, eyes watering, beads of sweat appearing at his hairline where his fringe parted at the side. He nodded. 'Had this cough for over a week now. Sweating and cold all the time.' He sniffed and stubbed out the cigarette.

'He coughs up blood,' Mitch added.

Dan glared at him as though it were a betrayal, but Mitch shrugged. 'I'm just sayin', man. You need to see a doctor. You need to get something for that. Maybe you've got fucking pneumonia.'

'Aye, with a bit of luck.'

Rosie let his words hang for a few beats, but she had to suppress the urge to reach across and touch his face, feel the heat of his forehead. In fact she wanted to do more than that. She couldn't watch a kid suffering, whether it was in some far-flung refugee camp or some teenage junkie shivering in a Glasgow street, without wanting to take them home and make their lives better. As if she could. It was a ridiculous notion, and what McGuire called her 'bleeding heart' had landed her in trouble more times than she could count. But wading through other people's misery most of her working life hadn't left her immune to it. Here she was, staring at this kid, because although Mitch had told her he was twenty-one, he was still just a kid, too young to be so screwed up. Before Dan had uttered a word about himself, she could tell by looking at him, that he was broken.

'Mitch is right, Dan,' Rosie said quietly. 'You need to see a doctor. Today.'

'I don't have one.'

'I'll sort that, don't worry. After we leave here.' She took a breath. 'Right, let's get something to eat.'

The young ponytailed waitress came shuffling across, chewing gum, and looked at the two junkies with mild disgust.

'Iced drink for me,' Mitch said.

'Me too,' Dan added.

'Eat something as well, guys. Come on. Humour me.' Rosie smiled at them. 'Don't make me sit here and eat a cheese toastie all by myself.'

'Aye, well, get me a sausage roll then, and tea.'

'Me too,' Dan said.

He looked slightly more relaxed and slipped off his jacket. Rosie could see the hollow of his shoulders and his ribs through the long sleeved T-shirt. She watched him, trying to pick her words. She might as well get to the point.

'Dan.' She glanced at Mitch. 'You know Mitch talked to me about you being Bella Mason's brother.'

Dan nodded. 'Yeah. That's right. Bella's – well, she was – my sister.'

He looked down at the table and clasped his hands together tightly, the knuckles white.

'It's never been mentioned before, Dan. In any of the interviews with Bella, she never mentioned you.'

'I know. Nobody knows about it. Just me and her.' His lips tightened. 'Well, maybe a couple of people. But they'll just deny it.'

'Really? Why would they do that?'

The iced drinks arrived and the waitress put them on the table. Dan took a long drink, his Adam's apple slipping up and down his skinny neck. He sniffed. 'They just would. I don't have my birth certificate. Lost it years ago. But nobody knows anything about Bella. All that shite in the magazines, stuff about her being discovered in some cafe as a thirteen-year-old, is crap. That's not what happened. I know what happened. I was there.'

'Where, Dan?'

'In the home. The children's home. Here in Glasgow.' He suddenly stopped and bit his lip, his face reddening. 'I fucking know everything, what they did to us. Perverts.' He shook his head. 'Not just me and Bella. Fucking loads of weans.'

Rosie's heart sank. What she was hearing, if it was genuine, was massive. But she'd heard similar tales before, from

Mags Gillick's little girl and her friend. The *Post* had exposed the men behind it, but not all the perpetrators, not the ones at the top because they were never fully unmasked for what they were. One of the High Court judges who was implicated in a child-abuse ring simply stood down to avoid publicity and an agreement was reached with the *Post* not to publish his involvement. Even now, years later, it sickened Rosie. And now this.

'Which home?'

'Eastwood Park. It's closed now.' Dan sipped some more of his drink as the waitress came over with the rest of their order.

Rosie reached across and touched his hand. 'I've written about that before, Dan. Not Eastwood Park, a different home. So I know these things went on. It was hard for people to believe, but it happened.'

'Too right it did.'

There was a lot to do here, Rosie thought. A whole life story to tell. She'd been surprised that Dan had come straight to the point so quickly, and she could imagine McGuire saying that what she had here were two hopeless heroin addicts selling a story on the back of a model's death. Prove it, he'd say. And it had better be solid proof – every line of it.

'When did you last see Bella?' Rosie asked, just to find out what Dan would say and to watch his face for any signs of a fairy story than to find out the answer, though nothing about him so far had made her think he was lying.

'Two months ago. She came to see me for my birthday. Well, it was a couple of days after my actual birthday. She came up to Glasgow and was staying in the hotel.'

'Which one?'

'That one up Great Western Road. Devonshire Gardens or something. Dead posh. She had a suite and everything.'

Rosie nodded. This at least was checkable. 'Okay, Dan. I want you to tell me about that visit. But before we get there, I think it's best if we start at the beginning. How do you feel about that? The beginning of you and Bella. Where you were born. What happened to your parents. Can you talk to me about that?'

Dan pushed away the empty glass and lifted the mug of tea. He glanced at Mitch.

'I think you should talk to her, man,' Mitch said. 'You need to. You'll not be right till this all comes out in the open.'

Dan wrung his hands. 'I don't know. I'm nervous. Fucking messed up, you know, with the heroin and stuff. I've been smoking heroin for the past four years. My life's a mess.'

Rosie listened patiently. He was rattling a little, and she knew she hadn't long before the pair of them would need to top up with something. She had to get to the start of the story.

'Dan, I'm sure Mitch told you that I'm working on this story about Bella. There's something not right about how she died. It's being dismissed as suicide, but why would a young, successful, beautiful girl want to kill herself? I don't believe it, but I can't do anything about it unless I can really look into Bella's life. If something bad happened, as you're hinting, I want to look at it and see if that's the reason she could have taken her life. But I need to know the facts of her early life to build up a picture.'

'Bella didn't kill herself. No way! That's not why she died.'

'How do you know?'

'Because I was with her in Glasgow that time, and she talked to me about going to the police. She said she'd already told Mervyn Bates. He was her mentor – well, actually her manager. They'd fallen out over it. She said she was going to the police about everything. The drugs, the abuse. Everything. When she came to see me, that was what we talked about. No way did Bella want to die. She wanted to tell the police everything. Me and her. We were going to do it together. But *they* stopped us.' Tears came to his eyes and he covered his face with his hands. Mitch put an arm around his shoulders.

Rosie watched, her tape recorder on. She needed to get him in some kind of order with this. He was making allegations, but not telling her any real details. 'Dan,' she said, squeezing his hand. 'Let's just take a moment here. Eat something and have some tea. Do you want to talk to me about the whole story? I can look into this harder than anyone. Nobody will stop me, I can promise you that. And nobody will get to you.'

'How do you know?'

'I'll sort it. I promise.'

'I want to do something about it. For Bella.'

'Then take your time and start at the beginning.'

He nodded and wiped away his tears.

CHAPTER NINE

Nothing had prepared Millie for this. Nothing could have. To be completely powerless to fight back, to scream at the injustice of it, to have any choices taken away from you. She felt like a prisoner, and she wasn't even there yet. She carefully folded the stiff blue notepaper – thank God she still had her handbag with some stationery inside – put it into the envelope, which she sealed, and addressed it to Bridget, the Irish nurse. She didn't care who knew now. She had nothing left to lose.

The door opened and Nurse Bridget came in, carrying a cup of tea. 'Thought you might like a cuppa, Millie.' She smiled warmly and put it on the bedside cupboard.

'I'd kill for some gin,' Millie wanted to say, but instead she thanked her. The painkillers took the edge off the craving, but if she could get her hands on a bottle of gin, she'd down the whole lot just to blot out today. The nurse fussed around the room, tidying everything away, opening the window a little.

Millie glanced out at the driving rain, and looked at her small suitcase in the corner, all packed and ready to go. They were taking her to a private clinic in the Sussex countryside, she had been told by the psychologist who had visited her yesterday. It was for the best, and she needn't be afraid. In a few months' time, if all went well and she responded to the therapy, she could go home. They aimed to give her the tools to cope with her condition, the shrink had told her.

Tools, Millie had thought. She'd never heard that expression before. The tools she'd used for the past twelve years were contained in a bottle of wine, champagne, gin or any other drink she could get hold of. For years nobody had noticed, because in most of the circles she moved in, the ladies lunched and drank, then topped up in the evenings with their husbands or lovers. But Millie knew she wasn't drinking to be sociable and to enjoy herself. Alcohol deadened the pain, and by the time she'd realized it was only making things worse, it was too late. She needed it. It had taken over her life.

'The car will be here shortly,' Bridget said, checking the watch on the breast pocket of her uniform.

A wave of panic rushed through Millie. 'I don't want to go,' she said, her chest tight with emotion.

'I know, pet, but maybe it's for the best. These people are highly trained. You'll be okay.' She held Millie's hand.

Millie nodded, unable to stop the tears. 'Will you come and visit me?'

There was pity in Bridget's pale blue eyes. 'I'd love to, Millie. But it's not really allowed. I mean, I'm not supposed to get involved with patients.'

'But you can see I don't want this.'

'I know, pet. But I have to be able to take a step back professionally. I'm sure you can understand that. You're just afraid. But you'll be fine once you're settled.'

Millie clenched her fists. 'Bridget. Please, listen to me. Before they come for me I have something to tell you. I have something for you.' She reached below her pillow and pulled out the envelope.

Bridget looked confused.

'There's a letter in here. Well, a statement from me.' She handed it to her.

'A statement?' She was puzzled now.

'Yes. I need to explain what happened. I have to tell someone what I saw.'

'What do you mean, Millie? What did you see?'

'That night. In Madrid. I saw it. Bella Mason. The girl—'

The door suddenly opened. A man and a woman came in. One was wearing a uniform, and the other a suit. They were here. Millie looked through her tears at Bridget, pleading with her eyes. Bridget slipped the envelope into the pocket of her tunic. 'Come on now, Millie,' she said, firm but sympathetic. 'That's your car to collect you.'

The uniformed woman picked up the case from the corner of the room and waited.

Millie swallowed. Her legs felt a little weak as she got off the bed, but she put up her hand to dismiss the woman in uniform who took a step towards her.

'Do you want me to get a wheelchair?' the woman asked.

'No. I do not want a wheelchair. I'm not an invalid.'

Millie attempted to hold herself upright, raising her chin defiantly. She could do this. She had to. She fought back her tears. She took a few faltering steps, the pain still in her hip, but she managed it. Bridget helped her on with her coat, as the other two waited outside in the doorway. As she stood opposite Bridget, Millie put her arms around her. 'Thank you,' she said. Then, when Bridget hugged her back, Millie whispered in her ear, 'Please help me. Please, Bridget. I have nobody. I'm not mentally ill, just so unhappy.'

The nurse released her, and kept her face friendly but without emotion. Millie nodded, biting her lip. There was nothing more she could do. She walked down the corridor, the Cuban heels of her leather ankle boots clicking on the tiles. She took it slowly, aware that some of the staff were watching her from behind the nurses' station. She didn't look in their direction but straight ahead, walking as though she were going to the gallows, because that was how she felt.

Outside, the driver in his grey chauffeur's uniform held open the back door of the black Jaguar. She nodded at him and slipped inside. She sank into the black leather seat and gazed out of the window at the first signs of spring: the crows' nests high up in the tall poplar trees, the sun breaking through the clouds. The tears came to her eyes and she let them spill onto her cheeks. She had never felt so helpless and so alone.

Bridget Casey opened the front door of her flat and put her heavy shopping bags on the hall floor. She was soaked after trudging from the bus stop and glad to get out of the downpour. She stood for a moment, exhausted, and leaned against the front door, enjoying the warmth of her house. Again, the image came to her of Millie Chambers walking down the corridor in the hospital towards the front door. She had held her head high, a beautiful but broken woman, trying to be proud amid the humiliation of being sectioned as a basket case. It was a horrible, degrading thing to happen to a human being, but in a lot of cases, it was the only way to stop someone harming themselves or others. Normally, nothing like that would get under her skin, and rich, privileged women like Millie Chambers were pretty low on her sympathy radar. Yet she couldn't stop thinking about the poor woman, the pleading in her eyes. What had been so wrong in her life that she had shattered like a piece of fine porcelain? Bridget wondered.

She had heard the conversation between the husband and the hospital's psychiatrist about Millie being bipolar or suffering from some form of schizophrenia. She'd recognized Colin Chambers all right. A big-shot. Handsome and quite charming, glad-handing all the staff when he'd breezed in the other day. But Bridget had stood outside Millie's door yesterday and heard him tear a strip off his poor wife once the doctor had left. That wasn't right. Not in her condition. Whatever else this big snob was in his high-profile life, he was a cowardly abuser. A pure bastard.

Bridget picked up her shopping and went into the kitchen, then put it away in the fridge and the cupboards. She took a ready meal out of the freezer and shoved it into the microwave, then went into the living room and switched on the lights and the television. She sat down, opened her bag and took out the white envelope. She laid it on the coffee table, unsure whether to open it or not. She shouldn't even have taken it from Millie. It was bad enough that she'd been thinking about the poor woman all day, but she couldn't get involved like this. If anyone in the hospital found out she'd taken a letter from a patient she'd be in trouble. She picked it up. She should rip it up now and be done with it. But Millie had said she'd seen something in Madrid. She'd mentioned the name of the model who'd killed herself . . . Bridget sighed. Maybe Millie *was* mentally ill, delusional and as raving mad as they were saying. She sat back, the envelope in her hand.

The microwave pinged. She stood up and went into the kitchen, tossing the letter into the bin as she passed it.

After she had eaten, Bridget sat flicking through the TV channels from soap to soap, not really watching them but just staring, almost catatonic she was so tired. She'd been working since eight that morning and could rarely stay awake beyond nine thirty. She yawned, then got up to go and run a bath. It would help her sleep. It had been a pretty hellish day.

As she watched the tub fill with water, she thought again of Millie Chambers. She'd be in that private clinic by now, probably all cried out and desperately alone, no doubt sedated and locked into some pristine room. It rankled with her. Something wasn't right about it. She took off her clothes, put on her towelling robe and went down to the kitchen. She took out the envelope from the bin, slid it open and began to read.

CHAPTER TEN

Rosie had woken up with TJ holding her tight, whispering that everything was okay, that she was just having a dream. She opened her eyes, and he was looking at her. He wiped away her tears. Her throat tightened, partly with sadness from the dream, but also because she was glad he was there. So many times, when she'd woken herself screaming or crying like this, she'd longed for him to fill the crushing emptiness that overwhelmed her.

'Still with the nightmares, then, Gilmour?' TJ said, as she lay back on the pillow. 'Do they happen as much?'

Rosie sighed, staring at the ceiling. She'd been embarrassed the first time she'd slept with TJ and had woken up crying. He was the only person she'd ever told about her childhood and how she'd been waking up with these traumas for most of her life. 'Not as often. A lot of it depends on what's going on in my life, mostly at work. If I'm under pressure, scared or upset, it seems to lie dormant until I go to sleep. Then it all joins together to create some drama stretching back to that day with my mother – when I saw her.'

'I dreamed about you sometimes when I was in New York,' TJ said, propping himself up on his elbow.

'Yeah?' Rosie gave him a sideways glance. 'Nightmares, no doubt.'

'Nah. Mostly they were erotic. In fact, I think I feel another one coming on now.' He pulled her on top of him.

They made love with hunger, losing themselves, as though it were for the last time. Then Rosie's mobile rang on the bedside table.

'Aw, fuck, Rosie! Leave it!' TJ said, breathless, as he clutched her hair. 'Please, leave it.'

For a second, Rosie felt her body slacken against him, the urge to answer the phone crashing through her. But, this time, she let it ring.

Afterwards, she lay in TJ's arms, exhausted.

'Come on, Gilmour. I know you're dying to get on your mobile. Don't pretend you're relaxing in the afterglow.' He nuzzled her neck. 'I'm impressed you stayed till the end, though.'

Rosie smiled, reaching over and propping herself up on the pillow, then checked her phone. A missed call from McGuire, and it wasn't even eight yet. 'It's my editor. I have to call him.' She sat up, swinging her feet to the floor, and pushed the call-return key as she walked naked to the bedroom door.

'I'll do some breakfast.' TJ yawned.

McGuire tossed the *Mirror* onto his desk. 'Get a load of this, Gilmour! Out of the fucking blue!'

Rosie picked up the paper, the front page headline screaming, 'TORY WIFE HIT BY CAR'. And beneath it a strapline, 'FORMER MINISTER'S WIFE IN HOSPITAL'.

'Christ! That changes things a bit,' Rosie said, as she read through the story.

'Sure does. Sit down, Rosie, we need to work out how we move on what we've got.'

Rosie sat on the sofa, still reading. 'There's a line in here from some witness saying Millie seemed a bit confused moments before she stepped off the pavement.'

'Or pissed. Or hungover.' McGuire picked up his mug of coffee and came out from behind his desk to sit opposite her. 'How much did we get from Pettigrew in Westminster re the state of the Chambers marriage and all that kind of shit?'

'Well, he's still digging away. The signs are that she's a bit of a lush, highly strung is what he's been told, but also very popular. A real beauty in her day, as we know from the pictures.'

Rosie had been delighted that José had once again come up trumps, sending her a picture yesterday of Millie Chambers in the foyer at the Hotel Senator in Madrid.

'There's no mention in the story of why she was in East-bourne,' McGuire said. 'And nothing about Madrid.'

'Well, our picture and information put her in Madrid just a day or so before this car accident. But, more impor-tantly, we can place her in the same hotel the night Bella died. I'd say we've no option now but to start moving on that. You never know what might come out.'

'Agreed. The statement here from her prick of a husband is just the usual waffle. He says Millie had gone to East-bourne for a little break, that it's one of her favourite coastal retreats, she having spent holidays there as kid. Bullshit!'

'Yeah,' Rosie said. 'Well, the smart money is on them having a punch-up and she buggers off to Madrid, then to Eastbourne.'

'Do you think she got off her mark smartish in Madrid after Bella took the dive?'

'Absolutely. She'd have to. Otherwise it would be all over the papers that she was there.'

'Well, it's going to be all over this paper tomorrow,' McGuire said. 'Right. Here's what I want. I'm using the pic-tures of her in the hotel, and saying we have proof that she stayed there. And also that she was one of the last people to see Bella alive. Fuck it! I might even use the fact that she was pished in the afternoon in the hotel cocktail bar – just to noise up Chambers.'

'Yeah, but we shouldn't mention anything yet about her

being there when Bella was in tears at the hotel. Everyone will follow our story, so let's have something exclusive again for tomorrow.'

'Okay. Great. Get back to Pettigrew and find out what the lobby gossip is on her being in the crash and in Eastbourne. I can hear the sound of Tory arseholes clanging shut.'

'Well, that's one way of putting it, Mick. But, listen, I got some great stuff from the alleged brother yesterday. I think he's telling the truth. We need to go through his interview.'

McGuire consulted his watch. 'Okay. After conference. But go and get something down on your screen about Millie in Madrid for tomorrow's paper. The *Sun* thinks they had an exclusive today, but tomorrow we'll show them all just what a fucking exclusive is.'

Rosie stood up. 'I can't wait to hear what Chambers says when I phone him for a quote.'

McGuire grinned. 'Yeah, but that won't be until I'm about to start the fucking presses. He won't be getting any time to prepare a load of fanny for a statement.'

She left the office with a spring in her step.

Rosie waited in her car for Dan outside the doctor's surgery in Hyndland. She was surprised he'd turned up, knowing how unreliable junkies could be. She'd made the arrangement with her GP friend Simon. It wasn't a request he had every day, but as one of Rosie's oldest mates, he'd agreed to see Dan.

She watched as Dan came out of the surgery, zipping up his jacket. He waved a prescription at her as he approached the car, and sat down on the passenger seat. 'He says I've got a touch of pneumonia.'

'Pneumonia?' Rosie said. 'Jesus, Dan. You're going to have to do something about your health here, pal. You'll need to make some changes, starting right now.'

Dan was staring out of the windscreen. 'He gave me antibiotics and said I've got to rest . . . But where the fuck am I going to rest? I don't even have a bed.'

Rosie said nothing, but her mind was already doing over-time, and she could nearly hear McGuire shouting.

'I'll talk to the editor about putting you up somewhere for a few days.' She started the engine. 'But your biggest problem is the drugs, Dan. I can't put you into a hotel or decent accommodation if you're going to be out of your box on smack all the time, bringing people back and stuff. It just won't work. What did the doc say about the heroin?'

Dan sighed. 'He said I need to go on a programme. He looked at my arms – I told him I don't inject – and he took some blood for tests. He asked me if I'd go on a methadone programme.'

'Have you thought about that before?'

'Aye. Bella talked about it, and she was saying something about getting me into a clinic. A private place. That was the last time I saw her.'

'You have to *want* to chuck it, Dan. That's the most important thing.'

'Fucking right I *want* to chuck it.' He wiped his nose with his sleeve. 'See, every time I wake up, Rosie, it's the first thing I think of, because I know if I don't get sorted with some smack soon – just a wee smoke – I'll be rattling. It's a shite feeling, being sick and having a pain in your gut because you just need it. I want to stop, but the smack makes life a bit easier. When I get some, I just sink away and nothing hurts me any more. I forget a lot of the crap, all that stuff I told you about. The heroin turns the volume down on it all. Know what I mean?'

Rosie nodded and said nothing. She turned the car around and headed back towards the city centre. They picked up his prescription at a chemist on Byres Road and went into a cafe nearby. Once they'd ordered some food and drinks, she went outside to phone McGuire. There was no answer on his private line, but she got Marion, his secretary, on the main number.

'He's at a board meeting upstairs, Rosie. Won't be out till after seven he says. Can I pass on a message?'

'No. I'll call him back later, Marion.'

Rosie stood outside for a moment while she made a

decision, then went back into the cafe. She sat down and took a sip of her coffee. 'Right, Dan. Listen to me for a moment. Can you do that?'

'Aye.'

'I want to talk to the editor about getting you into a flat or a hotel while we work on this investigation together. It's no good me trying to dig you out every day, not knowing where you're staying or if you're sleeping rough. You understand that? How do you feel about getting into somewhere, especially as you're ill? You need to be some place warm and you need rest with that pneumonia. It's not the kind of thing you can just shrug off.'

'I know. I've no money.' He looked at the table. 'And I need smack. I can't function without it.'

'What did the doctor actually say about the methadone programme?'

'That he'd phone you and talk about it.'

Rosie nodded. 'If I get you into a hotel or put you up somewhere, I don't want to be getting any phone calls that you've buggered off and taken everything that isn't nailed down.'

He glanced up at her and looked away. 'I'm not a born thief. It's just the way things are, these days.'

'I don't care, Dan. If I stick my neck out for you, I need to be able to trust you. Are we clear about that?'

'Yeah.'

'You need to do this for Bella. It's what she would have

wanted. She'd be proud of what you're doing right now, that you're going to talk to the police as soon as we can get you straightened out. But most of this has to come from you. You must know that you can make your life different.'

She watched as he bit back tears. 'I want to get better. I want to do the right thing. But I'm so fucked up inside if I don't have the heroin.'

'But that will get better. You know it will.'

He swallowed hard. 'What about Mitch? Can he come with me? I don't want to be on my own.'

Rosie pondered for a moment. Mitch was more of a wide-boy, and if they were in a hotel, she could just about guarantee he would steal something. But right now she didn't have a lot of choices. She needed this boy to function, and more than that, she wanted him to. Dan had got under her skin a little, despite her trying to keep him at arm's length. After his stories of the children's home, the rent-boys and the ritual abuse, she just wanted to hug him and make it better. If she left him alone now, in some hostel or sleeping rough, he'd be dead in a few days from the pneumonia. That was the only certainty. She took a step back from her emotions and changed the subject. 'I want to show you something, Dan. A picture.'

Dan looked bewildered. 'Sure.'

She went into her bag and pulled out photocopies of the CCTV pictures José had sent of the two heavies at the party on the night Bella had died. She unfolded one and placed it on the table, watching closely for any flicker from Dan. He was sickly pale as it was, but he went even whiter.

'Fuck! Where did you get that?'

Rosie didn't flinch, but Dan was agitated, squirming in his seat.

'You've seen this guy before? You know him?'

Dan's trembling hands went to his face. 'I don't know him. But I know who he is. He's an evil cunt.' He ran his hands through his hair, his body suddenly jangling. 'Fuck's sake! Where did you get this, Rosie? Tell me! Please!'

Rosie didn't answer. Instead she brought out another photocopy and unfolded the image of the squat guy who'd been with him that night. Dan shook his head, glanced over his shoulder, wringing his hands. 'Aw fuck! Do you know these fuckers? Where was this picture taken?'

Rosie sensed a meltdown coming, and she had to keep a lid on it while they were in a public place. She leaned across and took hold of his wrist. 'Dan. I need you to calm down. Please! You need to be calm in here. You never know who's sitting in the place. Okay? Now, take a breath, son.'

Dan's lip was quivering. 'Okay, I'll try. Just tell me.'

Rosie waited two beats, still holding his arm. 'This was taken at the Hotel Senator the night Bella died. These two guys were at the after-show party.'

Dan had already started to crumple before she finished her sentence, as though he knew what was coming. He began to weep into his hands. 'Oh, Christ, no! They killed Bella. I know it. If they were there that night, Bella didn't jump off that roof, I fucking know it. These evil bastards pushed her.' He sobbed, as Rosie squeezed his hand. 'They killed my sister. Oh, Rosie! I'm a dead man now.'

CHAPTER ELEVEN

Bridget sat in the park, enjoying the peace of mid-afternoon, now that the lunchtime joggers had gone back to work and the young mothers with pushchairs had headed off. The place was deserted, the only sounds the crows and the magpies fighting over a paper bag that had held a takeaway, ripping out the leftover food. She couldn't get Millie's letter out of her mind. She'd been glad when her shift had finished at two – she'd been awake half the night and had gone through her day on automatic pilot. She reached into her bag and took out the letter. She'd read it so many times, she could just about recite it by heart.

But she opened it again and began reading.

My name is Millie Chambers, and I am the wife of Colin Chambers, the former Conservative Home Secretary.
I am of sound mind as I write this, though there are those

who would tell you, and me, that I am not. But believe me, I am.

I write this statement as I am waiting to go into a private clinic to be treated as a mentally ill patient, even though I know I am not mentally ill. I am distraught, hurt that my husband has had me sectioned against my will. But I am not broken and I will not be silenced.

I want to describe here what happened at the Hotel Senator, in Madrid, the night Bella Mason died. I know what happened, because I was there. I saw it with my own eyes. Not the eyes of a mentally ill woman, but a woman who had all her faculties.

The fact is, I had come to Madrid to end my own life. If that qualifies me for being mentally ill, then so be it. But I can assure whoever is reading this, that I am not insane. My plan to take my life that night was born of hopelessness, desperation to escape the pain and misery of what has passed for my life in recent years.

First, I want to state categorically that I saw Bella Mason being murdered. I saw her thrown off the roof of the hotel by two burly men, whom I could identify if this statement is taken seriously, as I pray it is. I have nothing left but my honesty. They have stripped me of my dignity.

I was staying at the hotel for three nights, and there is proof of this as I booked with my credit card. On the third night, my plan was to end my life. Without going into the details of how I felt, suffice to say that the decision had been *made and I was at peace with where I was and what I was about to do.*

I stepped onto the roof for my final moments and stood in the shadows of a pillar, walking slowly to the edge. I stood there, smoking my last cigarette. I was crying, I suppose, because it had come to this.

Then I heard a commotion, and I saw Bella Mason come out onto the roof with three men. One of the men was arguing with her, an older man, telling her he owned her and that he could do what he liked with her. I distinctly heard Bella say she was going to the police, she'd had enough. I stepped back into the shadows, terrified of what was happening. I didn't see the older man disappear, but all I know is that when I peered out from the spot where I stood, I saw these two men wrestling with Bella. She was protesting and struggling, but she was no match for them. I stood there, rooted to the spot, my own suicide plan now completely irrelevant. I watched, panic-stricken, contemplating screaming, but too terrified to move. I regret now that I did nothing. In fact, I'm ashamed. Then I saw the men drag Bella to the edge and throw her off the roof. That is what I saw. Please believe me. I am that young girl's only witness in this world.

No matter how many times Bridget read it, the words that described Bella being dragged and thrown off the roof made her stomach knot. What if it were true? Sure, it

was written with the level of detail and accuracy of someone who was indeed of sound mind, but she was well aware
that even someone with a mental illness could produce
prose of astonishing accuracy. But what if it *were* true? Millie had been so desperate that morning, so troubled and
pleading . . . The letter could be the ranting of a mad-
woman, but it could also have been penned by someone
who wanted the truth to come out. There was another
page to the letter, and although Bridget had also read that
several times, it didn't have the same impact as the details
about Bella Mason. She read the last page again.

*And now to turn to the lies and secrets of my husband. I
have long since known he was a philanderer and an
adulterer. As questioning him resulted in beatings and
bruising, I stopped arguing with him about it some years
ago. My suffering is not important here, but the suffering of
innocent children is.*

*As Home Secretary, my husband was responsible for
dealing with complaints and reports that came from the
police and the Crown Prosecution Service of a sensitive
nature that might impact on government. Around 1993,
although I cannot be accurate about the dates – I believe it
was in the late summer or early autumn – I was privy to a
conversation with my husband and the Chief Constable of
the Metropolitan Police. The CC had been invited to dinner
at our house. Over the evening, various subjects were*

discussed, and I heard them discussing the reports on the CC's desk about a number of allegations relating to a sex-abuse ring, involving children, young people and senior figures some ten or fifteen years previously. I distinctly recall the words 'being procured from children's homes'. I obviously would never comment to him on these matters, but my understanding was that my husband was to look into these allegations. There were some names mentioned of senior political figures – one was a Tory activist and fundraiser by the name of Geoffrey Myers, and also the Liberal Democrat MP David Simpson. Both are now deceased. Celebrities were also mentioned, and I distinctly remember the name Mervyn Bates, who is some kind of showbusiness impresario and agent. I didn't hear much more about it, but did mention it to my husband later that night when everyone left, and he told me to stay out of his business and to keep my mouth shut about what I heard. I thought this reaction was a little absurd and over the top. I only wanted to tell him I was glad that he was investigating and I hoped the abusers would be brought to justice.

Weeks later, I overheard a phone call from my husband, who was in his study, talking to the Chief Constable. I heard the words, and I repeat them here, 'Well, just shred the fucking things, or make them disappear. That's what we've done here.'

I also heard him say, that he would not allow the allegations of 'some lowlife underclass vagabonds to bring

down the government, or in fact to taint it in any way'.
That was what he said.

I confronted him about this later that evening, and he
slapped me in the face. I have never mentioned it again
until this day. I do now simply because someone has to ask
the questions that remain unanswered. Nobody is going to
tell the truth about Bella Mason, because nobody knows
what happened that night, except me. I have no idea how
much authenticity there was in the police investigation, the
statements and complaints from people regarding child
abuse, but their voices too will never be heard.

Bridget sighed as she folded the letter carefully and slid
it back into the envelope, then into her bag. She looked
over her shoulder and shuddered. She was in possession of
something that could be the poisonous bile of a sick
woman, or indeed could be an explosive scandal that
would shake the corridors of power.

The watery sun was giving way to a pale grey sky and
the fading light gave the park an eerie feel. The guttural
caw of the crows made her skin crawl, and she quickened
her step towards the gates. As she strolled towards her
house, she considered her options. If she was the kind of
woman who was capable of blackmail, she could have
found a way to let Colin Chambers know that she had this
letter, and threaten him with it. She considered for a few
moments how much a man like him would pay for it. A lot,

she decided. Enough to get her out of the crumbling NHS and to let her fade quietly away into the background of a foreign land. She could reinvent herself somewhere like Spain or the Greek islands where she loved to spend her summer holidays. But Bridget wasn't that kind of woman, though she had to admit that a tiny part of her wished she was. No. She would go home and make her dinner, watch her soaps on telly, and a decision would come to her. The good Lord would see to that. He had always guided her path through life.

CHAPTER TWELVE

'Have you found that little junkie fucker yet?' Larry Sutton's Cockney voice barked down the phone. He was a great believer in putting the frighteners on with the opening line. No pissing around with small talk or howsit-going-mate. Just get to the fucking point – smartish.

'Not yet, boss. Sorry. No joy. Not a fucking sniff.'

Larry could hear the jitters in Big Ricky's voice, and that made him even angrier. Six foot two and built like Goliath, but didn't have the balls to fight his corner. He'd have respected him more if Ricky'd given him a sharp answer back, even though he'd still have got his face wasted for his cheek when Larry saw him.

'Well, you're fucking lucky you're up in fucking Glasgow and not down here standing in front of me, else I might rip that fucking bleached-blond barnet right off of your fucking head. What the fuck have you been doing up there? How hard can it be to find a fucking heroin addict in

Glasgow? The place is crawling with them, innit? If it weren't, I wouldn't be so fucking rich.'

He stopped his rant to hear just how shit Ricky's excuse was. Larry liked the sound of his own East End twang, and he loved to ram it home to the Jocks that they were nothing but a bunch of lowlife sheep-shaggers.

'He's nowhere to be seen, Larry. Me and Pete have been putting down markers all over the shop. But nothing's happening.'

'But you're a fucking Glasgow ned, Ricky. I thought you knew every lowlife cunt up there.'

'Well, to be fair, boss, I've been down in the Smoke for a while. Okay, I know the lads we work with at the top of the supply chain up here, but nobody deals with the junkies first-hand. They're usually lying in their own shit in some fucking smack den.'

'But he's been living in Glasgow for months, I've been told.'

'I know, I know. And I'm everywhere looking for him. One guy in a house in Ruchazie said he saw somebody called Dan in a hostel in the East End a few months ago. I've got a few feelers out, thrown some money around, but nothing's come back to me yet.'

'Well, somebody'd better get back to you soon, because if I have to send some other fucker up there to do your job, you'll be in the shit, my son. Are you fucking hearing me?'

'Yeah, boss. I hear you. Me and Pete are chasing down every fucking shithole we can find, but this little bastard seems to have disappeared. Maybe he's dead. He might have overdosed or something, happens all the time. You never see it in the papers or anything. They just shovel them into a body-bag and get rid of it.'

'Yeah, well, I really don't need to hear the story of a life in the day of some junked-up prick. I want Dan Mason, and I want him pronto. So don't call me back until you've got something good to tell me.' He paused. 'I'm giving you two more days. Now fuck off.'

Larry hung up and tossed the handset across the table, then sat back in his leather office chair, swinging his feet onto his desk. 'Fucking lowlife bastard,' he muttered. It had been over a week now since he'd disposed of that coked-up nut-job Bella Mason. Well, *his* hands were completely clean, and they would remain that way if the heat ever came to his door. But it had been his hit, all right, and he was quite proud of the way his boys had sorted it, even if the bird's untimely death did continue to grab the headlines in the shitty papers. The suicide of a young model at one of the biggest events in the fashion world hadn't been his suggestion, but he had to hand it to that creepy bastard Mervyn Bates for having the nous to inject a bit of theatre into the contract. Taking a swan dive off the hotel roof in Madrid was pretty inspired, even if it had involved a bit of legwork and forward planning to pull it off. Big Ricky and that gorilla mate of his Pete had done well. In and out like a couple of ghosts they were, down the fire escape and out of the way, while stunned people were trying to work out if they were imagining the corpse splattered on the ground in front of them. By the time the ambulances and cops arrived, Ricky and Pete were already out of Madrid and on the motorway north for France.

The newspapers, predictably, had all sorts of conspiracy theories. Did she fall or was she pushed, the usual crap. But the vultures on the tabloids were satisfied that Bella had done herself in, thanks to sly old Merv drip-feeding his sources that Bella had had a huge coke problem for the last couple of years, which he'd been trying to keep a lid on while getting her to clean up her act. Give it another couple of weeks and she'd be history, if she wasn't already. But there *was* a catch. Merv had told him over lunch last week that the job wasn't over. Bella had a secret brother, a heroin addict, somewhere in Glasgow. He had to be found and disposed of, too, because he knew too much. Fucking hell! Knew too much of what? Larry had asked. 'It doesn't matter,' Merv told him. 'Just get rid of him. You never know how much he knows about Bella, the coke *and* who was the supplier not just to her but to all the models.' Maybe Bella had told the brother everything. It was a loose end, Merv had said, and it needed sorting.

Merv had handed over the attaché case containing the remains of the seventy grand they'd agreed to get rid of

Bella. It was a decent pay-off, much more than an ordinary hit, but then again this little production was no ordinary hit. Find the boy, Larry was told, and there's another twenty big ones coming your way. It wasn't that Larry needed the money, though in this game you could never have enough. But he had to agree with Merv. He didn't like loose ends. Larry was the coke supplier for Merv and his girls, had been for years, and some little slack-mouthed junkie could end up making trouble.

Rosie was grateful that Dan was more composed now, even if it *was* down to the heroin he'd just smoked. If McGuire knew what she was up to, it would put him right off the edge. But it was nine at night, and she didn't want to disturb him at the backbench when he'd be putting the paper to bed.

After Dan's meltdown in the cafe, Rosie knew, more than ever, that she had to hold onto him – whatever it took. She had to get everything out of him. It was pissing down outside, and she couldn't risk leaving him on his own in that state. She'd got Dan to phone Mitch to meet them, and when she'd picked Mitch up she had to drive the pair of them to a tenement nearby to get a couple of tenner bags of heroin. Not only that, but she had to give them the money for it. She'd never admit this to McGuire, but she knew he wouldn't question her too closely. Deep down he really didn't want to know. She'd then taken them to a cheap hotel owned by a Pakistani guy, who wouldn't ask questions as long as he was getting paid an extra wedge. She'd used the place before, and to call it a hotel was stretching the truth, but at least Dan wouldn't be sleeping rough. In one of her usual rush-of-blood-to-the-head moments, she considered taking them to her flat for the night, but that was wrong on so many levels. Tomorrow she'd speak to the editor about renting a flat for a couple of weeks till this was all over.

Rosie boiled the kettle in the small, damp room, and switched on the electric fire to take the chill out of the place. It was clean enough, but with damp, furry patches high up in the corners and a threadbare tartan fitted carpet that might once have looked plush. Dan sat by the fire, warming his hands. Rosie ripped up the pizza she'd collected on the way there and handed each lad a slice, even though food was not high on their agenda. She needed to get more out of Dan tonight, because he could go to pieces any day now. She didn't have much time. She sipped her tea and pulled her chair closer to the fire.

'So Dan, can you tell me more about these two guys in the picture? Who are they and how did you meet them? I can see they scare you. Do they work for someone?' She took her tape recorder out of her pocket. 'Listen. I'm going to tape what you're saying here, because in due course when we use your interview, I want to get it right. Are you okay with that?'

Dan nodded. 'But if you're going to put something in the paper right away, I need to get the fuck out of Glasgow and far away. I'm telling you, those guys will be looking for me.'

Rosie nodded patiently. 'Don't worry. I'll sort that. Who are they?'

'Okay. I'll tell you.' Dan tore off a corner of pizza and stuffed it into his mouth.

Rosie waited. Mitch sat on the floor, his back resting against the sofa, staring blankly at the fake flames dancing on the electric fire.

'The big guy with the bleached hair, he's Ricky, and the other one is Pete. They're coke dealers who live in London. But they're from Glasgow. They work for some East End geezer down in London – a big-shot. His name is Larry something.' He frowned. 'I can't remember, but it'll come back to me. Larry is an evil bastard, loaded with money, a big coke dealer. I mean big-time. He supplies most of the coke up here. Heroin too. Nearly everything from Spain and places like that comes to him first.'

'How do you know all this?'

Rosie was surprised at how well informed Dan seemed to be. He was a nobody, a skinny heroin addict who at twenty-one was probably in the twilight of his life because junkies like him, ravaged by drugs and disease, rarely saw their thirtieth birthday.

'Bella told me,' Dan said. 'That Larry prick was at a

function one time in London, and I was there with Bella. Well, I wasn't with her, because nobody knew I was her brother. But I was at it too. It was a couple of years ago. I wasn't as into heroin as I am now, just using it now and again. Anyway, for this party thing, Bella had got me spruced up.' A half-smile played on his lips at the recollection, and he glanced at Mitch. 'New jeans and stuff, and a dead expensive shirt. I looked all right that night.'

'So this Larry guy was there?'

'Aye. Like I said, he's a big coke dealer. Bella was doing coke then, but not as much as she did recently. She admitted it to me when we were back staying in her hotel room that night – we were both wasted drunk. We talked about the old days, the home and stuff, and we were both greetin'.' Dan gazed at the fire. 'She said that Larry . . . Oh, I remember his name now – Larry Sutton. Aye. She said that Larry was the coke supplier for all the models who used. And they all did, to keep themselves skinny. Everyone was a cokehead in the fashion business. Larry supplied them all through that prick Mervyn. Big Mervyn Bates, her manager I told you about. He organized the coke for Bella and other girls. He's the real bastard. He's the one who took Bella away from me.'

Rosie watched as his mouth tightened and the muscle in his jaw twitched.

'What do you mean, Dan, he took Bella away?'

'From the home. From the children's home. Bella was thirteen, but she looked older. She was beautiful. Tall and thin, with these great green eyes. Everybody fancied her.' He smiled. 'And she fancied herself too. She said she was going to be a model. Any time someone asked her what she wanted to do when she grew up, Bella said she was going to be famous – a famous model.' He shook his head. 'And she was. She was famous all right.'

'So how did Mervyn Bates get involved?'

'He's an agent or something. I'm not sure. He's like the guy who pushes the models to the right agencies, and he gets a cut of the money. He became Bella's manager.'

'What, when she was thirteen?'

'No. Well, I don't know. But it was him who arranged for Bella to be moved out of the home and live with foster parents. He said she was a special kid and could go far in the world, but that she needed to get out of the home. I was there when he said that. I remember it.' He paused. 'I don't even know how he came to be around the home anyway. Maybe somebody got in touch with him and told him there was this beautiful young girl there. Who knows? I think they were all in on the pervert thing that was going on. Bastards.'

'You were there when he said Bella had to get out of the home?'

Dan nodded sadly. 'Yeah. Then it seemed to happen quite quickly. It was only about two months later that Bella was taken away.'

'But what about you? Could they not take her brother?'

'They only wanted one child. I don't know who the fuck they were. They took her down to England. It was Mervyn who set it up, but I'll bet they were all part of the whole fucking paedo thing that had been going on.'

'Did you ever meet the people?'

'No. Bella didn't even want to go. She was crying every day and causing fights, and saying she wasn't going without me. But they just took her one night when we were all sleeping. When I went into the canteen in the morning, she wasn't there. I took a flaky and started shouting and smashing things. They dragged me away.' He sniffed back tears. 'I didn't even get a chance to say goodbye to my sister. She was all I fucking had in the world. Everything that was done was about the paedos getting what they wanted. Bastards!' Dan buried his head in his hands.

Mitch patted his shoulder. 'Come on, mate. You're all right. You'll be all right.'

'I won't, Mitch,' he sobbed. 'I'll never be all right. Not after all that stuff. Fuck! I was only eight years old when the first greasy bastard got his hands on me. And I know Bella was only ten the first time they took us on the bus to that flat.'

Rosie waited until he stopped crying. 'Dan, do you want to talk about that just now? It's up to you. We can stop if you want. Take a break and do it in the morning.'

He wiped his nose on his sleeve, composed himself.

'Aye. I want to talk. You said we were getting the police, didn't you? I want to go to the cops with this and tell them everything, like I did before. When I was fifteen and still in Glasgow, I got arrested for shoplifting and then got done again for smashing a window and stealing jewellery. I told the cops then about the abuse, but I don't think they believed me. I tried to get some of the other people I knew from the home, but they'd all gone their own ways and it was hopeless. I did meet one guy, Tony, a year later, and he also went to the cops. I know that for sure. He made a complaint.'

'What was his second name?'

'Tony Calvetti.'

'Have you seen him since?'

'No. Don't know what happened to him. I only bumped into him by chance in one of the hostels here about eighteen months ago. That was when he told me he'd reported it to the cops. It was when he'd been arrested for assault. I haven't seen him since.'

'Was he a heroin addict?'

'Aye. Injected.'

Rosie wrote down the name in her pad. With a name like that he could be traced, if he was still alive.

She listened, furiously taking notes as Dan described in as much detail as he could remember the places, the areas and the people. He said some of them had English accents, were posh. One was an actor, but he was only young at the time. Bella had told him that politicians were involved, and that some were quite high up. But that was years later, long after Bella had been taken away, when she had tracked him down and they were reunited for the first time in ten years. Bella seemed to know more about the sexual abuse than him because the foster parents she was taken to were in London, and a lot of things happened there. So Merv was still very much part of her life. It was he who pushed her into the modelling game and got her the big contract so that she was already successful by the time she was sixteen.

He stopped and they all sat in silence. Outside they could hear a drunken argument and a bottle smashed on the pavement. The rain battered off the window. It didn't get much more depressing than this, Rosie thought. Then Dan went into the pocket of his jacket, pulled something out. It was like a little sackcloth purse. He took something out from inside and held it so that Rosie could see it. She hoped her jaw hadn't dropped. It was a recent photograph of Dan standing with Bella, their arms around each other, smiling for the camera. Dan was gleaming and happy, not as skinny as he was now, and Bella stunning and chic, in a white polo-neck sweater. They looked like twins.

'Christ, Dan. That's astonishing. The likeness between you. Who took the picture?'

'The concierge at the hotel – that Devonshire Gardens place in the West End. He was up collecting Bella's bags before she was leaving and she asked him to take a photo. Good, isn't it? She was so beautiful.'

CHAPTER THIRTEEN

From the kitchen, Bridget's ears pricked up as she heard the name Millie Chambers on the breakfast-television news. She dashed through to the living room in time to see the TV host holding up a copy of a tabloid newspaper's front page: TOP TORY WIFE IN MODEL SUICIDE HOTEL. She turned up the volume and stood closer to the television, concentrating.

The presenter was holding up the *Post* newspaper, which claimed they had proof that Millie Chambers, the wife of former Tory Home Secretary, Colin Chambers, had been a guest in the Madrid hotel on the night Bella Mason had fallen to her death from the rooftop during a post-fashion-show party. The Spanish police had confirmed it, and even had a grainy picture of Millie in the hotel foyer. Bridget strained her eyes. It was definitely her.

'Jesus protect us!' she muttered to herself. 'It's true! What Millie said in her letter was true. It wasn't the rantings of some mad alcoholic.'

Bridget sat down, looking at her watch, aware that she had a bus to catch in fifteen minutes and still had to walk to the stop. She had to do something, but she didn't know what. Her mind was racing. Poor Millie. She was lying in that bloody psychiatric hospital, sectioned and unable to fight back. Now it was all crystal clear. That bastard of a husband had put her there because *he* had something to hide. Millie was a loose cannon, and the way she'd been behaving, she could blow at any time. Bridget recalled that line in the letter: *their voices will never be heard . . .*

She stood up, went into the hall and picked up the bulky telephone directory. She scanned a page for the Dawson Institute, where they had taken Millie, and before she could stop herself she was dialling the number.

A voice answered.

'Hello.' Bridget put on her best, staff-nurse-in-control voice. 'I'm a friend of Mrs Millie Chambers. I'm wondering if it's possible to visit her? I haven't seen her for a couple of weeks.'

There was a long pause, and Bridget held her breath.

'Who is it, please?'

'My name is Bridget. I'm a close friend of Millie Chambers, who I understand is a patient there at the moment. We're friends from way back.'

'I'm not sure if she can have visitors, but I'll check for you. Could you call back in, say, half an hour?'

'Of course. That's no problem. And if she's not able to see me, perhaps I could talk to her on the phone.'

'I'm sure that can be arranged. But let me check first if she can see you. If you could call back later. Thanks.'

The line went dead. Bridget hurriedly pulled on her coat and hung her bag over her shoulder. She picked up her packed lunch from the kitchen worktop and was out of the door in seconds. For the first time in ages, she was filled with a sense of urgency and purpose. She checked the letter was still in her bag, then zipped it up to keep it safe. She'd photocopy it once she got to work.

Bridget slipped into the supplies room on the ward during her mid-morning tea break. She locked the door and used her mobile to dial the number of the Dawson Institute in Sussex.

'Hello. I spoke to a member of staff a little while ago and was asked to phone back. I was wondering if I can visit my friend, Millie Chambers.'

Silence, then: 'Actually, it was myself you spoke to. I'm afraid Millie is not to receive visitors at the moment, due to her treatment.'

Bridget's heart sank. 'Oh. I'm really sorry to hear that. Is she all right?'

'Mrs Chambers is fine, just not able to have visitors.'

'Would it be possible to speak to her on the phone?'

'Yes, and I've arranged to have a phone brought to her

room for a few minutes. Will you hold on while I transfer you?'

Bridget tensed. This was serious. They were putting her through to Millie. She knew that, the moment she spoke to a former patient on a personal matter, she would be crossing the line. If anyone found out, she'd be finished as a nurse. She had to make the decision now. Back out and leave well alone, a voice inside her head told her. What could she achieve anyway?

'Hello? Are you still there? Will you hold on while I transfer you?'

'Oh. Yes. I'm here,' Bridget heard herself saying. 'I'd be delighted if you could put me through.' A nervous flush rose up her neck, and she leaned back on the desk and took a deep breath. She could hear her heartbeat. 'Calm down,' she told herself. 'You're doing the right thing. Think of the letter.' A clicking noise in the background, then the voice, thin and frail.

'Hello? Bridget? Is that you?'

'Millie.' Bridget's voice was a loud whisper, even though she was in a locked office. 'Yes, it's me. It's Bridget. Can you speak right now? Are you alone?'

'Yes. I'm alone. I can speak.'

Then a silence, and Bridget could hear her stifling sobs. 'Millie, please. We may not have much time. I asked if I could see you but they won't let me.'

'I know.' Millie sniffed. 'No visitors. Oh, Bridget! I'm

locked in here. They've locked me away. Please help me.' Her voice was barely audible.

Bridget swallowed. 'I'll try, Millie. I have the letter. I've read it. My God, Millie! You poor woman! What do you want me to do with it?'

'I want you to expose them, Bridget. Go to the police, the press, anyone. Take my letter. I'll die in here. Take it as my last witness statement.'

'Don't talk like that, Millie. You're not going to die. I know you're a good woman, and I'll help you. I promise. But listen. A Scottish newspaper called the *Post* had a story on the front page today, saying you were in that hotel in Madrid where the model died. They actually had it in the newspaper. They said you were there.'

'The *Post* had that story? How?'

'I suppose they're investigating the death of the model, and they maybe got lucky and found out you were a guest. That's what it looks like. But they have a picture of you on the front page.'

'Oh, my God! Colin will be furious. There'll be trouble now. But you're right. We may not have much time. Bridget . . . I wasn't lying in the letter. I saw it. I saw them throw that girl off the roof.'

'I believe you. I really do. But you also mentioned the children. The sexual abuse?'

'Organized abuse of children. The complaints made, the dossiers, everything, it all disappeared, Bridget. My husband had them on his desk, given to him by the police, as I've said in the letter. They disappeared. I heard him say on the phone that he shredded them.'

'Jesus! I'm going to do something here. I'm not sure what at the moment, but please, Millie, don't think you've been abandoned. I'll do everything I can to help you.'

Silence, then more sobbing.

'Thank you. They're going to start some treatment in the next couple of days. I heard them talking about ECT. Christ almighty! They're going to do ECT on me without my consent. They're going to fry my brain, Bridget. Please don't let them do that. Please stop it! I'm only telling the truth. I know what I saw in Madrid, and I know what I heard all those years ago. I'm not mad.'

'I know you're not mad, Millie. I never thought you were.'

'They're coming now. I can hear their footsteps. I have to get off the phone. I can't talk any more.'

'Can I not visit you?'

'No. They won't let anyone in. I haven't even seen Colin. He's pulling all the strings . . . But please, please, Bridget, don't forget me. I knew I could trust you.'

'I won't, Millie. Don't worry. I'll do something about this. Just stay strong.'

Rosie was sitting on the sofa in McGuire's office as he paced up and down.

'I mean, for fuck's sake, Gilmour. If we put two smackheads up in a flat or a hotel room, and they thieve everything they can carry, I'll be in all sorts of shit. Can you imagine Weaver's face falling even further when I put that one to him?'

'Don't tell him, Mick. This is on a need-to-know basis, and the managing editor doesn't need to know. Just tell him it's a contact we have to protect. It'll only be for a few days.'

'Yeah, but what if they steal everything? Or get a few mates round to their new gaff. Next thing they'll fall asleep and burn the bastard place down. Junkies. You can't take your eyes off them.' He turned to look at her. 'But, knowing you, I bet you even considered putting them up in your flat.'

Rosie half smiled: he always saw through her. 'Course not.'

'Liar.'

'Well, it was only for a fleeting moment. Of course I wouldn't let them stay at my flat. But that boy Dan . . . Look, I know he's wasted with drugs, but the point is, Mick, he's been wasted since he was eight years old, from the first time some perv got his hands on him. He's a genuine victim. We have to look at it that way.' Rosie pushed her hair back as McGuire came over and sat opposite her. 'All that aside, his story is total dynamite, and that snapshot of him and Bella together is worth a fortune. Picture editors would kill their granny for it. And we've got it, as well as his story.'

'I know, and don't think I'm knocking what we've got. It's brilliant, Gilmour, but it's got danger stamped all over it. Especially now that he's saying some psychos are chasing him down. How are we going to protect him if he goes out on the street? We can't keep him locked up. Especially if he's a heroin addict.'

'He'll probably stay in the flat. His mate can go out—'

Rosie stopped. She didn't want to say that the mate could go out and score some smack for them, but the look on McGuire's face said it all. He put his hands up.

'Don't tell me. I don't want to know.' He glanced at his watch. 'Right. Get Marion to sort out a one-bedroom job for them, and get the paperwork done. I'll deal with the questions. But why do I always get this sense of impending doom when you come in here with a good story?'

'It's all part of the fun,' Rosie said, and stood up.

There was a knock at the door and Declan appeared, his hand up apologetically to the editor. 'Sorry to interrupt. Rosie, I've got someone on the phone saying they want to speak to you urgently. She's says she's got information on Millie Chambers.'

She glanced at McGuire, who spread his hands in submission. 'I have to take this, Mick.'

She headed for the door, rushed across to her desk and picked up her phone. 'Hello?'

'I'm looking for Rosie Gilmour,' a voice said.

'Who's this?' Rosie asked, glancing at Declan.

'Are you Rosie Gilmour? I have some information about Millie Chambers. Can I speak to Rosie?'

'Yes. This is Rosie.'

'Hello,' the voice said. 'I won't tell you my name just yet, but I have some very important information. Millie has asked me to pass it on.'

Rosie felt her heart skip a beat. 'Millie Chambers asked you to pass it on?'

'Yes. Your name was on the front page of the story that she was in the hotel in Madrid – the night that young model was killed.'

The accent was Irish, and she sounded like an older woman. She was well spoken and to the point. She was either a fantasist who had read the paper or she was the real deal. It was hard to tell on the phone.

'That's correct. That was my story. Look, rather than talk on the phone, can I meet you somewhere? I'm free now, if you are?'

'Well, I'm in the south of England so I'm quite far away. I'm in East Sussex – Eastbourne.'

Rosie knew the *Post* went into some London newsagents and at the airport, but it wasn't generally available. 'I see,' she said. 'How did you get the *Post* in Eastbourne?'

'Well, I couldn't find it, but I did see it on breakfast television this morning.' She paused. 'Listen. This is genuine. I'm no crank caller, please don't think that.'

'Of course I don't think that, not for a moment. I can

come to Eastbourne, but can you tell me a little more? Do you know Millie Chambers?'

'I do.'

'Really? Are you a friend?'

'Only a recent friend. But I can see how troubled the woman is. I . . . I'm a nurse. But, please, you mustn't tell anyone that. I'm trying to help her.'

'A nurse? Are you a nurse in the hospital where Millie is after being hit by the car?'

'I work at that hospital, but Millie isn't there any more. She's been moved.' She paused. 'To a private psychiatric hospital. She . . . she's been sectioned.'

Rosie felt a little punch of adrenalin. There had been no statement about Millie Chambers other than that she was being released from hospital. 'Sectioned? Under the Mental Health Act? Are you sure?'

'I am. Rosie, I spoke to Millie today.'

Rosie's heart sank a little. Christ! She could be talking to a psychiatric patient in the next bed to Millie Chambers and she'd come up with some story. But she had to play along with it. 'Is she all right?'

'No. She's far from all right. Can you come and see me? I need some help here to expose what's going on. Millie Chambers has asked me to go to the police with the letter—'

'What letter?'

'The letter she wrote before they took her away. She gave

it to me, pleaded with me to take it off her. It tells every-thing. She saw that model girl being murdered.'

Rosie wondered how fast she could get to Eastbourne. Even if this woman was a nutcase, she had to see her.

'I have the letter. It's signed by Millie. Please, you have to believe me.'

'I do, I do,' Rosie said quickly. 'But you must understand, this is an incredible claim you're making. I need to know your name. It won't go anywhere else, I promise. Of course I'll come down and meet you.' She could get the five o'clock flight to Heathrow. 'I can be there later today. But I need to know your name, for my own peace of mind. Do you understand?'

'My name is Bridget Casey. I'm a staff nurse at a hospital in Eastbourne. The District General. But if it comes out anywhere that I've helped Millie, I'll be in trouble. I'll get fired. Are you going to help, or will I go to the police?'

'No,' Rosie interrupted. 'Don't go to the police. We can talk about involving them when I get there. Just keep the letter safe and I'll be down this evening. Keep your mobile on, if that's the number you're phoning from. I'll meet you anywhere you want.'

'I live just outside Eastbourne.' She gave her address and Rosie wrote it down.

'That's fine. I can be there by this evening.'

'I'm scared, but I'm telling you the truth. I'm already too

far in. I was too far in from the moment I took the letter from Millie.'

'Don't be scared. Can you just tell me what she says in the letter?'

'I have to go in a second as I'm due back on the ward. She says she saw the girl being thrown off the roof. She says she was in Madrid to commit suicide herself and was going to do it. She was on the roof when it happened, and she also says things about a sexual-abuse ring and children years ago, that certain dossiers were destroyed by her husband.'

Rosie held her breath. Dossiers shredded by the Home Secretary? His wife in Madrid to commit suicide? She'd heard enough. 'Okay, Bridget. Don't be afraid. I'll be in Eastbourne by around eight tonight. I'll call you.'

Rosie wanted to ask her to fax the letter, to find some way of taking a photograph of the contents, of the signature, or anything that would make her feel it was authentic before she headed all the way to London on what might be a major wild-goose chase. Yet something told her the woman was genuine. But her story was so far-fetched that she knew she'd practically have to hold McGuire down to make him agree to let her go to Eastbourne in the middle of everything else she was doing.

'Okay. I'll be waiting for your call. But please don't think I'm a nutcase.'

She can read my mind, Rosie thought. 'I don't,' she said. 'I'll call you when I'm in Eastbourne.'

The line went dead. Rosie turned to Declan. 'I need you to put a call in to Eastbourne District General Hospital, and ask for Bridget Casey. Just ask if she's available, that's all. I'll tell you about it in a few minutes. I only want to know if she exists, okay?'

Declan nodded, writing the name on his notebook as Rosie headed back to McGuire's office.

CHAPTER FOURTEEN

Dan wrapped both hands around the paper cup of steaming hot tea to take the chill off his fingers. Despite the mid-morning March sun bursting through the clouds the bitter wind would cut you in two. The stone wall felt cold on his backside and he shivered, hoping Mitch would be back soon with some kit. He sniffed and shuddered, beginning to feel the tremors of a junkie needing a hit. He hated that feeling, and wished more than anything he could get off the rollercoaster before it killed him.

Especially now with Bella gone. One of the last things she'd said to him on the phone was that she was going to get him better. 'I promise,' she'd said. Those were her words. She'd had enough of all this shit too, and she hated the fact that she was doing more and more coke than ever. But she was ready to do something about it. They'd pull each other through it, she'd said. Now he was on his own. He'd vowed to himself that he'd get better for Bella, but such promises were always made under the comforting blanket of heroin, when everything seemed manageable. But when he woke up, felt the chill and the need for more smack, the only thing in his mind was how soon he could get it.

Dan wasn't ashamed of it – he was well past that – he was just sick of it. He wanted his life back. Whatever was left of him, he just wanted to have it back. He sighed and lit a cigarette. He really liked Rosie Gilmour. She seemed as if she actually cared about him, and he hadn't met anyone like that in his entire life, except his Bella – maybe Mitch too, but he knew that Mitch would still dip his pockets if he needed the money. He smiled: his junkie pal had just been up the town shoplifting and had headed down to Shettleston to offload the stolen goods in return for enough smack for a couple of days. Rosie was going to put them up in some flat.

He thought of that psycho Ricky coming looking for him and glanced over his shoulder, even though he didn't think he'd be out on the street searching for him, but you never knew. Paranoia was all part of the addiction. Dan's mobile rang and he took it out of his jeans pocket. There was no number. He put it to his ear, but didn't speak.

'Dan? Is that you, Dan?'

Somewhere in Dan's fuddled mind, he recognized the voice, but couldn't remember where from.

'Dan? You there? Is that Dan Mason?'

'Who's this?' he said cautiously.

'It's Mervyn, Dan. Merv . . . How you doing, son?'

A chill ran through him. Mervyn. Fucking slimy bastard. Dan began to shake from his knees right to the hand holding the phone. His mouth was dry. What the fuck was he going to say to this guy? What the hell did he want? Bella had detested him. She'd told him all about Mervyn, but made him promise not to mention anything to anyone until she had gone to the cops.

'Oh, right, Merv.' Dan managed to get his tongue off the roof of his mouth to speak. 'Hi, man. Yeah, it's Dan.'

'Dan, my boy! Christ, son! What can I say? I've been trying to get hold of you since . . . Since Bella.'

He paused and Dan waited, his mind a blur. Then Merv spoke again. 'You must be in bits, son. We all are.'

Dan said nothing, rage rising as he heard the quiver of emotion in Merv's voice. Faker. He took a breath and waited two beats until he knew he could get a sentence out. 'Yeah, man. Shattered. I just don't know what to do. I loved Bella. My heart's broken.'

'So is mine, Dan. Bella was like my own daughter. I've known her since she was thirteen.'

'I know.' Dan swallowed his rage. He wanted to say, 'Sure. You've known her since you abused her at thirteen, you pervy cunt.' But he composed himself, surprised at how he was managing it. He wished Mitch would hurry up and come back with some smack.

'We haven't even got poor Bella's body home yet, so we can't organize the funeral. I've been over this with the bloody

Spanish cops. They keep saying it's still under investigation. But for what? It breaks my heart, Dan, genuinely breaks my heart to accept that Bella took her own life, but that's what happened, and we all have to get our minds around it.'

Dan said nothing. But something was happening inside his head, as though he could suddenly see clearer than he had in months. It was like he'd just been given a hit and his senses were firing on all cylinders. Or maybe adrenalin pumping that was making him sharper. If only he could feel like this all the time. He had to be on the ball for the bastard, he knew. Why was Merv calling him? Dan was the secret brother nobody knew about, nobody wanted to know about. The last person to want to involve him would be this parasite bastard.

'You there, Dan?'

'Yeah.'

'I know this must be hard for you. Where are you, by the way?'

Dan took a short breath. That was it. He was looking for him. Big Ricky was looking for him. It felt like confirmation: what he'd thought was true. 'I'm not really anywhere, man. Nothing permanent. Just dossing about.'

'You in Glasgow?'

'Nah,' Dan lied. 'Was for a few days, but I'm just moving around.'

'It must be awful for you, but listen, Dan. I need to get together with you. We need to talk. About Bella.'

Dan waited a moment. 'What do you mean?'

'Well, there's a lot to sort out. Bella was a very wealthy girl, as you know. We need to sort something out between us. Where are you so that I can come and see you?'

'What do you mean, "sort out"?'

Silence, and Dan listened to Merv's breathing. It seemed laboured and he could picture his puffy red face and his fleshy lips, which were always too wet.

'I mean, I need to make sure you're sorted, so you can have a decent life. I know Bella would have wanted that.'

'Nobody knows about me and Bella.'

'I know that, son, and that's how Bella wanted it. I think maybe it would be best if we kept it that way, but she would have wanted to make sure you were set up.'

Dan didn't answer. He hadn't even given any thought to Bella's money. It had never occurred to him that he was her sole heir, her next of kin. Everything had happened so fast in the past week, but the sudden realization that he was all Bella had had made him feel a little surge of emotion, of belonging. This bastard wanted to pay him off, that was for sure. His hands were shaking a little and he took a breath. 'Yeah, maybe she would have wanted that right enough, Merv.'

'Of course she would. Now listen, son. Where can we meet? Don't worry about how you're fixed. I know you've got a lot of problems, so I'll come to you. We can get everything sorted and make sure you're all right. Are you in Scotland?'

'Not right now,' Dan lied. He had to talk to Rosie. He didn't know where to turn, but if this fucker was pushing him like this, it wasn't because he wanted to look after him.

'You're not in Scotland?' Merv sounded surprised. 'I thought you lived there.'

'Yeah, I did for a while, but you know how it is. I keep moving around. Trying to find a good place to be. Since Bella died, I've been in bits, man.'

'I know. But look. Tell me where you are and I'll come and see you. We can put you up in a hotel, somewhere nice, then get everything sorted for you.'

'Listen, Merv. My battery's out of juice,' Dan lied. 'I'm going to get cut off. Can you give me a bell tomorrow? I'll need to get this charged up.'

'Sure. Go and get your phone charged up and I'll call you. Don't worry about a thing. I'll come to you, and we'll look after you. I mean that, son.'

'Aye, right. Okay.' Dan hung up.

He felt like throwing up. He needed a hit and fast, but somehow, somewhere inside, he didn't want it. He needed to be in some kind of state to deal with this bastard. He needed his wits about him and, most of all, he needed to get off the fucking street. He dialled Rosie's number.

Rosie checked the time on Matt's dashboard clock as he raced through the traffic on Broomielaw and out towards the East End. She had a maximum of two hours to pick up

Dan and Mitch, take them to the flat she'd organized for them, then head to the airport. She was glad to see them standing smoking across from the High Court.

'Thank Christ they're waiting,' Rosie said. 'Dan sounded a bit spaced out when I talked to him on the phone. Let's get them holed up in the flat and, hopefully, they'll still be there in the morning. Marion has already been up and put some stuff in the fridge for them.'

Matt grinned. 'Like some hash?'

'Don't even go there Matt. My bum's already twitching.'

'Aye. It'll be a laugh if all you find when we go up in the morning is the bare floorboards and couple of fag ends.'

'Christ. Don't, Matt. They'll be fine.'

Rosie gave them a wave as Matt pulled into the kerb. She hadn't even told McGuire about Dan's phone call half an hour ago – that this Mervyn character had called Dan for a meeting. Whatever he wanted, she was sure it wasn't to give Dan a sympathetic hug. She'd already had Declan check as much as he could on Mervyn Bates. She knew the name, knew he was a big-time manager for models and other celebrities. But he was never in the limelight: he stayed in the background and pulled all the strings. If what Dan had said about him was true, he was one sick bastard. Proving it was another matter.

'All right, guys?' Rosie chirped, turning to face them as they got into the back.

'Not really, Rosie. Shitting myself is more like it. I didn't get time to phone you, but just after we talked and I told you about Merv, Mitch arrived. He says some geezer's been asking about me.'

'Really? Where?'

'Just asking about,' Mitch said.

Rosie glanced from one to the other. They'd both had a recent hit and looked a little spaced out.

Mitch sniffed. 'One of the boys I know told me while I was getting some gear down London Road. He was in a hostel last night and said there was a big bloke asking did he know Dan. My man twigged straightaway that he was some kind of nut-job, and he told him that he knew a guy called Dan but he left last week. The guy gave him a tenner for the information and said there would be a lot more if he could find Dan for him.'

'Jesus! Did he say what he looked like?'

'Aye,' Dan said. 'Mitch says he had bleached-blond hair. It'll be that fucker who's after me. Guaranteed.'

'Will the guy he spoke to dob you in?' Rosie asked.

'Dunno. Hope not. He doesn't know where I am anyway,' Dan said.

'I don't think he will,' Mitch said. 'But you know what it's like. If this big cunt comes up with a right few quid to hand over to a junkie, he might tell him anything. I wouldn't bet my house on it . . . if I had one.'

Rosie smiled, even though her insides were churning. 'Don't worry. Talking of houses, I'm taking you to a great wee flat we've got organized for you, but as I said to you last night, lads, please don't screw this up in any way. I've stuck my neck right out here with the editor, and said I want to look after you – and I do. But you've got to meet me halfway on it. I can keep you safe and secure up here, but you can't bring anyone back or any shit like that. You need to respect the place. You understand?'

'Aye. Course,' Mitch said, looking at Dan. 'We know what you mean. We wouldn't fuck you up, Rosie. I'll look after my wee buddy here. We'll be the happy couple.' He put a playful arm around Dan and gave him a squeeze. 'Won't we, darlin'?'

'Aye, right.' Dan shrugged him off. 'I hope we've got separate beds.'

'Don't worry.' Rosie grinned at Matt, who was trying to keep his face straight.

She turned around and looked out of the windscreen. Despite all of the crap, the messed-up lives and the fact that this pair of smackheads only looked towards their next hit, there was something in their demeanour of excited young boys going on holiday. She felt a little surge of affection for them both. Of course, like most drug addicts, they would probably steal the eye out of your head for a fix, but that wasn't how it was meant to be when they'd started out. It was all about their start in life, the chances they had, the environment, the crap they'd found themselves knee deep in as soon as they were old enough to be aware of it. They might choose to be shoplifting or selling their bodies for sex, but making the choice not to do so had never been possible.

Matt drove towards Finnieston and a new block of flats that had been recently converted from an office.

'Here we are, guys.' Rosie pointed. 'You're on the top floor. It's brand-new, so let's keep it that way.'

Matt parked and they all piled out.

'Come on. I'll show you where it is. Now, I need you to stay in until I get back. I have to go somewhere tonight, but I'll be up tomorrow.'

'Don't worry,' Dan said. 'We'll be all right.'

'Is there a telly?' Mitch asked.

Rosie looked at Matt, whose tongue was in his cheek, and she knew they were both thinking that the telly might be sold before they were even at Glasgow Airport. She hoped not.

CHAPTER FIFTEEN

Rosie lowered the window of the hire car and relished a lungful of sea air as they drove along the Eastbourne promenade. 'I could nearly get giddy on that, it feels so good. I wish we were on a wee holiday.'

Gulls screamed and swooped overhead, and the sun setting on the horizon made a dramatic skyline of the ancient white pier, its leggy boardwalk stretching out to sea.

'Yeah, me too, Rosie. This is not as mental as some of the last *holidays* I've been on with you. We've been here fifteen minutes and nobody's shot at us yet.'

Rosie laughed, conjuring up an image of their trip to Pakistan, being chased and shot at by the Taliban as they raced through the Swat valley. 'Don't worry. This will be a breeze, pal. The worst thing that can happen to us here is that this nurse is a screaming lunatic and we look like a couple of tits back in the editor's office.'

'Well, to be fair,' Matt joked, 'I only take the pictures. I just do what I'm told by you, boss.'

'Yeah, right.' Rosie rolled up her window as they approached a road sign. 'It says Pevensey there. You got that? Can't be very far now.'

Matt followed the direction of the sign and Rosie sat back, hoping against hope that Bridget was genuine. McGuire had looked at her in disbelief when she'd come back into his office straight after Bridget's phone call, but he knew how these things worked. He knew they couldn't risk not acting on the information. It was a case of either running it to the ground to prove the letter was a figment of the nurse's imagination or discovering they'd had the phone call that all reporters and editors dream of. While she'd been discussing it, Declan had phoned her to tell her that a nurse with the name of Bridget Casey did work at the Eastbourne hospital. It still didn't prove the letter was genuine, or that the woman she was going to meet was actually that nurse, but McGuire had accepted that even though she was up to her eyes in this investigation, she had to go all the way to Eastbourne to find out.

Rosie flicked back through her notebook and checked the address as they drove into the street. She'd decided to meet the woman in her home to get a better picture of who she was.

The end terrace house looked bright and welcoming from the outside, with neat borders around the mono-blocked pathway leading up to the front door. A perfectly clipped hedge either side of the gate gave the place a level of privacy that others in the cul-de-sac didn't have, with their open gardens and small driveways. Rosie pushed the bell. She glanced at Matt, then peered into the stained-glass window on the white door. 'Someone's coming,' she said.

'Does it look like they're carrying an axe?'

'Shut up, you. Get your game face on.'

Matt put on his 'understanding' expression.

The door opened just a little.

'Bridget?' Rosie asked. 'I called about twenty minutes ago?'

'Is that you, Rosie? I was in the shower.'

'Yeah. Rosie Gilmour, and this is Matt. He's a photographer. We work together a lot.'

'Oh, I can't have my picture taken.'

'Don't worry, Bridget. He's not here for you.'

The door opened a bit more and Bridget stood before them, a little flushed about the face and neck. She looked about fifty, a bit overweight, and neatly dressed in trousers and a baggy top. When she smiled, Rosie noticed the blue of her eyes and the warmth in her face. She hoped her gut instinct, that she was a good woman eager to help, was right.

'Come on in,' Bridget said, stepping back.

Rosie glanced at Matt, who gestured with his arm for her

to go first. They stepped into the carpeted hallway and walked behind Bridget towards the kitchen. She could hear the TV from the living room on her left off the hallway and glanced through the open door as she passed. It looked like any home – not her own, though, which was almost permanently messy, with clothes and shoes strewn all over the place.

'Lovely house,' Rosie said, as they went into the kitchen. 'Have you lived here long?' A bit of small-talk to ease your way, she thought.

Bridget picked up the kettle and held it under the tap. 'Well, as you probably gathered, I'm Irish.' She smiled again, and her eyes became half-moons, with laughter creases at the sides. 'I've been here since I came over to train as a nurse in my twenties, and that wasn't yesterday, but I've never lost my accent.'

Rosie smiled. 'It's a great accent. Nice area you live in too, with the sea and the town nearby.' Enough with the small talk, Rosie was thinking.

'Yes,' Bridget said. 'I love it.' She paused and there was a little awkward moment. 'Now. Cup of tea? Then we can sit down.'

Rosie was relieved she was getting straight to the point. Bridget motioned them to sit down, then disappeared into the living room and came back with a white envelope in her hand. She pulled up a chair and they all sat at the table, the house quiet, except for the gentle hiss of the kettle.

'Now.' Bridget touched her neck lightly with her fingers as though she could feel the colour rising in it. 'I want you to bear in mind, Rosie, that what I'm about to do here I have not done lightly. I have given this a great deal of thought, agonized over the implications for me if it ever gets out that I passed on this information.' She glanced from Rosie to Matt. 'I'd lose my job on the spot after thirty years of an unblemished career. But, worse than that, I could be end up embroiled in this and, who knows, maybe the police would get involved. I don't want any part of that. I don't want to be questioned by police, or anyone else. I'm only doing this because I feel heart sorry for that poor woman.'

She stood up as the boiling kettle clicked off. The envelope lay on the table, and Bridget brought over cups, milk and sugar, then poured water into the teapot. She carried it across, sat down and poured the tea, sighing and shaking her head. 'She really was a poor soul when she came in that day after the accident.'

'She'd been hit by a car in Eastbourne, hadn't she?' Rosie asked, even though she already knew.

'Yes, but once she came round, it was clear that she had a lot of other issues.' She lowered her voice. 'She's got an alcohol problem, and I'm sure she knows that, though she never said anything to me. Maybe it all goes together, but she was awful sad. Crying all the time.'

Rosie nodded sympathetically. 'Did you see her husband,

Colin Chambers? I mean, did you know who Millie was when she came in injured?'

'Yes, I did see him, but, no, I didn't know who she was.' Bridget shook her head. 'I wouldn't have known her from Adam. I vaguely recognized him when he arrived. But I'll tell you this, Rosie. He's a right snob, underneath his breezy attitude. Millie looked crushed when he came into her room. I'd been talking to her a little before it. She was mostly crying, and I assumed it was the delayed shock from the accident, but when he came in, he dismissed me, like I was a servant.'

'Did you hear anything between them? Any conversation?' Rosie asked.

'Not straightaway, as I had other duties on the ward, but at one point I went past and he was really laying into her, calling her a drunk and this and that. Terrible way to talk to anyone, never mind your wife.'

Rosie nodded slowly, wishing she would get to the nitty-gritty. 'So when did she begin to confide in you, give you the letter?'

'Well, that didn't happen until the morning they were coming to take her to the psychiatric hospital, the private clinic the husband had arranged for her. I'd heard her crying, sobbing actually, and I went in and brought her a cup of tea while she was waiting for the car. She looked so lonely, so forlorn, sitting there, her little case all packed.' Bridget shook her head. 'It was as though they were just

packing her off somewhere because she was an embarrass-
ment. Don't get me wrong, I think she could do with a bit
of counselling, or help with her drinking problem, but I'd
say most of her problems stem from that gobshite of a husband – if you'll pardon the French.'

Rosie was impressed by how quickly Bridget could go
from being delicate, polite middle-aged woman talk to
Dublin pub-speak.

'Well, he's got a reputation for being a bit of a bully.'

'That doesn't surprise me.'

'So had she'd actually written this letter in the hospital?'

'She'd just finished it when I came in with the tea, and
we didn't have a lot of time. Suddenly she grabbed my wrist
and said she had a letter there and wanted me to have it.
She gave it to me there and then, and for a second I
didn't know what to do. I just looked at her, but then she
burst into tears. What could I do? She looked so abandoned,
so desperate. I took the letter and put it inside my uniform.
A few seconds later the door opened and it was the people
to take her away.' Bridget sipped her tea. 'Poor woman was
crying her eyes out. I gave her a hug and she held me so
tight I was nearly crying myself.'

'What a shame.'

'I know. Just shows you that you don't know what goes
on in these highfalutin' places. Anyhow, the letter. When I
finally opened it, which wasn't until I came home that
night, and even then I was reluctant, I nearly died when I

read it.' She slid her thumb across the seal and opened the envelope. 'At first I couldn't believe my eyes, and thought maybe Millie had lost her mind – the things she was claiming in the letter . . . Afterwards, when I went to bed I couldn't get her out of my head all night. Then in the morning when I was watching TV, this . . . your front page story suddenly came up, that she was in the hotel the night the model died. I nearly had to be brought round when I saw it. Millie was telling the truth. She must have been. I was so taken aback, but I knew I had to do something to help.'

Bridget handed the letter to Rosie, who began to read it. She glanced up at Matt. 'This is unbelievable!' She read it to the end, then again, more slowly, trying to take in the part about the documents and the child-abuse ring. It was dynamite. Even if Millie Chambers was mentally ill and had made it up, it was still an incredible accusation to make against a government minister and a police chief, that they had colluded to stifle a police investigation into child sex abuse. It wasn't that far-fetched, as Rosie's own experience, with her exposé on the children's home in Glasgow a couple of years ago, had told her. But could it really have been more widespread?

'So, you called Millie in hospital?' Rosie asked.

'Yes. I decided it was my duty to do something about this, and to be honest, at that point I didn't care what happened to me. My heart and my gut were telling me not to allow the woman to be abused in this way, because that was what it was – abuse. Millie was a witness to a murder and that has to come out. If it wasn't for me seeing your story on the television that morning, I might have thought differently, but that confirmed it for me. I had to take action. I phoned Millie. They said she couldn't have visitors, but they put a phone at her bedside so I could talk with her. The poor woman was crying her eyes out, pleading with me to help her. She even said they're going to fry her brain with ECT electric-shock therapy.'

'Jesus!' Rosie screwed up her eyes, glancing at Matt. 'Do they still do that? I thought they stopped it years ago.'

'Yes, on the NHS they did, but this is a private clinic. They can pretty much do what they want in those places, and Millie doesn't have a say because she was sectioned.'

'How awful! Is there any way she can get out even into the grounds?' Rosie's rush of blood mentality was already thinking about going in there and rescuing her. She caught Matt reading her mind and rolling his eyes.

'I don't know. I suppose she'll get outside for some fresh air. But they might have started the therapy now, so she'll be locked up if they have. God knows what's happened to her.'

They sat in silence, the sun streaming through the kitchen window to highlight the yellows and the greens of the walls and tall plants. They had to do something to get to Millie. The letter was explosive, especially because it had her signature. But she knew the lawyers would be all over it: although the signature could be authenticated with the credit card from the Madrid hotel, they would still insist that allegations like these needed a face-to-face.

'There has to be a way to get to her,' Rosie said.

'What do you mean? Go in and see her?'

Rosie sighed. 'Well, yes. But . . .'

'You mean to get her out of there?'

Rosie felt a little embarrassed, and Matt, arms folded, was shaking his head. 'I suppose I do.'

'But that would be breaking the law! She's been sectioned under the Mental Health Act, so it's illegal for her to leave, and obviously illegal for anyone to aid and abet that.'

'I know, I know,' Rosie conceded, her heart sinking a little.

They sat in awkward silence.

Then Bridget pushed her chair back. 'But, tell you what, I'm game if you are!'

From the corner of her eye, Rosie could see Matt puffing his cheeks and blowing out an exaggerated sigh. 'Then let's talk about it,' she said.

CHAPTER SIXTEEN

Larry Sutton was raging. Mervyn fucking Bates! How in the name of fuck could he have known him for ten years and not twigged he was a nonce? Granted, Bates had only been on the edge of his radar most of the time, in the way that these rich showbiz cunts were. Larry knew pricks like Bates would never willingly associate with a gangster like him, someone he'd view as a lowlife thug. But he wouldn't be the first former public-schoolboy to call on guys like him when he needed a bit of muscle or someone taken out of the equation. And it happened more than people probably imagined. Rich, privileged wankers didn't do their own dirty work. Never had. They always turned to the great unwashed to pick up the pieces if they fucked up and some big problem needed sorting.

Not that it was ever an issue for Larry, the way he worked. His empire in the corner of east London had been built on terror and violence, and everyone knew Larry Sutton didn't shrink from a challenge. He wouldn't flinch if he was approached to do a hit on someone – anyone. Obviously, if it was some bastard's grandmother, he'd draw the line. But basically he was up for hire, if the price was right.

He'd only met that cokehead model Bella Mason once at a party. Sure, his troops supplied coke to her and the other girls Bates had on his books, but Larry didn't want to know the nitty-gritty of their stupid lives. Fuck that. Bates paid the money up front and supplied the coke. Supply and demand, Larry told his troops. It was just like any other business, from the chip shop to the grocery store. But this information changed everything. He reflected on his meeting yesterday.

Larry had very little patience with that polecat Marty Brown at the best of times. He was like a fucking fishwife, with his gossip and stories, and half the time you could take anything he told you with a big pinch of salt. But when he'd called yesterday to ask for a meet, saying he had some very big information to impart about Merv Bates, Larry reluctantly agreed to see him. You never knew what it might be.

They'd met in one of Marty's bars in Bethnal Green, and as they'd sat in the empty back room in the late-afternoon gloom, Marty had poured him a whisky. 'Larry,' he'd said. 'That Mervyn Bates. I've been told something about him.'

'Yeah? What?' Larry didn't want to spend all day on this, but given that he'd just bumped off one of the world's biggest models at the behest of Bates, he felt he had to listen. He knew how the grapevine worked, and suspected that perhaps Matty had got wind that Larry was behind the death of the model, that maybe it was a hit and he'd been asked to do it. But if he did suspect that, he wouldn't be stupid enough to mention it at this table. Nobody would ever mention it, not if they wanted to see their next birthday. But somebody like Marty, even though he was a bit of a tit sometimes, was useful and picked things up on the quiet.

'Did you know that cunt's a nonce? A fucking kiddy-fiddler?'

Larry kept his expression impassive, but it wasn't easy. He sipped his drink and put the glass on the table, feeling the whisky burn all the way down his gut. Of all the people he despised in the whole world, it was anyone who could look at or touch a kid in any kind of sexual way. They deserved to die, was Larry's view – and not in a quick way. If he had his way, he would round up all the fucking child abusers and take a flame-thrower to the lot of them. He'd be doing the world a favour – no doubt about it. With every pervy bastard who died, it would be justice and payback for the memory of his best mate, Spider Willard, who'd taken his own life four years ago because he couldn't escape the nightmare of what those monsters had done to him as a skinny little kid. Larry had met Spider in Borstal when they were doing their first detention at fifteen, and even then he could see there was something not right about him. There was a rage inside him, a real fucked-up rage that he couldn't control. His temper was on such a short fuse that the slightest insult could send him into a frenzy of violence. Yet beneath it all was this really solid, lovable bloke, who would die rather than betray you. They'd become the best of mates and that had continued right through jail till they were eighteen. Later, when they were released, they were the young thrusters pushing their way round London, winning turf and getting respect.

One night when Spider had been blind drunk he'd broken down in tears and told him what had happened. He'd been serially abused from the age of ten by people in charge of his children's home and others they'd passed him around to. He'd said he couldn't get over it and that for years he'd wanted to die each morning when he woke up. By the time he was around sixteen, he'd decided to get on with his life, or what was left of it. Spider was heavily into uppers and downers. He needed them to sleep, he'd said, and then to wake up. Only Larry knew his secret. Then, one day, he didn't wake up.

When Larry had broken into his flat late that afternoon, he'd found his best pal in a pool of blood, a handgun in his mouth. He'd shot himself and left a note. To say Larry was heartbroken couldn't cover it. Spider was all he had and he loved him like a brother. Of course, life had to go on, but he never really got over it. With every deal Larry made, he used to go to Spider's graveside and tell him how well they were doing. So he was always happy to take a hit on a pervert, and every time one got sent to prison, he'd get word to his mates inside, and justice was dealt out in the cells or the canteen. He instigated most of the brutal attacks on sex offenders in the Scrubs. It was one of the things he'd have put on his CV if he could. Mervyn fucking Bates.

'Who told you this, Marty?' Larry asked calmly.

'Somebody very much in the know, Larry,' Marty replied. 'Listen, mate, you know I wouldn't come to you with this if I didn't know it was true. I'm only telling you because I know you deal with the cunt.'

'You know fuck-all, Marty.' Larry leaned across the table. 'And you'd be wise to keep your fucking mouth shut about what you think you know.'

Marty put his hands up defensively and his face went suddenly pale. 'Larry, man. For fuck sake! Do you think I'm going to be shouting about anything I been told about anybody? I only got told about it yesterday and my first thought was to let you know. Give you the chance to cut the fucker loose. Everyone knows how much you hate nonces.'

'Who told you?'

'It was a bird I've been shagging for a couple of weeks. Her cousin is in the showbiz side of things. Public relations or whatever crap they call it, but she knows Merv. She told him she'd heard things about him. That he was a pervert who used young girls, and has done for years. Pays for it all the time, and no cunt's ever exposed it. Not even the papers.'

Larry said nothing, but inside he was shaking with rage. He'd only ever done one hit for Bates, and that was Bella Mason. He'd done it because the money was great, and plus the fact she was a wasted junkie, who would be dead before she was twenty-five anyway. If he hadn't done it, someone else would have taken the job, knowing he'd knocked it back, and he couldn't afford to have that kind of thing getting out. But the bigger problem was that he'd been supplying Mervyn Bates with coke for years. So much money had changed hands. Bates used to invite him to dinner and for nights out, but Larry had always kept his distance as he didn't want to be going around with the pricks who surrounded showbiz. But this changed everything. He swallowed his whisky and put his hand over the glass when Marty offered a refill. Then he stood up.

'Well, cheers for that, mate. It's good to know who to watch your back for. I never liked that Merv anyway.' He shook Marty's hand, pulled on his Crombie and walked away, feeling Marty's eyes burning his back all the way out of the bar.

Now Larry sat staring out of the window of his office three floors up, overlooking Brick Lane market. He had to get this into perspective. He didn't have to like the people who hired him for a contract. Business was business. He couldn't afford to get personal on every job. But this gave him the creeps. He had to do something.

He got up and left his office, coming down the stairs and out of the fire door into the side street where his driver had parked the Jag. As he got into the back, he punched in a phone number on his mobile.

Mitch had told Dan it'd take him an hour tops to nip across to Shettleston and pick up some more kit from the dealer. He knew Dan wasn't happy about being left on his own, especially as Rosie had told them not to go out. But they were running low on smack and it was best to have some hash back-up. Sitting about, watching television, he and Dan had been in and out of a drug-induced stupor, feeling out of sorts at the loss of their usual routine: foraging to make enough cash. Dan hadn't taken very much heroin, and said he was trying to to cut things back a bit. But Mitch knew that was easier said than done, and they didn't want to wake in the morning, then have to go searching for gear. He made his way along the Shettleston Road and headed for the tenement block where his dealer was on the top floor.

There was a queue of the usual suspects in various stages of desperation. A couple of them were fighting on the stairway, and one skinny, grey-faced girl sat shivering on a step. Most of them would be pushing heroin themselves to pay their debts, so it was impossible for them to get out of the vicious circle. Mitch wanted to be in and out of the place quickly before it got dark. He had money in his pocket, so he pushed past everyone to the top of the stairs and eased his way in.

His dealer was busy in the kitchen sorting one of the junkies out with some tenner bags, and Mitch stood in the hallway. He saw Tam, the wee junkie from Govan, glance at him from across the kitchen, but he didn't speak. It was Tam who'd told him some blokes were looking for Dan, but that was two days ago. Mitch nodded to him, but Tam turned away, then disappeared. He might have been on first-name terms with every smackhead in this place, but none of them were friends. That wasn't how it worked.

Eventually Mitch caught his dealer's eye and he motioned him over. The dealer sorted him out with three tenner bags and some hash and he handed over the money.

'What's this? Money? You not been on the rob this morning, Mitch?' the dealer said, a fag dangling from between his lips as he spoke.

'Nah, man. Did a wee bit of work for someone and made a couple of quid.'

His dealer gave him a sly look, then turned away. Their business was done.

Mitch went downstairs, past the two who were still brawling, and wove his way to the front door. Outside, it was already getting grey and he would have to step on it to get back to the flat quickly. Suddenly, he stopped in his tracks. He hadn't noticed the big black jeep as he was going into the tenement and it wasn't the kind of motor you saw in these parts. He spotted Tam, leaning in the window, then looking furtively over his shoulder and walking briskly away. Mitch felt the hairs on his neck stand on end.

The driver's door opened. It was the bleached-blond hair he saw first, and a chill ran through him. The passenger door opened and another guy, built like a bull, got out and looked straight at Mitch as he moved quickly around the car towards him. The blond bloke opened the back door of the car.

'C'mere, son! In you get!' He took a step towards Mitch and the other bloke closed in from his left. 'Don't even think about trying to run on your junkie legs. Get in!'

'What for?' Mitch felt jittery.

'Just get in, before I fucking snap you in half to make you fit.'

'But I haven't done anything. Listen, man. I need to go. I'm in a hurry.'

The blond guy's lips curled into a snarl. In one seamless movement he took a step, reached out an arm and grabbed Mitch by the hair. He dragged him the two feet to the car and threw him into the back. Then he and his mate got in, the blond on the driver's side, and they drove off, wheels screeching, as he closed the passenger door.

'What the fuck, man? What's this about? I promise you, I've no idea what this is about. I don't want any trouble.'

'Shut your fucking mouth and listen, you prick.'

Mitch could hear himself whimpering. He felt sick with terror. As they drove out of Shettleston Road and towards the city centre, the blond guy spoke, and Mitch met his eyes in the rear-view mirror.

'Dan Mason,' the blond guy said. 'Where is he?' He raised his eyebrows. 'And don't even think about trying to ask, who he is, because we know he's your junkie mate and we know you've been with him for the past few days. What are you, a couple of bent shots?'

'Naw,' Mitch said.

'Shut it. Where's Mason?'

'I don't know, man. I haven't seen him for a week.'

The car braked quickly and Mitch was almost thrown against the back of driver's seat.

'Listen, you wee prick, have I got to drag you out of here and beat the shit out of you? Because that's no problem.'

'I don't know. I hardly know him at all. What's he done? He's just a wee smackhead and, yeah, I helped him a couple of times, but I haven't seen him for ages. Honest.'

He could hear the big man sigh as he gave a sideways glance to the gorilla sitting next to him. They said nothing and kept driving, Mitch looking out of the window as they drove across the bridge towards Kinning Park. He wanted to ask where they were going and his stomach churned as they drove under the arches below the bridge and into a used-car parts workshop. The blond parked and both men got out quickly.

The door back opened and Mitch was yanked out by the hair, the gorilla punching his face three or four times until he could feel himself passing out. Then he came to as they stood him up beside the car, punching him in the ribs.

'Don't make this hard for yourself, son. All you have to do is tell us where to find him, and we'll stick a few quid in your pocket and that's it all forgotten about. How hard can that be? It's not as if you junkies are all best mates. Who gives a fuck about each other? Come on!'

Mitch felt his eye swell shut and he could barely make out the blond man's face swimming in front of him. He tasted blood and suddenly sick rose up, and he vomited.

'Fuck me!' the blond man jumped back quickly. 'Mind the fucking shoes, you cunt.'

'Please, big man. Let me go.'

'Where's fucking Dan Mason?'

'I don't know. Honest. I don't know.'

'Tell us or you're going to die. Where is he?'

Mitch felt another blow to the side of his cheek and something cracked, then a knee hit him between his legs and he buckled. 'I . . . don't know.'

'You fucking liar. You're a lying junkie bastard. Where is he?'

As Mitch slumped to the ground he was barely aware of them kicking him any longer. After the first couple on his stomach and the final boot on his chin, he thought his head would come off. He opened one of his eyes briefly and could see the sky turning from grey to black.

Dan sat flicking through the TV channels, checking his phone constantly. Nothing from Mitch. It crossed his mind that his pal had decided it was getting too dodgy to be around him and maybe done a runner. He hoped not. He liked Mitch a lot, and he was all he had right now. But even though Dan was spaced out for much of the time, he knew how these things worked. Junkies came and went with each other, depending on who was the best chance to work with and score some smack. But Mitch had seemed different, like he really wanted to help him. He looked at his phone again. Nothing. He checked the time. It was gone nine and dark outside. He was shit-scared. Mitch wasn't coming back. Dan was on his own. He punched in Rosie's number.

CHAPTER SEVENTEEN

Rosie's phone was blinking with two missed calls and a message from Dan by the time she got off the plane in Glasgow and into Matt's car. There was also a text message from her Strathclyde Police detective contact, Don, asking to call. She'd ring him later.

'Dan. It's me,' she said. 'You okay?'

There were a couple of beats of silence, then his voice, weak. 'I'm scared, Rosie. I don't know where Mitch is. He went out this afternoon and hasn't come back. I've heard nothing from him. I can't believe he would run out on me. Something's happened, I know it.'

'He went out? I thought the two of you were supposed to be staying in the flat, Dan. What happened?'

'He wanted to get some more kit.'

Rosie bit her tongue. Junkies didn't work inside the same parameters as everyone else. She'd assumed they had enough gear to keep them going, but she didn't even want to enter into the discussion. She took a breath. 'Okay. Don't worry, Dan. We'll see what we can do. I'll be there shortly, just sit tight.'

'I've no kit left. I'm rattling.'

Shit. This was not good. Rose had worked with heroin addicts often enough to know that withdrawals were not pretty and not something to do without professional help. The middle of an investigation was not the time to go cold turkey.

'Try not to worry. I'll see you shortly.'

Her next call was to her detective friend, Don. 'Hey, Don. How're you, pal? I've a message here to call you.'

'Rosie! Long time no see? You're obviously up to something.'

'You really don't want to know right now, Don. That I can promise you. So, what's new?'

Silence. Rosie waited.

'Can you talk?'

'Sure.'

'Listen. We've got a situation here where your phone number has come up on a victim's mobile.'

Rosie's stomach dropped. She said nothing. It could be one of various drug addicts, small-time crooks or random punters she'd dealt with over the years, but right at this moment she knew it could be only one person: Mitch.

'A victim?' Rosie asked. 'Of what?'

'Really brutal assault. Somebody beat the shit out of this

guy and it looks like they left him for dead. Down under the arches by the Clyde.' He paused. 'It seems you were one of the last people he talked to on his mobile. His name is Mitch Gilland.'

She heard the disappointment in Don's voice that she hadn't come clean with him straightaway. She cleared her throat. 'Don. I'm working on something really big, and I know you understand that I can't talk about what's going on. But you know I'll always mark your card or pass anything on to you when I can.'

'You don't have to apologize, Rosie,' Don said. 'I know the score. But the scrapes you get yourself into, I'm more worried about you than this junkie who's fighting for his life right now up at the Royal.'

'Is he really that bad?'

'Pretty much. Internal bleeding. And these guys . . . I mean, their system is so low anyway, from all the drugs, that they have nothing to fight back with.'

Rosie swallowed the sudden lump in her throat. Poor Mitch. This was obviously someone looking for Dan. She felt awful. But the hard-bitten journalist in her wondered if he'd told his attackers anything. Sometimes she hated herself for that side of her.

'Don, I can meet you a bit later at O'Brien's, or for a coffee somewhere and tell you some things about this. You're right. Mitch is someone who was helping me. He tracked somebody down for me who I needed to talk to and right now we're protecting him. I thought we had the two of them protected. But Mitch went out of the place they were staying.'

'Yeah. Well, you can't expect anything but chaos around junkies. And, right now, he's part of a police investigation. It's not my case. I overheard the boys talking in the office, and someone said it was your phone number. So you'll be getting a call from the cops, no doubt. This is your friendly early-warning system kicking in.'

Rosie was relieved that he was so calm about it. 'Thanks, pal, but I won't be able to tell them anything. Honestly. Not a single thing.' She looked at her watch as Matt pulled up outside the flat. 'Look, I have to go but why don't we meet later? I'll call you.'

'Sure.' Don hung up.

Rosie's mobile rang. It was McGuire.

'Mick,' Rosie said, 'I'm back, but on my way up to see Dan.'

'What's going on, Gilmour? I'm choking to get my hands on this letter.'

'I know. But there's been a problem.'

'What?'

'It's Mitch, Dan's mate. He's been beaten up really bad. He's in the Royal.'

'Christ almighty! What about Dan? I thought you had this pair under house arrest.'

'Dan's all right. He's in the flat. But Mitch must have gone out for some reason.'

'Aye. For fucking drugs, most likely. Look at the bastard now. Honest to Christ. Bloody junkies. Rosie, go and talk to Dan and settle him down, then get right down here. I need to see the letter. Is it good? How was the woman? She's not a loony, is she?'

'No. Far from it. I'll tell you when I see you. I have to go.' She hung up.

Rosie let out a long sigh as Matt switched off the engine. 'Don't tell me I'm going to miss my dinner again,' he said sarcastically.

Rosie shook her head and smiled, but her nerves were becoming more frayed by the minute.

Rosie had read the letter from Millie so many times on the plane from London that she had memorized every line. With each read, she became more intrigued. On any level this was the most incredible property for a newspaper to have in their hands, and she couldn't wait to compare the signatures with the copy from Millie's signed credit-card receipt from the hotel. The confession that a former cabinet minister's wife was depressed enough to travel to Madrid to commit suicide was explosive enough, but the claim that she had witnessed a murder was mind-blowing. But it was the allegation she made about the child-sex-abuse ring that appealed to Rosie more than anything. Could it really be possible that police and the political hierarchy had been aware of the abuse and covered it up? It seemed unbelievable, and would be desperately hard to prove. She took the stairs two at a time from the *Post* foyer to the editorial floor and didn't stop to nod to anyone as she headed to McGuire's office.

'He's waiting for you,' Marion said. 'He's been like a cat on a hot tin roof all day.'

'Why you working so late, Marion?'

'So much to do, I decided to put in a couple of extra hours.' She went back to her computer screen.

Rosie knocked on the editor's half-open door and walked in.

'Gilmour! Thank Christ!' He stood up behind his desk. 'First, how's Danny Boy doing? Is he still with us? He's not going to renege, is he?'

'No. He's okay. He's sorted.'

McGuire gave her a stern look. 'I sincerely hope you've not been out scoring heroin for him, Rosie. I mean, seriously.'

Rosie put her hands up in surprise.

'Would I ever, Mick.'

She managed to keep her face straight, but when she'd seen the nick Dan was in when she'd got to the flat, she'd known she had to do something. He was seriously rattling, crying and sweating and shaking like a leaf. He needed something badly. He pleaded with her to take him to a house where he could get sorted, but she had to sit him down and explain what had happened to Mitch. He was even worse after that, sobbing, bordering on hysteria.

She knew it wasn't safe to go to any of his usual haunts for smack, and she sure as hell didn't want to go anywhere else.

There was only one thing for it. She'd phoned her GP friend, Simon. At first she hadn't planned to tell McGuire but, given the way he was looking at her, and that she didn't know how any of this would pan out, she decided it was better to come clean. 'Listen, Mick—'

'Christ! When you start a sentence, "Listen, Mick," it's usually trouble, Gilmour.' He motioned her to sit down, then came out from behind his desk and sat on the leather seat opposite her. 'Now, you listen to me, Rosie. I need you to be honest with me. No fucking about. Too many things have happened in the past that you kept me in the dark about. I'm not saying I want to know every cough, spit and fart of how you go about your job. In fact, some of it I'd rather not know. But right now we have a junkie unravelling in a flat I'm paying for, and another one about to pop his clogs in the hospital. *And* the wife of a fucking Tory ex-cabinet minister claiming she witnessed a murder. Honest to Christ! I feel as if I'm going to wake up sweating in a minute.'

Rosie put her head back and looked at the ceiling. 'If I'm honest, I do too.' She pushed out an exhausted sigh. 'So. Here's what I had to do. I got my GP pal to take Dan on as a patient. It wasn't the usual protocol, but he did it for me as a favour. He's already seen him anyway and recommended a methadone programme at the time. So he's started him on methadone.'

'Christ almighty. I'm not even going to ask if the doc's stepped over the line.'

'He hasn't. He's just bent the rules a bit. He gave me a prescription for him. I took Dan to the chemist and got him sorted with that. He's got some to take at the flat too.'

'So he won't need heroin?'

'Well. He shouldn't. That's the whole point of it. It will take away the tremors and the horrors and give him much the same feeling as a heroin hit. But it's even more addictive than heroin, and definitely not the answer in the long run.'

'I don't care what happens in the long run, or how he sorts himself out. Pardon my being a callous bastard of an editor, but I need this kid functioning on some kind of level, at least till we get this in the paper.'

'You're all heart, Mick. Don't worry. He'll be fine. He's making sense and he won't be as anxious. But I need to keep an eye on him.'

McGuire looked at her, indignant. 'Well, you're not moving in with him. That's for sure.'

'No, of course not. But I need to be around a lot, and if I'm not, then we need to get someone to babysit him a bit. I'm thinking Declan. He's a good kid.'

'Yeah. Okay. Whatever. Just sort it. Now where's the letter?'

Rosie took it out of her bag and handed it to him. He sat back and read it quickly, letting out a low whistle, his eyebrows dancing, knitting in concentration and disbelief. 'Fucking hell! This is unbelievable!'

He stood up and went across to his desk, brought over the credit-card photocopy with the signature and placed the letter on the coffee table between him and Rosie. They both leaned over it, but could see straightaway that it was the same.

'It's exactly the same signature, Mick. Totally.'

McGuire folded his arms and sat back. 'It is. It has to be the same person. I've spoken to Pettigrew down at Westminster but he's not got a whole lot on her. She is a bit of a flaky type, as I told you, but these allegations are right off the scale. What's this stuff about a child-abuse ring? Are we really supposed to believe that?'

Rosie gave him a sharp look. 'We don't have to go too far back, Mick, to see what happened here in Glasgow. And a certain High Court judge, who was allowed to slip away quietly because this newspaper had an attack of the shits when it came to telling the truth, the whole truth and nothing but the truth.'

McGuire looked guilty. 'You know, Rosie. I hated myself for that, but the decision would have been taken out of my hands. I should have fucking resigned.'

'No, you shouldn't, Mick. It was one of those things. You win some, you lose some. You said as much to me at the time when I was cracking up over it. I drew a line under it, but the last thing I'd have imagined was that it could possibly be more widespread. Do you think it's possible?'

'Who knows? But we really need to take it seriously. If this woman isn't a complete head case, we have to pull out all sorts of stops to get to the heart of this.' He paused. 'What's the nurse like? What's she saying?'

'She's a good type. She knows her stuff, and has been a nurse for all of her professional life. She's in her fifties. I'd say she's a pretty good judge of character, and she completely believes Millie Chambers is telling the truth. More than that, she wants to help her.'

Mick picked up the letter and was reading it again. 'How can she help her? Millie Chambers is locked up, is she not?' He spoke without looking up from the page.

'Yes, but she wants to help her get out.'

Rosie watched Mick put down the letter. They sat for a long moment in silence.

'Meaning what?' He looked up at her slowly.

Rosie swallowed and took a deep breath. 'Er . . . Meaning she wants to help her to get out of the hospital?'

'You mean escape.' McGuire sat back, his hands clasped across his stomach.

'Well. Yes.'

'You mean help a woman sectioned under the Mental Health Act to escape psychiatric care.'

Rosie pushed her hair back.

'It's not exactly helping her to escape as such, Mick. The idea is that Millie gets out of the place under her own steam. Bridget knows the hospital. She's already spoken to Millie, and Millie has told her there are times in the day when they go out for some fresh air in the grounds. Bridget worked in the clinic for a few weeks when she was younger and said there is a way out of the place, if Millie could find it. A gate. Somewhere at the back of the building.'

McGuire shook his head. 'And then what happens?'

Rosie shrugged. 'Someone would be there to meet her in a car.'

'Who?'

Rosie couldn't help smiling. 'Who do you think? Batman?'

'Oh, fuck me, Rosie!'

Rosie stretched out her hands, pleading. 'Have you got a better idea, Mick? I mean, we wouldn't have helped her escape the confines of the grounds as such, we would just pick her up on the public road. There's no crime in that. She wants to do it.'

'You mean you've already bloody agreed to it.'

Rosie bit her lip. 'I said I'd have to run it past you.'

'Yeah. My arse, Gilmour.' He stood up and walked back behind his desk. 'Honest to Christ, some days I don't know if I'm coming or going. I don't know where the fuck this is going to end, Gilmour, and that's the truth.' He sat down and looked across at Rosie.

'You can deny all knowledge of it if the shit hits the fan, Mick. As it surely will.'

He burst out laughing. 'Oh, don't worry about that, pal. I will.'

'So I can go ahead?' Rosie stood up.

McGuire went into his drawer and took out a foil packet of pills he used for his ulcer. He popped one into his mouth and knocked it back with some water, then sighed. 'Bring me the full story on Millie Chambers, Rosie. We need that. Get everything out of her. We'll deal with the lawyers when the time comes.'

Game on. Rosie was glad she'd decided not to tell McGuire that the cops were looking for her because of the attack on Mitch. No point in giving him anything else to irritate his ulcer.

CHAPTER EIGHTEEN

Millie had been lying awake in her room, gazing out of the window at the darkness, desperate for the morning light to spread across the sky. She hated night time, always had. Especially the dead of night, just before dawn, when she used to lie in bed suffocated by her anxieties, dreading the day ahead while wishing to be out of the blackness. It was one of the reasons she'd started drinking so much at night, hoping she could pass out till the morning, but she never did.

Last night was different, though. Her sleeplessness wasn't the usual dread, but it had worsened over the past few days when they'd been talking about the schedule for her electric-shock treatment. Millie had raged and bawled her eyes out until she'd finally collapsed from exhaustion when the psychologist and nurse tried to convince her it was for the best. They'd said it would change her outlook. So why had the NHS stopped using it routinely? she'd questioned furiously. They hadn't bothered to answer that. They didn't have to. They were holding her prisoner. The decision was made.

She'd demanded to see her husband, but was told that Colin had insisted in letting them get on with the treatment. He would see her after the first few sessions, once she was showing signs of improvement. Damn them.

But last night Millie hadn't been crying or lying terrified in bed. She had a plan, and nothing was going to stand in her way. For the past two days, since Bridget had phoned her and told her the agreement she'd made with Scottish reporter Rosie Gilmour, Millie had had a new lease of life. She knew if she got caught, she'd be locked up with even more stringent security measures, but she was determined that wouldn't happen. She'd never felt more driven in her life. It was exhilarating, as though she were standing at the top of a rollercoaster waiting to take the plunge, a heady mixture of nerves and excitement. She'd been flushing her medication down the toilet over the past two days, and none of the staff had noticed. In fact, she had been flushing at least half of it away ever since she'd got there, once she'd realized what they were doing.

When she'd first arrived, distraught, strung out and traumatized, she had been glad of the painkillers and sleeping pills. They took the edge off the alcohol cravings. But the medication was making her groggy and listless, and if she was going to survive this, she couldn't do it in a drug-induced stupor. Now she was ready. Over the past couple of days, when they'd let her and some of the other patients outside for their daily dose of fresh air, Millie had been slipping around the back of the building. Yesterday, she had found the gate Bridget had told her about.

It was just after lunch, and as she sipped her tea at the table by the window, Millie relished the sun streaming down on the sea of daffodils splashed across the lawn. Daffodils were the first sign of spring and they had always to her been a sign of hope. They were the first flowers that Colin had given her when he'd arrived at her digs, carrying a bunch behind his back, a lifetime ago. And now here she was, planning her escape from the loony-bin she'd been cast into by the man she had once loved more than life itself. 'Don't go there,' she told herself. 'That chapter is over and done with.' Now her life would be about truth, not for her but for that poor weeping girl, Bella, and for the abandoned children.

Millie checked the pocket of her coat again. She had to leave with only the clothes she was wearing. Her little suitcase stood in the corner to be left behind, like all the other trappings of her life. If she walked out of here now and was successful, she would leave everything behind. The truth was, she hadn't even agonized about it. It had been over for so long, but she hadn't realized it. She had clung to the hope that the misery would end, and Colin would again become the man he was when she had met him. How deluded she had been.

A knock on the door brought Millie out of her reverie, and a young nurse stuck her head in. 'Time for a bit of exercise and fresh air, Millie. Are you up for that? It's a beautiful day.'

'Of course,' Millie answered, as cheerily as she could. She stood up and took her coat off the hook behind her bathroom door. 'I can't wait to get out there.'

'Good for you,' the nurse said. 'You're in good spirits today, Millie. Great to see you like this.'

'Yes,' Millie said. 'It's the sight of the daffodils. I do so love the spring, don't you?'

'Oh, yes. My favourite time of the year.'

The door opened wide. Millie pulled on her coat and walked, a little slowly, out of the room into the long, polished corridor. She was wearing her flat shoes and could hear them squeaking on the tiles as she walked past the nurses' station. She had to make this work. As she went towards the door, she saw some other patients in the corridor. She hadn't spoken to any of them: she hadn't wanted to be drawn into conversation about their lives and how they'd got there. But she did give a friendly smile to anyone who looked in her direction. Most of the patients were very tranquil as they moved outside, blinking in the sunlight, but their faces were pale and drawn, with glazed eyes from constant mood-altering medication. Millie wondered what they made of her. As she did most days, she had put on some make-up and tried to hide the dark shadows that had become a part of her life in recent months. She felt good inside. That was all that mattered. She walked towards the big oak tree to the left of the building, stopping as though to look at the greenery.

'It's Millie, isn't it?

The voice from behind startled her, and she turned sharply. She gave a weak smile, hoping it signalled that she wanted to be alone. The last thing she needed right now was a friend.

'Yes,' she said.

The older woman smiled back at her, her papery skin wrinkled. Her snow-white hair was wispy and unkempt and gave her an eccentric look. 'I've been watching you.'

Millie looked at her, but didn't answer. She changed direction and walked away from the side of the building in an attempt to steer the other woman away from where she was really headed. She was conscious of the time.

'What are you in for?' the woman asked.

Millie gave her a bewildered look but said nothing.

'Drink? Drugs? You punch someone?' The old woman gave her a mischievous look.

Millie shook her head and smiled. 'For a bit of a rest. Things got difficult.'

'Drinker,' the woman said, with a tone of accusation. 'Knew it as soon as I saw you.'

'Thanks for that,' Millie said. She let out a sigh. 'Actually, if you don't mind, I'm trying to take in a bit of sunshine and enjoy the plants and trees. I quite like my own company.' She took a step back.

The old woman folded her arms and shrugged. 'Fair enough.' She took a step towards her. 'But if I were you,' she whispered, 'I'd get the fuck out of here.'

Then she burst out laughing, a loud, cackling guffaw, as though someone had flipped a switch in her head. Millie walked quickly away, but could feel her heart beating faster. She could hear the woman laughing hysterically behind her and was afraid to turn back. But she was heading in the wrong direction. She glanced around her, then took the path along the front again and walked briskly, as though she was trying to exercise. At the far end of the building she slowed down and turned.

People were still milling around, walking in the grounds as they did every day. Millie was slipping away from them. She went around the back of the building, eyes darting everywhere in case a car or delivery van came up to the tradesmen's entrance. But there was nothing. She walked to the very back of the building and saw the gate. She'd already checked it and knew it was locked with a padlock the size of her hand. She would have to climb over, and she would have to be quick. She didn't have a watch on, but by her reckoning she'd been out ten or fifteen minutes and they only got twenty-five in total.

She looked over her shoulder, then at the gate, praying that Bridget would be on the road at the other side. Her heart was pounding. The tension was almost like it had been when she'd stood on that hotel roof in Madrid, but that time she had come to kill herself. Now she was about to reclaim her life. Sweat trickled down her back as she put her foot onto the first rung of the iron gate. It was old with pointed spars. She began to climb. She hadn't climbed a gate or a tree since she was a teenager, and it was harder than she'd anticipated. Her foot slipped on the iron rung and she almost lost a shoe. 'Shit,' she murmured. 'Keep calm.'

She was at the top, and all she had to do was negotiate how to get over it without tearing herself to pieces. She lifted one leg over carefully, feeling for a foothold. So far, so good. Then the next. She was over. She was barely breathing as she looked down and thought of jumping, but it was nearly ten feet high and she was afraid she'd break her ankle. At last she found her footing. One more move and she was low enough to jump. She slipped and fell to the ground, her knee bashing on the grass. Pain seared through her. She pushed it away and stood up.

The road was across a verge and through a clump of trees. She could see it. She struggled to her feet, in agony as she bent and pulled herself through the undergrowth. Then she was on the country road, on a straight, with a bend at the rise of the hill. But no car. Where was it? 'My

God,' she heard herself say. 'They'll be looking for me in the next ten minutes.' Her mouth was dry with panic. She looked back at the gate, then at the road ahead, and thought of sprinting away.

Then suddenly, racing round the bend, a car was coming towards her. Please let it be Bridget. She kept her head down just in case. The car screeched to a halt, and the driver's window lowered. But she could see Bridget waving from the passenger seat.

'Millie!'

'Oh, Bridget! Thank God!'

'Quick, get in. We must hurry.'

The back door was pushed open and Millie limped and stumbled across the narrow road, then flung herself into the car. A young woman with dark hair and startling blue eyes greeted her. 'Hello, Millie. I'm Rosie Gilmour. What a pleasure to meet you.'

Millie's face lit up with a smile, but tears of relief spilled out of her eyes.

CHAPTER NINETEEN

It had taken them nearly six hours to get just across the Scottish border, where Rosie had booked them into a small hotel. It was owned by a former detective inspector from Glasgow, whom she had known since her early days on the *Post* when part of her job was to build up police contacts and cultivate mutual trust. It wasn't every friendly cop you could do that with, but she had made a good connection with Bertie Shaw. He'd moved down to the Met in his thirties and at one stage worked with the Royal Protection Squad, but they had kept in touch. He'd taken early retirement a few years ago to live the life he'd been promising his wife as soon as he'd plucked up the courage to take the leap into the unknown. The old country-house gamble had paid off, and the hotel was more of a hideaway for a discerning traveller than a mass-tourism venue, which suited Bertie and his wife, who loved to cook. It wasn't the first time Rosie had stashed someone there: the *Post* had smuggled people out of the High Court after a major case, and on one occasion a prisoner who'd been freed after serving two years for murder, when he was acquitted on appeal.

Bertie was old school and knew his stuff when it came to complete discretion. He could also handle himself, as Rosie had found out when a couple found not guilty of murdering their landlord, who were giving their exclusive to the *Post*, got drunk and, to everyone's horror, the man pulled a gun. Bertie had stepped in and sorted him out in no uncertain terms.

Rosie hadn't wanted to take Dan and Mitch to Bertie's hotel when she was working out where to keep them safe: she didn't want to give him the aggro of two smackheads messing up his place. But a couple of middle-aged respectable women were no problem, and the hotel, nestling two miles off the beaten track at the edge of a wood, was a perfect hideout.

Rosie came out of the shower in her bedroom and checked her phone. Another missed call from TJ. She felt a twinge of guilt. Their relationship wasn't one where they kept each other informed of their every move, but she'd forgotten to call him last night to tell him she was heading south. TJ knew the story she was involved with, and he would understand, but she, more than anyone else, was always irritated when her calls or messages went unanswered. And now she was doing it to the man she didn't want to lose.

She looked at her watch on the bedside table. She'd arranged to have dinner with Millie, Bridget and Matt at seven thirty and didn't have enough time to give TJ the attention of a phone call. She texted him a message explaining and promising they'd get together over the weekend. 'Keep this up,' she told herself, as she stood up and let the bath towel slip onto the floor, 'and you'll screw up your relationship again.' She sighed, glancing at her naked body in the wardrobe mirror. More than anything, she would love to be heading out for a night with TJ, where they would drink too much then fall into bed and lose themselves in each other.

Her mobile rang, and she picked it up: Declan. 'Howsit going? I hope you're not going to give me bad news. Is Dan all right?'

'Yeah. He's fine, Rosie. I'm just checking in to tell you a couple of things. Dan's been taking his methadone religiously, and I'm up here like Mary Poppins, keeping him sweet. He's a good guy.'

'Are you managing okay, Declan? Sorry to land you with a junkie.'

'Yeah. I've had plenty of experience, Rosie, so babysitting a smackhead is no big deal.'

'What do you mean, plenty of experience, Dec?' Rosie was curious. She didn't know much about Declan other than that he'd been raised in one of the Glasgow housing schemes.

'My brother John was a heroin addict.' Declan paused.

'We lost him the year before I joined the *Post.* He was only twenty-four. Broke my ma and da's hearts. They didn't last too long after that.'

'Christ!' Rosie said. 'I'm really sorry. I had no idea about your brother. I wouldn't have put you in this position if I had. Are you sure you're okay?'

She knew from Declan's voice that the pain was still raw, and she didn't want to ask any more. but she inwardly chastised herself for not having found out a bit more about the smart young reporter who sat opposite her. She made a quiet vow to take him out when they got back and see if she could be more supportive. So many people carried such a lot of misery on their backs. You just didn't know what was going on in their lives. Half the time you were too busy to notice anyway.

'I'm fine,' Declan assured her. 'I'm probably your best bet to look after Dan right now. It's not everybody at the paper who'd be comfortable with a heroin addict to babysit. But he's all right. He's not misbehaving, and I'll bell you if anything happens. But one thing, Rosie. He's had a call from some guy called Merv, and he seemed a bit upset by it. I didn't ask him anything, but he says you know about him. This Merv guy wants to meet him in the next couple of days. He said he'd come to Glasgow, but I heard Dan tell him he wasn't in Glasgow.'

'Oh,' Rosie said softly. 'Tell Dan he did well. If Merv calls back, tell Dan to stall him. I'll be up tomorrow morning, all being well, and we can work something out. Don't worry.' She paused. 'And, Declan, thanks.'

'No sweat, Rosie.' He hung up.

As they sat at the table in the small private room off the restaurant, Rosie could see that Millie was a little edgy. She probably needed a drink. Whether she was an out-and-out alcoholic, Rosie had no idea. Millie hadn't spoken a great deal on the journey up, other than to declare that the letter was genuine and she was going all out to do what she could to expose everything. But right now she looked like a woman who needed a drink, and it didn't take much soul-searching for Rosie to decide to take a chance. They could probably all do with a drink. As long as they kept a lid on things, and Millie didn't start asking for large gins in the next half-hour, they'd be all right.

She ordered a bottle of wine from the waiter as he took their dinner order, and saw the relief in Millie's face when it arrived and the waiter poured her a glass. What the heck? Rosie thought. A couple of bottles of wine isn't going to kill things, and it would loosen her up a little. She needed the interview, chapter and verse, on tape tonight, as she knew McGuire would be on the phone before midnight.

'Here's to you, Millie.' Rosie raised a glass. 'To your courage.' She turned to Bridget. 'And yours, Bridget. Few people would go out on a limb the way you have.'

Millie sipped her wine. 'Thanks.' She glanced at Bridget, then Rosie. 'For believing me.'

Over the meal they drank two bottles of wine between the four of them, and Millie wasn't showing any immediate signs of wanting more. But now it was time to get her on tape with everything she knew.

'Are you ready to have a longer chat, Millie?' Rosie asked. 'About everything? All the stuff from Madrid? I want to ask you about what you said in the letter regarding the sexual abuse.'

Millie nodded. The alcohol had made her face a little flushed, which emphasized her high cheekbones. She was still a fine-looking woman, Rosie thought, but there was a sadness in her expression, as though life had not measured up to the promises and dreams she'd once had. Rosie pulled her tape recorder out of her bag.

'I'm going to tape our conversation, Millie, if that's okay. The newspaper's lawyers insist on it, these days.'

'I know how these things work. That's fine.'

She seemed relaxed, and Rosie assumed she was probably still backing herself up with a couple of painkillers to take the edge off her anxiety. But she was perfectly lucid and looked keen to go ahead.

Matt looked at Rosie, then at Bridget. 'Why don't I take you for a drink in the bar, Bridget, while they talk? You can tell me about growing up in Ireland. I've got relatives from Dublin.'

Bridget smiled. 'I'm happy to do that.' She turned to Millie. 'Is that okay with you?'

'Yes,' Millie said. 'And thanks.'

Millie's eyes moistened a little and Rosie could see she was still fragile, despite the strong front she was trying to put up. For a few moments they said nothing as they watched Bridget and Matt walk towards the bar. Then Rosie switched on the machine and placed it in the middle of the table between them. 'Millie, I want to ask you first if you can tell me what took you to Madrid. I'd like to know about your life. You said in the letter that you were suicidal, and it was a shocking thing to read. But you must have been very low to feel like that, so can you tell me what happened?'

Millie looked at Rosie, then beyond her, as though she was trying to figure out where to start. She took a deep breath and let it out slowly, shaking her head.

'So many things, Rosie. It's hard to know where to begin. But what I can say is that by the time I went to Madrid I had made up my mind to end my life. I know it sounds dramatic, but I just didn't want to go on. I was living with Colin in a marriage he didn't want any more. He'd stopped loving me a long time ago.' She bit her lip. 'In fact, I think after the second miscarriage, he had begun to resent me. He wanted children as much as I did, and not being able to carry a child was something that I had never even considered, so it was a huge blow to both of us when I lost the first. But when it happened a second time, Colin changed.

I think he blamed me.' She sipped her wine. 'Anyway, he became distant, began to stay out late, not just with work but all night. He'd stay in the flat we had in the centre of the city, and it wasn't long before the rumours reached me about women.'

'It must have been very hurtful, given your losses.'

'Of course. I had all that grief to deal with, and on top of it, the realization that he didn't want me any more. We would have furious rows that he would initiate, and now when I look back, it's clear it was just so he could go out and slam the door. The rows became more frequent, and Colin became more aggressive. He hit me. More than once. But the first time it happened . . . I think that was when I started drinking seriously.' She swallowed and tightened her lips. 'I was so lonely. I felt so abandoned, and the only way I could get through the evenings on my own was to drink. It got worse and worse, and sometimes I'd pass out on the sofa and Colin would come in and drag me to bed. I must have disgusted him. I can see that now. But the marriage was over.'

Millie looked down at the table, fidgeting with her napkin.

'Then, a couple of times over the years, I took a handful of pills on top of the alcohol.'

'You were attempting suicide then? When was that?'

Millie seemed perplexed. 'Twice in the past five years. Pretty half-hearted attempt. On both occasions before I passed out I was on the phone to Colin, telling him what I'd done. I – I suppose I can see why he lost patience.' She sighed. 'I just wanted him to see me, to notice me, to understand that I was falling to pieces. I needed help. But I don't need to be locked away. Do you know what I mean?'

Rosie nodded and listened as Millie went on to describe her descent into depression. She still had to be the political wife, appearing on his arm at functions, conscious that he was watching what she drank. She'd never made a spectacle of herself, but away from the glare of other people, their evenings always ended up in a brawl back at home, with Colin becoming more and more violent. Of course, she could have just left, Millie admitted. But she'd kept holding onto the hope that the Colin she'd fallen in love with, when they were young students at Cambridge, would come back to her. She knew they had come from very different backgrounds. Millie told her she was actually born in Glasgow but had moved to Manchester with her Scottish parents when she was a baby. She was working-class and had had a poor upbringing compared to Colin who had inherited a fortune from generations of privilege. She'd managed to get to Cambridge University on a scholarship to study English literature, and though she'd always felt she didn't fit in, none of it mattered once she and Colin had met and fallen in love. She shook her head, as she said she still couldn't comprehend how it could all have gone so wrong, how it could have come to this.

Rosie watched as Millie sniffed back tears, then began to talk about Madrid: she had seen a girl on her own, crying in the hotel bar in the afternoon. 'She was just a waif,' Millie said, 'but very beautiful. The bar was completely empty, and I sat there watching her, feeling miserable, downing drink after drink. I was on the verge of going over to ask her if I could help when the door opened and in came this entourage. I still had no idea who she was, but the barman mentioned that she was called Bella Mason. I vaguely knew her name and face from newspaper pictures. And that was it. She got up, gave me a slight smile and went out into the street. I followed a little later and watched as they all flounced around her taking pictures. But I had my own problems. I knew what I was going to do.'

'You really had made your mind up?'

'I'd made it up before I left London, Rosie. I felt I had nothing to live for.' She paused, as though remembering. 'All I had were memories. So I walked around Madrid, going to the cafes Colin and I had gone to, drinking, crying, just feeling so isolated and alone. None of the things I yearned for in life were ever going to happen. Not Colin, and there was nobody to leave behind, no children who could have given me a reason to live.' She sniffed and dabbed her cheeks with the napkin. 'Goodness, look at me. Maybe deep down I was desperate for someone to stop me, but right at that moment, when I went onto the roof, there was nobody. I had made my mind up. I was smoking my last cigarette.' She clasped her hands on the table. 'Then it all happened. I had seen this party on the rooftop when I was making my way up there and I had no idea what it was, but I saw through the little porthole window on the door that Bella Mason was in there. Everyone was fussing around her, like she was holding court, and she seemed happy enough and smiling. Then for a brief moment she looked across the room and our eyes met. I have no idea to this day what that meant, but we actually locked eyes for a couple of seconds, and I can still see her right now. You might think I'm truly mad, Rosie, but something tells me that that moment was somehow meant to be. I had no idea what was about to happen to her, but something drew the two of us together for a few seconds. Do you think that's even possible?'

Rosie had no idea, but she was loving Millie's words. There was a headline on almost every line, and she could see McGuire doing somersaults if the lawyers allowed him to publish this story. But there was a long way to go.

'I don't see why not. It was a strange moment, given what happened next.' Rosie raised her eyebrows, gesturing for Millie to continue.

Her expression grew dark. 'So I went outside through the fire door. I was crying. I was so sad, Rosie. My heart was so badly broken that I felt the pain in my chest for everything, for my dead babies, for Colin, for all the plans I'd made over the years. I knew I was a drunk and I didn't even want to find the road back. It was easier just to go.' She composed herself. 'I was just seconds from stepping off that roof when I heard the door burst open, then raised voices and arguing. I stopped and stood there, barely breathing. I automatically stepped back from the edge and slipped into the shadow behind a pillar and peered out. I had a clear view. I could see three men. One with weird bleached-blond hair, another built like a tank – they were like bouncers. The third was older, with a goatee beard and glasses. And Bella. The older man had his hands on her shoulders and he was shaking her. She was crying and he was saying that he owned her. What a peculiar thing to say. I have no idea who he was, but that's what he was saying. And the poor girl was sobbing, and she was saying she was going to the police, she was going to tell them everything, that she'd had enough. I stood there, my heart in my mouth, afraid to move. Then, to my horror, these two burly men grappled with the girl and they were pulling her to the edge of the roof. I wanted to step out and shout to them, and when I think back now, I'm ashamed I didn't. Even if they still threw her off the roof, at least I'd have done something to stop them. Even if I didn't succeed, and they also killed me, then at least my death wouldn't have been so self-centred. I watched as they dragged that poor girl to the edge, and she was fighting for her life every second, and just a minute earlier I had been going to end mine. I felt ashamed and angry, and I almost called out.

But the next thing . . . they threw her off.' Millie's hands went to her face and she wept.

Rosie reached across and touched her wrist but said nothing.

'My God! That poor girl. She was so sad, and yet she was fighting for her life right until they killed her.'

They sat in silence, and Rosie watched as Millie wiped her tears.

'Then I ran,' Millie said. 'I ran and ran, and I've haven't stopped running since. I'm ashamed of that too, Rosie. I could have come forward in Madrid and talked to the police. But I was in such a state emotionally I just couldn't have coped. I hate myself for that now.' She looked Rosie in the eye. 'I'm not running any more. I'm going to tell the truth and I'm going to do it for Bella. Are you going to help me, Rosie? Are you really going to expose these people?'

Rosie nodded. 'Yes, Millie. I am. You can be sure of that.'

Millie reached across and grabbed Rosie's arm. 'Thank you.' She swallowed. 'Could I please have another drink? Just one?'

Rosie smiled. 'Of course. I need one too. One drink and then we'd better get ourselves to bed for the night. You must be shattered.'

'I am. And I know they'll be looking for me.'

Rosie tried not to think about that.

CHAPTER TWENTY

Rosie scanned Dan's story one final time before sending it to McGuire. It was a harrowing read, and she'd felt more involved than she should have as she wrote it. But reading it now made her smile inside. It would send the rest of the media into a frenzy in the morning when it was splashed all over the front page of the *Post*. The story was so good, it had more or less written itself. There had never been as much as a sniff that Bella Mason had a long-lost brother, never mind one who was a heroin addict, living rough in Glasgow. Nobody would see it coming, because the last couple of days the Bella Mason story had been a series of the same old follow-ups from the police investigation that Bella had been a depressed cocaine addict. But Rosie's 'exclusive' had it all: the loving siblings dumped in a children's home by their mother, the separation a few years later when Bella was plucked from obscurity and thrust into the glamorous world of modelling, and how they'd lost contact for more than a decade.

Rosie and Matt had hammered up the motorway from the hotel that morning after McGuire had told her he planned to blast Dan's story over the next couple of days. She'd put aside Millie's interview from last night and left her and Bridget in the more than capable hands of Bertie Shaw. She pulled on her jacket, and pressed the send key, emailing McGuire's private account with the message that she was going up to see Dan in the apartment. She didn't tell him the rest of her plan.

Rosie was conscious of the ward sister at the Royal Infirmary giving Dan the once-over. He looked every inch the heroin addict, with his gaunt face and skinny frame.

'Now, I can't have Mitch being disturbed for too long,' the sister said, as she walked ahead of them down the corridor towards the room at the end. 'He's not a well boy. He's in a lot of pain, and' – she glanced at Dan – 'with all the underlying problems, he's lucky to be alive.' She sighed. 'I despair of these young people nowadays, so many of them lost to drugs.'

'I know,' Rosie agreed, because she couldn't think of anything else to say, and wanted to keep on the sister's good side.

Dan looked a little sheepish as he walked beside her, but Rosie was glad to see he was definitely in better shape mentally now that he was on the methadone. She knew it was only replacing one addiction with another, but at least she didn't have to sit outside drug dens to get him through his day. The antibiotics were working too and he wasn't coughing his guts up as he had been when she'd first met him.

Dan had told her as they drove to the hospital that he was determined to change his life. Rosie knew that if this story were ever to have a happy ending for him, he had to quit drugs – and soon. There was a shedload of money coming his way, once he could establish for the authorities that he was Bella's only surviving relative and therefore heir to her fortune. He would either use it to change his life for the better or he'd be dead in six months. Right now, it wasn't worth a bet either way.

The sister opened the door to Mitch's room and they stepped in. Rosie tried not to gasp when she saw him. Mitch lay on the bed, his face almost unrecognizable, puffy and bruised, with stitches across his forehead and a bandage around his chin and up to the top of his head. The crumpled white sheet stopped below his bare chest and there were wires connected to a machine at the side of his bed. You could count almost every one of his ribs.

'Fuck's sake, man,' Dan whispered. 'Look at the nick of him.' He turned to the sister. 'Is . . . is he going to die?'

She gave him a matronly smile. 'He's been through a lot. And the doctors are surprised that he's actually hanging in there. He's not out of the woods yet, but it looks like he's survived the attack.' She frowned. 'The addiction is another matter. Right now that's not an issue as he's fully medicated for pain. But the boy has a long way to go.' She stepped back. 'I'll leave you for a few minutes.'

Rosie stood back as Dan went across to Mitch's bedside. His tears were instant as he sat on the chair and reached out, taking Mitch's hand. 'Aw, mate! I'm so sorry. I'm so sorry, man.' He pushed Mitch's fringe back with his other hand as he pleaded with him through tears. 'Listen, Mitch. You need to get through this. You're my only friend in the whole fucking world. I love you, man. Don't fucking die on me.'

Rosie swallowed hard, watching as Dan's tears dripped off his chin and he stroked Mitch's forehead. She pictured them as innocent boys, playing football in the schoolyard, blissfully unaware of what lay ahead and how their lives would turn out. Whatever their dreams had been, here they were, a couple of junkies who'd be lucky if they saw their next birthdays. Mitch's eyes flickered and his lips slowly moved to a smile.

'Can you hear me, Mitch?' Dan said. 'I'm here. I'm right beside you. I'm going to help you. We can get through all this shit because we're mates. Don't forget that. I need you here, man.'

Mitch squeezed Dan's hand and a solitary tear spilled out of the corner of the swollen, black mass where his eye should have been.

They took the lift to the ground floor, and Rosie stopped at the kiosk at the edge of the canteen to pick up a couple of bottles of water and some chocolate bars for Dan. The methadone was working, but it did nothing for the sugar cravings. She waited in the queue, handed over her money, then she and Dan walked towards the exit. A sudden uneasiness – paranoia or instinct – swept through her and she quickened her step. The corridor was busy and a couple of times she bumped into people walking briskly towards her. She wanted out of there fast, into the safety of her car. As they got to the automatic sliding glass doors, a voice called, 'Dan!' Rosie's stomach turned over. 'Hey, Dan!' The voice again. Dan stopped in his tracks and turned around.

'Don't stop, for Christ's sake. Keep going.' Rosie grabbed his arm and pushed him to walk faster. 'Hurry, Dan. Let's get out of here. Keep your head down.'

As they stepped outside Rosie felt someone burly bump into her, almost knocking her off her feet. She looked up and her gut flipped when she saw the bleached-blond hair.

'Hey, Dan. Where you been, wee man?'

Dan looked at Rosie, his face even whiter than normal. She pulled him away, and just as the guy came after her, a police car pulled up in front of them, like a gift from God, with its blue lights flashing. Rosie rushed quickly towards it and stood at the passenger door. She pretended to be looking at her mobile phone so as not to arouse the suspicion of the cops, but she knew they were safe as long as she stood there for a second. Her own car was only twenty feet away and now she was glad she'd taken the risk of parking on a double yellow line. Suddenly an ambulance screamed into the entrance and people scattered in all directions to keep the path clear.

Rosie pulled Dan away and they jumped into her car, her fingers trembling as she tried to get the key into the ignition. She headed out of the throng around the entrance, the police already out of their car. Another ambulance arrived and the road behind her was blocked. As she drove towards the exit, she looked in her rear-view mirror and could see the bleached-blond thug sprinting towards some parked cars. She prayed his was far enough away to give them a start.

'Fuck, Rosie!' Dan said, as she screeched out of the car park and down High Street. 'That was him. That's Ricky. The big blond cunt.'

'I gathered that,' Rosie said, trying to sound calm. 'Don't worry, there's nobody behind us.'

She drove down to the lights and turned right up towards the M8. She pulled her phone out of her jacket and punched in McGuire's private mobile. 'Mick. It's me. There's a problem.'

'What problem? We're all set for tomorrow. All guns blazing, Gilmour.'

'Listen. I need to get out of here. Fast. That big guy I told you about, the one who's looking for Dan, he's here. We just saw him.'

'Fuck me! Where? At the flat?'

'No. At the Royal. Just outside. He saw us.'

'The Royal? What were you doing up there?' McGuire paused. 'Fuck's sake, Rosie. You went to see Mitch! Christ almighty!'

'I know, I know. But Dan wanted to see him. Look, never mind that. We need to act now. I'm heading for the border. I need to take Dan out of here.'

'Is the bastard following you?'

'I don't think so. Not so far. But I didn't want to hang around Glasgow. I'm on the motorway. Is that okay?'

McGuire snorted. 'Like I've got a fucking choice?'

'Sorry, Mick. It had to be done. I'll just hole up in the hotel for the night, the one where Millie and the nurse are. I'll come back up in the morning, early doors. Can you get Matt to hook up with me?'

'Christ, Rosie! You're fucking off the scale.'

'It'll be fine. I'll call you in a couple of hours in case there's any problem with my story.'

'The story's great. It's you that's the bloody problem.' He hung up.

Larry's mobile rang as he was about to sit down to a late lunch with his driver. He looked at the screen. It was that clown Ricky. He didn't have the patience for this.

'Ricky.' Larry's tone was sharp. 'I'm about to eat. You'd better not be disturbing me with bad news.'

'Good and bad news, boss. I saw Dan Mason.'

Larry poured a little red wine into his glass and swirled it around. 'What do you mean, you saw him? Are you telling me you saw him, but you haven't got him?'

'Well, yeah, boss.'

'Fuck's sake. Get to the point, Ricky. My steak's getting cold.'

'You see, boss, he turned up at the hospital to see that Mitch geezer we gave the going over to.'

'You mean the one you beat the shit out of but still got no information from, you tit.'

'Yeah,' Ricky said sheepishly. 'But we were staking out the hospital in the hope something would happen, in case the Dan boy came. And he did. Pete was inside and clocked him going up to the ward and asking for Mitch. Then, when he was leaving, I was stood outside. I called out, "Dan," and the little prick turned around. Thing is, boss, he was with this bird. She just about shat it when the boy turned, and she ushered him away. I'm nearly a hundred per cent sure it was him.'

'What bird? What are you talking about? He was with some bird?'

'Don't know who she is. Nice-looking. Not a junkie. And older than him. Maybe thirties.'

'So who the fuck, was she? Maybe a copper?'

'Don't know.'

'So what happened?'

'They saw us, obviously, and as I say, the bird rushed

away. We would have grabbed him, but she seemed to sense the danger and made for a cop car that had just pulled up, so we had to stand back. Then, there was some sudden emergency at the door of the hospital, with ambulances arriving, and it all got a bit chaotic.'

'So you fucking lost them, you prick.'

'Yes. I'm afraid so, boss.'

'Fucking Christ almighty! Talk about fucking amateur night! Did you see her car?'

'Yeah. It was a Vauxhall Vectra. I got the number plate.'

'Gimme it. I'll get it checked.' Larry wrote down the registration on the back of his hand. 'Okay. So what happened next?'

'We jumped into our motor, but by the time we got out of the car park – I mean it was fucking mental, boss, queued up because of the emergency – by the time we got out into the road, she was nowhere to be seen.'

Larry sighed. 'Okay. Just stay where you are and keep looking. I'll get the number checked. Now fuck off and let me eat my lunch.'

Larry hung up, then scrolled down and punched in the number of a copper on his payroll. 'Jack? You all right, mate? Listen. I need you to check a plate for me.' He reeled off the number.

CHAPTER TWENTY-ONE

Colin Chambers had been screaming down the phone at people for so long that his head was pounding. How hard could it be to keep a patient locked up in a psychiatric ward? The whole fucking point of sectioning someone was to save them from harming themselves or being a danger to the public, but his bloody wife was out there somewhere, walking around. If it had been an NHS hospital he'd have expected no less, but this was costing him a fortune.

He had torn a strip off the hospital manager once the news began to sink in that Millie had disappeared. It was the same routine every day, he was told. Nobody had ever gone missing before, the manager had said, by way of apology. He assured Colin that an investigation was under way. The staff were being questioned closely and would be dealt with if any dereliction of duty was found. The manager had been surprised when Chambers had instructed him not to report the matter to the police. He told him it was a private matter, and the last thing he wanted was some story appearing in a newspaper that would frighten his poor wife. He had done his distraught-husband routine rather well, he mused, once he'd slammed the phone down.

Earlier in the morning, he'd called in his closest aides and instructed them to do whatever they had to do to find her. They'd already tried to track down the location of her mobile from recent calls, but the last place it had been switched on was in the private hospital. It had been dead since then. They were able to check her phone records, though, and found she'd had an incoming call from a number they tracked to Eastbourne. It had been from a mobile, which belonged to someone called Bridget Casey from Eastbourne. Who the hell was she? He told them to find out. They'd just come back with the information that she was a nurse at the District General, but when they'd rung and asked to speak to her, they were told she was at home ill. She wasn't at the house, so one of his men had broken in and found nothing suspicious. Whoever the hell she was, she must have had a hand in Millie's escape.

To some, Millie was a pathetic soul, and was out there somewhere and vulnerable. But that didn't matter a damn to Colin. She was a nervous wreck and on the verge of a breakdown, and the very fact that she had buggered off to Madrid without telling him showed how unhinged she had become. He had been right to get her locked up for some treatment. It wasn't that he wanted her back – he'd given up the ghost of their marriage a long time ago, and she didn't even attract him any more: It was over. Millie was a seriously loose cannon. She knew too much.

She'd been around and would have been in a position to hear things while he was Home Secretary. Especially during that unfortunate time when allegations began to emerge about a sexual-abuse ring. The claims were far-fetched, the police had told him. He should bear in mind that the kids making the claims were mostly from criminal backgrounds and were already young offenders. They were not to be trusted. Colin had been a little uneasy about it in the beginning, but once names had begun to emerge in political circles, it was important to silence it, shut it down.

His closest advisers in the civil service suggested it was easier simply to shred the dossiers. It was his decision in the end, but everyone knew it was the civil servants who were the nuts and bolts of the government. They covered your back and they made things disappear. You just had to keep denying things. But every bloody time Millie was pissed she brought up the conversation she had overheard between Colin and the Chief Constable of the Met. 'What about those kids?' she'd kept moaning. 'You knew about it. I heard you talk with the Chief Constable,' she'd bleated one night. She'd received a hard slap for being so presumptuous and spying on him. But still she went on about it. It niggled him that she was out there now in a position to damage him, and was bitter and twisted enough to do it. But he consoled himself with the fact that she would be roaring drunk somewhere, not making sense to anyone. With any luck, they'd get her picked up in the next couple of days.

His phone rang on his desk and he answered it.

It was a private eye. 'The mobile phone of that nurse has been traced to a location in the borders. She must have made a phone call,' the voice said.

'The borders? How come? Whereabouts?' Colin barked.

'The only place for miles is a country hotel. We have the name of it. Unless she's lost her phone, I'd be surprised if this lady isn't staying there. Perhaps Mrs Chambers too. I know it's a long shot, but it's all we have.'

Colin took a few moments to process the information, then he spoke. 'Okay. Do what you have to. Let me know when you find out any more.'

Rosie was glad Dan had crashed out in the passenger seat and was comatose most of the journey towards Carlisle. He'd been flapping after they'd made their getaway from the hospital car park, and had broken down in tears over the state Mitch was in. When they arrived at the hotel, Matt in his car following Rosie up the long, leafy driveway, Dan woke and looked around him, bewildered. 'Where are we?'

'Just this side of Carlisle, Dan. Don't worry. Nobody knows

we're here. The owner is a friend of mine, and I've already got someone else here out of the way. We're safe, trust me.'

'Are you sure?'

'Yeah.' Rosie opened the door and got out. 'Come on. Matt's here too. He went to the flat and picked up some things for you.'

Dan gave Rosie an anxious look, and she knew what he meant. 'Yeah, don't worry. He's got your meth as well.'

'All right, mate?' Matt smiled at Dan.

'Aye. Hope so, man.' Dan looked glumly back, his shoulders slumped.

'Come on, guys, let's go inside.'

Rosie hadn't considered the fact that Dan and Millie Chambers would be in the same place at the same time. But the goalposts had shifted, and now she had to decide whether it was wise to introduce them to each other. Millie would probably be able to handle it – she would take a sympathetic, motherly view of Dan. But Dan would probably freak out if he learned the full details of Bella's death at this stage. She decided it was best to leave it till later.

'This is Dan.' Rosie gestured towards Dan, as Bertie Shaw greeted them on the doorstep.

Bertie gave him the long, slow look of an ex-detective, taking in every inch of his skinny frame. Dan seemed slightly intimidated and shifted from one foot to the other, glancing at Rosie.

'Okay, son?' Bertie stretched out a hand. 'Come on, we'll get you settled into your room.'

Dan and Matt walked ahead along the shiny wooden entrance hall and Rosie hung back to chat to Bertie.

'I hope he doesn't set fire to the bed, Rosie.' Bertie raised his eyebrows, half kidding, half serious.

'He'll be fine, Bertie. He's very well behaved. He's a bit of a poor soul, actually. Harmless.'

'Yeah, well, he might be. But I'll be making sure the money's well locked away in the safe. You can't trust guys like that. They don't have any rules, as long as they get their fix.' He lowered his voice. 'If I'm honest, looking at the cut of him, I'd give him two years maximum. Skin and bone, Rosie. He's on the last leg of his journey.' He shook his head. 'Poor bastard. He looks scared.'

'He is, Bertie. He's terrified. As I was saying, the guys I told you about are looking for him. They caught up with us in Glasgow, so I wanted to get out of the area as quick as possible.'

Rosie hoped Bertie wasn't going to renege after saying he'd put them up for a couple of days to escape the heat.

'Of course,' Bertie said. 'There's always some bastard on the street who'll betray your trust for money and grass you up to the bad guys. Well, he'll be okay here for a couple of days. We're not busy. We've got about four guests in total – a couple checked in about an hour ago. And we've got a few rooms booked for the weekend. Some anniversary party.' He smiled. 'Definitely a bit different from dragging villains out of their beds in Possilpark at two in the morning.'

Rosie chuckled. 'Yeah. And I bet you'd give it all up just to be back in the action.'

'Oh, aye.' Bertie chortled. 'That'll be right. Give me my pinny and a full breakfast for four to cook, any day of the week. I'm loving the life. Honestly.'

'Really? You don't miss the action?'

He shook his head. 'Nah. Only thing I miss is taking some bullying hardman and running his head into a wall when I had to get some answers.' He grinned. 'But you can't do that any more. Too much political correctness.'

Rosie smiled as she watched Bertie go past Matt and Dan, and take the stairs two at a time.

Colin Chambers sat in his study in the darkness, transfixed by the glow of the fake flames from the gas fire. He swirled whisky in a heavy crystal tumbler, the aroma of the malt and the cask in his nostrils. He took a sip and swallowed, feeling it burn all the way down. How in the name of Christ had it come to this? Colin could hear a voice inside his head plead. He pushed it away and took another drink.

But an image of Millie in her twenties, barefoot on the beach, her hair billowing in the breeze, came to him. It was their first date, when they were Cambridge students, and he'd driven her to Dorset in his old Triumph convertible. He'd fallen in love with her there and then, and that single image had stayed with him, no matter how bad their lives together had become. But he didn't want what she'd become. Millie wasn't the girl he'd fallen for and hadn't been for the past fifteen years. She was dragging them both down and he despised her. He couldn't bear being in her company, and didnt want to go anywhere near the fact that she couldn't even have his children. She should have pulled herself together after she'd lost them and got on with her life, but she'd wallowed in self-pity, drowning herself in booze. He couldn't live with her like that.

Now, though, she was in a position to harm him – and not just him: the child-abuse investigation could bring trouble for a lot of his people, and nobody even knew if it was true.

He downed the last of his whisky and took out his mobile phone. It was time to do what he had to do. His aides had called earlier to say that they'd established where Millie was. Colin had asked if they were certain. He was told they didn't want to spell out how they did business. Rest assured, they'd told him, they knew where she was. It was time to issue their further instructions. He punched in the number.

CHAPTER TWENTY-TWO

It was always going to be grim, bringing Millie Chambers and Dan Mason together. One was grieving for the sister he'd been grieving for most of his life. The other was the last person to see her alive, and a witness to her murder. It was a difficult truth for Dan to have to hear, but he had to hear it. Rosie wasn't looking forward to it, but she'd talked with McGuire that afternoon from her hotel bedroom, and he had decided that it had to be done.

Rosie lay back on the bed, listening to the sound of the steady drizzle on the windows. She reflected on her conversation with McGuire.

'We have to put them together, Rosie,' McGuire said. 'It's pure theatre.'

'Jesus, Mick,' Rosie moaned, 'it's not a TV drama. Forgive me if I don't share your excitement. I know the value of having them together, but this is all a bit raw for them.

Dan hasn't come to terms with Bella's death. I don't know if he's ready to hear what happened to her. And Millie—'

'Gilmour,' McGuire interrupted. 'You're not his social worker, for Christ's sake. I know you get a bit emotionally involved with some of this shit and that it makes you who you are. I admire that. But I'm the editor, and I'm the one who makes the call on how to get the best out of the story. I want everything wrung out of it. Plus, we need some good pics.'

'I know you do and I know exactly what needs to come out, but what I'm saying is, we need to tread carefully. Dan could fall to bits if this suddenly gets dropped into the conversation over dinner.'

'But it would be great colour.'

Rosie pushed out a frustrated sigh. 'Not if he goes to pieces. We need him in some kind of shape.' She paused. 'Listen. Let me handle it my way. We'll still have plenty of colour and emotion. I just don't want to jeopardize what we've got. I have to keep these people together until we can get the full story in the paper. By the way, what are the lawyers saying about Millie's story?'

'They're fine about her testimony of what she saw that night in Madrid, but they're twitching a bit about her claims that Colin Chambers beat her up. And they're positively shitting themselves over the child-abuse allegations and the shredded documents. That basically accuses the entire Met of negligence and a cover-up.'

'Not really, just the former Chief Constable – and he's

dead. We need to use that line, even if we have to find a way to tone it down.'

'We will, Gilmour. I'm still discussing with the lawyer whether to use the material first and ask questions second. But I think we have to show a bit of our hand in the interests of balance and accuracy.'

'Oh, that old thing . . .' Rosie said sarcastically.

'Right, Gilmour. I have to go. Just deal with it as you think best. It's your call on how you do it, but I want both of them told tonight exactly how they're connected. That's going to be my day two after Dan's splash and spread tomorrow. By the way, it's looking terrific. We'll punt this all over the world. Have a glass of wine on me.'

'Yeah, great,' Rosie said half-heartedly. She wished she could be more enthusiastic. McGuire was right, she was a bleeding heart, but none of this crap got any easier.

Rosie knocked on Dan's door. 'It's me,' she said.

He opened it, pulling on a shirt, and she glimpsed his torso, the skin so white it was almost translucent.

'You about ready to go down and eat, Dan?'

'Yeah. I took some of the meth a wee while ago, so I fell asleep. Just woke up and out the shower.' He glanced over his shoulder, a look bordering contentment in his eyes. 'It's nice here. Like being away on holiday.'

If only, Rosie thought. 'Listen, I need to talk to you for a second. Can I come in?'

'Aye, sure.'

He stood back and Rosie stepped inside. She saw the sudden concern in Dan's eyes. 'Can you sit down a wee minute, Dan? I've got something to tell you, and it's going to be hard for you to hear.'

Dan sat on the edge of the bed, the colour draining from him. 'What's wrong, Rosie? Have those bastards found us?'

'No, don't worry. Nothing like that.' Rosie sat beside him. 'It's about Bella.' She swallowed. 'And how she died. I have something to tell you, and I wanted to do it in private, before I take you to meet someone.'

This wasn't how McGuire had wanted it done, but it was Rosie's call.

Dan looked confused. 'Meet someone? What do you mean, Rosie? Tell me what happened. I'm shaking here. What happened to Bella?'

Rosie put her hand up. 'Just calm down a bit. I need you to be calm and listen. Okay?'

Dan nodded. 'I'm all right.'

Rosie ran her hand over her brow and pushed her hair back. She leaned a little closer to Dan and took his hand in hers. 'I have solid information that Bella did not commit suicide, that . . . that she was thrown off the roof of that hotel in Madrid.'

Dan's eyes widened, like a rabbit caught in headlights, and he stared unblinking, holding his breath. Rosie watched, afraid he was going to pass out. Then his lip trembled. 'I knew it. I fucking knew it, Rosie. How do you know? Tell me, please.' He was beginning to crumple.

Rosie squeezed his hand. 'There was a woman on the roof that night too. She's the woman I told you about, who is also staying in this hotel. She's in hiding, and I'll explain that later. But she saw what happened to Bella.' Dan's eyes scanned her face, urging her to continue. She swallowed. 'She saw two men. Three, actually, in the beginning. Bella was arguing with one of them. Then . . .' Rosie almost couldn't bring herself to say it, '. . . then the other two men dragged her to the edge and threw her off the roof.'

Dan looked confused, as though he were waiting for something else to be said, then he dissolved into tears and jumped to his feet. 'Oh, fuck, Rosie! I knew Bella didn't kill herself. She would never do that. No way. Where is this woman? Why didn't she help her? Did she really see it?'

Rosie stood up and took him by the shoulders. 'She saw it all, Dan. The woman wasn't well herself, she was depressed, and was actually going to take her own life. That's why she was on the roof.'

'What? Who is she?'

'She's a British woman. You're going to meet her shortly. But don't be accusing her of not helping Bella. There was nothing she could do, and that's not going to help anyone right now. I want you just to put that out of your mind. She's quite fragile, so try to understand that, okay? But I need you to listen to her, and I want you to know the truth. I also need you to identify a photograph of someone.'

Dan nodded, tears spilling out of his eyes. 'I knew Bella didn't kill herself. Please, Rosie, we have to find out who did.'

'That's why we need your help. Now, I know this is hard for you to take in, and I'm so sorry I had to break it to you like that, but you need to know where we are now. You need to be strong.'

He wiped his tears with the back of his hand. 'I'm all right. You know something? There's a part of me that feels a bit better because Bella didn't kill herself.' He swallowed. 'But she didn't have to die. She shouldn't have died. It's – it's not fair. After everything that happened to her! She wanted to live. For both of us.' He broke down and sat on the bed.

Rosie watched him for a long moment, then reached out and stroked his hair.

She sat beside him.

'Come on, Dan. You need to be strong.'

He threw his arms around her and sobbed on her shoulder.

Rosie saw something like panic flash across Millie's eyes when she walked into the restaurant with Dan. She was already seated with Matt and Bridget at a secluded table, away from the other few diners. Rosie had gone to Millie's room earlier after breaking the news to Dan: she knew she would be equally shocked to meet him. She'd been upset, but more nervous than distraught, the way Dan had been.

Millie stood up, and Rosie was surprised to see her make her way towards them. She stopped and all three of them stood still, Millie trying to control the tremor in her bottom lip.

Rosie broke the silence. 'Millie, this is Dan Mason. Bella's brother.'

Dan looked from Millie to the floor, then finally looked up again.

'Hello, Dan,' Millie said softly. She stretched out her hand. 'I . . . I'm so sorry for what happened to your sister.' Dan took it, and she covered his with the other, holding it for a few seconds. 'I saw her only briefly, twice on that day, and I can see now that you were the image of each other. She was very beautiful.'

'Sorry,' he sniffed. 'I miss her. Bella was all I had. We had a lot of plans.'

Dan was handling it better than Rosie had hoped. 'Come on,' she interjected. 'Let's have a seat and we can talk over dinner.'

She went to the table and beckoned Dan to sit next to her, Millie opposite. Matt gave her a so-far-so-good look. The waiter arrived alongside them and Rosie turned to everyone. 'I think we could all do with a drink.' She ordered some wine and beers.

Over dinner, with a couple of beers inside him on top of his methadone, Dan was more talkative than depressed and spoke animatedly about himself and Bella as young children. How their mother had been a single parent and had put them into a home when he was only five. He still remembered the day that had happened. Bella had taken on the role of his protector; though she was a skinny little thing, only four years older, she was fiercely protective of him when they were placed in care. She had refused to eat when they'd split them up because of Dan's age, and the home had to allow them to have beds next to each other. It was only for the first few weeks, Dan said, until he'd stopped crying for his mother and Bella had made him understand that the boys had to sleep in another dormitory. But most of the time they'd been inseparable. He talked of how everyone spoke of Bella's beauty and the boss of the home said that, with a face like hers, she could have anything she wanted in the world. It was when Bella was almost thirteen, Dan said, that they'd taken her. Some guy from showbiz or modelling said he could put her on the front page of every magazine.

Rosie let him tell the story about how Mervyn Bates had arranged for a couple to foster Bella. They'd wanted only one child, so Dan had been abandoned while they carried Bella off, kicking and screaming. He didn't see her after that until she tracked him down twelve years later. Millie listened, fighting back tears, and Bridget sat shaking her head and telling them about how children being split up happened all over Ireland on a daily basis for decades. It was a shame, she said, that would haunt the country for ever.

Rosie was pleased with how the conversation was going, and decided it was time to bring out the photograph that had been faxed to her. She placed it on the table and turned to Millie.

'Millie, is this the man you saw on the roof that night?'

Millie pulled it closer to her, peering at it. 'Yes. It was dark, but although I was in the shadows, I could see him. It was the arguing I heard first, which made me realize who it was coming from. It was him.'

Rosie turned to Dan. 'You know this guy, don't you, Dan?'

Dan nodded. 'Fucking Mervyn Bates. Merv the perv. I know him. I remember him from when I was just a wee boy coming into the home. But it was Bella he was always fawning over. I met him with her one time after she found me. He's a fucking creep.' He looked at Millie. 'He killed Bella? Is that what you're saying, Millie?'

'He was the one who was doing the shouting. He was in charge, but then he disappeared and left Bella with the two other men. It was they who . . .' Millie trailed off and she looked at Dan, her eyes filling with tears. 'I wish I'd had the courage to do something, Dan. I'll never forgive myself.'

Dan shook his head. 'They'd have killed you too.'

'I went there to kill myself. But when I realized what they were doing to Bella, all thoughts of my own suicide were gone, and I just wanted to get away so that I could be the person who witnessed it. If they knew I'd seen it, you're right, they'd have killed me.'

Dan nodded, but said nothing.

CHAPTER TWENTY-THREE

Something woke Rosie from a restless sleep. She opened her eyes, blinking in the darkness, and lay there, holding her breath, just listening. There was a rustling sound, and at first she wondered if it was the tall trees outside her window, but her eyes, now getting used to the dark, shifted to the door. She thought she heard a click, like a door handle being turned or opened softly, and sat up in bed, focused on her own door. Then silence.

Instinct told her something wasn't right. Before she could even think it through, Rosie was out of bed, pulling on her jeans and a T-shirt. She stepped towards her door, but suddenly there was another sound. This time a thud, then what sounded like muffled cries. Then nothing.

Every nerve in her body stood to attention. She knew Millie's bedroom was on the other side of the landing facing hers, and in between there were two other rooms. Rosie had noted earlier that the rooms next to her were unoccupied, so if she wasn't imagining this noise, it must be coming from Millie's room. She eyed her mobile on her bedside table, considering for a moment whether to phone Matt or Millie, or even Bertie. But what if she was just panicking? These old houses always had cracks and noises. It could be anything. She found herself slowly turning the handle on her door, and pulling it gently towards her.

The landing was in darkness, but by now her eyes were used to the blackness and she could make out Millie's bedroom door at the other end. It was closed. She stood there, barely breathing. She should go back to bed, but she had to check, just listen at the door. She tiptoed out of the room on bare feet and padded along the corridor, holding onto the banister. In a few seconds she was at Millie's door, her heart pounding.

She was about to turn the handle, when the door opened. She barely had time to register her surprise before a hand reached out and dragged her into the room, another hand covering her mouth. The door behind her closed and the key was turned. Someone was holding her tight and she could feel the solid body behind her, the hand squeezing her mouth so hard she couldn't breathe. She made muffled sounds as she struggled. Another hand punched the side of her head and she felt dizzy for a few seconds. But she recovered quickly and saw Millie sitting on the side of the bed, gaffer tape over her mouth and her hands tied behind her back. In the darkness she could see Millie's eyes, distraught and terrified. A man was standing over her, a handgun with a silencer pointed at her head. He wore a black ski mask. Rosie kept struggling and the man behind her freed her, but stuck tape over her mouth. Then the gunman came towards her, and she could smell cigarettes and alcohol on his breath.

'If you want to stay alive, you'll keep your mouth shut,' he whispered. 'It's not you we're here for. But if you get in our way, you're fucking dead. Am I clear?' He pushed the gun into Rosie's temple.

She nodded, trying to peer at the eyes through the narrow holes in the mask. She felt her hands being roughly bound behind her, and the man holding her pulled her arms back so hard she squeaked in pain. He slapped her again and her eyes burned. Her legs buckled but she kept her balance as he pushed her against the wall. He took a step back, then suddenly, before Rosie could stop herself, her foot went up and kicked him hard between his legs. It was madness, and she knew it as soon as she heard him grunt and bend double.

'What the fuck!' The gunman was across the room in a second and grabbed Rosie's hair. He pushed the gun into her bruised face. 'You want this, you stupid bitch?' Then he hit her on the side of the face with the gun and she fell to the floor. She was conscious of movement in the room, the stifled cries of Millie, who was being dragged out of the door. The man Rosie had kicked was on his feet now, gasping. As he left, he landed a swift kick to her ribs, forcing the breath out of her. She curled up in agony in the doorway, as she saw them rush across the landing and haul Millie downstairs towards the front door. Rosie crawled on her belly to the landing, then heard the unmistakable click of a gun, and the lights were suddenly full on. She blinked in the glare.

'Just stop right there.' Rosie recognized Bertie Shaw's voice. 'Put your gun down and let the lady go, if you value your life.'

His voice was calm, matter-of-fact, as though he did this sort of thing every week. He went to the beefy guy and pulled the mask off his face. Rosie peered down at him. She'd seen him at a table on his own earlier in the restaurant. He'd been a guest. It had all been planned. Christ almighty! Right in front of their eyes! She couldn't believe they'd tracked them down to here. It must be somebody's phone.

Suddenly Matt was standing over her in his jeans, chest bare, his mouth open in shock. His camera was by his side. He pulled the tape off Rosie's mouth.

'Get a picture of him, Matt.' she said.

Matt dropped to the floor and lay beside her. He aimed the camera at the scene in the hallway. 'You okay, Rosie? Christ! Your face! You're bleeding.'

'I'm all right.'

'Leave the lady alone.' Bertie's voice again. 'Then walk

out of here and nobody will be any the wiser. Just go to your boss and tell him you failed.'

Suddenly the gunman pulled Millie to his chest and grabbed her in a stranglehold. He held a gun to her head.

'Your call, big man. She dies in the middle of a robbery in your hotel, it's not good for business. Now fuck off and let us get on with our work. We're taking her with us.'

Rosie could see Bertie stand his ground, but she knew he would have to put down the gun. Those bastards were on a mission, told to bring her back or kill her. They didn't give a damn what they did.

'Now, I'm opening this door and I'm walking out of here. Have you got that, big man? Just go back to cooking. This is not your fight so butt out.' He pressed the gun harder to Millie's chin and she whimpered.

Bertie lowered his gun. The man opened the door and they backed out into the darkness. Rosie lay there, while Matt rushed into his bedroom to take pictures from the window. A moment later she pulled herself up to a sitting position and touched her face. It was swollen and her eye was almost shut. There was a searing pain in her ribs, and she groaned. Bertie looked up from the hall.

'Rosie, are you hurt?' He took the stairs two at a time.

'Just slapped around a bit. But I'm okay.'

'I'm sorry, Rosie. Fuck! I couldn't stop them. They were obviously told to bring her back alive if they could, but if they couldn't then just to kill her. I'm so sorry.'

'Don't be, Bertie. Honestly, it's not your fault. You risked your life there. Thanks.' As Rosie sat up, she felt a little tearful.

Bertie gently lifted her to her feet. 'Come on, let's get you sorted. You hurt anywhere else apart from your face?'

'Yeah.' Rosie grimaced, her breath catching. 'He kicked me in the ribs. I think he cracked one at least. Can barely breathe.'

'Let's get you to your room.'

A bedroom door opened and Bridget came out, clearly bewildered. 'What's happened Rosie? Where's Millie? I just heard the commotion.' She rushed towards Rosie and helped take her weight as they limped to her room.

'She's gone, Bridget,' Rosie said. 'They took her. Chambers must have sent them.'

CHAPTER TWENTY-FOUR

Matt loaded Rosie's bags into the boot of her car, as she limped up to him. The sharp pain when she took a breath had been confirmed as a cracked rib, by Bertie's GP friend. The doctor had dropped in as a favour to him and, to Rosie's surprise, he didn't ask any questions about how she'd been injured. He prescribed painkillers and a couple of weeks' rest. Fat chance, Rosie thought, as she thanked him while he put a couple of butterfly clips above her eyebrow where the fat man's punch had opened up the flesh. 'You'll live this time,' the doctor said, as he gave her a stern look, and she couldn't help but smile, wondering just how much Bertie had confided in him about his hotel guests.

Rosie's first phone call at six thirty that morning had been to McGuire, who was immediately on edge when he answered.

'This can only be bad news, Gilmour. I'm barely out of bed.'

'It is, Mick. It's Millie Chambers. She's gone.'

'What? She did a runner?'

'No. She was kidnapped from her hotel room. Middle of the night. Chambers must have organized it.'

'Fucking Christ almighty! What happened?'

Rosie described the scene as he listened, and she could hear him almost breathless with disbelief.

'Are you all right?'

'I've got a cracked rib. Bertie got one of his doc pals to call over and that's what he said. Oh, and my good looks are a bit on the swollen side,' she joked.

'Jesus, Rosie! This is fucking serious!'

'Yeah, well, I think Millie Chambers will know that, wherever she is.'

'Where do you think they took her? Back to the laughing academy?'

'I suppose so, but I don't know how the hell we're ever going to find out now.'

'What about the nurse? . . . What's her name? Bridget? Is she okay?'

'Yeah. She slept through it. But we need to get out of here now, so we're heading up the road. Bridget isn't coming. She says she's going home in case Millie gets in touch. She doesn't want to be too far away from her if she can help in some way. She's a lovely, caring woman, Mick, and right now she's the only friend Millie's got. But Christ knows where they've taken her.'

'Do you think they'd take her to another clinic?'

'No idea. Depends on how Chambers wants to play it. If it gets out that she went walkabout, he'll be able to say she's back safe and sound now. If he puts her somewhere more secure, he's going to look dodgy, considering he's said she went in voluntarily. He won't want people to know she's been sectioned.'

McGuire was silent, and Rosie could almost hear him think.

'You know what, Gilmour? I think we need to lean on this Chambers fucker. He can't have it all his own way. We need to put some heat on him. We should think about fronting him up and telling him what we've got. Actually, kidnapping Millie might have been his biggest mistake.'

'I agree, but it's proving he was behind the kidnapping that's the problem.'

'Well, who the fuck else would kidnap her? It's up to him to explain that. He's in the shit and he must be feeling it now. All we've done in the paper is reveal that she was in the Madrid hotel on the night of the murder, but he'll be suspicious that we have more. And he'll be right. That's why he's gone to such lengths to track her down. How did it go last night?'

'Great. It'll make a terrific piece, Millie and Dan together.

He was really upset when I told him how Bella died, but he's more determined than ever to help us.'

'Good. I need you up here as soon as, Gilmour, so we can work out where we go next. Can you write that piece from last night on the way up?'

'Sure,' Rosie said. 'I'll have it half done by the time I get to Glasgow.'

She was struggling with the pain in her ribs, but when McGuire was fired up like this she wanted to keep it that way. The lawyers would have a fight on their hands if they tried to stand in his way.

'And what about Dan?'

'I'm going to have to take him back to the flat. Bertie has suggested coming along with us as a minder. He's driving my car up. He can stay with Dan while I'm working and getting things sorted. I don't know if Chambers has any idea that Millie is talking to us, but given that he's already tracked her down, he must have some sharp people working for him so I think it's good to have Bertie on our side.'

'Is this cop-turned-hotel-owner a bit mental? By that, I mean is he like that big Bosnian ghost?'

'You mean like Adrian? No. Bertie's all right. He was brave enough to take on these guys this morning, but he had to back down or Millie would have been shot. I think we should bring him with us.'

'Okay. Fair enough. Maybe he can come into the office and rustle me up a full English breakfast.' McGuire chuckled.

Rosie was waiting for Bridget when she came out of the hotel and walked towards them. The car Bertie had arranged to drive her back to Eastbourne was already waiting.

'Are you sure you want to go home, Bridget?' Rosie said, as she approached. 'It might be a good idea for you to disappear for a couple of days and come to Scotland with us. I can get you put up in a hotel.'

'Not at all,' Bridget said, folding her coat over her arm. 'I'll be fine. Those animals got what they came for. Poor Millie. I can't help thinking of her back in some hospital. I'm going to my house and back to work, as if everything is fine. Maybe Millie will find a way to get in touch.' She narrowed her eyes. 'These people haven't won yet, and if I've got anything to do with it, they won't. I hope you can do your story, Rosie. Expose the lot of them.'

'We will, Bridget,' Rosie said. 'And thanks so much for getting in touch. We wouldn't be anywhere with this investigation if it wasn't for you.'

'No, Rosie. You wouldn't be anywhere with it if it wasn't for Millie and her courage. She's the one who was brave enough to stand up and be counted. I was only the messenger.'

'Nevertheless,' Rosie said, 'I'm very grateful you came to me and nobody else.'

'I'm confident I've done the right thing. I know you'll bust a gut to get something done.' She stepped forward and gave Rosie a motherly hug.

'You take care, Bridget. Call me when you get home.'

'I will, and I'll be in touch as soon as I hear anything from Millie – I hope she'll find a way to call me.'

Rosie went to the car where Dan was in the back seat, staring out of the window. 'You okay, Dan?'

He nodded.

'Right.' She turned to Bertie, pain stabbing her ribs. 'You ready to roll?'

'I was born ready, Rosie.'

They drove off with Matt behind them.

Millie hadn't screamed or struggled when they'd pushed her into the back seat of the car. She hadn't even cried. Not as much as a whimper or a sob came out of her, even when they roughly peeled off the tape from her mouth. She vowed to show them nothing: no emotion, no anger. She just sat there, gazing out of the side window as they'd driven out of the back roads leading to the A74 South. She assumed she would be taken to London or to Sussex, back to the Dawson Institute, but she never asked. The only time she nodded was when they stopped at a motorway service area so she could use the toilet. They had warned her not to do anything stupid, and they stood outside the entrance waiting for her. She could have run there and then in front of everyone, she could have kicked up a fuss that would have brought some kind of reaction, but she'd made up her mind to be passive. If she had caused a scene and the police were called, they'd have been told she was a patient who had been sectioned, so it wouldn't have made any difference.

All she could do now was to hope that Rosie Gilmour and the newspaper would take up the fight on her behalf. She would be calm and co-operative, and she continued to be so even when she saw, after eight hours, that they were heading in the direction of the clinic. No doubt they would move quickly now to begin the ECT. Inside, she was terrified and lonely, on the edge of screaming. But she wouldn't. She wondered if Colin would visit, but it was now seven in the evening. She was glad, and she made herself put any thoughts of him out of her mind. She owed it to that poor young man, Dan, to be strong and to do everything she could to keep it together. And she owed it to Bella who, even though she knew it was irrational, she still felt she had failed. Of course it was a ridiculous notion that she should step in and risk her life to save a total stranger, but it didn't make her feel any less guilty.

When the nurses came and went with, they did so with quiet organization and few words. They gave her medication, which she assured them she had taken, but when they left, she had taken it from the inside of her jaw where she'd lodged it and flushed it down the toilet. She would escape again. She would find a way. But, first, she had to let Bridget know where she was so that she could relay the information to Rosie. She was one gutsy woman – especially when she'd kicked out at the kidnapper.

They brought Millie her evening meal, and she sat at the little table by the window in her room, picking at the fish pie. It was decent enough but it was a prison meal, even if it was for a well-heeled prisoner. She would have loved a glass of white wine, and a bottle would have been even more welcome, but Millie managed to keep a lid on her cravings. She knew she wasn't an alcoholic, despite the drunken benders she frequently went on: they were all about escaping from what her life had become. Now she had to be firing on all cylinders. She glimpsed out into the corridor, the polished floors and the quiet activity of nurses and staff going about their business. She ate her meal and gazed out of the window at the blaze of daffodils in the fading evening light.

Then she became aware of a figure in the doorway. The woman with the snowy hair whom she'd met in the grounds the morning she escaped stood watching her, a roguish smile playing on her thin lips. Millie said nothing but smiled and blinked in acknowledgement, hoping she would go away. But she stood staring. Then she took a step inside the room, and Millie began to feel a little uneasy.

She wondered who had locked her up in here, and how long ago.

'I see they brought you back,' she whispered, coming a little closer to Millie. 'I knew they'd get you. But at least you lasted longer than me. Good on you. I heard you climbed the gate.' She grinned.

Millie didn't know what to say. But the woman wasn't threatening, so she smiled back.

'They found me in four hours,' the woman said. 'I was just sitting in a cafe and in they came. The bastards.'

'Really? I'm sorry to hear that.'

'Yep. You must have had help, though. I had no help. I just climbed the gate and ran like blazes. Stupid, when I think of it.' She came even closer so that she was standing over Millie. 'I heard one of the nurses whispering that you were away up north or something.'

Millie said nothing, but the woman looked lonely. She motioned her to sit down. 'How long have you been here?' she asked.

The woman folded her arms and crossed her legs, her linen trousers creeping up to expose wrinkled shins. 'Lost count. But it's a very long time. Years. I'm not even sure what age I am now. All the medication they give me made me a bit of a loony. I forget a lot of things.'

'Years?' Millie raised her eyebrows. 'It's supposed to be a clinic for people to rest. People who've had a breakdown come here for some therapy.'

The woman nodded.

'Yes, that too. But it depends on who you are. If you've got enough money, you can stick anyone in here for keeps. And they can do what they like with you once you've been sectioned – like me.' She gave Millie a whimsical look. 'That's what's happened to you, I'd say. I know who you are. I watched the news. You're the Tory wife. They were all talking about you when you came in. And when you did a runner . . .' she cackled and broke into a chesty cough '. . . the place was in uproar. It was brilliant!' Then her face became serious. 'I'm sorry they caught you. But that's it now. It's not like the movies, you know. You're not Papillon. You can't keep escaping. Eventually you'll realize you're stuck here.'

Millie sighed. 'I know. Do you have any family?'

She shook her head. 'None that will admit to it.'

'Why are you here?'

She shrugged. 'I kept trying to do myself in.'

'Oh.'

'But I wasn't very good at it. Otherwise I wouldn't be here, would I?' she said, with a slightly mad glint in her eye.

'Why? I mean, I don't want to pry, but why did you want to kill yourself? Sorry. If it's too difficult, please forgive me – forget I asked.'

The woman looked through her, the grey eyes a little glazed. 'They took my baby away. A very long time ago.

That's what caused it. The shrinks in here told me that, as if I didn't bloody know.'

'My God, how awful! What happened?'

The woman pinched the thin skin on the back of her hands. 'Scandal. I was only fifteen. My parents were stinking rich, respected upper middle-class and all that stuff. Like your Tory toff husband. But I was the rebel daughter. All the schools and the money they spent on me, the life they had planned for me – probably the husband they'd find for me – I ruined it for them. Fell for a local boy at the fairground one summer.' She shook her head. 'Thought it was true love. But of course it was just for that one summer. I never saw him again, but he left a baby in my belly.'

'Oh,' Millie said.

'Yes. Bit of a shock. Anyway, that was swiftly covered up and the baby was snatched away from me the moment the little thing popped its head out.' She swallowed and her face tightened. 'I screamed so much for so long that I couldn't speak for days. Then I just stopped speaking. That was it. They shut me away. I was damaged, stained. Soiled goods. Nobody would want me.'

'But where are your family?'

'My parents are dead now, obviously, but they just kept putting me in various institutions. You see, the problem is, I stole a baby. Only for half an hour. I was fifteen. I just wanted a baby to hold. Christ! My heart was broken, and nobody could see that.' Suddenly tears rolled down her cheeks.

Millie could do nothing but sit and watch and fight back her own tears, the longing for her own child, the memory coming back of how her body wouldn't allow her to carry a baby longer than three months. She reached across and touched the woman's thin arm. 'I'm so sorry.'

She nodded and wiped her tears with hands.

'Are they not able to help you here? I mean with counselling and the things you need?'

'They tried. They gave me a lot of that ECT, and maybe it helped for a while, but I don't think so. My head's a bit frazzled with it. They do nothing now, just give me food, lock my door at night and put up with me. It's like a posh prison. It *is* a posh prison, actually. I'll never get out. All my family money is in trust, and they just fork out the fees every month, probably by standing order. That's what I am. A standing order. Nobody comes to see me. They've forgotten about me.'

'Do you want to go out?'

'I don't know any more. Maybe.'

'I'm sorry,' Millie said.

'What about you?' The woman asked. 'You going to escape again, Papillon?' Once more the wicked smile.

'No. My husband has had me sectioned. I run, they'll get me again.'

The woman nodded. 'They're all sectioned in here. But it's a con.'

Millie looked at her, and wondered if she could chance confiding in her.

'Do you think you'd be able to do something for me?'

The woman shrugged.

'If I can. Don't know.'

'They lock my door at night so I can't go anywhere, and I don't think they'll let me use the phone. I think they were tracing my calls from here, so I can't risk it anyway. But I need to get in touch with someone – a friend who cares about me. Could you help me with that?'

The woman gazed at her for a long moment. Then she stood up and stared blankly out of the window. 'The daffodils are lovely, aren't they? I remember we used to plant them in our gardens at school. I was so happy then . . .' She trailed off, looking as though she were in another world.

Millie's heart sank. How stupid to ask someone who'd been locked up for years if they could help. The woman walked out of the room, and Millie felt hopeless.

A few minutes later, the woman reappeared, put her hand into her pocket and brought out a pen with a small notepad.

'Give me the name of the person you want me to contact. And tell me the message.'

Millie looked up at her. Her expression was stern and determined. Millie scribbled down Bridget's home and mobile phone numbers.

'Thank you. Please just tell her where I am.'

The woman took the pad, stuck it into her pocket and walked away without a word. Millie stared after her, wondering if she was part of a game the old woman was playing, not knowing if she would hand it over to the nurses, make the call or flush it down the toilet.

CHAPTER TWENTY-FIVE

Rosie was in her office, off the editorial floor, so she could put together the piece from last night's interview with Millie and Dan.

'Fuck's sake, Rosie! I thought you were coming straight to my office when you got back. Look at the state of you.' McGuire had come in without her noticing.

Rosie sat back and grimaced. Her swollen eye was still almost closed and her head was thumping, partly from lack of sleep, partly the build-up of tension. Her cracked rib sent a searing pain through her when she took a breath. McGuire looked at her in disbelief.

'What the fuck's going on? Right. We need to get you up to A & E.'

Rosie raised her hand, and took a shallow breath., trying not to strain herself.

'No, Mick. Honestly, I'm fine. I've already seen a doctor. I told you, he came to Bertie's hotel before I left and had a good look. He said I've got a cracked rib, but there's nothing you can do for it except wait till it gets better.' She tried to straighten, but was conscious that her face showed the pain. 'It catches my breath a bit. Once I get this piece over, I'm going home for a hot bath and a rest. It'll be a lot better in the morning.' She looked up at him. 'I thought I'd come in here first and rattle out the story before I saw you. It's good stuff.'

McGuire stood with his hands in his pockets and was silent for a moment. Then he ran a hand through his hair. 'Well, that's what I came to tell you about. The lawyers are seriously bricking it over Millie Chambers and the child-abuse cover-up claims.'

'Christ, Mick! They haven't seen the bloody copy.' She was indignant. 'Even *you* haven't seen it!'

'I know. I'm sure it'll be brilliant. But you know the score, Rosie.'

Rosie shifted in her seat, trying to make herself comfortable. 'Yeah. I know. Claiming it and proving it are two different things.'

'Read me your intro.' McGuire planked himself onto the chair opposite her, his feet on the desk, his hands in his pockets.

Rosie glanced at her screen and read aloud: 'A former Tory cabinet minister covered up a police investigation into a child-abuse ring involving senior public figures . . .'

McGuire pursed his lips. 'That's just a bit nuclear.'

'It's what the claim is, Mick, and it's not being made lightly. What are the lawyers saying?'

'I spoke to Hanlon last night, and McKay did a conference call with the two senior partners this morning. They're both of the view that, without more evidence, we'll get our arses sued *and* we'll lose in court . . . big-time. Hanlon agrees it's a bit risky.' He folded his arms. 'Can we tone it down a bit? Get a form of words that hints at something?'

'Hints at what, though? Like being a little bit raped? Listen, it's not going to work unless we tell it like it is.'

'We need to get some more evidence.'

'Some of it is nearly twenty years ago, Mick.' Rosie had already considered this, and knew it was almost impossible to track down either a victim or an officer who had investigated the crimes. But she wanted to see Millie's story on the screen first and to hear if the lawyers looked like they were on board. Only one person she knew could perhaps dig something up. Mickey Kavanagh. 'I can make a call to a good mate of mine who worked at the Met for a while. The crimes will all be before his time, I suppose, but he has a lot of contacts.'

McGuire nodded, but he didn't seem very impressed, and Rosie had the sinking feeling that he was throwing in the towel already.

'Okay. Give him a shout. But, remember, we've already got two belters of stories waiting to go, Dan's, and Millie's witness to the murder. We can hang onto the investigation for a bit.'

Rosie looked him in the eye. 'But you're not giving up on it?'

'Of course not, Gilmour. But you know yourself – we need more evidence. Anything that can say, first, such an investigation took place, and second, we've tracked down any officers or victims. That's paramount.'

'Millie said the files were destroyed.'

McGuire stood up. 'Of course they were. That's what guilty fuckers in positions of power do, and that's why we have to make sure they don't get away with it. Now, make your call to your mate, and get home to bed. This story will still be here in the morning.'

'I won't let it go away, Mick.'

'I know you won't.' He winked, then left the room.

Rosie picked up her mobile and punched in Mickey Kavanagh's number. He answered after five rings.

'Mickey. How are things down in the Smoke?'

'All human life is here, my lovely,' he replied. 'And some of it, if I had anything to do with it, would not be.'

Rosie enjoyed Kavanagh's outlook on life. 'You doing something unpleasant?'

'You could say that, Rosie. Been doing a bit of undercover work, as usual, and digging up a few complete bastards for the plods. Honestly, I sometimes wonder what's happened to the modern plod. Some of them couldn't find their arse in the dark.' He paused. 'Anyway, how the hell are you? We need to get a night out and you can tell me your stories. I'm still surprised the diamond smugglers or the Taliban haven't got you yet. You were lucky to get out of Pakistan a couple of months ago – but then you never listen to me.'

'I do listen to you. In fact, I'm phoning again to pick your detective brains re: that model death in Madrid. It's growing arms and legs. Is that okay?'

'Fire away. If I can help, I will.'

'Colin Chambers.' Rosie said.

'Arsehole,' Kavanagh replied.

'John Garvey, former Chief Constable of the Met.'

'Arsehole,' Kavanagh said. 'I was only here the last couple of years before he retired, but I've heard a few things about him. So what is this? Word association? I can say "arsehole" to loads of people.'

'I'm working on a mega-story. Not just about Millie and the hotel in Madrid. Bigger than that.'

'With Chambers and Garvey at the heart of it? Yeah. In your dreams, Rosie.'

'I seriously am, and I need your help. By the way, why do you say Chambers is an arsehole, and the other guy?'

'Well, Garvey was a crook by all accounts, and lined his own pockets all his life. He croaked it five years ago, and most of the guys who turned up at his funeral were there just to make sure.'

'Okay. What about Chambers?'

'As Home Secretary, he was the guy who ordered inquiries into Met officers after the riots and stuff. But he turned a blind eye to rogue cops beating people up and officers that were plain racist who should have been out the door. He's a wanker. And a powerful one.'

'Interesting. Listen, Mick. I've got good information that Garvey covered up a child-sexual-abuse investigation because it came too close for comfort to a lot of establishment figures.'

'You mean they were involved?'

'Yes.'

'I've never heard of that. When was it?'

'Might have been twenty years ago.'

'Before my time. But what did Garvey do? Please tell me he was a pervert.'

'I don't know anything about that. But he covered up the investigation at the behest of Colin Chambers, who was then Home Secretary.'

Silence.

'Christ, Rosie! If that's anything like true, you'll never get it in any paper in a month of fucking Sundays. Who's telling you this? You got victims?'

'Well, no. Chambers' wife is telling me.'

Silence.

'Fuck me! His wife? The flaky woman who was hit by a car in Eastbourne a few weeks ago? She's a bit of a pisshead, is she not?'

'Well, there is that.'

'So how does she know?'

'She claims the Chief Constable was a dinner guest on a few occasions and she overheard the conversation about this investigation and was horrified. Weeks later she overheard her husband telling him on the phone to shred the files.'

'She heard that? How did she know it was him and not his imaginary friend he was on the phone to, though?'

'She said she took the call from Garvey and passed it to her husband.'

'And she's going public to say this?'

'Yep. Er . . . if I can find her.'

'What do you mean, if you can find her? Have you spoken to her?'

'Long story, Mickey, but yes. I had her with me for a couple of days while she spilled all the beans, and then she was kidnapped.'

'Kidnapped?'

'Yeah. I'll tell you later when I get a chance. But is there anyone at all down there who would throw the slightest bit of light on this? I realize that some of the officers may be retired or dead, and I don't even know how many worked on it. All I have is her claim. And a young guy who says he was aware of kids being taken from the children's home where he was, but that was in Glasgow. He was abused, but doesn't know if it was an organized thing.'

'Did he go to the cops?'

'Yes, he did. When he was about fifteen. But he became a bit of a drifter after that.'

'Where is he now?'

'I have him somewhere safe – I hope.' She paused. 'He's a heroin addict.'

'Fuck's sake, Rosie! You don't half keep some strange company.'

'Not just any heroin addict, though, Mickey. He's Bella Mason's secret brother.'

'You mean the model who jumped from the building in Madrid? That Bella Mason?'

'That Bella Mason. Yes. And he says after they were split up as kids, she lived down south and knew about the organized abuse.'

'Christ almighty!'

Rosie could hear a landline telephone ringing in the background.

'I need to go, Rosie, but leave it with me. I'll see what I can find. But it's a tough one. I've never even had a sniff of anything like that and, as you know, I've got mates everywhere. Nobody has ever mentioned a thing about child abuse.'

'Okay. I understand, but I'd be very grateful if you could just put a couple of calls in for me.'

'Sure. I'll phone you once I've made a few enquiries.' He paused. 'But, Rosie, watch what you're doing. You could get burned on this.'

'I know.'

'You always know, but you keep doing it. Just be careful.'

He hung up.

Bridget had been awake since six after a restless night, her mind flooded with dark scenarios of Millie. They could just get rid of her, but she consoled herself that things like that only happened in the movies. Colin Chambers was a powerful man, but he couldn't afford to harm his wife, she decided, especially after the story in the newspapers about her being hit by a car, and Rosie Gilmour's story that she'd been in the hotel when Bella Mason died. He'd be scrutinized too closely to do anything, especially if what Millie had said about the child-abuse investigation was true. Colin Chambers had too much to hide to do away with Millie.

She finished her coffee and looked at the clock. She still had ten minutes before she had to leave for the bus to work. Her stomach tightened a little at the thought of going back after disappearing for a few days. She'd phoned in sick, but when she'd called yesterday after arriving home to say she'd be returning to work this morning, one of her friends had asked if everything was all right. Then the nurse said the hospital manager had been asking if anyone had had a proper chat with Millie Chambers while she was there.

Suddenly the shrill ring of her house phone in the hall startled her as she was about to leave. She went through and picked it up, but didn't speak. There was silence at the other end of the line, but Bridget could hear breathing.

'Is that Bridget?' The voice was thin, an older woman's.

'Who's this, please?'

'I need to speak to Bridget. Is that you?'

'But who is this?' Bridget protested, edgy.

'I have a very important message from Millie Chambers for Bridget. I don't have much time.'

Bridget stalled for two seconds. 'Yes. I'm Bridget.'

'Millie Chambers told me to phone you to let you know that she's in the Dawson Institute. She said to tell you they took her back.'

Bridget's heart beat faster. 'How do you know this? Have you seen her? Is she all right?'

'A lot of questions.'

'Please. Tell me.'

'I'm in there as well. I'm crazy too, so they say. But she gave me your number. Listen to me, Bridget. Millie is all right. Okay? I have to go in case they catch me.'

'But—' Bridget tried to speak, just as she heard the line go dead.

CHAPTER TWENTY-SIX

Rosie watched Dan pace the living room at the flat, his knuckles white as he gripped the mobile to his ear. Beads of sweat broke out on his top lip and he was beginning to hyperventilate. If this was how jittery he was on the phone to Mervyn Bates, what the hell would he be like in a face-to-face? Especially if he was wired up to record the conversation. She glanced at Bertie, who seemed to be thinking the same thing. But if they were going to take this forward, McGuire had told her, they'd have to allow the face-to-face with Dan and Mervyn.

They'd discussed if it was time to get the police involved, and Rosie had considered phoning Don, her contact in Strathclyde Police, to alert his mates down in Scotland Yard. But it was too early, she told the editor. There were too many loose ends to bring in the police yet. The investigation would be taken out of their hands – and it could end up in the shredder, like the child-abuse investigation at the heart of it. This was a big story and it was theirs for the proving. Leave the cops out. McGuire agreed, but only with the proviso that the meeting took place over a coffee in the foyer of the Holiday Inn in Glasgow. It didn't get any more public than that.

To Rosie's surprise, Dan agreed to it immediately. 'I want this fucker off my back,' he'd said. He seemed to have grown in confidence now it had been established that he was Bella Mason's brother. Declan, who'd been digging things up at Martha Street register office for the past three days, had tracked down their births, their mother's name and their father's. Rosie couldn't work out whether it was the fact that, in due course, Dan would be in line to receive a fortune, which he could either blow on heroin or use to change his life, or whether it was just because he had a birth certificate in his hand that he seemed so much more in control. He'd kept unfolding it, looking at it again and again when she'd brought it to him. It seemed to legitimize him somehow. A piece of paper. He wasn't just some gutter-junkie stumbling around. He was Dan Mason. His sister was Bella Mason, and he was going to let the whole world know how proud of her he was. Mervyn Bates wasn't going to stop him.

Rosie hoped he hadn't upped his methadone, but Bertie had assured her that he himself was keeping a careful watch, staying overnight and dishing out Dan's dosage as prescribed.

'Okay, Merv. I'll see you there. Tomorrow. Two fifteen.' Dan hung up, then turned to them, wiping the sweat from his lip. 'Fuck me, man! He's coming up here. What a smarmy cunt. Trying to sound like he really gives a fuck about Bella and me.'

Rosie handed him and Bertie mugs of tea. Dan sat beside her on the sofa.

'You did really well there, Dan. But you seemed a bit nervous.'

Dan's hands trembled as he put the mug on the table. He held them out in front of him. 'Shitting myself, Rosie. Look at my hands! Shaking like fuck! But I'm all right.' He looked at the three of them. 'I want to do this. It's the least I can do for Bella.' He took a cigarette from a packet and lit up, sucking the smoke and coughing. 'It's not about the money or anything like that. Fuck the money! I don't even know what I'd do with it. That's for later on. But you know what, Rosie? I don't know if it's the methadone helping me but I feel better. I don't know when or how I'll ever be able to get off it, but it's making me feel I can have a bit of my life back. I feel I can get through this. It's like I can hear Bella telling me I'll be all right.' He shrugged and sniffed, glancing at them. 'Does that sound fucking stupid?'

'Not at all,' Rosie said. 'I'm so glad you feel stronger. But putting yourself up for him tomorrow is dangerous, you know that. You saw what happened when those two thugs came after us at the hospital that day. They want you out of the equation. What we're trying to do here, and what you're going to try to do tomorrow, is get Mervyn Bates to give you the opportunity to *be* out of the equation. Once he knows you have proof of who you are, he'll be crapping himself. He has two choices. Get you done in, or pay you off. My problem is, I don't know which he'll go for.'

Dan nodded. 'I'll tell him I'm going away. That I'm going to Spain or Morocco or Greece or something, and I need some money. I'll say he'll never see or hear from me again.'

'What makes you think he'll go for that? Look what he did to Bella.'

'I know, but I'm depending on you to get this cunt arrested very quickly before he gets the chance to fucking do me in.'

'I'm working towards that. But we need tomorrow to go well.' She leaned forward and touched his arm. 'We can pull out of this now, if you like, and move on. See if we can find another way to get to him. I want you to know that. By the time you meet him tomorrow, it'll be too late to pull out. You do understand that, don't you?'

'Aye. I do. But if I pull out now and disappear, I'll be looking over my shoulder for this fucker for the rest of my life.'

Rosie nodded.

'I know.'

Bridget pulled on her coat and buttoned it as she stepped outside the hospital into the drizzle. She was glad to see the back of that shift, and she almost said it aloud as she walked across the car park to the main exit, reflecting on how her day had unfolded.

The other nurses on her ward had greeted her with the usual warmth when she'd arrived that morning. It had felt good to be back. Now that she'd passed on the information from this morning's phone call to Rosie, she could take a back seat and get on with her life. She knew she'd done the right thing in taking Millie's letter and acting on it. That was what had kept her going. She only hoped that some kind of justice would come out of it for those children, poor Bella and, of course, for Millie.

She'd only been a couple of hours into her shift when the phone on the nurses' station had buzzed and she'd been asked to go and see the hospital administrator. She'd felt a little nervous as she made her way along the corridor and knocked on his door. A voice had summoned her in. Bridget stepped into the room and was surprised to be greeted not just by the administrator, but two men in suits sitting on opposite him.

'Bridget. Thanks for coming, I know you're busy.' The administrator made eye contact with her. 'You feeling better now?'

'Yes, thanks.' Bridget cleared her throat. She tried hard not to glance at the men, but she knew they were studying her and she felt her neck redden.

'Bridget. These two gentlemen are making some enquiries

on behalf of Colin Chambers. You remember Millie Chambers, the lady who was knocked down in the town centre?'

Bridget glanced quickly at the men, then away. 'Of course I remember her. She wasn't badly hurt, though. Only stayed a few days.'

'That's right,' he said slowly, looking from her to the men. 'Can you remember the day she left? She was going to some clinic or other, suffering from exhaustion – anyway, not our problem. But you were there with her just before she left, as I recall. I came into the room and you were with her.'

Bridget felt her chest tighten. 'Yes. That's right. I'd taken her in a cup of tea. She was all packed up, waiting for transport.'

'How was she?'

'How was she?' Bridget threw it back at him, along with a puzzled look. 'What do you mean? Is something wrong with her?'

He shook his head.

'No, no. Just trying to check a few details. Did she speak to you about anything? I understand she was quite upset while she was here.'

Bridget gave a little shrug, hoping she seemed distant enough to hide her inner panic. 'Understandable if she was a bit weepy, I suppose. The shock of the car accident. She was on heavy painkillers. Combination that can make a person a bit tearful.'

He nodded slowly, and looked at the two men. They said nothing and the room crackled with tension. Bridget didn't know how much longer she could keep this up. Sweat trickled out of the back of her hair.

'Did she say anything to you, Bridget?' one of the men chipped in. Bridget turned towards him and looked surprised. 'Say anything?'

'Well, yes. I mean, like, did she talk much to you over the few days, confide in you in any way?'

Bridget puffed, a little impatient. 'Sorry, I don't know what you mean. The lady was in a crash. She was a patient, and had been a bit emotional. But to be honest I'd only seen her a few times – in and out of the room. With her being a former cabinet minister's wife, we wanted to make sure she was comfortable. So, no. She didn't confide in me. Why would she?'

The other man piped up: 'You knew she was going to the clinic, right?' He didn't wait for an answer or reaction. 'Did she by any chance get in touch with you in the days that followed?'

Bridget screwed up her eyes, confused. 'I'm sorry. I really don't know what you mean. I'm a nurse on a ward. Patients come and go. They don't get in touch with me after they leave.' She smiled politely. 'That just wouldn't be right, would it, sir?'

'So she didn't get in touch?'

Bridget sighed and looked at the administrator. 'No. She

didn't get in touch. Now, if there's anything else I can help you with I will, but the ward is very busy and I've just returned from sickness, so I don't want to leave them short-staffed.' She turned to the men, then to the administrator. 'I have no idea why you're asking these questions, so if you don't mind . . .'

Her legs felt a little weak. She glared at the administrator, and he turned towards the men. 'Okay, Bridget. Thanks for your time. That'll be all.'

She walked towards the door, feeling the eyes of everyone on her.

Bridget headed for the supermarket instead of going for the usual bus as she'd no fresh food in the house. She whizzed around with her basket, her head still going over the interrogation earlier. Who were those men? They'd looked like private detectives, ex-police or something. A couple of shady characters, anyway, and she hoped she'd given them short but polite shrift. She didn't like the way they'd looked at her at all.

She came out of the supermarket and headed up the high street towards the bus stop. The rain was coming down heavily now, and she quickened her step. She walked up to the top, then looked right and left before she stepped into the road to cross to her bus stop.

It happened so quickly she couldn't even move. The car seemed to come from nowhere. It was racing towards her, lights blazing, and she stood rooted to the spot, her legs refusing to move. Her mind was still trying to register it. The road had been clear when she'd stepped off the pavement. She barely knew it hit her. But just as it did, she became aware that she was flying through the air, and there was a sudden terrifying realization that they had come to kill her. She could hear screams somewhere close as her head hit the road – then nothing.

CHAPTER TWENTY-SEVEN

Dan was in the back of Matt's car, alongside Bertie, as they drove out of Finnieston and along Broomielaw in the direction of the Holiday Inn. He stared out of the window, listening to Rosie from the front seat.

'Okay, Dan, so you're clear about everything, yes? How are you feeling?'

'All right,' he replied. 'Bit nervous, but I know what I'm doing.'

Dan didn't want to say that his insides had been turning over so much that half an hour ago, in the flat, he had considered taking the two jellies he had in his jeans pocket that he kept for emergencies. The prescription tranquillizers were common currency among junkies and did the job if you couldn't get a hit of heroin when you desperately needed it. The methadone was getting him through what were maybe the first stages of rehab for him, but with so much shit flying around with this Merv bastard, he really wanted something else. But he couldn't risk the jellies. They'd make him more relaxed for sure, but he could end up spaced out and running off at the mouth. He had to be sharp enough to go along with what Rosie had suggested. Get the fucker to admit that he knew Bella was Dan's sister and to offer to pay him off for his silence, then bail out. The car pulled in at the Clydeside.

'Probably best you get out here, Dan. You never know if Merv's got somebody watching in case you arrive with anyone. So you just walk up there and go in. By the time you get there, Bertie, Matt and I will already be nearby. If we're in the foyer or having a drink at the bar, don't even look in our direction, okay?'

Dan nodded as he opened the door. He felt Bertie's big hand grip his arm and give it a squeeze. 'Don't worry, son. We'll be watching for you.'

Rosie turned to face him. 'Good luck. Once your meeting's finished, just walk out of the hotel and we'll be parked right at the door. I've already arranged it with the concierge – he's a good contact of mine and throws me some information now and again, so don't worry.'

She reached for his hand, and he squeezed it hard, swallowing his emotion.

Dan could hear the roar of the traffic above as he took the short walk under Kingston Bridge towards Argyle Street. He shuddered a little as the wind swirled around him, and stopped for a moment to compose himself. He was on his own now. This was the biggest thing he'd ever done in his life. He reached into his pocket and his fingers caressed the photo of himself and Bella the last time they had been together. Without even looking at it, he could see her face smiling, the pair of them happy, with their arms over each other's shoulders in the fancy hotel. The image brought tears to his eyes and he sniffed them back.

He turned off Argyle Street and into the hotel's car park. He looked up at the tall building and reached inside his shirt to switch on the tape recorder and the camera hidden in the lapel of his bomber jacket. The automatic glass doors opened as he approached and a middle-aged couple came out with their suitcases. Dan paused for a brief moment, took a deep breath, then walked into the lobby. He glanced around the area that led up to the bar and the restaurant. Four or five business types were sitting at tables, going over papers and drinking coffee.

Then his eyes fell on Merv. His head swam and he felt cold and clammy. He thought he was going to pass out. He tried to catch his breath but it wouldn't come. 'Calm down, for fuck's sake,' he told himself. He managed a deep breath and let it out slowly. When he looked at Merv again across the room, he was staring right at him. A mixture of rage and fear burned through Dan and he found his body squaring up as he lifted his chin in acknowledgement to the big fucker, then walked towards him.

'Dan!' Merv stood up, his hefty frame just as Dan remembered. 'My boy. I'm so sorry, son, for your loss.'

Then, to Dan's surprise, Merv held out his arms and pulled him into his chest. Jesus! He could smell the pervy bastard. Dan didn't hug him back.

Eventually, Merv stood away from him, his face a mask of fake sympathy behind the wiry beard. 'When you walked in the door there, son, it was like Bella had come back to us.'

Dan said nothing, but he wished to fuck he'd stop calling him 'son'.

'Sit down, son. Have a drink. Well, a bit early for a drink, maybe. But a coffee or something.'

'Just a soda and lime, thanks, Merv.'

Merv waved at a waitress and ordered, including a coffee for himself. Dan sat down on the wicker chair. He glanced at the silver attaché case beside Merv. 'So.' Merv pulled his chair closer so his knees were almost touching Dan's. He leaned forward, hands clasped. 'I know it's a tough question, Dan, but how are you? I can't tell you what it's been like for me. Losing Bella . . . It was like my own child was taken from me. I was in bits. Still am.'

Dan nodded. Lying bastard. He opened his mouth to speak, but Merv kept going: 'Bella had so many problems with drugs. I did everything to get her off coke, once I knew it wasn't just a case of a few lines at a party. It was a serious habit. You did know that, didn't you?'

Dan nodded, but said nothing.

'And, of course, I know how much she worried about you and the heroin, Dan.' Merv sighed. 'What a mess young people are making of their lives, these days. Such a waste.'

Dan waited, hoping for an in from Merv, but he kept rabbiting on.

'You know that night when she . . .' he paused as though choked with emotion '. . . when she took her own life, I'd decided to take matters into my own hands. As soon as we got back from Madrid, I was going to more or less force her into rehab. She was that bad with the coke, Dan. Honest to God. But I didn't think she was suicidal.'

Dan sipped his drink and placed the glass on the table. 'She was all right the last time I saw her.'

Merv's shock and surprise showed on his face. 'You saw her? When? You mean that night in London when she had you down for the show?'

'No. In Glasgow. She came up to meet me,' Dan said, hoping he was sounding calm. 'She was great. We went to the shops and she bought me some clothes. I stayed with her in the hotel.'

'Really? She didn't tell me that. Well, I can't be up to date with everything my girls do, and they're entitled to their free time, but she should have told me.'

'Why?'

'Why?' Merv was suddenly irritated. 'Because anything could have happened to her in Glasgow. Don't take this the wrong way, Dan, but you're a heroin addict. I don't know who you mix with. Anything could have happened to Bella, meeting you.'

They were silent for a moment, and Dan sensed a change in the atmosphere. 'She wanted to see me. It was fine. We just stayed in the hotel. Had dinner.' Dan looked Merv in the eye. 'Bella was all I had. My sister. You know that, and you know how much we meant to each other, Merv. When Bella found me that time a couple of years ago, it was the best day of my life. I'd thought I was never going to see her again.'

Merv shifted in his chair, half smirking and half sympathetic. 'You weren't part of her life, son. You may have been her brother, in the early days, but the reality is, this was a lifetime ago. Bella wasn't part of that world any more. And, I don't want to insult you at this time, but *you* certainly weren't part of her world.'

'But she never forgot me, and I never forgot her. I was just ashamed to go looking for her. That's why I didn't contact her. I . . . just didn't know what to do.'

'Bollocks.' Merv was angry now. 'The truth is, you were a cheap little junkie who would have stolen from your sister if you'd had the chance.'

Dan caught his breath, his lip trembling. 'That's not true! I would never have done that! I loved Bella!'

'Well, Bella had long forgotten about you. She was a supermodel. She was famous worldwide. Doors opened everywhere for her. You were not part of her life. You should have accepted that and stayed away from her.'

'It was her who contacted me, Merv. She found me!'

Merv drained his coffee cup, and Dan noticed his hands were trembling when he put it down. He was rattled. What the fuck would happen now?

'Okay,' Merv said. 'I'm going to keep this simple and brief. Come closer to me.' He lowered his voice and beckoned him.

Reluctantly Dan leaned towards him. He could smell the coffee on his breath, mingled with the faint smell of after-shave or cologne.

'I want you to listen to me, Dan, and listen good, because I don't have a lot of time to fuck about here.'

Dan held his breath.

'Bella made a lot of money in her day. She was a million-aire at least twice over. You knew that, didn't you? That's why you more or less stalked her. To get her money so you could blow it all on heroin.'

'That's not true.'

'Yes, it is, and now you want to get your grubby little junkie hands on her fortune, you fucking little shit.'

Dan felt dizzy with rage and frustration. He wanted to punch the bastard in the face, but he couldn't. 'I don't,' he protested. 'I don't want that. I'm trying to get clean. It was Bella who looked for me and, actually, you're the one who keeps phoning me. Why you doing that?'

'Because I know what junkies are like. I know how they bleed people dry. Fucking leeches. I know you want money, so I'm going to give you some. Then I want you to get to fuck out of my life and go back to who you were, a junkie waster. You can blow all the money on heroin for your gutter mates. You'll be rich for as long as it lasts. It's up to you what you do with it. But once you get the money, you never, and I mean never, regard yourself as Bella's brother. Ever again. Do you understand that?'

'I *am* her brother.'

'You were once, but I told you, Bella forgot about you. So you forget about her. She's dead now. She can't help you.'

'You can't make me do anything.'

'Oh, really?' He grabbed Dan's wrist tight. 'Listen, you little cunt! I can make you disappear. Any fucking day of the week!'

'Like you made Bella disappear?' Dan was shaking now and close to tears.

Merv's face was crimson with fury. 'Don't be so fucking stupid. Is that what you're going to do? Make stupid accusations? Go to the press? The cops? Who's going to believe a junkie? Now listen. I've opened a bank account in your name, and I'm going to deposit a massive sum of money in it, more than you've ever dreamed about in your pathetic little life. Three hundred fucking grand. How does that sound, son? Think of all the heroin you could buy.'

'I don't want heroin. I'm trying to come off it. And I don't want your money. Bella was my sister. People should know that.'

'Nobody gives a fuck about you or who you are. Listen to me, pal. Junkies die every fucking day of the week, you'll just be another one.'

Dan sat in silence. This wasn't how he'd expected it to go. He thought there would be some talk, then an offer of money. But the bastard was threatening him. He knew the tape was recording it all, and he should feel good about that, but he felt weak and abused, and somewhere inside he was beginning to buckle. He glanced around the room and saw Rosie, Bertie and Matt sitting at a table at the far corner. He felt lightheaded. This bastard was serious. Merv would kill him, just like he'd killed Bella. What if Rosie couldn't save him? Panic rose in his throat.

'I need to go to the toilet,' he said. 'I feel a bit sick.'

'Need a hit? Like your junkie sister? Don't even think about doing a runner.' He jerked his head in the direction of the front door. 'Look. You know that guy with the blond hair at the door and his mate?'

Dan looked and a shiver ran through him. It was Ricky and Pete.

Merv snarled, 'Yeah. I know you recognize him. He's the bastard who was outside the hospital that day you were with some bird. I know for a fact that she's a journalist tart, Rosie Gilmour. Scum.' He sniggered. 'Are you really so stupid that you think getting cosy with a journalist is going to help you? What do you think you can do? Expose people, you stupid little tit? I'm already onto her, and I'm on to you and your fucking scheme. You're not going anywhere. You can go to the toilet, but if you leave, you'll disappear. Those guys have been looking for you for three weeks, but, lo and behold, you were here all the time. Not down south, not anywhere but Glasgow. Right here. So now you're like a rat in a trap. The only way out for you, pal, is to take the money and run. And keep your mouth fucking shut. Because if you open it I'll hunt you down. Do you hear me?'

'I need to go to the toilet.'

'Hurry up. It's down that corridor there.'

Dan stood up on rubber legs and immediately wanted to sit down again. He felt claustrophobic. Trapped. A cornered rat. He wanted to run across to Rosie, but it would give the game away. But the game was up anyway. This guy would never let him off the hook if he took his money. He walked out of the foyer and down the corridor towards the toilet. Then, suddenly, he saw a fire exit half open. Before he could stop himself, Dan had pushed it open and run outside into the rain. He had to get away. He ran as fast as his jittery legs would carry him.

CHAPTER TWENTY-EIGHT

Rosie had spotted the thug with the bleached-blond hair loitering in the reception area, and she'd alerted Matt and Bertie. But there was nothing they could do except keep an eye on him and his mate. Dan had seemed to be doing okay, until he'd suddenly stood up. They'd assumed he was going to the toilet, but when he didn't come back, she sent Matt to look for him. Her fears were confirmed when he'd arrived back, shaking his head. They slipped out of another exit and got into Matt's car.

'Looks like he's done a runner,' Matt said. 'Maybe his bottle just crashed.'

'But he's got nowhere to go,' Rosie said, her stomach in knots as they drove around the car park for the second time, looking in every space and behind wheelie-bins, in case he was hiding. 'I can't understand it. That big bastard must have said something to him to put serious frighteners on him. He must have had some kind of meltdown.' She looked out of the passenger window, guilt washing over her. 'Christ! I should never have involved him.'

'Don't be daft, Rosie. He wanted to do it. You heard him last night. He was determined to go through with it.'

'I know, but he's a drug addict. Maybe the methadone gave him a bit of bravado, but once it got scary he felt he was in over his head. I wish he'd given us a sign or something.'

'But, Rosie,' Bertie said, 'you don't know what was being said to the lad. Maybe Mervyn Bates already knows about you and threatened you too. Don't go over the top worrying till we know where he is.'

'But how the hell are we going to find him?' Rosie said. 'He won't go to his normal places as he knows those guys will get him. And they *will* find him if he's walking around, scared. He doesn't even have any methadone, he'll be rattling in the next two hours. Jesus! What a bloody mess!'

Rosie's mobile rang, and she saw it was McGuire. She glanced at Matt. 'Brilliant timing,' she muttered, then answered it.

'How did the meeting go with Dan and that pervy bastard, Gilmour?'

'Er . . . Mick. There's a problem.'

'Fuck! Don't tell me somebody's dead.'

'No. It's Dan. He's disappeared. Right in the middle of the meeting with Merv. We were watching him from the bar. He got up, and we thought he was going to the toilet, but he didn't come back.'

'Oh, fuck! Have they grabbed him or has he just done a runner? Do you think he'd run out on you?'

Rosie sighed, frustrated with herself and wondering if she could have made a better plan. 'Jesus, Mick! I just don't know. We went over the plan a dozen times. When his chat was finished he was to stand up and head for the front door. But he suddenly goes the other way. Then I spotted that bleached-blond thug and his gorilla mate at the entrance. They seemed to appear from nowhere.'

'Did it look like they went after him?'

'Not straightaway. They just stood there, because they didn't know he was going to disappear. Then Matt went to look in the toilet. But there was a fire escape door open close to it. I think he's run out of that. Maybe had some kind of panic attack.'

'Shit! That's the problem with junkies. I know you feel for the guy, but the point is, you just don't know what you're going to get.'

'But he was calm enough before he went in, and as we were driving up towards the hotel he was determined to go through with it. He'd had the methadone and was compos mentis. I never expected this, Mick.' She paused. 'I'm really worried about him. He's out there somewhere and those bastards will hunt him down.'

'So what do you think happened?'

'Don't know. Maybe Mervyn Bates made some kind of threat. He must have done something to scare him.'

McGuire was silent for a moment, then said, 'Or maybe he's onto the fact that Dan was talking to you and has made him a bigger offer to keep his mouth shut. He could be with them right now.'

It had never occurred to her that Dan would double-cross her.

'But that would never work. Merv won't let him live under any circumstances, because as long as Dan's alive he's in a position to reveal that he's Bella's brother, and detail the abuse that Bella told him about. Merv will have to eliminate that threat no matter what. He'll do him in, Mick, just like he did Bella.'

'So, what now?'

'I've not got a lot of options. But as soon as I think of something I'll give you a shout. I'm going to look for him.'

'Rosie, be careful. Don't you think you should call your mate in the police? See if we can talk to them about it?'

'Maybe. But I want to have a look first.'

'Well, just watch yourself. Phone me in an hour and we can talk again.'

'Yeah.'

'And, Gilmour, this is not your fault, so don't start all that beating yourself up shit.'

She hung up, dread making her nauseous.

Rosie was glad to see Mitch sitting up in bed and trying his best to smile when he saw them come into the room. His face was still puffy around the eyes and he had bandages on his arms. He glanced at Bertie, then back to Rosie.

'Mitch, this is Bertie Shaw. He's a good friend of mine. He's helping on the story. You can trust him.'

Mitch nodded as Rosie, Matt and Bertie stood by his bedside. He grimaced as he shifted his position a little. 'Where's Dan?' he asked.

Rosie moved closer to the bed. 'That's why we're here, Mitch. He's disappeared.'

'What? How?'

'He had a meeting with that Mervyn Bates – the guy who was Bella's manager.'

Mitch nodded.

'Well, the meeting was in the Holiday Inn and we were watching from the bar. But Dan went to the toilet and never came back.'

Mitch shook his head and blew out a sigh. 'Fuck!' he said, his lips barely moving. 'Fuck's sake!'

'Mitch,' Rosie touched his arm. 'I need your help here. You know Dan will be in danger if I can't get to him soon. Those guys are after him, and he's out there in the city on his own. Have you any idea where I can go looking for him?'

Mitch sighed wearily. 'Aw, man! Poor wee bastard! He'll be shitting himself. You need to find him, Rosie.'

'I will. But where will he be? He won't go back to his usual haunts and dealers, because those guys will have been onto them. That's how they found you that day, by going round the houses.' Rosie paused. 'So is there anywhere at all you think he might be?'

Mitch was silent for a moment, then he moved his head slightly for Rosie to hand him his mobile phone. 'There's a wee guy up in Ruchill – in a flat there. It's a real shitehouse, but if Dan's out in the street and got nowhere to go for some gear, he might go there as a last resort.' He moved again and his face contorted with pain. 'I can't remember the address, though. Somewhere up near Bilsland Drive, a cul-de-sac. But you can't just go asking around or you'll get lynched. If I could get out this bed I could take you there.' He tried to sit up, but slumped back down.

'You can't, Mitch. No chance of that. You've a bit to go before you can even get on your feet.'

Mitch scanned some numbers on his phone. 'Look. Take this number. When you get to Bilsland Drive, phone this guy. He's a fucking wee polecat, but tell him to give you the number of the house. Say you're a mate of mine. He owes me one. That's all I can think of, Rosie. It's about the only other place Dan knew for drugs. He took me there one time and we bought some kit on tick till we got the money to pay. But it ended up costing us double. It's that kind of place.'

Rosie punched the number into her phone, then turned to Bertie and Matt. 'Might be our only option, guys.' She squeezed Mitch's arm. 'Thanks, Mitch. I hope it works. You just relax and we'll let you know how it goes.'

'You need to find him, Rosie. Dan's like a wee boy sometimes.'

'I know,' Rosie said. 'By the way, how's it going in here with you?'

'It's all right. Free morphine and stuff. Not bad. They've had some rehab guy in to talk to me. Said they're going to get me a bed in some place. I'm up for that.'

'Good,' Rosie said, trying to get to grips with his outlook when free morphine and a spell in rehab were a goal worth achieving.

'Find my wee mate, will you, Rosie?'

'Sure I will.' Rosie said, as he closed his eyes.

CHAPTER TWENTY-NINE

Rosie knew the street well enough. She had plenty of bleak memories of knocking on doors at houses like this, wondering what kind of picture of despair and poverty would greet her on the other side. It passed for a life here in the north side of Glasgow – the poverty, the drunkenness, the gang fights. But that was before the heroin explosion took the ghetto to a new level. Now, like so many of the housing schemes across the city, where being poor and out of work was normal, the streets were a breeding ground for heroin. Mothers buried daughters barely out of their teens. Hope had all but vanished, except for the dealers on the corners or in some of the dens who would make enough to get them to hell out of it before they were caught by the police.

Heroin didn't have the whiff of glamour that coke had, where nightclubs buzzed with it and cokeheads felt they'd reached a level of success by doing a few lines on a night out. Heroin was the dark refuge the desperate sought when all hope was gone. And once they'd been wrapped in that warm blanket or, more recently, in that of crack cocaine, there was seldom a way back. In this street there was probably only one small-time heroin dealer, but there would be several heroin dens, where junkies dumped themselves of an evening. Dan would be no stranger to places like this. Why hadn't he phoned her? His mobile was in his pocket and he had her number. She kept looking at her phone, willing it to ring.

'Okay, let's try this punter now.' Rosie punched in the number as they pulled into the kerb. A couple of kids eyed them suspiciously. They wouldn't be able to loiter here too long.

'Who's this?'

'Hello? Is that Jimbo?'

'Who's this?'

'Jimbo, I'm a pal of Mitch Gilland. You know him? He gave me your number. I'm looking for someone. Where is the place he sometimes comes to?'

'Aye, I know Mitch. He's all right. Where are you?'

'Bilsland Drive.'

'How do I know you're not the polis?'

'You don't, Jimbo. Listen, pal. Can you just help me out? I need to find someone. Really fast.' Rosie paused. 'Mitch says he'll weigh you in as soon as he can.'

'Mitch is in the hospital. I heard he got a right doin'.'

'That's right. He did. You know who did it?'

'Naw. Just heard it was some fuckers not from here. Mitch is all right.'

'Have you seen his mate Dan?'

'Naw. But I only came in here this morning. I was down in Shettleston last night.'

'Listen, Jimbo, can you just give me the address?'

'All right, then, but it didn't come from me.'

'Of course not. Mitch said you can trust us.'

'Okay. It's number one two nine. Ground floor. It's got an aluminium door on it, but it's not fixed right. You just push it hard.' He hung up.

Rosie looked up at the numbers on the houses. They were at number fifty-seven. 'Along here a bit, Matt. It's number one two nine.'

'What if this bastard's alerted them, Rosie? We'll get our heads cleaved off.' Matt said, as they drove towards the house. 'This feels a bit crazy. Dan might not even be there.'

'I know, but it's the only place we can try. Most of the people inside will be out of their box, so it should be okay.' Rosie turned to Bertie. 'What do you think?'

He shrugged. 'As long as we're in and out. If it looks too dodgy, we pull out straightaway.'

'Right. Let's go.'

Matt parked the car beside the house, and Rosie looked over her shoulder as they got out. They definitely didn't look like they were there to score heroin, so they wouldn't have too long before the jungle drums beat that there were strangers about. Inside, her gut was telling her this was a fruitless mission, but she had to feel she was doing something. The longer Dan was out there, the bigger the risk. They picked their way through beer cans and Buckfast bottles. The close stank of piss and vomit. They went towards the aluminium door.

'Locked?' Rosie wondered, noticing no handle.

'No,' Bertie said. 'Look at the bottom. It's not attached properly.' He stepped forward and leaned against it. Nothing. Then he leaned again and this time gave it a hard push. The door made a scraping noise and opened enough for them to squeeze through. Rosie followed Bertie into the bare wood hallway.

The distinct stench of a rotting corpse hit her like a punch. She'd stumbled across enough in far-flung lands to recognize the stomach-churning reek anywhere. 'Christ! There's a body somewhere, Bertie.'

He nodded. 'Was about to say that myself.'

The hall was dark and bleak, but a door was ajar at the far end. They tiptoed and could hear the unmistakable mumbled conversations of junkies. They stopped.

'I'll go first,' Rosie said. 'Don't want to spook them.'

She went towards the door and pushed it open, gasping as she put her head around the door and saw inside. A pall of smoke hung over a torn sofa and two emaciated faces were sitting smoking heroin. Another girl sat on the floor against the wall pulling a band tight against her arm, trying to find a vein to inject. Two other junkies were passed out on the floor. She walked in, but nobody looked up. Bertie and Matt followed, and stood there, taking in the scene. One guy eventually looked at them, his eyes dreamy, and half smiled, then lay back to doze on the sofa, cigarette burning in his hand.

'He's not here. Let's try the other rooms.' Rosie backed out. 'There's something dead in this bloody house, though. I can smell it. Putrid!'

They followed the direction of the stench.

'I'm going to throw up,' Matt said, zipping his bomber jacket over his mouth. 'Holy fuck, Rosie!'

The stench was coming from the door at the far end of the hall. Rosie looked at Bertie and Matt. It was already feeling like a wasted trip, another image to haunt her sleepless nights.

'Let's try.' She pushed open the door and the smell almost knocked her off her feet. 'Oh, Christ!'

Bertie coughed and Matt had to steady himself against the wall. Inside, among the mountain of rubbish, beer cans and debris, a woman lay on a sofa, her face blue and beginning to swell. She had been dead for at least a day, by the look of her. But the sight of the toddler on the floor beside her, eating out of a box of Frosties, made Rosie's head swim.

'Oh, Jesus wept!'

The toddler looked up out of dark-circled eyes and, for all the misery it sat in, smiled at them.

'Shit!' Bertie said suddenly. 'Look, Rosie. Behind the sofa.'

Rosie glanced down to see Dan out for the count, his face deathly pale, a bubble of saliva at the side of his mouth. Her legs felt so heavy she couldn't move.

'Fucking hell!' Bertie said. He dived across to him and dropped to his knees, feeling for a pulse under his neck, and slapping Dan's face at the same time. Nothing. Rosie watched, unable to move or speak, the baby still staring at her. Bertie was wiping the saliva from Dan's mouth and opening it gently. He bent over to give him mouth-to-mouth.

She heard herself murmur, 'Please don't die, Dan. Please, God, don't let him die.'

Bertie pumped Dan's chest, then breathed into his mouth alternately. Dan's head flopped from side to side, not responding. Then suddenly he gurgled. Bertie turned him onto his side. He made a grunting sound. 'He's alive! But maybe not for long. Let's get him to fuck out of here.'

Bertie picked him up and held him in his arms as they made for the door. Rosie glanced back. 'What about the baby? We can't just leave her in the middle of this shit, Bertie.'

'We can't take her either, Rosie. Come on. Let's get out of here and call the cops for her as soon as we get to the car. Go!'

They were in the hall when two young guys came through

the half-open aluminium door. They didn't look spaced out and one was brandishing a machete, the other a knife.

Rosie glanced at Matt. Suddenly, Bertie slung Dan over his shoulder, reached into his jacket pocket and pulled out a gun. 'Out of my fucking way, ya pair of fannies, if you don't want to die in the next three seconds.'

They stopped in their tracks, put their hands up, the machete clattering to the floor, and stood with their backs to the walls as Rosie and Matt slipped past them, then Bertie, carrying Dan. Matt could hardly get the keys into the car door, he was trembling so much. Rosie sat on the passenger seat and twisted round to Dan as they sped out of the street. His eyes were flickering, but he was deathly pale. 'We need to get to the hospital, fast.'

CHAPTER THIRTY

Rosie sat in McGuire's office, only half listening to him. She was still trying to take in what they'd witnessed in the stinking junkie hellhole. It wasn't the first time she'd stepped into somebody's tragic story. She'd been in refugee camps when people had died in front of her, or children they'd been photographing would be dead by the time she and Matt had got back to their hotel. Her work was about walking into and out of people's lives. She should have been used to it but she wasn't: she couldn't get the picture of the dead woman on the sofa out of her head. Who would tell the story of her short life? And what of the wide-eyed toddler who had already seen too much? She knew only too well that you could never erase a moment of trauma. It shaped who you became. She hoped the baby was young enough to forget.

'You're not listening to me, Gilmour.' The editor clicked his fingers. 'Come on. Snap out of it.'

Rosie blinked. 'I *am* listening, Mick. I just keep thinking about the dead woman and that wee kid.'

'Well, don't worry about the kid. He or she's better off out of it, and will get a real chance at life now. I know you're a soft touch, but that drug-addict mother cared so much for her baby she was mainlining in front of it, probably since the day it was born. What chance would the wee thing have had in that shithole of an environment? Look at it this way. You did the kid a favour barging in there. You've probably saved its life.'

Rosie shrugged half-heartedly. 'I suppose you're right. I'll try to see it that way.'

'Good. What about Dan? He's going to make it, isn't he?'

By the time Rosie had left Dan's bedside, he was awake and lucid enough to talk to her. He felt awful that he'd let everyone down and couldn't understand why it had happened. He told her he'd had a panic attack, and before he knew what he was doing, he was running through the streets of Glasgow and heading up to Ruchill. He was in tears, apologizing, saying he was no good, that he'd been trying to be strong but he was shit at it. Rosie had to reassure him that nothing was lost. She knew he was in the safest place right now, so she'd left him, as the doctor had said he would be kept in overnight.

'Also, what's the score with this Bertie bloke? Christ, Rosie! You can fairly dig them up. He just produces a handgun out of his pocket? I thought you said he was a hotel owner in the borders. Why is he getting so involved? I know he's an ex-cop, but is he a bit of a nutter?'

Rosie smiled for the first time that day, as she reflected on her conversation with Bertie at the hotel when she'd confided in him who the guests were and the dangers they brought with them. He was up for a bit of action: he was glad to have put his police career behind him, but he sometimes missed the buzz.

'He's straight as a die and was a great copper in his day. He was part of the Royal Protection Squad at one time so he always had a gun in his jacket, just in case. Believe me, he's the kind of guy you'd want on your side when your back's to the wall. He says he'll stay in now till we get our story in the paper.'

'Good stuff. As long as we're not paying him an arm and a leg.'

'I'll just put it on my hotel expenses,' Rosie said, only half joking.

McGuire gave her a look, and changed the subject. 'Anyway, this Merv bastard. What do we do with him now? Where is he?'

'He's staying at the Holiday Inn. My concierge contact called me half an hour ago. Said he's booked in at least for the night. His boys will still be hunting for Dan, so he might be here for another day.'

McGuire sat back and narrowed his eyes. 'I think it's time we monstered the fucker.'

'I was hoping you'd say that. I think we really need to move on him.'

'What about the tape Dan was wearing? Where is it? Has he still got it?'

'Sadly, no.'

Rosie had hoped McGuire wouldn't ask about it until she'd at least tried to find it.

'Fuck's sake! Where is it?'

'Dan said he had it when he went into that house, but he didn't have it when we took him away. I didn't look for it at the time because we thought he was dying, and it didn't occur to me to see where the tape was. Bertie was giving him mouth-to-mouth.'

'You're not as heartless as you need to be, Gilmour. The tape is a priority. What you going to do?'

'I'll think of something.'

'I don't want to know what you're thinking, Rosie. But I don't want you wading back in there and upturning the sofas in search of it. Are we clear on that?'

'Sure,' Rosie said. She didn't tell him that Bertie was already planning to go back and look for it. 'So let's give it till tomorrow. Then we'll go up to the Holiday Inn and see how we go with big Merv. You okay with that?'

'Right. I want you to go home now. I need to think where my next story is going. Also, we have to see what we can do about Millie Chambers. The nurse Bridget says she got a call – that right? She's back in the same place?'

'Yeah,' Rosie had almost forgotten she'd told him about Bridget's call, she was so wrapped up in the pace of the last few hours. She'd tried Bridget's mobile several times but got no answer.

'Okay. Go home. Relax. Build a jigsaw or have a drink with that JT bloke.'

'It's TJ.'

'Aye. Well, what kind of name is that anyway?' McGuire stood up. 'I want you relaxed, not staring into space. You looked a mess when you walked in here.'

'Cheers, Mick.'

'You know what I mean. I don't want you overdoing it with all the crap that's happened. We've a lot to do yet, so rest tonight. Tomorrow we'll be ramping things up a bit. And I want to rattle Colin Chambers' cage very soon too.'

Rosie called Bridget's number, but there was still no answer. Her landline was ringing out too, and at six in the evening she'd have expected her to be at home. She'd said she was a creature of habit: after work it was always dinner, TV soaps, then an early night with a book. It bothered Rosie as she drove into the car park off Woodlands Road, on the way to her flat in St George's Cross, and took out her notebook. She was looking forward to dinner with TJ. But she had to reassure herself before she could take a night off. She scanned the pages until she found the phone number for the Eastbourne District General Hospital, punched it in and asked for Ward Seven. A woman answered.

'Hello. Is it possible to speak to Bridget Casey?'

Silence.

'Hello?' Rosie said. 'Sorry to trouble you. I'm looking to speak to Bridget Casey. Is she still on duty?'

There was a long pause and a chill ran through Rosie.

'Who is this, please? Are you a relative?'

'No. Actually, I'm a friend.'

Another silence.

'I'm sorry. But I'm afraid I have bad news for you. Bridget . . . er . . . Bridget was involved in a car accident yesterday.'

Rosie pressed the phone to her ear. 'Oh, my God! I didn't know. Is she all right?'

Another thumping silence.

'I'm sorry. But . . . I'm really sorry to tell you that Bridget is dead.'

'Jesus!' Rosie murmured. 'What happened?'

'It was yesterday afternoon. She had finished her shift and was heading up the high street in the town. She seemed to step out in front of a car. Police are investigating. It was a hit-and-run. Imagine not stopping when a woman is so badly injured . . .'

Rosie was hearing the words, but all she could think of was Bridget hugging her the morning she'd left.

'Hello? Are you still there? Do you want to speak to the ward sister on duty?'

'No. I'm sorry, I have to go.'

'If you want to leave a number, we can keep you informed of funeral arrangements.'

'Thanks. I won't leave a number. I must go.' Rosie hung up.

She punched in McGuire's private number, still in disbelief.

'Rosie.'

'Mick. It's Bridget. She's dead. I just called the hospital ward she works in and they told me. Knocked down by a car last night. Hit-and-run.'

'Fuck me!'

'Somebody did that deliberately, Mick.'

'I know. Poor woman.' He paused. 'Look, Gilmour. I'm sorry you've had this news on top of everything, but try to get some rest tonight. We really need to take the gloves off tomorrow.' He hung up.

She sat in the car and switched off the engine, numb with shock as she stared out at the rain bouncing off the street. Poor Bridget. All she'd wanted to do was the right thing.

Rosie lay in a hot bath with a glass of red wine, as TJ sat with his feet up on a chair in the corner, listening as she described the past few hours.

'These people are bad bastards, Rosie. I hope you get to nail them.' He sipped his wine.

She was surprised. No lecture? It wouldn't be the first

time she'd fallen into TJ's arms when she was traumatized, depressed, or scared in the middle of an investigation, but almost every time, while he was there with an understanding hug, there was always the lecture on how she had to live her own life and that her job was dragging her down.

'What? You're not going to tell me to throw in the towel? That I can't go on living like this, through other people's misery?'

TJ got off his chair and knelt beside her. He pushed a strand of her hair behind her ear, and stroked her face. 'Nope. No more lectures, Rosie. There were a lot of long days and nights in New York when I wondered if I'd ever see you again. And if I did, on what terms.'

Rosie looked at him, wondering what was he going to say? Was this the point where he would say that he'd he come to the conclusion that they could never be together like normal people, but that he would always be there for her as a friend?

'So I made the decision. If I came back here and we hooked up again, I'd have to take a step back. We're never going to be normal, you and me.' He smiled. 'Because you're not normal, you crazy woman. You're not happy unless you're up to your knees in someone's misery. And I decided that rather than whinge about it or try to change you, I'd just accept what you are. If I'm honest, I'm not even sure I'd want to be around you if you chucked the job. You wouldn't be you without it. So, we are what we are.' He paused. 'I love you, Rosie. Whatever happens to you or to us, just know that. Nobody else will ever love you the way I do.'

Rosie swallowed the lump in her throat, but the tears still spilled out of her eyes, and she gave way to them. 'Christ, look at me. I haven't cried for ages, and now you've got me blubbing.'

'You did cry,' TJ said playfully. 'A few nights ago – again. In your sleep. I just didn't feel the need to wake you and tell you.'

Rosie smiled through her tears. 'I don't remember it.'

TJ stood up, unfolded a towel and held it out. 'Come on. I'm starving.'

She stood up, and he wrapped her in his arms.

CHAPTER THIRTY-ONE

Rosie looked at her watch as she waited in the cafe on Woodlands Road for Don. It was only nine, but she was already feeling the tension of the day ahead. On top of that, she was knackered after a restless night. To her surprise, she'd dropped off as soon as her head had hit the pillow, probably due to the couple of large glasses of wine she'd had with TJ. But she'd woken up in his arms, with him murmuring words of comfort. Another nightmare – vivid pictures of Millie, Bridget and Dan flying through the air from a high building. But it was her mother who lay on the ground when Rosie ran down the stairwell, pushing doors open until she was outside. Her face was wet with tears, and she couldn't get back to sleep afterwards.

She was glad to see Don coming in the doorway.

'You're on the go early this morning, Rosie.' He slipped into the booth.

'I know. Listen, thanks for coming. I've been meaning to

see you for days to explain some things to you, but everything's happening so quickly.'

'You look like you've been up all night. What's up? What the fuck happened to your face?'

'I got punched by some thug. I'll come to that in a minute. I'm a bit frazzled, chasing down a very big story, and I feel as though the walls are closing in on me.'

'Is it to do with that wee junkie Mitch getting a going-over?'

'Yeah. I'd hoped to talk to you about it before now.'

Don raised his eyebrows. 'But you wanted your story in the bag first.' He put his hands up. 'Perfectly understandable.'

'I'd have told you because, believe me, you'll want to know about this, but it's only between us for the moment. You okay with that?'

'Sure.'

The waitress came over and he ordered an espresso. Rosie asked for a mineral water – she was already two coffees down and another would leave her jangling.

'So, what's happening? I don't think anyone's interviewed Mitch yet. To be honest, nobody seems to be that bothered about it. Junkies get beaten up for all sorts of reasons – debts, thieving.'

Rosie puffed out her cheeks. 'I'm sure the city's junkies will sleep easy in their cardboard boxes knowing that Strathclyde's finest have them high on their list of priorities.'

Don chuckled. 'You know what I mean. They'll never tell us anything we can act on anyway. Guy probably doesn't have a clue who did him over. Have any of our guys been in touch with you yet for a statement, given that your number was on Mitch's mobile?'

'Not so far, thankfully,' Rosie said. 'I don't want to talk to the cops yet. Well, apart from you.' She changed the subject. 'Anyway, Mitch was helping me track down the brother of Bella Mason – the model? We've been working on the tip that she didn't kill herself, that somebody threw her off that roof.'

'So why are you involved? She's from London.'

'No. She was born here and brought up in a children's home after being abandoned by her mother. She was taken to live in London when she was thirteen. Got fostered by some couple. Some model impresario saw her and the rest is history.'

'So what's the big story there?'

'Several things. She has a secret brother, a junkie, living rough in Glasgow. Amazing story, Don. We tracked him down.'

'Ah. So that's why Mitch was involved.'

'Yes. But that's not all. You know Colin Chambers – remember? The former Tory Home Secretary.'

'Yeah. I remember him.'

'Well. You won't believe this, but his wife was on the roof of the hotel that night in Madrid.'

He was incredulous. 'What? You kidding me?'

'No. She was going to commit suicide.'

He half smiled. 'So was it a suicide convention? Are you sure you've not been drinking?'

'Seriously, Don. She was on that roof. She came to Spain to kill herself, but then she witnessed what happened.'

'Really witnessed it?' His face turned serious. 'You're not kidding me, are you?'

'No. She told me herself. I've got it all.' Rosie put her hand up. 'Look, it's a long story, but she didn't go to the police and kind of freaked out after what she saw. I can't go into all that right now. All you need to know is that she saw it. I don't want you to do anything official about this, not right now. But she will talk to the police when the time is right. And she can identify the guys who did it.'

'Rosie, you really can't sit on this kind of information.'

'I know. It's already proving too hot to handle.' She pointed to her swollen eye. 'I know we'll have to involve the police, but the problem is whether we can trust them.'

'Christ! What are you talking about? Can you trust us!'

Rosie explained to him about the child abuse, and about Dan, what he'd said had happened to them in the home. He listened, shaking his head in disbelief.

'I see what you mean.' He drained his coffee cup. 'You need to talk to your editor. I'm not even going to mention our discussion to anyone because I know what will happen. They'll be down at the *Post* before lunchtime, beating the soles of your feet with rubber hoses.'

Rosie smiled. 'Thanks. I just wanted to alert you. I'm going to the office now, so we'll be making a decision later. But that Mervyn Bates character – you've seen him in the papers, some kind of agent for models. He's a pervert, and we're going to nail him to the wall. Then the cops can have him.'

Don stood up. 'Okay. I'm fine with that. I need to go. I've got to meet the procurator fiscal about a court case. Give me a shout as soon as you can. Just don't leave it too late, Rosie. If there's any truth in all these things you're telling me, all sorts of people will be trying to smother the story.' He leaned down and kissed her head, then was gone.

A few minutes later, Rosie left the cafe and walked quickly to where her car was parked in a side street. By the time she noticed she was hemmed in by the black Mercedes parked across her, it was too late. Someone was behind her, poking what felt like a gun into her back. She stopped in her tracks, feeling the blood drain from her face, as the rear door of the Merc opened.

'Get in,' a voice said behind her. 'Don't turn around. Just get in the car.'

'Wh-what's going on?' She glanced along the street, cars parked nose-to-tail, but not a damn car actually moving. She could make a run for it. Nobody was going to shoot her down in the street.

'Don't even think about it.'

'What? You going to shoot me in broad daylight?'

'If I have to. Get in the car.' The gun poked harder and she jerked at the pain in her back. She had no option. Christ almighty! This was really happening. She took a step forward, her legs like jelly. In the back she could see a well-dressed man in a dark Crombie coat, silver hair, looking out at her, his mouth tight. She got into the car.

'What is this? Who are you? My boss will be phoning me in about five minutes, wondering where I am.'

'Then switch your fucking phone off, sweetheart.' The Cockney accent sounded like something from a soap.

Sweetheart? Rosie watched in horror as the guy with the bleached-blond hair got into the passenger seat.

'I see you recognize Ricky.'

Rosie said nothing. She couldn't peel her tongue off the roof of her mouth.

'Dan Mason,' the man next to her said. 'You've done a good job hiding the little fucker. My boys here have ripped up this fucking shithole of a city looking for him.'

Rosie tried to swallow, tried to keep her nerve.

'So,' the man said. 'Is he dead?'

Rosie felt a flush of rage rise in her. 'No, he's not, but it's not for the want of these two bastards trying.' She turned to him. 'You won't get away with this, I'm telling you. Or what your chimps did to Mitch. Cowards. I don't know who you are. Some big-shot from London determined to kill an innocent wee guy who's got nothing. That's real balls, that is.'

The Cockney reached across and slapped her hard on the face. It stung and she fought back tears. They were going to kill her and dump her somewhere. But she wasn't going out without a fight.

'Fuck you!' Rosie spat, desperate to touch her face, but refusing to show him her pain.

'No. Fuck you, Rosie Gilmour. One thing you don't do is talk to me like that. You don't know who I am, do you?'

Rosie swallowed. 'What do you want with me? You can't make me disappear. People will be all over the place looking for me. I was having a coffee with a police detective not ten minutes ago in the cafe round the corner.'

'Yeah. We saw him come out. He looked like the filth.'

'So, what do you want?'

He sighed. Looked a little bored. 'Let me tell you something, Rosie Gilmour. I'm going to give you a break.' He went into his coat pocket and brought out a recording device. Matt's recording device: the one he'd fitted to Dan before his meeting with Mervyn Bates. She looked at it, puzzled, then at him.

'Your boy Dan dropped this in that shithole he was in, and one of my lads picked it up.'

Rosie said nothing. She waited, barely breathing.

'I listened to it. His meeting with big Merv. You know Merv? You met him?'

Rosie shook her head.

'He's a pervy cunt,' the man said. 'I only found that out the other day. This tape here confirms what I was told.'

'So what's he got to do with you?' Rosie asked, but she already knew. Whoever this character was, he'd been sent by Mervyn Bates to track down and dispose of Dan, the only link to Bella and the abuse she'd suffered. Dan could ruin Bates.

'Are you going to expose this fucker Merv, then? He's got a lot more coming to him than that. But exposing him is a good start.'

Rosie didn't know how to react. This guy had just slapped her in the face and now he was talking as though he was on her side. She said nothing. He handed her the device.

She looked at him and at the backs of the heads of the chimps in the front.

'Go on. It's not a fucking trap. Take it. Expose this fucker. But make it fast, because you're running out of time.'

Rosie looked at him, confused. 'What do you mean?'

'You'll know soon enough. Get Mervyn Bates all over your paper. I want to see him publicly ruined, first and foremost.'

Rosie sat for a moment.

'Why?'

'Fuckin' hell. You don't half push your luck, girl. Just do as I tell you and fuck off out of here. Oh, and don't even think about reporting this to the cops, or I really will get rough with you.'

He reached across her and opened the door – she caught a whiff of his aftershave. Rosie didn't stop to take a look, but got out and teetered away on shaky legs as she closed the door behind her. She looked around her as the Merc pulled into the traffic and down the street. She stood with the tape recorder in her hand, then got into her car, her hands shaking, and locked all doors. Her mobile rang and she jumped.

'Gilmour. Where the fuck are you? I said nine thirty.'

'I'm on my way, Mick. You won't believe what just happened.'

CHAPTER THIRTY-TWO

Marion looked up from her screen as Rosie walked towards the editor's office. She pointed at her cheek and gave Rosie an enquiring look. In her rush to get back to the office, still barely believing she had Dan's tape in her pocket, she'd completely forgotten about the stinging pain in her cheek where she'd been slapped.

'Me and my big mouth,' Rosie said to Marion, touching her still-burning cheek.

'I'd like to see the other guy.' Marion smiled and went back to her screen.

Rosie went into McGuire's office as he finished a phone call.

'What's with the face?' he asked.

'I got a right hard slap, Mick.'

'What? Who from?'

'You won't believe it when I tell you.'

'Sit down.' McGuire motioned her to the sofa, then got

up and came round from behind his desk. 'But before you tell me about that, Gilmour, here's the sketch. We're going with Dan's story tomorrow. Chapter and verse as he told it to you. If we had the tape to back it up the lawyers would be a lot happier but, fuck it. I'm not hanging onto this any longer. Time to rattle cages.'

Rosie pulled the tape out of her pocket. She put it on the table and couldn't help the triumphant smile on her lips.

'What's that?'

'What does it look like?'

'A tape?' The editor's eyes widened. 'Dan's tape? Please tell me it is.'

'It is. I haven't listened to it yet, but I'm told it's great.'

McGuire sat back, shaking his head in disbelief. 'Fuck me, Gilmour! Where the hell did you get it? Is somebody dead?'

Rosie grinned. 'No. If you give me a second, I'll tell you.' She touched her face. 'That's where I got the slap.'

'Tell me.'

Rosie described how she'd left the meeting with her cop contact only to be kidnapped briefly into the back of a Merc. She explained what had happened.

'And this fucker just hands you the tape? That's insane. And these two bastards who chucked Bella off the hotel roof were in the car? You must have been shitting yourself.'

'Well, it was a bit nerve-racking,' Rosie said.

'Who the fuck is he?'

'I don't know. Gangster from London. Obviously he handles the gorillas who did Bella Mason, so I think it's safe to assume that he was behind it. Doesn't take Sherlock Holmes to work out that he must have done the hit for Mervyn Bates.'

'Fuck! That's dynamite. You're sitting in the back of a car with him, and you got out alive? What is this bastard doing helping a reporter?'

'It's the most bizarre situation I've ever been in. I couldn't believe it when he handed the tape to me. But he must have plans of his own for Mervyn Bates, because he said he wants the newspaper to ruin him first. He's using us to get what he wants. But I don't know why.'

'I don't give a fuck that he's using us. We need that tape.'

'But what if this guy is the man who organized the hit on Bella?'

'We'll leave that to the cops to sort. Right now, he's done us a good turn. Switch the tape on, I want to hear it. This is totally off the wall.'

'We need to get him done, Mick. He's as guilty of shoving Bella off the roof as his two henchmen.'

'We will, Gilmour. That's for later. We've got a splash and a spread ready to jump into the paper, thanks to this bastard. It's a means to an end.' He paused. 'And the tape is actually our property anyway. We've only got back what was rightfully ours.'

'That'll sound great in the High Court, Mick.'

'We'll cross that bridge when we come to it.'

Rosie switched on the tape. Thoughts of Bella's final moments were already kicking in, as was guilt: Rosie appeared now to be working with the model's killer. She wished she could justify the means to the end as readily as McGuire.

The foyer at the Holiday Inn was busy with a crowd of Japanese tourists checking in. Rosie and Bertie picked their way around the throng at the reception desk, returning the friendly nods and smiles of the queue.

'I have this terrible urge to start whistling "Colonel Bogey", but I don't suppose it would go down too well.'

'Not a good idea.' Rosie stifled a laugh. 'That's all behind us now.'

'I've still never forgiven them for what they did to Alex Guinness in *Bridge Over the River Kwai*.'

'Don't mention the war.' Rosie smiled, nodding to the tourists. 'Right. Let's see where you're going to sit.'

'Are you sure this Merv's going to be around?'

'Not really, but my contact said he was here half an hour ago, then disappeared to his room. He's not been out of the hotel since yesterday, according to my man. He'll be waiting to see how his boys get on hunting for Dan.'

She told Bertie to sit a few tables away from them, in case anyone got rough. She ordered some tea, but didn't have to wait long because Mervyn Bates emerged from the lift and strode across to the bar, barking into his mobile phone. Rosie exchanged glances with Bertie, who nodded and went back to his newspaper. She watched as Bates sat down, still talking, then mouthed to the waiter to bring him some coffee. He put an attaché case on the table, opened it and brought out some papers. Rosie was nervous and took a slow breath, bracing herself. 'Don't hang around,' she told herself. 'Just go for it.' She watched as he put down the phone and the waiter brought his coffee. Then he placed a sheaf of papers on his lap and began to study them. She got up and went towards him.

'Mervyn Bates?' she said, as she reached the table.

He looked up, startled.

'Mervyn?'

He was waving his hand dismissively. 'What? Can I help you?'

'You're Mervyn Bates. The agent. I've seen you on the telly.'

He let out a bored sigh. 'Yes, well, thanks for that. But, to be honest, I'm very busy. So—'

'You're Bella Mason's agent. That's right, isn't it?'

He rolled his eyes. 'Yes. But, look, dear, I'm honestly up to my eyes. I need to get on with some phone calls. I'm here on business and I've no time to spend in idle chat. So, if you'll excuse me . . .'

'I know what business you're here on, Mervyn.' Rosie

stood her ground, letting it hang in the air for a moment. 'That's why I'm here.'

Bates looked across at Reception, then over his shoulder, as though searching for the concierge to throw out the intruder.

'Look,' he said irritated, 'what the hell is this? Can you not take a gentle hint? I'm busy.'

'Okay, Mervyn. I'll get straight to the point. Bella Mason. The sister of Dan Mason.' She paused. 'Are the bells ringing now? I'm Rosie Gilmour, from the *Post*. Right now, I'm your worst nightmare.'

His face went chalk-white above his wiry, patchy beard.

'You do remember Dan, don't you? He's the kid you left behind when you plucked Bella from the children's home.'

'I don't know any Dan Mason and I've no idea what the hell you're talking about. Okay, so you've read the stories about Bella. Yes, I took her from the children's home and gave her a life. I made her the model she was. Now, can you leave me alone? My heart was broken when Bella killed herself, and you barging in here asking questions and dragging it all up isn't helping.'

'She didn't kill herself. You had her killed.'

Bates shook his head vigorously and went to pick up his cup, but his hands were shaking so much he put it down again. 'For goodness' sake. Are you on some kind of drugs?'

'No, but Bella was. Drugs that you supplied. You turned her into a cokehead so you could use and abuse her, the way you did when she was underage.' Rosie stopped for a moment, surprised he hadn't got to his feet and demanded help from the hotel staff. 'And when she was going to expose you, for all the years you sexually abused her and the other kids, you had her killed.'

'You're off your fucking head!'

'No, I'm not. You were on the roof that night in Madrid.'

'I'm not listening to this any longer.'

'You were seen by someone. Someone witnessed the murder. I have it all, Mervyn, and it's going in my newspaper. But in the interests of balance and accuracy I came up here to give you the right of reply – a chance to say something before we go to print.'

He opened his mouth to speak, but nothing came out. Rosie raised her right hand and signalled for Matt to come across and take a picture. They would be in trouble for this as it was forbidden to photograph someone in a public place against their will, but she'd deal with the Press Complaints Commission later. She already had the encounter taped and the camera on her jacket was filming him, but it wouldn't be great quality.

'It's over, Mervyn. If I were you I'd phone the cops.'

'I bloody *will*! I'll have you removed from here and arrested.'

'Go ahead.'

His lip trembled and he looked over her shoulder. His face fell even further. Rosie glanced around to see the crook from this morning coming towards them. She looked at Bertie, who was already on his feet.

'Larry!' Bates said, trying to appear calm. 'Thank God you're here. I'm getting fucking harassed by this stupid woman.'

Rosie turned around as the man who'd slapped her face this morning was almost at her side. He looked through her, then at Bates. She had said enough.

'Okay, Mervyn. I'll take it that's a no-comment, then.'

'You'll hear from my bloody lawyers, madam.'

'I'm sure I will.' Rosie took a couple of steps towards the gangster. As she passed him, she couldn't resist the urge to slap his face, and she'd done it before she could stop herself. She heard Bertie and Matt gasp from twenty feet away. Larry looked at her and half smiled.

'That's for this morning,' Rosie murmured. 'He's all yours.' She walked past him, her legs like jelly.

'What the fuck, Rosie!' Matt said, as they went quickly across the foyer and out of the automatic doors.

'Couldn't help myself.'

'You're a fucking headcase!' He laughed nervously. 'Come on. Let's get out of here before he comes after us.'

'He won't.'

CHAPTER THIRTY-THREE

Larry Sutton felt the sting on his cheek from the reporter's slap, but it brought a smile to his lips. Ballsy little bitch. He could've got Ricky to grab her at the door and pull her fingers off one by one, but he had to admire her chutzpah. He'd let it go if she did her job. Right now he had a score to settle. Even before he sat down, he could smell the fear coming off Mervyn Bates. It was seeping out of his pores. But Bates was looking at him with his five-grand cosmetic smile, trying his best to be in control.

'What the hell was that, Larry? You know that reporter bitch?'

Larry turned his mouth down, a little bored, and sighed. 'I make it my business to know things, Merv. You should know that by now.'

'So what brings you up here, man? Can I get you a drink?'

Bates waved the waitress over, and Larry ordered tea. He sat back, staring, knowing the agent was waiting nervously for an answer as to why he was there.

'You up checking on your boys?' Bates asked.

'Well, I was up to see what the fucking score is, Merv. They've taken about three fucking weeks to get this job done, and then they phone me yesterday to say Dan's done a runner.'

The waitress brought a pot of tea, and Larry watched as Bates poured it with trembling hands.

'You been at the drink, old son?' Larry said playfully. 'You're shaking like a fucking leaf. What's the matter? What about that reporter bird? Did she unnerve you?'

'She's a fucking nutter, Larry. Comes walking in here from nowhere and starts making all sorts of accusations.'

'Yeah?' Larry lifted the cup to his lips and sipped. 'Like what?'

Bates gave a frustrated sigh. 'Just crap. You know what it's like with these fucking gutter tabloids. They're always looking for a story.' He took a breath. 'But the thing is, Larry, she comes in here and tells me she has some woman who witnessed what happened on the hotel roof in Madrid.'

Larry screwed up his eyes, confused. 'What? Not fucking possible, mate. She's bluffing.'

'But how do we know that for sure, Larry? I mean, your boys were the ones who did the recce and organized the whole thing. Surely to Christ they did a sweep of the place to make sure nobody was out there?'

Larry rolled his eyes. Knowing Ricky and Pete, they probably hadn't bothered their arses looking in every nook and cranny on the roof of a hotel. 'Well, they would have done a search. But who's going to be on the roof of a hotel at nearly midnight? I thought you said the party was inside a closed-off function room on the roof.'

'It was.'

'So who was on the roof? A guest at the party?'

'How the fuck do I know? It might be a load of crap. Maybe this reporter's just fishing to see what she can dig up. She said the witness is a woman and that she's going to talk to the police.'

This was not good news, but Larry did his best to absorb it and keep his face impassive. He hadn't come here expecting anything like this. He'd come to deal with Mervyn Bates − to ask him some questions and see if he squirmed. But this information might mean that, after a bit of digging, some bastard had been savvy enough to work out who was who in the hit that night. And, ultimately, that could lead all the way to his door. Fuck that for a game of soldiers.

'Anyway,' Larry played it down, 'I'm not going to bust my tits worrying about some reporter's bullshit. I've got some questions I want to ask you, Merv.'

'Questions? What about? You got paid for the hit, didn't

you? Expenses all covered? And, don't worry, I'll still weigh you in for the work you've done trying to find Dan Mason.'

'Yeah.' Larry nodded slowly. 'I want to ask you about him, actually.' He looked Bates in the eye. 'And his sister.'

Bates shrugged. 'Not much I can tell you. Other than the fact that they were a couple of snotty-nosed kids in a children's home in Glasgow when I came across Bella. What a fucking beauty she was. Only thirteen, but you could see she was made for great things in the modelling world. So I saw to it that she got out of that place. Got her a new life. Made her a fucking star.'

'And you raped her, when she was still a kid.'

Larry watched as his accusation hung in the air like nuclear fallout.

Bates looked almost dizzy with shock. 'What?'

'You heard me. You raped the girl when she was only thirteen or fourteen. That's the real reason you took her away.'

Bates' mouth dropped open and his bottom lip twitched. 'What a monstrous allegation, Larry! What the fuck are you saying that for?'

'Yeah,' Larry said, leaning forward. 'Monstrous. Good word that, to describe what you did to her.'

'I – I—'

Merv tried to protest, but Larry interrupted, putting his hand up. He leaned forward and dropped his voice to a loud whisper. 'Listen, you pervy paedo cunt, don't fucking insult my intelligence, or I'll get Ricky to take you outside and cut your fucking balls off.' Rage rose in his chest. 'You think I'm just some fucking lowlife gangster who lets the fucking world wash over him? How do you think I got this far in my life if I didn't make it my business to know what was going on?'

'B-but—'

'Shut it. One thing I'm very cross with myself about is that I didn't know what you were. I've done jobs for you over the years. Some of them I didn't particularly like doing, but business is business. And all that time, I didn't realize you were a fucking paedo. Little girls you lured into your web with talk of money and fame. You did that, and I didn't even have a fucking clue. That makes me very angry.'

'I didn't, Larry! It's not true. I don't know who's telling you this.'

'Well, one of the people who's saying it is Dan fucking Mason. And while he was here, laying all his cards on the table as you sat there shitting your pants, he was taping the whole conversation.'

'Wh-what?'

'Yeah, mate. Done up like a fucking kipper you are.'

'How do you even know this? He came in here and did a runner. He's a lowlife junkie.'

'Shut it. You don't get to ask questions. You don't need to know how I know this, but I've heard the fucking tape.'

Bates was silent for a moment. Then he glared at Larry. 'So where's the fucking tape? Show me. Name your fucking price, if that's what this is about.'

Quick as a flash, Larry leaned across and grabbed him by the throat. 'Don't you *ever* talk to me like that, or I'll squeeze the fucking life out of you.'

Bates managed to squeak, 'Sorry,' and Larry released him.

They sat in silence, Larry trying to compose himself. He was going to deal with this, but not right here in the middle of the hotel.

'So,' Bates said, 'what do you want, Larry? Just tell me.'

Larry looked at him with contempt. 'I want you to tell me the truth. That's all. The truth. Did you rape Bella Mason when she was a kid?'

Bates looked down at his hands and Larry watched as he picked at his fingernails. When he looked up again, tears were filling his eyes. 'Larry. I swear to God—'

'The fucking truth!'

He took a breath and let it out slowly, beads of sweat on his forehead. 'I didn't rape her, Larry. You have to understand . . . Please let me explain. Bella was fourteen, going on bloody twenty. She was already doing well in the modelling game. I was looking after her, but she was a feisty little bugger and I know she was a handful for her foster parents. She was already going out with boys and coming home late and stuff. What I'm trying to say here, is, yes, okay, we did have sex. But it wasn't like she was a kid.'

'She was fourteen. She *was* a kid.'

'She wanted it.'

Larry had to bite his lip to stop himself upturning the table, as an image of Spider came to him, of the night when he'd confessed about the rapes, saying that his attackers had told him he wanted it.

'She wanted sex with a . . . What age would you have been then, Merv? Forty-five? A fourteen-year-old beautiful little girl wanted sex with a poncy, hairy-faced cunt, pushing fifty?'

'It wasn't like that. Bella and me were close. We had become so close. I loved her, Larry. I really loved her.'

Larry rolled his eyes. 'Oh, fuck me, Merv! Bring out the fucking violins. You loved her? You paid me fucking seventy grand to get her thrown off a fucking roof! You *loved* her!'

'She turned, Larry. She became toxic. She was a fucking cokehead, wasted half the time, out of control. All the other birds knew it. It was only a matter of time before she self-destructed. She'd have lost her looks before she was thirty, and she'd be history.'

Larry shook his head slowly. He'd been supplying this bastard with coke for all of his model birds for the past ten years, and now he was sitting there saying that. 'She was a fucking cokehead because you supplied her.'

'That's not true. She was already into it before I found out. I thought if she was going to do it, I'd better manage it. That way she wouldn't get photographed in the tabloids up some fucking alley in Hackney.'

Larry sat back. He'd heard just about enough, but he wanted to put one last thing to him. 'Merv. There were others, weren't they? Other kids. You went to parties and stuff in London, organized by nonces like you, showbiz pals, politicians, all sorts of bastards.'

He said nothing. Larry let him squirm.

'Just tell me. This is the day you get it all off your chest.'

Larry watched as Bates crumpled, first his lips and his cheeks twitching, then the tears in his eyes. He put his head in his hands.

'I'm just . . . I'm weak. Maybe I'm sick, Larry. I don't like who I am.'

Larry nodded. He stood up. 'Neither do I, mate. I don't like who you are, either.'

'Where are you going?'

'Out of here. I need to get some fresh air, away from the stench that surrounds you, you filthy, stinking pervert. I'm going back to London. But that reporter bitch, believe me, she's onto you, so if I was you, I'd fuck off somewhere far away before the cops start looking for you. You're finished.'

Larry stood for a few seconds and watched in disgust as Bates folded into his hands and wept. He walked outside into the fresh, crisp air, where Ricky was standing at the entrance smoking a cigarette. 'All right, boss?'

'Yeah.' He jerked his thumb over his shoulder. 'Deal with that piece of shit before the night's out, then head back down the road. I hate this fucking place.'

CHAPTER THIRTY-FOUR

Rosie picked up one of the last copies of the *Post* from the stand at Glasgow Airport, as she and Matt headed for their flight to London. The splash headline with the 'World Exclusive' banner said it all: AGONY OF BELLA AND HER SECRET BROTHER. The picture of Dan and Bella, smiling, arms round each other's shoulders, was probably making its way to media outlets around the world by now, if the *Post*'s lucrative syndication arm was doing its job. There was a strapline at the foot of the page, directing readers to pages four and five: MODEL RAPED AS A CHILD. By the time she'd left the office last night, McGuire had the kind of triumphant swagger that you only saw at times like this. Rosie had seen the make-up of the front page and inside spread before she left, and as she walked through the front door of the building, she'd stood on the steps and allowed herself a moment. This was what she lived for. It shouldn't be, but it was.

'Some front page, Rosie! I reckon today's paper will be the biggest circulation the paper has seen in a long time. It's flying off the shelves. Couldn't even get one in my local shop this morning.'

Rosie flicked to the spread as they stood in the newsagent's queue.

'You can't fail, really, if you've got the face of one of the world's top models on your splash and a story to take your breath away. I'm well pleased with it.'

'How was Dan when you saw him last night?' Matt asked, as they made their way to security.

'He was on good form. The most relaxed he's been in a few days. Mitch is getting out of the hospital today and Declan is picking him up and taking him to the flat. I think they'll be okay on their own.'

'Did you search the house for tenner bags?' Matt joked.

Rosie smiled. 'No. I think he just feels like there's a load off his back. He's had to live with this secret all his life, and now he can shout who he is from the rooftops. I really hope he gets on now and makes his life better.'

'He'll be in for a fortune once it all gets sorted.'

'Yeah,' Rosie said. 'That'll be the real test. Whether he uses it to change his life or blows it in a year. But he's a good kid. I think he'll do all right.'

But, right now, the story had moved on. She was looking forward to a showdown with Colin Chambers. It wouldn't be a warm reception. She hoped the flowers she'd sent to

Millie at the clinic would get to her. Given that her husband had had her locked away, all phone calls and mail would be monitored, so she couldn't risk a call. But a bouquet would seem innocuous enough. She'd asked the local florist to put a simple message on the card. She hoped that 'Thinking of you' would be enough for Millie to understand she hadn't been abandoned. She simply put 'R' as the sender.

As she sat in the splendour of the Garrick Club, Rosie was more than impressed that Mickey Kavanagh had come up trumps. He'd been sniffing around for the past week and found that Colin Chambers was a creature of habit. He lunched at White's every Monday afternoon, and on Fridays he could be found in the Garrick, relaxing with his mistress, an actress who was currently starring in one of the West End theatres. Kavanagh had also established that Chambers would visit the actress's flat on a Thursday, late afternoon, and wouldn't emerge until mid-evening. Rosie didn't ask how Kavanagh had sourced the information – she didn't want to know. She'd laughed when he told her he was buying her lunch at his club, assuming it was some pub used by his ex-copper pals in the city. But here she was, sitting in the members' dining room, the walls adorned with portraits of theatrical legends going back a hundred years.

'You just don't strike me as the private members' club type,

Mickey, especially one like this,' Rosie said, as the waiter unfolded a crisp white napkin and spread it on her lap.

Kavanagh grinned as he was handed a menu. 'If I was paying for the membership myself, I wouldn't entertain it. But it's financed. And, by the way, this crumpled suit I'm wearing is a classic sign of old money.'

Rosie chuckled. 'You get your membership paid for?'

'Well, it's got to be done. I don't just move in lowlife places, pet. I have to be able to swan around everywhere, keeping tabs on all sorts of scallywags – and some of them are from the top drawer.'

'I'm well impressed.'

'So you should be, and since I'm buying lunch, that dinner in Glasgow is getting more expensive by the minute.'

'I don't have a club I can take you to in Glasgow – but the Auchengeich Miners does a right good pie and mushy peas on a Friday. Only thing is, you've got to unfold your own napkin.'

'Good.' Kavanagh clinked his glass of water with Rosie's. 'Get it sorted. Christ! I can't believe I'm not even having a drink.'

'You can drink away. Don't mind me. I just want to be totally on the ball when I front up Chambers.' Rosie glanced around, but only three other tables were occupied.

'Well, you'll not have long to wait because, don't look now, he's right behind you. He'll go to his usual table, if I'm not mistaken.'

She didn't look, but in a few seconds, a tall, lean, well-dressed man walked past her, a leggy thirty-something shimmering brunette, with a pert bottom, striding behind him.

'That's his bird,' Kavanagh said. 'Quite tidy.'

'His wife is beautiful, Mickey, and a lovely woman. Tragic figure, really, when I think of what's happened to her. I'm looking forward to giving this bastard a roasting.' She drank her water, eyeing Chambers with contempt.

After lunch, Rosie and Mickey sat in leather armchairs in the dimly lit members' bar, sipping green tea. They'd watched Chambers and his girlfriend shift a bottle of red wine and had seen him get up, walk towards the foyer with her, then return on his own. Mickey said that was what he did every week. Lunch with the woman, then an hour reading newspapers and going over papers from his attaché case.

'He's on his second brandy,' Rosie said. 'I'm going for it. I don't imagine he's going to invite me to join him, so I won't pussyfoot around him.'

'Okay, sweetheart. Break a leg, as they say in these parts.' He winked. 'And don't do anything that'll get us thrown out, no matter what he says to you. He's an arrogant bastard. He'll probably suggest you should be horsewhipped on the steps for your sheer impertinence.'

Rosie smiled as she got up, but her heart was going like an engine. She reached into her jacket and switched on the tape recorder, then slung her handbag over her shoulder. She walked across to where he was reading *The Times*, the paper covering his face.

'Mr Chambers?' Rosie said.

He lowered the newspaper, his face twisting with impatience as he stared up at her.

'Mr Chambers, my name is Rosie Gilmour.' She smiled coldly. 'I'd like to talk to you.'

His expression changed from bewilderment as the penny dropped. He shot a furtive glance around the room. 'Who?'

Rosie let it hang for a moment, then looked him square in the eye. 'Oh, I think you know my name, Mr Chambers, so can we cut the crap? You need to hear what I've got to say.'

'Who the blazes are you? What business have you to barge in on me at my club? That's the bloody problem, these days. They let anyone in here. Now, if you'll forgive me . . .'

He was about to lift his paper to his face when Rosie stepped a little closer and thrust a copy of the *Post* at him. 'You don't want to read that fusty old rag. Have a look at a decent tabloid. Your wife was all over it a couple of weeks ago. Don't tell me you've forgotten already?'

His face paled. 'I can have you removed from here in less than five seconds, madam.'

'But you won't. It's not smart. I'm here for a quote for my newspaper. For the exclusive we're about to run – an exposé on you and your web of corruption, and the dossiers of child-abuse allegations you made disappear all those years ago.' He opened his mouth to speak, but Rosie put her hand up. 'It's too late now for some kind of tantrum. You're finished, Chambers. Luckily for your copper mate, who was in it with you, he's already dead. But you? Your number's up, pal, and that's the message my editor wanted me to deliver to you.'

He seemed too stunned to speak. Rosie decided to throw the kitchen sink at him, to provoke a reaction.

'You know something, Chambers? It's people like you who ruin lives, and if you're not ruining them, you preside over the people who do. You covered up and hid crimes to protect your toff friends, while vulnerable people were abused by them and anyone else with money. And your wife, Millie. What a lovely woman, wasted on a piece of shit like you.'

His face turned crimson, and Rosie put her hand up to stop him speaking.

'Yes. She's told me the whole story. How you broke her. You're the worst kind of human being, Chambers, the worst. You even kidnapped your own wife and locked her away. What kind of monster does that? It might be too late for her, but I have it all, chapter and verse, on tape, and our lawyers have said we can go ahead and publish.' She could feel sweat on the back of her neck and her hands were shaking by her sides. 'So, if you're smarter than you look right now, you'll at least say sorry publicly. Or you could deny everything, but this is your only chance to tell the truth. And if you've got any scrap of decency, you'll sign the papers to release your wife from that prison. You have one last chance to do something right in your privileged, selfish life. You failed all those children. You failed the woman who loved you. You, Mr Chambers, are a failure, and my newspaper is going to tell the world exactly what you are.' Rosie took a breath, waiting for a reaction.

Chambers stood up, beads of sweat on his top lip, a little unsteady on his feet. 'My lawyers will be in touch with your editor, you lowlife little tart. It's not me who's finished, it's you.' He strode off.

'Not drinking your brandy, sir?' Rosie shouted to his back. 'Oh, well! No point in it going to waste.' She downed the remains in one, feeling it burn all the way down. She didn't even like brandy, but that one hit the spot. She knew Matt would be standing outside, hosing him down with his camera as soon as he stepped out of the doors. Job done.

CHAPTER THIRTY-FIVE

Rosie peered at the red-brick terraced houses in Hackney for the right number, as Matt drove along the shabby street. She knew it was a long shot, but it had to be done. Even if the guy did still live there, it was unlikely he'd be willing to relive the story of the abuse he had suffered. But, right now, he was the only thread she had that might back up the retired detective's revelations and those of Millie Chambers. Kavanagh had managed to dig out one of the cops involved in the investigation, but he didn't want to meet a journalist in person. Instead, he passed on the name and address of a victim he'd interviewed.

'There it is,' Rosie said. 'Number one three eight.' She took in the grimy net curtain on the downstairs window and the paint peeling off the once-white front door. 'Looks a bit rough.'

'The whole street looks rough,' Matt said. 'It's like they're all living on top of each other in these rows of houses. So depressing.'

'No more depressing, I suppose, than a tower block in Glasgow, or the tenements. It's how half the population lives in cities. The boom of the eighties and nineties obviously never made it out here. My pal Mickey says it's a lot of second- and third-generation immigrants. They were Irish and Polish mostly, to begin with. But now it's a mix, with a big Asian population too. It's a hard life for a lot of people, if this is home.'

Matt parked the car and she gathered up her bag. 'Okay, let's go. Don't bring in all your toys. Just one camera, in case we get lucky.' She got out of the car.

Rosie rapped on the door and they waited. No answer. She gave the knocker a more emphatic rattle, and they stood for a while.

'Wasted journey?'

'Never wasted. It might have worked.' She sighed. 'Come on. Maybe we'll find a greasy spoon for a coffee and come back later.'

As they walked down the path, they stopped when they heard chains and locks being released. Then the door opened a fraction. Rosie swung round, back to the step. Through the six-inch space she could see a balding man, with a blotchy, boozy face. 'Hello,' she said. 'Sorry to bother you. We're looking for James Gallacher. Is that you?'

The man nodded. 'Yeah. What is it?'

Rosie caught a whiff of stale food from the open door. 'Is

it possible to come in and talk to you? My name is Rosie Gilmour. I'm a journalist.'

The man looked a little confused, stared at her, then beyond her, but said nothing.

'Mr Gallacher, I'm investigating a paedophile ring in London some years ago. Could we please come in? I don't want to talk on the doorstep.'

'Who gave you my name? I don't know what you're talking about.'

Rosie's heart sank a little, but gut instinct told her he was lying, perhaps afraid and ashamed. He wouldn't give her much longer. She'd better make the next couple of sentences count.

'Mr Gallacher, I can't say right now where your name came from, but it was a reliable source, and I'd like to talk to you about it. I know things like this from the past can be painful, but I also know that the police interviewed a lot of people who gave statements about abuse, and in some cases brutality, by some high-profile members of society. I want to expose that, and I'm trying to trace victims. My newspaper would like to unmask the people who did this, who ruined lives. The victims didn't have a voice because there was an elaborate cover-up. I'm hoping to expose that.'

He said nothing. Rosie took a step back. 'Okay, Mr Gallacher. I'm sorry to have bothered you. But if you do want to talk to me just let me know.' She handed him her card. He took it. She looked at Matt and they turned away.

'Wait!'

Rosie glanced at Matt and they turned as the chain was detached and the door opened. He stood before them, a portly, shambolic figure, in an old yellow V-neck sweater, with straggly chest hair poking out, grey tracksuit bottoms and slippers. 'Come in.'

There was a smell of grease mixed with old food. Overflowing bins were stacked up along the hall. Rosie could feel her feet sticking to the carpet. They walked into the living room. She stopped in her tracks when she saw the chainsaw on the coffee table. Matt shot her an anxious glance.

'Excuse the mess,' James Gallacher said. He bent down to lift the chainsaw and Rosie felt a little wobble in her stomach. She glanced at the living-room door, wondering how quickly they could escape. He looked at them as though reading their minds. 'I was just cutting down some trees in the back garden. I'll put this away.'

Rosie saw the relief in Matt's face and almost burst out laughing as James disappeared into the kitchen.

'Sit down,' James said, as he came back in. He sat on a threadbare armchair next to the old fireplace.

Rosie and Matt squeezed onto a space on the couch between mountains of newspapers.

'Mr Gallacher. Er . . . can I call you James?'

'Yeah.'

'Thanks, James. Okay. As I was saying, your name came

up because we're investigating this case and we've spoken to some contacts who were looking into it at the time.'

'I thought so. Detectives?'

Rosie shrugged but said nothing.

'Well,' James seemed perplexed, 'they did their job, I suppose. But nothing happened. All that talking and statements and meetings, but fuck-all. Sorry for swearing. It's a long time ago, but I still feel angry. No, worse than angry.'

'James,' Rosie said, trying to tread carefully, 'can I ask you to go back there in your mind and talk to us about it?'

He looked at her in disbelief.

'Go back there? Do you think I've ever left it behind?'

'Sorry,' Rosie said. 'I don't mean to be insensitive. But some victims of abuse I've spoken to in the past had kind of put it out of their minds and tried to live a life, and that's why I said "go back there".'

'It's alright.' His lip twitched. 'Maybe some people can do that, and I tried to as well. Because life goes on, and nobody really cares that much about your problems after a while. We were abandoned, simple as that. But you have to live your life. I tried. Believe me, I tried. But you need only to look around you to see it didn't work. My life was fucking wrecked. I've got a drink problem. Haven't had a drop for six weeks, but I'm dying for some, and that's the truth. It helps me get by. It's not that I relive it every day, but I relive how shit my life became because of the abuse . . . All the people I let down because of my drinking. I lost everything.'

Rosie said nothing, but took out her notebook and the tape recorder. 'Do you mind if I tape our conversation? You see, we have evidence from people that senior figures in police and government destroyed evidence, such as dossiers of victim statements and police work. But I have no first-hand accounts from victims. I think this abuse may have gone on nationwide. Not just in London.'

'I wouldn't be surprised. But I only know about London. I was only twelve when it happened. Just a wee boy in the children's home.'

'Can you tell me your recollections?'

He said nothing for a long moment, and Rosie watched as he sat staring at the empty hearth. 'The first time I was taken out with the rest of the bigger boys and girls, I was told it was a party. The older guys, they were fourteen and fifteen, said it was good fun, that you got money and great food, a trip up to London in the minibus. We were taken to a building in the city centre. It was beautiful – even the corridors and the smell of it stay with me. Then we were taken into this house and there were loads of people there. I don't mean just a dozen or so. The house was full of people in several rooms, like big living rooms. We were taken into a room with tables of cakes and pizza and all sorts of sweets and drinks. We just got in and ate everything we could see. Then some of the bigger boys disappeared. We didn't think anything about it. There were football magazines and games, and they said we could take them back with us.

But halfway through the evening it all changed. That was the first time for me.' He stopped and they sat for a few moments.

'What happened?'

'One of the people, a butler or something, came in and took me to another room. There was a man in there. I thought I'd seen him before, maybe on the telly or something, but I'm still not sure. He was dead rich-looking, well-dressed in a suit and tie. He smiled at me and said what a lovely boy I was, then asked me some things about myself. I told him I liked football and was in the school team and he said maybe one day I would be a famous star and play for Arsenal. I told him I wanted to play for Real Madrid, and he laughed and kind of ruffled my hair. He asked me to sit down beside him. It seemed a bit strange, but he was a nice man. Then he touched my hair and face. Kind of stroked me like this.' James demonstrated, his fingers tracing his face. 'I just sat there not knowing what to do. Then he touched my thighs and in between my legs, over my trousers. I felt my face going a bit red, and looked at him, but he said it was all right, that he was just being friendly and that he was going to be my special friend. He would do anything he could do to help me become a footballer. He said he would get me a Real Madrid shirt. I can still remember that moment, picturing myself in a Real Madrid shirt. It was the only thing on my mind. Sounds fucking strange when I say that, but as a wee boy obsessed with football, a Real Madrid shirt was like gold to me. I had all their football cards and knew every player and could pronounce their names. And this guy was going to buy me a shirt.' He shook his head, almost with disbelief. 'Then he leaned across me, opened my trousers and put his hand on my pants. It was a very strange feeling. That's what upsets me about it to this day. He touched me and I could feel myself getting hard. Then he put his hand inside and began to masturbate me. I suddenly ejaculated and I felt embarrassed and ashamed. It was just horrible. Like something in my life had changed and I would never be the same person ever again.' His eyes were filling with tears.

'That's awful,' Rosie said. 'But you mustn't blame yourself. It's common for victims of abuse to react the way you did.'

'He gave me a five-pound note and said next week he'd have the shirt for me. I pulled my trousers up and he said I could go. I just walked out of the room and didn't know what to think. I was ashamed of myself.'

'Did you ever see him again?'

James nodded. 'There was no choice. You just got told on the Friday afternoon that you were going up to the party. A few of the boys were quite looking forward to it because they came back with money and stuff and we spent it all on sweets. But it was like madness. So when I went up the second time, it wasn't a week later, it was two or three weeks. Same thing. Taken into the room and this time he was there again. But he had the shirt for me. He handed it to me and told me to open it, and when I did it was the most exciting thing to have those colours actually in my hand and to imagine pulling it on and going out to play football on a pitch, just like my heroes. Then he touched me again and asked me to touch him. He opened my trousers and this time he put me in his mouth. It was disgusting. Afterwards, we went home, and the next Thursday I ran away for the first time. It was so that I wouldn't be there on the Friday. But they brought me back and I had to go again and again. It was always the same man. One time he raped me. But I know I wasn't the only one that stuff happened to. There were other boys, and they went with a few men.'

'Can you remember any names or any of the faces?'

'No. But somebody said one of them was a politician. Like an MP or something. Labour, I think, but I don't know that for sure.'

'Did you ever tell anyone? Did the boys or girls ever talk to each other about it?'

'No, never. It was never mentioned, but we all knew when we came home on the bus what we'd been doing. Nobody ever spoke on the way home. We just sat there, dead quiet.'

'What did you tell people about the Real Madrid shirt?' Rosie hoped it wasn't too intrusive a question, but she needed to know.

'I never wore it. Not once. Didn't even try it on. Didn't show it to anyone. Just took it back to the home with me and put it under my mattress.' He shook his head. 'I've still got it. I mean, how fucked up is that?'

'Seriously? You still have it?'

'You want to see it?'

'Yes.'

Matt, she knew, would be visualizing a picture.

James returned a couple of minutes later with a carrier-bag and pulled out the shirt. It was at least twenty years old. The style and year could be checked. Of course, it proved nothing, but it was good to have it.

'Can I ask why you kept it, James? It must have been a painful reminder.'

'I don't know, really. I couldn't bear to throw it away because I loved it so much, yet I couldn't even try it on.' Suddenly he was crying. 'I know, in the bigger picture of everything I've said to you, how fucking stupid that sounds, but sometimes that single thought of the top makes me cry. I was just so innocent. Just a little boy with all these stupid dreams of playing football for Real Madrid. But after those encounters, my life completely changed. I changed. I became angry and troublesome. When I left the home, I took to drink. I trained as an apprentice joiner, but because of my alcoholism, I amounted to nothing. I lost my marriage to a great girl who, to this day, doesn't know what was wrong with me.'

'So when did you go to the police?'

'When I was about fifteen. One of the other guys was going, and we went together.'

'Can you remember which police station?'

'Romford. The home was near there. We talked to various officers and they came to see us at the home. It all got a bit difficult then, but the trips stopped. That was it. It never happened again. But nothing ever came of it.'

'Do you ever see any of the boys now?'

'No. When I left, I moved away, up to Derby, and married a Scottish girl. We stayed there for years and had two kids, but I drank so much I blew the lot. I don't even see my kids now.'

James gazed at the football shirt, and she wondered how many more innocent young lives and dreams had been shattered because nobody thought they were important enough to matter.

CHAPTER THIRTY-SIX

Mervyn Bates clicked his small suitcase shut, his hands trembling. 'Calm down,' he told himself. 'You'll be out of here in half an hour. Out and away, too far away for anyone to come looking for you. They wouldn't know where to start.' He had always had a contingency plan. He called it his nuclear survival plan, in the event of the walls ever closing in on him. He hadn't expected to put the wheels in motion from a hotel in bloody Glasgow, but today he had to. After the visit from that head-case reporter and her disturbingly accurate accusations, he knew the game was finally up. He'd have to disappear, and quick. If he'd needed any more convincing, the visit from Larry Sutton had left him in no doubt. It wasn't just his reputation that was about to be destroyed, he would be dead meat if he stayed another night in this city.

He'd decided not even to risk going to the airport, and had got his PA in London to book him on the overnight sleeper to Euston. He'd told her just to shut up and book it, and not to ask bloody questions when she expressed surprise that he wanted a train, not the morning flight. Then he'd asked her to reserve the Eurostar to Paris, from where he would fly to Thailand in the evening. He knew the place well. He had friends there of a kindred spirit and he could quietly disappear. He was loaded with money and could live out the rest of his life with nobody to ask questions about his sexual desires or preferences for young kids. Mervyn Bates didn't even ask himself the question that the bitch reporter had put to him: had he raped Bella Mason? That was in the past. He hadn't felt bad about it then and he didn't now. He was moving on with his life, and nobody was going to drag him down.

He finished the remains of a bottle of mineral water, looked at his watch and stepped out of the hotel bedroom. He walked along the corridor and went down in the lift to the foyer. He glanced furtively around the place, busy with some kind of function, then slipped through the throng and out of the automatic doors into the driving rain. There was no taxi at the door, and he was about to turn and go back in when he felt something in his back. Even though nobody had ever stuck a gun in his back, he knew exactly what it was.

'Let's go, Merv. Don't make a fuss.'

Bates felt his whole body go limp as he recognized Ricky's voice. The gun was pushed harder into his back and urged him in the direction of a car a few yards along from the entrance. Ricky opened the back door, and he got in without protest. As they drove out of the car park, Bates opened his mouth to speak, but nothing came out. Then he croaked, 'Ricky. Listen, mate. This is crazy.'

'It's just business, Merv.'

'Ricky,' he could hear his voice shaking, 'you're a smart guy. You don't have to do this. I can make you a rich young man. The two of you. You know that. Just please take me to the station and let me go. You tell Larry you missed me, and by tomorrow afternoon there'll be a hundred grand in your bank account.'

He saw Ricky glance at the driver, a small smirk on his face, and wondered if he was getting through. This pair of Neanderthals could be bought, no doubt about it. All they knew was money. They could barely string a sentence together. But they didn't answer.

'Ricky,' Bates said, leaning forward so his head was between the two of them. 'No way is Larry paying you more than a hundred grand. You're just dog shit to him. He'll be giving you a few quid to get rid of me, but ask yourself, what's the point? Take my money and you can just fuck off abroad somewhere . . . I mean—'

By the time he saw the fist coming from the front seat, he was already dazed and slumping back, his nose cracking and opening up, blood gushing.

'Fuck's sake, Ricky! Aw, Jesus, man! There's blood everywhere.'

'Shut up, Merv.'

He was barely conscious, wiping the blood away as vomit rose in the back of his throat. The car turned away from the city centre. He had no idea where they were going. This was his first time in Glasgow since the days he used to come up for charity work, when he'd first spotted Bella Mason. After he'd taken her away, he'd never come back.

The car pulled off the main road and into a layby next to the river. This was not good. The driver stopped. Ricky got out and opened the back door. He didn't speak, just leaned in with his big arms and dragged Bates out. His legs buckled so Ricky and the driver pulled him to his feet. He was dizzy with panic. They were going to beat the shit out of him and probably leave him for dead. But, no. The driver had a rope. They turned him around roughly and pushed him face down onto the car bonnet, then pulled his head back and stuck gaffer tape over his mouth. He couldn't breathe through his nose for the blood and he started gagging. He was beginning to pass out. He felt his hands being tied behind his back, and then the rope go around his ankles. Now he was being dragged along the cobblestones towards a ledge, and he could hear the flow of the river. They held him over the water and all he could see was the inky blackness.

A mobile rang and they stopped, leaving him dangling over the edge. Ricky took it out of his pocket. 'Yep. Sure, boss.'

Bates felt the mobile being pressed against his ear, and he could hear the voice of Larry Sutton.

'This is what should happen to all the cunts like you, Merv. Every last one of them. But I can't do them all, even though I've done a few. You're a bastard, Merv, and you'll rot in Hell. This is for Bella Mason. I hope you can see her face as you drown, you evil, twisted fucker.'

The words were ringing in his ear as Ricky pulled the phone away from him and they started to ease him, feet first, over the side. Bates found himself wondering if he would float, or maybe even be found. He felt piss run down his legs, puked and choked. Still they said nothing. He heard a big splash in the water and wondered what it was. Then there was a sudden, fierce tugging at the rope. He realized that something very heavy was attached to him as he hit the water and disappeared.

Colin Chambers sat in his study, behind his desk, the ice melting in his large malt whisky. He poured himself more. He had been on the phone to his assistant and had signed the necessary papers releasing Millie from the hospital, with the final say going to the Harley Street psychiatrist, whom he knew would go along with his wishes. He opened his drawer and took out some photographs of Millie and himself when they were young and in Madrid, sitting in pavement cafes, laughing and drinking. Millie was carefree and eager then, and the sound of her laughter could make him forget everything else.

Where had it gone wrong? Was it his greed for power once he'd become an MP, determined to make it to the top? Or was it Millie and her failure to produce their child? It wasn't her fault, but he needed someone to blame, and he had never forgiven her.

He was a bastard, but Millie had become a liability with her drunken episodes. He had stopped loving her. Now she was reduced to threatening him. That reporter was some piece of work coming in and shouting him down in his club. But she wouldn't have done that unless she had something solid. He knew how these things worked. There had already been a call put to his secretary asking if he had a comment for the story in the *Post* about those bloody dossiers. He could never answer that. There was no answer.

It had seemed the right thing to do at the time, and it hadn't been his decision alone. He had spoken to the Prime Minister, but he could never admit that, even now. You couldn't spread the blame. It had been his decision. He could have said no. What about all those children? They were so remote from him, troubled kids from housing estates and children's homes. It was a different world. He couldn't have people like them bringing down the government with their accusations. Perhaps he should have been braver – but he just hadn't cared enough.

He pushed his hand into the back of the drawer and fumbled until he felt the velvet cover and the hardness inside it. He pulled out the revolver and methodically unwrapped it, then opened the barrel and checked it was loaded, though he knew it would be. His father's old army revolver. He picked up the photograph of Millie and himself in Madrid and looked at it one last time, then put the gun to his head.

The shot echoed around the empty house as the photograph slipped out of Colin's hand.

CHAPTER THIRTY-SEVEN

Rosie stirred in TJ's arms at the sound of the mobile ringing. She eased herself away from him, not wanting to wake him.

'Don't be creeping about now, Gilmour. I'm awake. It's not even eight o'clock. Who's phoning at this time? . . . As if I didn't know.'

Rosie turned her head towards him, as he lay, one eye open and his lips moving to a smile. She ran a hand down his cheekbone, and traced the line of his lips as she put the phone to her ear.

'Hey, Rosie! Sorry if I woke you, but I thought you'd want to know this.'

It was Mickey Kavanagh, his first-thing-in-the-morning gravelly twenty-a-day voice.

'No problem, Mickey. What's up?'

'Colin Chambers shot himself last night.'

'Christ! Really?'

'Yep. The cops won't be putting it out this morning officially, but my mate in the Branch called me, as I'd been talking to him re your stuff in the past few days. So your little chat at the Garrick must have struck the right chord.'

Even though a dead Colin Chambers was much easier for her than a live one, Rosie couldn't help the pang of guilt. 'Cheers, mate, for telling me I drove a man to suicide.'

'Fuck him, Rosie. He drove himself to suicide. You just helped him over the last hurdle.'

'Oh, thanks. I feel better now,' Rosie said sarcastically. 'Christ, Mick. Can't believe he did that. What a cowardly bastard.'

'Typical of his type. Falling on his sword as he finally realized his number was up. He would never have admitted it, Rosie. Make no mistake about it, if he thought there was any way he could trash your allegations, he would have done it. But he knew he was done up like a kipper. He'd been hiding behind this all his life. Good fucking riddance is what I say, and so should you.'

'Yeah,' Rosie said half-heartedly. 'You're right. It's one bastard off the face of the earth. Listen, Mickey, I'd better go and phone my editor. We'll want to run with our piece full-on now.'

'Sure. That's why I phoned you, darling. Give me a shout if you need me. And give yourself a pat on the back. Okay?'

'Yeah,' Rosie said, as he hung up.

She sank back on the pillows as TJ's hand stretched over and caressed her stomach.

'What's up?'

'Colin Chambers shot himself last night.'

TJ let out a low whistle. 'Good,' he said. 'The world can do with a lot fewer of those bastards.' He leaned over and kissed her cheek.

'I have to phone the editor.' She punched in McGuire's number.

'Gilmour. What's up at this time of the morning?'

'Mick. It's Colin Chambers. He shot himself last night. He's dead.'

There was a long moment of silence, then McGuire spoke. 'What a fucking result, Rosie!'

'I thought you'd say that.'

'But it is, though. You can't libel the dead, so now we've got him and the Chief Constable at the time, who's been dead for years. We can more or less trample all over the fuckers, as long as we don't accuse the whole of the UK police force.'

'Yeah. It's definitely a result.'

Silence.

'Gilmour, I hope you're not going to start all that guilt shite on me. I know what you're like. I bet you're already agonizing because you gave him it straight at your meeting in the Garrick. Am I right?'

'Well, a bit. I can't pretend I'm happy to have assisted someone in ending their life, Mick.'

'What about the bloody lives that were ruined by his actions? What about them? Robbed of their innocence and their voice. Come on, Gilmour. Don't give me your crap. Get down to the office pronto and let's get about this, all fucking guns blazing. Are we clear?'

'Sure. Of course. I'm glad he's dead. I'm just feeling a bit guilty for my part in it.'

'Fuck that. We'll have a historic splash and couple of spreads tomorrow, and Colin Chambers will be rotting in Hell where he belongs. Now piss off and let me get my breakfast.'

Rosie thought about it for a moment. 'Yeah. You're right, Mick. We should be celebrating.'

'That's the spirit.' He hung up.

CHAPTER THIRTY-EIGHT

Millie sat in her room, staring at Sky News as though she were watching the story of someone else's life unravel. But it was *her* life they were dissecting, hers and Colin's. Well, mostly it was Colin's. It was *his* picture that flashed up with the breaking news tag that the former Tory Home Secretary had been found dead of gunshot wounds in the study of his London home. There were no suspicious circumstances, the police had said, as they usually did when they didn't want to say outright that a person had taken their own life. But Millie knew that all the newspapers would be saying it loud and clear tomorrow morning. There was no revelation, no speculation as to what could have driven her husband to take his own life, just the breaking news that he'd been found dead by his housekeeper when she'd arrived that morning.

Earlier, when Millie's door had been gently opened and her psychiatrist had appeared, accompanied by a nurse

and the hospital manager, Millie had immediately wondered what was going on. She'd assumed this was the day
they were going to give her ECT, and part of her had
resigned herself to it. She knew that Rosie Gilmour
wouldn't abandon her, especially after the flowers and the
cryptic note had been delivered, but she had no control
over when the ECT would happen. Time was running out.
But then, from their expressions as they'd stood over her
bed, Millie had sensed grim news.

When the psychiatrist had pulled a chair up at her bedside and told her calmly that her husband had been found
dead in their home, and that it appeared he had taken his
own life, Millie had looked at him, but said nothing. She
felt nothing. Not sadness, not anger, not even any sense of
loss. She didn't flinch. So much so that the psychiatrist had
asked her if she fully understood what he had told her. She
nodded. Then, after a few moments, she had asked how he
had done it. There was a gun at the scene, the police had
said. And a note for her. Somewhere inside a part of her
that had been dead for a long time, she felt an odd comfort
that, in his final moments, he had acknowledged her, after
all these years.

After a few moments of silence, but for the sound of feet
shuffling and awkward clearing of throats, the psychiatrist had told her the next part. She was free to leave the
hospital. The section order under the Mental Health Act
had been lifted because her husband had signed a paper

saying he was willing to withdraw his agreement to it, and the medical evidence that the psychiatrist had found over the past few weeks suggested that she was fit to be released back into the community. Millie hadn't reacted to this either, but inside she was smiling.

'I'd like to go home now,' was all she said, and the manager told her he would arrange for a car to take her to wherever she wanted to go.

Two hours later, Millie stood on the steps outside her front door where a young WPC stood guard and gave her a sympathetic smile of recognition. The officer asked if she would be all right to go inside alone, and Millie nodded. She stepped aside as Millie slipped her key into the lock and pushed open the door. She could hear the whirr of cameras behind her, and had been told to expect them by the hospital manager as she'd been preparing to leave the hospital. She'd seen them crowded together from the top of the road, when the car had turned down towards the house. Dozens of them, and a TV crew. She didn't care. They can photograph me all they like, she thought. Nothing can hurt me any more.

She stepped inside and closed the door behind her. The light from the stained-glass window on the high ceiling sent a cobalt sheen to the white walls of the hallway and she stood for a moment, transfixed by the shaft of colour. Then she walked across the oak floor and pushed open the study door. Cigar smoke lingered in the air, and she could imagine Colin sitting on his leather chair beside the fire with a whisky in his hand. So many nights she'd longed to join him and talk things out, but they'd become so distant that it had seemed impossible. She stood gazing around the room, every corner a memory, every bookshelf, photograph, school sporting trophy of Colin's . . .

She hadn't seen this room sober for months. Everything had been a blur almost, between the depression and the alcoholic stupor her life had become. But now she saw it clearly. She looked across at his desk, where there was a whisky glass, almost empty, and behind it, bloodstains. Her heart lurched. She pictured Colin lying there in his blood. She steadied herself. Then she saw the cream envelope and noticed his writing: *Millie.* The police had informed her that they'd put it back on the desk once they'd established that Colin had committed suicide. She went across and picked it up, held it in her hands, almost reluctant to open it. Then she slit it with the paper knife she'd given him as a gift many years ago and took out the letter. It was written in fountain pen, so typical of Colin even in his final moments, such a snob and a stickler for form. She began to read:

My darling Millie,

I'm sorry. Where and how can I ever begin to tell you I'm sorry? I think you know it's too late for that. It was too late

*long ago for me to say sorry to you for all the wrong I had
done, for not understanding you in your grief over the
babies. I'm so ashamed. The truth is, I've always been
ashamed and I'm such a coward I couldn't even face that,
because I know that I singularly ruined your life as well as
mine. And my shame is even greater, because I only realized
this in the last couple of days when it has all come tumbling
down. When the reporter came to me and told me about the
dossiers and the revelations that would come out over my
part in their destruction, the shame of my entire life
overwhelmed me.*

*I know I cannot go on. I'm too much of a coward to face
what is going to happen when the story comes out. I cannot
face it. I cannot face you because I had you locked away in
a hospital, as though you were mad, because you were a
threat to me. What kind of man does that? It is my greatest
shame. I know you will never forgive me, and neither should
you. I hope your life is better without me in it. I have no
contribution to make, not to you, to myself, or to anything
I touch. But I know that in my heart I have never stopped
loving you.*

Colin

Millie sat on the chair he had occupied in his final
moments, and gazed at the photograph of them in the cafe
on Madrid's Plaza Mayor, so happy together. She looked at

the letter in her hand and read it again. She'd felt a physical pain in her chest at *never stopped loving you*. If only she could have got through to him. But he was what he was. He had killed himself because he had been found out. It wasn't because he had let her down; it wasn't because of her. He could have come back to her at any time and told her he loved her, and she might have thrown herself into his arms. But he hadn't. He had killed himself because of the dossiers, because he had been rumbled. 'I won't weep for you, Colin Chambers.'

She went into her bag and took out her mobile phone. She punched in a number and was glad to hear a familiar voice.

'Rosie, I'm home.'

Larry Sutton waited in the office of the plumbers' merchant that he part-owned with one of his oldest associates. It *was* a plumbers' merchant, as the sign above the door said, but it was also the location for secret meetings, out of the way of any of the bars or clubs where he normally saw his associates. Most of Larry's drug deals were done from this very office, and had been since he and Kenny had started working together all those years ago. Fair play to Kenny, he had actually learned a trade when he'd come out of Borstal. But within five years, watching the way his old muckers Larry and Spider swashbuckled their way around the East End, he quickly realized that being up to your arse in mucky water was a lot harder than being the middle man.

The plumbers' merchant's was also the scene of the punishment and interrogations that were part of the business. The secret was not letting whoever Larry had summoned there know whether he was getting sent on a job or having his fingers chopped off.

That had been the score when Larry had summoned Ricky and Pete. He told them he was well impressed with their work in Madrid and Glasgow, even though he was pissed off with Mervyn Bates. He was grateful for the way they'd disposed of him, and now they'd get their reward.

Kenny had left the office fifteen minutes ago, as arranged, and everything was in place. Larry had brought someone from Belfast for the job, someone who didn't ask, never flinched, and just got on with it, as long as the money was agreed. He looked at his watch. He was out there somewhere in the yard waiting for Larry's text.

Larry heard the car, then Ricky and Pete sharing a joke as the doors were slammed and they came up the narrow steps to the office entrance. There was a knock at the door.

'It's Ricky.'

'Come in, lads.'

The door opened, and in came the big frame of Ricky, his blond hair gelled and glistening under the fluorescent ceiling light. Pete was quieter, thicker-looking, as though he might have had bolts in his neck at one time.

'So, lads, how was Merv the perv in his final moments?' Larry chortled.

'Squealing like a fucking pig, Larry. I'd say he'd shat himself before he hit the water.'

'Good enough for the cunt.' He turned to them and looked them in the eye. 'Are you sure there was nothing left behind? You weighted him down enough so he won't pop up for a few weeks, and when he does it will take them weeks to ID him?

'You bet we did, boss. It was clean as a whistle, and we walked away. Came straight down the road, like you said.'

'Have you seen the papers today?'

'No, boss.'

'Well, it's all over the front page about Merv and his part in that Bella bird. I told you what he'd done, didn't I?'

Ricky nodded. 'Yeah, boss.'

'That reporter did the story in her paper in Scotland, but it's all over the news now. Merv's office said he's disappeared.' He smirked. 'That much I can confirm. They seem to think he's on the run, and the cops are supposed to be looking for him because of what's been said in the papers. But they'll not find him, if you boys have done your job right.' He raised his eyebrows, waiting for their nod.

'We have, boss. He's not going to surface for a while, if ever.'

Larry took a breath. It was time. He leaned forward, hands clasped on the desktop. 'You see, lads, the problem is, this fucking model story is so high-profile now. I mean, it was a big deal when she went off the roof, and the whole world decided she'd jumped. But now, with this reporter digging stuff up, finding that fucking junkie brother before we did, his story's all over the papers. The cops are going to be all over it.'

Larry looked from one to the other. Their faces were as blank as ever. He pushed a button on his mobile phone, sending the text to Billy.

'Well, what I'm saying is the cops will be asking all sorts of questions. The paper said they have CCTV footage of the hotel and tomorrow they're going to reveal the identity of the two men who were seen with her on the roof.' He glanced at them again. 'The paper also said there was that drunk woman on the roof, the Tory guy's wife. She said she was there to top herself, but she saw everything. She's going to be singing like a canary to the cops. She saw the two men.'

Larry took a breath, waiting for it to register with them. Finally it did. But as Ricky and Pete looked at each other, the door opened, and in walked Billy Brown, with a small squat henchman at his back. Ricky began to panic and shifted in his chair, moving to stand up.

'Stay where you are, Ricky.' Larry said. 'Listen, boys, you know how this works. It's just business. I need to protect the firm. I need to protect myself, because you're going to get pulled in as soon as this hits the papers.'

'Larry, for fuck's sake, man! You don't think I'd ever grass you up?' Ricky's flushed face made his hair seem even more bleached. 'No way, man. Never in my fucking life would I do that.'

He looked at his mate, who was grey.

'Come on now, Ricky. You know the score, son. You know I can't take that chance.'

Larry raised his eyes to Billy standing behind them and blinked his instruction.

'B-but, Larry . . . Aw, fuck, man . . . Please, ma—'

The last word was muffled as the bullet went into the back of his neck. A second went into Pete's. The look of disbelief was still on their faces as they slumped to the floor, blood bubbling out of the back of their heads and spreading into a pool.

Larry stood up and buttoned his coat. 'You all right to clean up here, Billy?'

'No worries, mate. Jake here's a dab hand with a feather duster.'

The smile and the glint in Billy's eye gave Larry the creeps. But he had his uses. He handed him the bag containing ten grand in used notes and walked out. 'Close the door behind you, boys.'

CHAPTER THIRTY-NINE

Rosie sat on the sofa in McGuire's office, watching him have two animated conversations at the same time. One was on the phone, to the *Post*'s parliamentary correspondent, Pettigrew, at Westminster, and every few seconds he shouted across to the lawyer, who was sitting beside Rosie. The managing editor, McKay, sat on a leather easy chair, wearing his usual funereal expression. But McGuire's bullishness made Rosie feel sure there would be only one winner here. He finally hung up and stood at his desk.

'Officially, the government are not saying much at all, only that they'll take the allegations seriously and act accordingly. But Pettigrew says the jungle drums are beating all over Westminster. Of course, those crimes happened on the Tory government's watch, so our current upholders of all that is just in the current Labour government will be happy to give them a good kicking, while thanking Christ it wasn't them in charge.'

'It probably happened on their watch too, Mick. This isn't a one-off. Organized sexual abuse will have been going on for a very long time. So much of it was swept under the carpet, as if it was just the way things were back in the day. But they can't get away with it.'

'But the dossiers,' the managing editor chipped in, 'or alleged dossiers, because, remember, if we're asked in court whether we've seen them we'll have to say no. Do we actually have proof? Millie Chambers didn't see them either. She's making allegations arising from a conversation she says she heard between her husband and the then Chief Constable of the Met. And you can bank on her getting torn to shreds if she stands in a witness box, given that she's a self-confessed piss-artist. And, of course, she's also a woman scorned.'

There was a stony silence for a few seconds, then Hanlon spoke.

'But who's going to take the *Post* to court? Not Colin Chambers or the Chief Constable, who have snuffed it – as you know, you can't libel the dead. I'm satisfied we're safe enough with this the way Rosie has written it. She hasn't implicated any other government minister or police officer, or even any public figure. Plus Rosie has the victim's account, and he's happy to be identified. The detective who gave her the name doesn't want to be involved, but once the story hits the paper, you can guarantee more people will come forward . . . victims as well as police.'

'Totally agree, with you, Tommy. People who were afraid or too ashamed until now will take heart from our victim's story. We can't lose.'

'You don't think we should hold fire, Mick, till Rosie gets an identified cop talking.'

'No way,' McGuire said, indignant. 'For Christ's sake! We've got Colin Chambers blowing his brains out in his home. We've got his wife telling us her tale of woe, with her own suicide bid, and we've got her on tape talking about the abuse allegations. For fuck's sake! We've even got Chambers' confession, or as good as, on his suicide note. What more do we need?'

McGuire's phone rang again, and he answered it. He rolled his eyes at Rosie as he listened for a couple of minutes. Rosie looked him, and he gave her a 'don't worry' look. As he hung up, he said, 'That was the MD. The Tory Party chairman has been onto him, asking about the level of accusations and if we have solid proof. What a wanker!'

'Exactly,' Rosie said. 'He's just shitting himself in case any other names come out. I'm prepared to bet that our story will flush out a few once it hits the streets tomorrow.'

'Well, let's hope so, Gilmour. But even if it doesn't, we're sound enough on this. Right, Tommy?'

'I'm cool with it, Mick. I've seen the layout and the copy. Go for it.'

McGuire went behind his desk. The meeting was over. 'Okay, guys. Thanks for coming in. I've got a paper to put out, and it's going to be a belter.'

Everyone stood up and the managing editor left the room, saying nothing. Hanlon and Rosie followed him.

'You need me to stay around, Mick?' she asked.

'No. Just keep your phone on in case there are any developments. Have a few drinks and relax, Gilmour. This is what it's all about.'

Larry Sutton sat on the terrace of his villa high on the hills overlooking Marbella. He sipped his malt whisky, swirled the ice and relished the taste in the back of his throat. It had been a tough couple of days, and he had the feeling it was going to get a lot tougher. If that bitch reporter had everything she said she had, the cops would be all over him once her paper came out tomorrow. He lit a cigarette and watched the smoke circle up into the blackness, the rustle of the palm trees in the breeze the only sound.

He hadn't taken pleasure in getting rid of Ricky and Pete, but that was how these things went. He couldn't rely on them to keep their mouths shut if it was true there were CCTV photos of them and the testimony of this Tory fucker's wife. He was fairly sure Ricky wouldn't have buckled, but his mate might have, so he'd had to get rid of both to be on the safe side. It didn't feel good. No doubt, the cops would come looking for him, but they'd need real proof, and he wasn't going to sit around London, making it easy for them. There was nothing to connect them, and Billy would see to it that Ricky and Pete were unrecognizable in the burned-out car.

But the knowledge that he'd done away with Mervyn Bates was a different matter: he raised a glass to his old friend. 'We're working our way through them, Spider, one by one. Here's to you, mate.'

CHAPTER FORTY

The Catholic church in Eastbourne was busier than Rosie had expected, full of people ready to sing some of the old hymns she'd grow up with and belted out at primary school. Bridget's light oak coffin was on a pedestal at the front, and Rosie ushered Dan into a pew. He'd asked her to take him to the funeral: he wanted to pay his respects because Bridget had been kind to him.

As the priest approached the altar and the congregation rose to their feet, Rosie heard the click of high heels in the aisle. She turned to see Millie Chambers, dressed in figure-hugging black, looking like a fading film star. She smiled and slipped into the pew beside Rosie and Dan. She reached across and squeezed Rosie's hand, then put a comforting arm around Dan. It was a touching picture of two lonely people who had lost so much of who they were, but were finding themselves again day by day.

After the service Millie invited them to come in her chauffeur-driven car to a nearby seafront hotel, where they sat, surrounded by old people, drinking tea in the conservatory overlooking the pebble beach.

'Poor Bridget,' Millie said. 'I feel so responsible. I *am* responsible. If I hadn't involved her by asking her to take the letter, she would be at work today on the ward, doing something she loved. But I got her roped into my own bloody story. I feel awful. Maybe some things are best left alone.'

Rosie knew it was the truth, and guilt was gnawing at her. 'There's no point in us all feeling bad, Millie, because it happened. Now we have to live with it,' she said. 'Bridget felt she was doing the right thing, taking your letter and acting on it. Look what she's achieved! She's helped expose all these wrongs – the children who were brutalized and abused. It's all over the media since our story this morning, and if some good comes of it, then Bridget's death won't have been for nothing. I'm proud of her.'

'She was kind,' Dan said, 'someone I could have relied on when I felt alone.'

Millie put down her cup and turned to him. 'But you're not alone, Dan. You're a lovely young man, with so much ahead of you, despite all the terrible things that have happened. Please don't ever feel alone. I'm in London, and I'll help you any way I can. I'll always be here for you, because you, as well as Bridget, did a very brave thing by coming forward.' She squeezed his arm. 'So, please, don't be a stranger. Come and visit me. In fact, you should move out of Glasgow – it's dragging you down. Come to London – or anywhere else you won't be surrounded by the people who would pull you back into drugs.'

Dan nodded. 'That's what my drugs counsellor says. I need to get away.'

'Well,' Rosie said, 'we're going to the lawyer this afternoon – Bella's lawyer – and he'll put you right about your sister's estate. I know it's hard for you to take in right now, but you won't have to worry about money.'

Dan sighed. 'I don't really care about the money. I'd give it all back to have one more day with her. Me and Mitch are hoping to get a flat together, once things are sorted out. We can help each other stay clean.'

'Stay in touch with me, though,' Millie said. 'We can be friends for each other.'

He smiled. 'I hope so.'

Rosie had left Dan at the flat in Finnieston with Mitch. She'd arranged with the owner for him to rent it for six months. It would be a good test to see if he could manage his own affairs, especially with his new-found wealth. At the lawyer's in London earlier, he had been surprisingly unmoved when the lawyer told him the extent of Bella Mason's wealth. With the various sponsorships and other deals, she had accrued a fortune of three and a half million pounds. Some of it was tied up in investments, on the advice of Mervyn Bates, but Bella was the sole signatory and it was her money. So now it was Dan's. Three and a half million.

'What am I going to do with all that money?' he asked, bewildered.

'You live the life Bella wanted for you, the one they took away from her,' Rosie told him.

He couldn't wait to get back and celebrate with Mitch. Life was going to be so different, and it was a lot to take in.

It was nine in the evening, and Rosie had left the office and was driving back to her flat when her mobile rang. She hoped it wasn't McGuire. Everyone was chasing her story, and it was the number-one item on all the TV news bulletins. She'd already passed on the information about the Dawson Institute in Sussex, where Millie had claimed people were locked up for years, although there was very little wrong with them. The *Post*'s sister paper in London would investigate it. Time for her to stand back and take a breather. She was going out for the dinner with TJ that she'd put off twice in the last couple of weeks. She needed to feel some of his security and love around her.

She picked up the phone. It was Don. She'd arranged to meet him tomorrow to pass on the full dossier of her investigation. He'd turn most of it over to Scotland Yard, but it would be a feather in his cap to be the one to pass it on.

'Rosie, where are you?'

'On my way home, Don. Been a long day. I'm seeing you tomorrow. What's up?'

She heard him clearing his throat, and a too-long pause before he spoke.

'Rosie, er, listen. It's that wee heroin-addict mate of Dan Mason's. Mitch? The guy who got the beating?'

'Yeah. What is it?'

'Rosie, I hate to break this to you, but Mitch has been found dead. Overdose. In a flat in the Calton.'

Rosie stopped the car and her stomach sank.

'Aw, Christ, Don. Are you sure? I saw him a few hours ago.'

'Yeah. Afraid so. Positive identification. One of the officers who worked on the beating he got that day flagged it up when the news came in. It was just another dead junkie for our books, then he suddenly said he recognized the name. It's him, all right. I'm sorry. I know how you get close to these things.'

Rosie pulled into the side of the road and sat, feeling numb.

'You there, sweetheart?'

'Yeah.' She swallowed. 'Can't believe this. I have to go. If you get any more information on it, give me a shout, Don.'

Rosie stared out of the windscreen, trying to work out what had happened. Poor Mitch. Images flooded into her mind of their first meeting. Mitch trying to be cocky, promising he could deliver, drinking his Coca-Cola iced drink, desperate for his next hit. How he'd taken on the role of big brother to Dan. She'd really believed he and Dan could work through their addiction. But she should have known better. The problem with junkies who had stopped using for a while was that a single hit could overwhelm their system and shut everything down. She shook her head and punched in TJ's number on her mobile.

'TJ, it's me. Listen. I'm going to be a bit late.'

'What's up? You stuck at the office? Shall I move the table back a bit? Are you all right?'

'Yeah. Well, no. I'll tell you later. I have to go and see someone. Be with you in an hour.'

Rosie turned round and drove back through the town towards Finnieston. Some things were better left alone, she'd thought at Bridget's funeral. And perhaps they were. If she hadn't dug up Mitch, he never would have found Dan, and if she hadn't found Dan, none of this would have come out. She wouldn't have the story of the year, and Bella Mason would be just another celebrity who couldn't take the heat. None of it was about winning, for Rosie. It was about the truth. But there were always losers when you shone the light in dark places. It wasn't only the guilty who perished. Was it all worth it? Right now, she didn't know.

She parked outside Dan's flat and let out a deep sigh as she pressed the buzzer. She was relieved when she heard his voice.

'Dan it's me. You all right?'

'Aye, Rosie. I'm just on my own,' Dan breezed. 'Mitch went out a couple of hours ago to meet his cousin up from England. He's not back yet. I said we'd go out and get a pizza – celebrate. So I'm all ready. I've got my new shirt on. Come on up.'

The door buzzed and clicked open, and Rosie walked in, her legs as heavy as her heart as she climbed the stairs. She wasn't a counsellor. She was a journalist, and her job was done. She should walk away right now, she told herself. But she didn't.